WOOING ERIC

Eric felt every limb in his body turn to water. Margot was gazing at him in a thoroughly intimate way, almost as though he were her lover. Those cornflower blue eyes seemed hot as they caressed him. Their eyes locked and, to his dismay and wonder, Eric saw Margot's face coming closer and closer to his. He realized with a shock that she was going to kiss him.

He was off the bench before he knew it. He walked a few steps away, then quickly turned and walked back, not daring to look at her.

It was just his imagination, he thought. She had not been about to kiss him. The idea was absurd. Ladies did not go about kissing strange men. And they certainly didn't go around trying to kiss someone like him!

The Vow

MARY SPENCER

HarperPaperbacks
A Division of HarperCollinsPublishers

This is a work of fiction. The characters, incidents, and dialogues are products of the author's imagination and are not to be construed as real. Any resemblance to actual events or persons, living or dead, is entirely coincidental.

HarperPaperbacks *A Division of* HarperCollins*Publishers*
10 East 53rd Street, New York, N.Y. 10022

Cover illustration by Jacqueline Goldstein

First printing: March 1994

Printed in the United States of America

HarperPaperbacks, HarperMonogram, and colophon are trademarks of HarperCollins*Publishers*

❖ 10 9 8 7 6 5 4 3 2 1

For Paul, who, sitting at his end of the rowboat, patiently listened to all the reasons why I couldn't possibly submit this book for publication, then looked at me over his fishing rod and stated that if I didn't submit the thing, he would. Thanks, honey, for having faith in me, especially while the clock on your three-day fishing license was running.

Special thanks goes to my sister, Rachel Thompson, a.k.a. Lady Amée Renée Cateline Marchand of the Society for Creative Anachronism, kingdom of Caid, for all the help and historical information. I couldn't have done it without you, Rache.

Prologue

To Sir Garin Stavelot, Lord of Belhaven

Greetings, friend, from the battlefield. I regret I did not return in time to bid thee Godspeed, but the delay proved the success of my search. The rebel's faithless servant indeed had a price and confessed the plotted treason of Terent of Ravinet. No sooner was the confession made, however, than we were set upon by Terent's men, intent on killing every one of us at the meeting place. De Arge and I alone escaped with our lives; the rest were killed, including Terent's servant. Thus our proof of his treachery is gone.

The time hath come, friend Garin, for thee to do as thou hast promised, and quickly. The danger is imminent now that Terent knows we are aware of his treason, and it is certain he will do all in his power to carry out his plans without delay. Therefore I beg thee to make all haste in securing my child under thy protection. I have sent her a missive instructing her to make ready to receive the one whom thou wilt send to her. Please God the messenger may not be waylaid by Terent or his men.

I shalt come to Belhaven as quickly as I may. If evil should befall me ere then, I beg thee, Garin, be a father to my beloved child, as thou didst promise me when last we took leave of one another. I trust thee alone with this, my most precious treasure.

I send thee my gratitude and love. By the king's seal thou wilt know these things are also his command.

This, from thy friend and brother-at-arms,

Sir Walter le Brun
Written at Shrewsbury
20 August 1403

1

The strong, damp winds had come up without warning a few hours before nightfall, bringing with them the threat of a summer storm. Already, in fact, masses of black and gray thunderheads were swallowing up the stars above, blotting out the light of them and the moon, saturating the night with darkness and humidity.

It was past midnight and the town of Belhaven was closed shut and locked tight. The sight of the first cloud had long since sent most of the townspeople scurrying to secure themselves, their families, and their belongings indoors, for summer storms in northern Britain could, on occasion, mete out a good deal of damage. The winds preceding this storm promised just that as they gained strength with the approaching clouds, and they wouldn't die down, most likely, until long after the clouds had finished their work.

To the lord of Belhaven, however, the winds and the coming storm were a blessing. He stood on the balcony of his bedchamber, dressed only in a robe, and delighted in the winds that buffeted and cooled him. It was late summer and the weather had been hot the past few days, and, though the temperature was still warmer than usual even now, the storm would offer a pleasant respite from the heat.

Another strong gust whipped Sir Garin's long blond hair off his shoulders and fluttered the robe around his legs. He smiled. The wind brought the scent of lavender with it, probably from his wife's garden, which was planted in the inner bailey directly below him, and the sweet smell reminded him again of how glad he was to be home. The sound of the gusts playing violence with the forest trees nearby was, he decided, the finest sound in the world, for it was his forest and they were his trees and he was home after having been gone warring.

He surveyed as much of Belhaven as he could from his high balcony and frowned to think that it had changed so much in only eight months. Had he been gone so long? Aye, the look on his lady's face when he had ridden to her yestereve across the bridge and through the gates had told him it was so. He would stay home now, for a while at least. King Henry would have to ask another of his vassals to fight with him, for Garin had vassals and serfs of his own to look to, as well as many pressing matters that required his attention. Indeed, it was one such matter that had kept him awake this eve, long after he and his lady had sought their bed.

He turned over in his mind once more the petition that had arrived that afternoon, and felt anew the anger and fear its contents had at once wrought in him. Knowing that he must soon make a decision concerning it had driven him to the balcony and to the solace of the winds and the coming storm.

"My lord?" he heard behind him, and turned.

His wife, dressed in a thin white night shift, her long black hair fluttering loosely down her back, stood at the opening of their bedchamber looking like a beautiful, unworldly apparition. For one brief moment an image of her as she had been when he had first set eyes on her flashed through his mind. She had been ten and five years of age then, running barefoot with her cousins through her father's gardens on a warm summer day, her coal black hair unbound and flying like a midnight banner behind her as she raced headlong, unknowingly, right into his heart.

Seeing her now he wondered anew that such a one as she had ever wed with such a one as he.

"Canst thou not sleep, Garin?" she asked sleepily, wrapping her arms around her shoulders in defense of the winds and giving a little yawn.

"Nay, lady, I've too many thoughts in my head to sleep yet. Did I wake thee?"

She grinned at him sheepishly. "I missed thy body next to mine, sir, and *that* is what woke me. Indeed, it is what hath wakened me every night since thou left me. Now thou'rt home again I refuse to be denied."

Garin laughed and reached one arm out to pull her close. "Come, then, and I shall gladly give thee what thou hast missed." He opened his robe, pulled her snugly up against his chest, and closed the robe around her, wrapping his arms about her waist to keep it secure.

"Ah, I've missed thee, Elaine, my love. What a long time I have been away from thee and from Belhaven."

"Aye, my lord. Far too long. Now tell me what disturbs thee and keeps thee from thy slumber ere the rain comes and drives us from the balcony."

He set his cheek against the softness of her hair. "'Twas the missive that came today," he admitted.

"It brought bad news, my lord?"

"It did. 'Twas from Walter le Brun. He is still at the side of the king, helping to sort out this trouble with the traitor. Before I left we'd heard rumors of treason involving Terent of Ravinet, and le Brun hath discovered they are true."

Elaine stiffened. "The king bids thee go again?"

"Nay, nay, lady," Garin reassured her with a squeeze. "God's my life, I'll not leave thee again for long, not e'en by command of the king. 'Tis not in me to do so. But hear me well, beloved, for Ravinet means to cause great trouble for the king, and for le Brun as well, and 'tis our sworn duty to give aid against the fiend as best we may, in whatever manner we may, regardless the sacrifice."

She lifted her head to look into his solemn face.

"Tell me, Garin, for I hear the worry in thy words. Tell me very quickly."

His voice, when he spoke, was grim. "Ravinet means to take Margot le Brun hostage and force her to wed with him." Elaine gasped, but Garin went on. "Thou dost understand what this means, dost thou not, my love? She is Walter's only child, the inheritor of all his lands. If she becomes the wife of Ravinet, she becomes his pawn against her own father, and naught would stay that demon from using her well," he finished bitterly.

"Ah, no." Elaine shook her head sadly. "The poor child!"

"No longer a child, but a woman full-grown and by all accounts most lovely. The king himself claims to be besotted with her, and for her sake as well as for the sake of his kingdom he hath required that she be taken and kept safe from Ravinet. Before we left Shrewsbury 'twas decided by himself and Walter and I that if the charges against Ravinet prove true, then Margot should be fetched at once to Belhaven and kept here in our care."

"Indeed, my lord," Elaine said truly, "I shall be glad and more to have the lady Margot stay with us, for I remember well what a sweet and lovely child she was, but if thou'rt not to go, who shall be the one to fetch her?"

The stark look in his eyes told her better than words how greatly the answer troubled him. "Eric shall go, at the request of both Walter and the king. He knows it not, yet. Indeed, he knows nothing of the danger the lady Margot is in, but 'twas decided many weeks ago that he would be the one to bring her to safety."

"Eric!—" Elaine repeated with shock. "Nay! I'll not allow it, and so His Majesty may have my head! He and Jaufre have but just returned with thee! 'Twould be unjust to send him away again after being home only one day!"

"My, my." Garin chuckled at his gentle wife's vehemence. He lifted a hand to touch her heated cheek. "And such a pretty head, too, to offer the king's executioner. Calm thyself, my heart. Faith, I like it no better than thee, for where Ravinet and his dogs are involved there can only be danger, yet we needs must accept what is. 'Tis God's own truth Eric is a fine, rare lad. Of that no man could be in doubt. If only thou hadst seen him in battle, my love! A true leader—e'en his brothers followed his will. When the bearer of the standard fell in the enemy's midst, I looked and saw that Eric had reached and lifted the colors before they touched ground. The men all around had begun to waver, thinking the battle turned against us, but the brave lad lifted the standard high and shouted, 'Forward men! For Henry and for England!' 'Twas a grand sight to see how they cheered and followed him into the fray. After all was over both the king and Prince Henry commended the lad and invited him to join their train."

"But he did not," said Elaine.

Garin frowned. "Nay, he *would* not. 'Twould have been a great boon for him, but he declined them by saying he'd sworn eternal fealty to me, and that naught save death should part us. I could have wrung his stubborn neck! The lad could easily achieve greatness, but that damned eternal fealty will be the ruin of him!"

Elaine lifted a hand to Garin's chin and caused him to look down at her. "Garin, thou knowest full well how he feels! He is determined to be indebted to thee, and he loves thee too well to leave thee. Didst not say that he looked to thy safety and comfort above all during thy battle stay?"

"By my troth! That he did, lady. He coddled me like a damned babe! 'Twas all I could do to keep him from tucking me into bed each eve. Betwixt his brothers and him I was almost turned mad. Henry began to think I could no longer do for myself, and so, in jest, he told me to my face."

Garin did his best to sound angry, Elaine knew, but she could hear the pride and pleasure hidden beneath his words. He was a giant, powerful man, a gruff man, and a stern lord, but he was also a man who loved his children. From their cradle on he had been a father who had taken an interest in every part of their lives, loving each of them equally, never setting one above the other and always full of pride in the things that made them unique, yet even so, Eric was special. He had been from the very moment he had come to them, and Elaine could vividly remember all that Garin had told her about the day when he had brought Eric home, hungry, cold, and dirty.

He had only been a few hours old when Garin had found him in the nearby forest, abandoned and squalling loudly, probably left there to die by a peasant family who couldn't feed yet another mouth. Garin had been out riding in an effort to console himself, for she, Elaine, had given birth only hours before to their second child, a stillborn son. So distraught was she that it had been necessary to sedate her. Garin had stayed by her side until she lapsed into an exhausted sleep; afterward he had escaped to the peace of the forest to master his own grief.

The crying of a baby had drawn his attention. He found it beneath a tree, a wrapped bundle lying on the muddy ground, emitting the healthiest screams Garin had ever heard from a newborn babe. He dismounted and gently picked the bundle up, cradling it in his arms. Sharp pangs of grief shot through him as he pulled the covering from the baby's face and looked upon the angry, red, wrinkled visage; such a contrast it was to the still, blue face of his own dead child.

But this child was not dead. A large healthy baby with masses of black curls sticking damply to his head, still wet from birth, the child actually appeared affronted at having been left to die, and he wanted the world to know it. He seemed determined not to leave this life without a fight, having so recently only entered it, and he screamed with his determination. Garin was soothed by the baby's fierceness, and holding a live child in his arms, as he would have done had his own child lived, was a comfort beyond reason.

He offered the tip of his little finger to the child to suckle, and the baby responded gratefully, sucking so hard that it actually stung.

"Well, my little fellow, thou'rt hungry, indeed. Poor little man. Did they not feed thee even once to ease thy suffering before they left thee here? The dogs! Verily, I would kill them for such evilness could I find who abandoned thee."

The babe stared thoughtfully while Garin spoke, but realizing after a moment that the finger on which he suckled wasn't providing the desired nourishment, he began to cry again. Garin chuckled at the demanding orphan and took him to his horse. He mounted carefully, cradling the child securely in one arm.

"Now then, lad, thou art mine by right of domain, for these are my lands on which thou hast been abandoned." He started his horse toward the castle.

He continued to address the unhappy child as he rode. "A very gift from God thou art, and I love thee already, for thou'rt a fierce warrior, indeed, whom I shall make mine own. Hush, now, child. I'm taking thee to nourishment, i'faith."

Thus Garin had brought the child to Elaine, who, waking from her stuporous sleep accepted the baby as though he were hers. Her breasts were painfully heavy with early milk and the hungry creature suckled eagerly, needing her so much and causing her to fall completely in love with him. She fingered the dark curls so like her own and found it easy to think of him as her natural child. Garin named him Eric and announced that he was, indeed, now theirs. The memory of her dead baby still pained Elaine, but in the ensuing days, months, and years, Eric eased the pain until it faded entirely.

"Garin," Elaine asked softly, "why must it be Eric who goes? Why canst thou not send another?"

Garin shook his head. "The king wishes him to go for all his ability, and Walter wishes him to go because his daughter loves him." Meeting her immediately questioning eyes, he clarified, "Walter claims that the lady Margot is in love with our Eric, and has been e'er since they first met each other, ten years past. Dost remember the time I speak of, love?"

"Ten years ago? When thou found her hiding in our chambers at court? When the other children had been cruel to her because of her halting speech?"

Garin nodded. "Aye, and she was crying, poor child, and was even more afeared when I found her, for she thought me a giant! What a delicate, sensitive child she was. I sat her on my lap and asked her why she was crying and how had she come to be hiding in our chambers, and she was so frightened that her stammer grew even worse. I could barely understand her, but well enough to learn that the others had teased her and run her off. Eric and Jaufre entered the chambers and found us thus. Jaufre was closer to her age and I asked him to play with her, but, being the stubborn ass he hath ere been he flatly refused to play with a girl." Garin laughed at the remembrance. "Eric was ten and three and nearly full-grown, as I seem to remember, but he offered, most readily, to entertain the little girl. Thou knowest he was ever a kind lad, and good with the younger children. Margot was all too happy to go with him and dried her tears at once. He took her to shoot arrows, I think, an activity which evidently caused her to develop a love for him which Walter claims hath lasted these many years, though the two have not seen each other since. 'Tis well," he added thoughtfully, "for she is to choose a husband for herself from amongst our sons once she arrives safe at Belhaven, and if she loves Eric beforehand 'twill bode well for their union, methinks."

With a sound of angry surprise Elaine pushed at her husband's broad shoulders. "Thou hast promised a son of mine in marriage without consulting me!" she nearly shouted at him. "I'll have no child of mine treated thusly! I will *not* have it, Garin!"

Garin grinned at his wife. "Thou wilt have it, madam, else thou wilt go against the word of the king, who has declared that the lady Margot shall wed with one of our sons as soon as may be so that Terent of Ravinet will be most thoroughly discouraged in his efforts. Henry would rather she be safely wed to one faithful to the throne, my love, and that must seem quite reasonable, even to thee."

"It is wrong to make thine own son wed against his will, my lord. That is how it seems to me."

"My loved one," he said softly, soothingly, "if Eric doth not wish to wed with the lady Margot I shall not force him. Thou must know that of me, at least. I wish our children to know the happiness we have had in their lives." He kissed her gently. "But she is reputed afar to be a great beauty, as well as the heiress to all of Walter's lands and titles and wealth. Surely no son of mine would be such an idiot as to turn her away!" He kissed her again.

"No son of thine would be such an idiot," she agreed when he lifted his mouth to kiss her throat and shoulders. "And no son of *mine* would wed for naught but love."

"Love is not the only cause of marriage, my darling," he murmured, thinking, at the moment, of desire, "and our stubborn Eric would not wed e'en for that were he to set himself against the union. 'Twould take more than love to force him to it."

His wife shook her head at him, as though pitying him for such foolishness. "Thou dost not know much of love then, my lord," she whispered, smiling.

"Not know much of love, lady?" Garin nuzzled the soft, scented skin beneath her ear. "Thy memory is sorely lacking. Methinks I should demonstrate to thee anew my vast knowledge of the subject." Taking her up in his arms, he moved toward their bedchamber.

"'Tis time and since thou wast in bed, anyway, my lord." Her sigh drifted back to the balcony as they went in.

The winds continued to gust, and in a few minutes the first drops of the promised rain began to pelt the balcony where they had stood.

2

"*What does it say,* Margot?" Minna asked, peering over her lady's shoulder.

"Hmm?" replied Margot, deep in concentration as she read her father's words.

"The missive, my lady, what doth thy father say?"

"In a m-moment, Minna. Be quiet now," Margot instructed gently, not turning her eyes from the document.

Minna sighed and picked up an ornate silver brush from the dressing table where Margot sat. She began to brush her lady's honey-colored hair, a laborious task as Margot's hair was so long and fine. Like silk thread, Minna thought with a twinge of jealousy, and so unlike her own dull brown locks.

But then, thought Minna, everything about Margot was perfect, and any lady would look plain by comparison, especially one as plain as herself. The fact that Margot seemed to be completely ignorant of her beauty helped to soothe Minna's feelings, but not much. What wouldn't she give to have such perfect, glowing skin as smooth as the ivory that Sir Walter had brought home from his last battle? And what wouldn't she do to have eyes the hue of cornflowers, or lips the color of fine pink roses? Minna sighed and continued brushing.

Margot, meantime, frowned over the document in her hands and read it through once more.

To the Lady Margot le Brun of Reed,

My sweet daughter, I send thee my love and greetings. I am alive and well and desire that thou shouldst not worry for my sake. All will be finished soon with the traitor Glendower and those who plot with him against the king, and I pray that we shall see each other soon.

With this missive I send thee a command and ask that thou fulfill it with neither question nor worry. It is this; I desire that thou shouldst reside for the present under the protection of Sir Garin Stavelot of Belhaven. Thou wilt remember that he hath been my close friend these many years, and that we trained together under Montfiort for our knighthood. He knows that I worry for thy safety while I am absent from Reed and hath willingly agreed to keep thee under his care until such time as I may come to thee. We have also agreed that when thou hast reached Belhaven thou shalt choose for thine husband one of his eligible sons. I believe, from what thou hast said in the past, that this shall meet with thine approval.

Sir Garin will send his finest men to escort thee safely to Belhaven, and even now they may be journeying toward Reed. Thou must prepare for travel in all haste and secure Reed under the supervision of John the Steward. Until thy escort arrives I desire that thou shouldst stay within the walls of Reed. Do not disobey me in this, beloved. I would not have thee be afeard, but merely to do this for me, thy father, who worries for and misses his only child.

I send thee my love and blessings and a final request to take care in all things until we are together again.

Sir Walter le Brun
Written at Shrewsbury
20 August 1403

She set the document aside and stared at the polished steel mirror before her. Conflicting emotions warred as she tried to make sense of her father's words. Was he in danger? Was she in danger? He had been careful to reassure her while in the same moment making it plain that something was very wrong. He had told her not to worry, yet had commanded her to stay within the town walls. Never before had he limited her freedom in any way, and she was used to doing as she pleased whenever she pleased. Today, for instance, she had promised Cook that she would visit the nearby forest to gather wild mushrooms. He had been so delighted that she hated to disappoint him. Well, she would go outside the walls just this last time and would take the dogs and some men with her for protection, and she would finish the task quickly and be home soon. After that she would obey her father and stray no farther than the village gates.

A sudden thrill rushed through her when she remembered his words about choosing a husband from among the Stavelot sons, and she flushed with pleasure as she thought of her beloved Eric. She had always known they would be together one day, and now her dreams were going to come true. Of course, Eric probably wouldn't even remember the little girl he had once entertained so many years ago. He had taught her archery that day, and Margot conjured up a memory of him helping her to pull back the string on his own giant bow, his strong arms easily doing the task, and of his pretending to be impressed as though she had done it herself.

Smiling, she gazed at her reflection in the mirror. Would he be pleased with how she had grown, she wondered.

"Wilt tell me now what Sir Walter wrote thee, Margot?" Minna interrupted her thoughts.

Margot folded the missive and placed it in a wooden box that lay on the table. She smiled up at her friend.

"We are g-going on a journey, Minna, thou and J-Jace and I. My father wrote to t-tell me to prepare in haste for those who come to escort us."

Minna stopped braiding Margot's hair. "A journey!" she exclaimed. "To where, my lady?"

"Belhaven!"

"Belhaven!" Minna repeated in a shocked whisper. "Is that not where thine Eric lives?"

"Yes, yes, yes!" Margot jumped up and grabbed Minna by the hand. She twirled her around, laughing. "I am g-going to be wed to my Eric and so we are going to Belhaven! Oh, Minna! I always knew he and I would be together!"

She stopped as suddenly as she had started, and grasped the stunned Minna by the shoulders. "There is much t-to d-do today, and so I m-must be finished with my promised task to Cook by midday. Fetch my working clothes, the blue surcoat, and quickly now!"

Shortly, Margot was dressed and ready, her hair fixed in one long thick braid that traveled down her back and past her waist. Her attire was simple but suitable for the task ahead. She collected a wide-brimmed hat, wicker basket, and pair of leather gloves before leaving her chambers.

Descending into the nearly deserted great hall, Margot was greeted by Jace, her father's young jester, who was also her constant companion, being only one year older than she.

"Hallo, Margot lady," he called as she approached him. "What's for today?"

"Good morn, J-Jace." She set the wide-brimmed hat upon her head. "We are going to p-pick mushrooms in the forest, but thou'rt not well d-dressed for it, i'faith." She surveyed his velvet tunic and soft leggings with a frown.

"Mushrooms in the forest?" he repeated. "Thou dost not love me if thou wouldst make me wet my feet." He lifted a foot to show that it was encased in a soft shoe as well.

She struggled to tie the hat beneath her chin. "I know it rained heartily last eve and that the ground is s-sure to be w-wet. But thou must come with me, Jace, for I need escort and Sir B-Basil will be short of m-men, so thou must m-make up for one."

"I am not one to protect thee, Margot lady," he replied with a pout, and indeed it was true, for he was rather slight. "I wish to remain here, where 'tis dry."

Margot laughed. "Nay, Jace, what w-would I do if I was set upon by knaves and had not thee to give me c-courage?"

This made him thoughtful but didn't remove the pout from his face.

"And," she added enticingly, "we shall take King and Prince with us for sport. Wouldst thou not like to match one of thy falcons with them?"

Now his face lit up. "King and Prince? Indeed I would. I shall fetch my best bird and come."

In less than half an hour they set out with an escort of six fighting men, including Sir Basil himself, and two large mastiffs trotting happily alongside.

Their destination was not far away and they

reached it shortly; Margot dismounted and left Jace to exercise the dogs as she went about her task. Sir Basil and his men spread out to guard the area while she lost herself among the cool, dark trees.

Black Donal had been watching his prey with great care that morning. What a little fool! She had given herself to him without even knowing it. But how *right* it was. How exactly right. He'd never dreamed capturing her would be such a simple matter. From his well-hidden vantage point he and his men had seen her leave her escort to go alone into the forest, a perfect place to take her without incident. He would simply have to wait until she wandered far enough away from her guards, and then she would be his. Terent would be pleased, indeed, that he had fulfilled his task so quickly.

"Mount up, men," Black Donal bellowed to the camp, taking hold of his own steed with heavily gloved hands. "We're away, and now!"

Margot had lost all sense of time, though she was sure she must not have been gone for more than an hour, for surely Sir Basil would have come to fetch her before that much time had passed. Worse, she couldn't see through the trees to where she had entered the woods. Panic rushed through her, but she sternly reminded herself that one good scream would bring the dogs running and Sir Basil and his men following. She turned around and around, looking in all directions. *There,* she thought, relieved at finally finding a landmark. Moving toward it, she began her way back.

"Ho, there, lass!" a voice behind her boomed. "What dost thou here?"

She whirled and found herself facing a strange man. How had he come to be there so suddenly? She hadn't heard him walking through the leaves.

"S-sir!" she stammered. "What a fright thou g-gavest me!"

He laughed and strode to where she stood holding her basket, one gloved hand crossed over her breast.

He was very tall and lithe, she saw, and moved gracefully; a handsome man with brown hair and beard and mustache, dressed as a hunter.

"'Twould be a shame indeed to scare away such a pretty little rabbit," he said cheerfully, grasping her hands firmly in his before she could jump away. Her basket fell to the ground.

"How d-dare thee!" Margot exclaimed, shocked and offended. She struggled to loose herself without success.

"Now, now, mistress," her captor chided, holding her fast. "What would be thought if a hunter such as I let a pretty catch like thee go without having at least a kiss to show for it?"

"I am n-no catch for th-thee, sir! I am th-the lady M-Margot le Brun of R-Reed!"

He laughed heartily at that, eyeing her clothing. "Oh, aye, mistress! And I am Henry Bolingbroke, most happy to make thy acquaintance!" He shook his head. "Nay, pretty rabbit. Lady Margot of Reed would ne'er wander alone into the forest unprotected. 'Twould be right dangerous, dost thou not think?"

Margot drew breath to scream, but he seemed to realize her intent and clasped a firm hand over her mouth before she could make a sound.

"Why, if the lady Margot ever did such a foolish thing," he continued pleasantly, his arms tightening around her struggling body, "she might find herself kidnapped by knaves, or ravished by a passing knight, or even murdered by a wandering hunter, certes if she was foolish enough to dress herself in the clothing of a peasant."

She tried to scream against his hand, but it was no good. All sound was completely stopped. His arms were painfully strong against her, his grip cruel. She began to cry, partly from fear and pain and partly from rage.

He brought his head closer and spoke warmly against her ear, his soft voice full of warning. "One can ne'er be too careful, can they, my dear? The world is filled with evil men who will do any and all for a price. Thou wilt henceforth remember that, wilt thou not?" He stared into her fear-widened eyes. She nodded slowly.

"Very well, little rabbit. I am going to turn thee in the direction of thy guards, and I am going to release thee. When I do 'twould be well if thou ran to them swiftly as thou canst, lest I change my mind and keep thee for myself." He chuckled. "But before I set thee free, I will exact payment for the valuable lesson I have given thee this day. Mayhap it will serve as a reminder in future." And with that he simultaneously withdrew his hand from her mouth and lowered his head to kiss her. It was a painful kiss, purposely brutal. She fought to free herself, but his fingers bit into her arms, holding her in place for this punishment. Her lips were cut against her teeth and she could taste blood. When he finally released her she crumpled to the ground at his feet.

Margot looked up at him through her tears and saw him shakily draw his hand across his mouth. For the one second she stared his face held regret. Then she leapt to her feet and ran.

Sir Basil and Jace were calling her name. The sound of the dogs barking met her as she ran wildly, pushing past trees and bushes in a frantic, desperate rush. She was blinded by tears and had no sense of direction, only a determination to get as far away from that madman as she could. Suddenly, thankfully, King and Prince came bounding into view. Behind them were Sir Basil and Jace.

In moments the men-at-arms were searching the forest for the man dressed in hunter's clothing, while Sir Basil gently led the distraught Margot to the clearing. Jace held her hand tightly as they made their way to the horses, his face paler than hers. Then they were on their way back into the safety of the walls of Reed.

*   *   *

"Be damned!" Black Donal exploded, slapping his thigh with a clenched fist. His horse paced nervously beneath him and he tightened the reins. "The bitch!"

His men surrounded him, mounted as well. They were deep in the forests of Reed, only steps from where the lady Margot had been a few minutes before. There was no sign of the lady anymore, and no sign of the hunter they had spied flying away on his horse just as they had arrived. Two of his men had taken chase but had returned empty-handed. Now several fighting men of Reed and two barking hounds were rapidly approaching, and Black Donal and his men had no choice but to retreat and return to their waiting place.

"Fiend sieze her, the little witch!" Donal's fury was boundless. "But I'll have her yet, I vow, and when I do 'twill be most pleasant to see Terent exact revenge for all the trouble she's caused me."

They turned and rode away full speed. Hours later Sir Basil's men returned to Reed with the Lady Margot's empty wicker basket, reporting that they had found no sign of the hunter in the forest.

3

Aleric woke slowly, groggily. His first clear thought was that someone quite heavy was sitting on his head, but when he carefully reached his hand up to touch his throbbing temple, that thought was dispelled. Moving his arm made his whole body ache, and he vaguely wondered where he was and why he felt so dizzy. Drawing in a much-needed breath of air, he managed only to fill his nostrils with moist dirt, and realized that he must be lying facedown in a wet field.

While his memory made its unhurried return, he was jarred by the warm laughter of a familiar voice.

"Come now, little brother. I've not killed thee with that tiny tap, have I?"

Aleric groaned in reply and in vain tried to empty his mouth of dirt. A giant hand took hold of the back of his hauberk and gently, if quickly, tossed him onto his back.

His eyes, caked with mud, creaked open, and when the world ceased its spinning he saw the smiling face of his brother looking down at him.

"Nay, Eric," he said, his voice rasping, "thou hast not killed me. But tell me, is my head still attached to the rest of me?"

Eric threw his head back and roared with laughter, and even though he was sure he was at least half-dead, Aleric smiled too, though rather foolishly.

"Aye, lad, thy head is still attached to thee." Eric chuckled. "Though what good it does thee there I dare not say."

He reached down again, grasped Aleric by the front of his tunic, and with one hand swept him off the ground and placed him on his feet as though he were doing nothing more strenuous than plucking a daisy. Eric dwarfed his younger brother by more than a foot and, in fact, was the tallest member of the entire Stavelot family. His father was closest to him in size, being another giant of a man, but his three brothers weren't able to match his height or width, to say nothing of his sister, who was a blonde image of his petite mother.

Aleric swayed unsteadily, but Eric held him until he could stand on his feet without falling down. He knew that Aleric, who had just turned seventeen, wouldn't stand for being coddled like a child.

Aleric was in training to be a knight and insisted that he would reach his goal by the time he was eighteen. Eric himself had been knighted at the age of sixteen, being already larger and stronger than most men and having accompanied his father and older brother into battle against one of old King Richard's foes. He had conducted himself so valiantly in the victorious fight that Richard himself had knighted him in front of the assembled warriors. His latest conquests at Shrewsbury had equally endeared him to both the king and Prince Henry, and all Aleric could speak of now was being exactly like his older brother.

Eric had promised to train him, and train him he would, though in his heart he believed Aleric would do better to study his beloved poetry, for Aleric would always be short and slender and smart. The rather gentle blow Eric had just delivered the boy had felled him. Had they been on the field of battle Aleric would have long been dead, run through with his enemy's sword.

"Come, Aleric." Eric smiled encouragingly, and handed him his mud-caked sword. "Thou hast had enough practice for one day. Does Father see thee rattled by my hand again he will have me skinned like a rabbit for dinner. Thou'rt his favorite, lad." Eric clapped his arm around Aleric's shoulder and led him toward his waiting squire. "Thou knowest full well he would be angry if he knew I was training thee for battle, for he declares thou'rt his scholar, and rightly so. If thou wouldst please him thou wouldst try to be a scholar, instead of a knight."

Aleric's anger sounded clearly through his dizziness. "I shall be a knight first, and then a scholar." He shook off his brother's arm. "Thou art a knight. My other brothers are knights. My father and uncles all are knights."

"Aye, Aleric, but I would rather be a scholar than a knight," Eric said truly.

Aleric stopped, making Eric stop as well, and stared hard at his giant brother. "Thou art making jest of me! I mean what I say!"

Eric fixed his brother with an amused expression. "Do I ever make jest of *thee,* brother, thou wilt know it! Dost not know that I envy thy book learning and thy many skills which I do not possess?"

Aleric gave him a look of pure disbelief. "What skills?" he demanded.

Eric shrugged, took a moment to call to his squire to come to them, then turned back to Aleric. "Thou'rt a better archer than I. In fact, thou'rt the best of the family. Better even than Father."

Aleric tried not to smile at this offhanded compliment.

"Archery," he said huffily, folding his arms across his chest, "is a sport for weaklings. Any child could do it."

Eric looked momentarily surprised, then turned his eyes heavenward and mockingly supplicated, "God make me a child again, then!"

Aleric, unsure of how to respond to his brother's teasing and still make his feelings on the subject firmly understood, was saved by the arrival of Eric's eager squire.

"By the blessed body o'God it rained well and good last eve," Eric declared, pulling off his gauntlets and handing them to the waiting squire. "And the wind blew like the Fiend, himself, eh, Geoff? Now thou must needs take care to rid my armor of all this mud."

"Aye, my lord, that I will," promised Geoff. He efficiently collected the dispensed bits of armor and swords from both Aleric and Eric and went to pack them neatly away.

Two horses waited nearby, a dappled mare and a giant roan destrier, contentedly munching the wet grass, but the field was otherwise empty of company, save Geoff.

"The wet has kept away the other knights' practice," said Aleric. "'Tis well for me, so Father will not know."

Eric gave him a strange look. "Thou shouldst tell him, lad. I cannot like doing this without his knowledge, though I promised thee I would, and will."

Aleric shook his head. "Nay. I'll not tell him 'til I'm full and ready. Father's wrath requires some forewarning." He looked toward the village. "Can we not walk back, Eric? I would know what damage the village has had from last eve's winds."

"As would I," Eric agreed with a curt nod. He turned to yell at Geoff. "Take the horses back, lad. We'll walk. Take care to rub Bram down well and make him comfortable." He smiled at his brother. "Come, then, Aleric, let's be on our way. We've been out long enough to worry Mother. Since Jaufre and I have come home she flutters over us like a hen over her chicks."

Aleric gave a short, unsympathetic laugh. "I'll not feel sorry for thee on that head, Eric. All the while thou wast gone 'twas I she fluttered o'er. 'Tis thy turn to be treated like a child."

"That is treatment I will bless and welcome," Eric assured him. "I'm done with sleeping in the cold and wet, and going without food and comfort. Mother may coddle me to her heart's content and I'll ne'er grow weary on't."

Aleric shot a sideways glance at his brother. "What was it like, Eric, to be in battle? Wast scared?"

Eric nodded with a grim smile. "Aye, God's my life, I was scared. Many a time I thought I would know death and wanted to turn craven and run." He sobered. "But I was angered, as well, lad, with what I believed wrong, and it gave me the mind to go on. E'en though I was scared."

"Please God I may see such a battle someday," Aleric said hopefully.

Eric shuddered. "Nay, Aleric, nay. Please God thou wilt not. That will be my prayer."

They had neared the gates of Belhaven, and Aleric looked up and saw a familiar figure striding toward them.

"Here comes Jaufre," he announced simply, causing Eric to look up as well.

Eric couldn't help but smile. Jaufre was not only his brother but also his closest friend, being only two years younger than he. He was a big man, though nowhere close to Eric's size, and they were opposites in appearance. Eric was the only Stavelot, other than his mother, with dark hair and coloring. The rest were blond and fair, including Jaufre, whose long hair fell well past his shoulders. Jaufre was generally considered to be the handsomest of the Stavelot sons, and the most reckless.

"Hey, lads!" he shouted in greeting as he neared them. "Out rolling in the mud, God save us! Best not let Father see thee thus attired. I believe he might knock thy two empty heads together."

"Why? Is he in the village surveying the damage?" Aleric asked with undisguised fear. "Mayhap we should go through the north side, Eric."

"Nay, lad, he is not like to see thee here," Jaufre reassured him. "He waits in the hall, wanting to see the three of us together. He sent me to find the two of thee and bid thee hie to him right quick."

Eric's forehead wrinkled in a frown. "Is aught amiss, Jaufre?"

"I do not know," he replied honestly, "though I think it may have to do with James getting married. I overheard Mother saying to her ladies something about having to prepare for a wedding feast soon."

"James married!" Eric declared as the three started forward together. "He did not speak of a lady love when we last took leave of him. He seemed ready to serve King Henry for a good while, I thought."

"Mmmm." Jaufre nodded. "Mayhap he doth not know he is to be wed. Mayhap 'tis an arranged marriage."

"Ugh!" Aleric emitted with feeling. "If that be so, mayhap his bride will be ugly as an old brown hen! I wonder why Father and Mother would do such a thing to our brother."

"Most marriages are arranged, Aleric," Eric said. "It doth seem time and since that James should have been wed, though I, too, am surprised that Mother and Father would arrange his marriage. They were a love match, after all."

"Aye, but being the eldest, James must produce an heir," Jaufre conjectured, "and that is best done with a properly titled lady. If Mother and Father left it to his choosing he might very well bring home a lady of unsuitable breeding."

"Surely they cannot care for such things as standing," Aleric argued. "I certainly don't."

"No, but thou need not worry, lad, being the youngest," Jaufre countered with a grin. "Thou canst choose any lady who strikes thy fancy, and welcome to her. But poor James hath responsibilities, and, God forbid it, should aught happen to keep him from fulfilling them, then our own dear Eric must do so."

Eric grimaced. "Nay, Jaufre, not I. Thou knowest full well I've sworn eternal fealty to our Father. I'll not marry."

"What! Never!?" Jaufre exclaimed with mock dismay. "Thy bed will be cold and lonely, lad, without a lovely maid to keep it warm."

Eric laughed. "That it will not be, not with so many willing maids nearby."

"Oho!" Jaufre crowed, clapping both hands over Aleric's ears. "Thou'lt give the lad ideas, Eric, and Mother will wring thy ears off thy lecherous head!"

Aleric shook Jaufre off. "I am not a child," he informed his elder brother in very offended tones. "I know about women."

"Oh, my pardon, sir," Jaufre apologized, bowing politely. When he straightened he winked at Eric over their little brother's head and they continued strolling through the village, laughing and talking.

Two particular residents of Belhaven watched the progress of the young lords with special interest.

Dortha, the elder, stopped her work and rested her hands and chin on the handle of the rake she'd been using to make neat piles of windblown straw.

"I'm so glad Sir Eric hath returned safely from battle." She sighed, gazing at him with undisguised longing. "'Tis a long time he hath been away."

Her sister, Alois, a pretty buxom girl, looked up from where she worked at pitching the piles of straw into a wheelbarrow.

"Shame on thee, Dortha! Best keep thine eyes off that one. He'll never offer thee marriage."

Dortha laughed pleasantly. "Marriage is not exactly what I want from him."

Alois's eyes widened. "Dortha! Thou hast not— *not* with that giant! A tumble with a man that size could kill thee!"

Dortha smiled at her little sister with what seemed

like a touch of sympathy. "Nay, Alois. He is not rough as some others are. He is very gentle and sweet and—most satisfying," she emphasized with a long sigh.

Alois shook her head. "I can understand not what thou seest in him. He is not even pleasing to look at, so dark and black and homely he is. Now if he was as beautiful as Sir Jaufre . . ." She looked approvingly at his approaching figure.

"Good day, mistresses," Eric greeted, nodding and giving Dortha a wink.

"M'lords." She smiled in return and curtseyed. Alois followed suit.

"The winds have caused thee much work, I see."

"Yes, m'lord," Dortha agreed. "Our father bade us gather the straw by nightfall and return it to the goat shed, but 'tis indeed a grievous task for two poor maids."

Jaufre gently lifted Alois's dimpled chin with one long finger. He let his eyes wander appreciatively over her pretty face and ample figure.

"*Poor* is not at all the word I would use for thee, mistress," he said, and Alois blushed.

"Nor I for thee, Dortha," Eric assured that young lady with a grin. "Thou hast grown even prettier in the past eight months. We are bade by our father to attend him now, but mayhap, if time permits, I will come back this eve to help thee with this hard work."

She smiled prettily and curtseyed again. "I thank thee, m'lord." She glanced up at him suggestively. "'Twould be most pleasant."

"Most," Eric agreed, a promise in his tone.

Jaufre sighed heavily. "It will never be enough. Mayhap I shall come as well, to see the job is quickly done."

"Mayhap I will soon be ill, if the two of thee do not cease this cooing and turtledoving," Aleric added with disgust. "Hast forgotten that Father is waiting?"

"Nay, lad," Eric said. "We'll away. Good day, mistresses."

Jaufre let one of his fingers gently caress Alois's cheek before pinching her chin softly and following his brothers.

"By the Rood, Aleric! Thy knowledge of women is indeed overwhelming," he teased when he caught up to them. "That romantic tongue of thine will be sure to have them swooning at thy feet."

Aleric reddened and began walking a little faster. "Keep thy teasing for thy lovesick maids, Jaufre. I've no need for it!"

Eric and Jaufre strode behind him, laughing.

They got no farther than several steps, however, before they were attacked by a band of dirty screaming urchins who had been playing at knights and squires when they saw Eric walking by and realized this presented an opportunity that could not be passed up. Within seconds Eric, Jaufre, and Aleric were surrounded by fierce little boys brandishing wooden sticks as swords and demanding surrender. Some of the youngsters attached themselves to their captives' long legs to prevent them from escape, and one healthy attacker leapt upon

Aleric's back and wrapped his arms firmly around his neck.

"Get off, little fiend!" Aleric demanded, turning around and around in an effort to dislodge the determined boy. "Eric, call off thy pack of brats!" he demanded of his laughing brother.

"Hold, men! And jab the noisy one to keep him quiet!" came a commanding voice from the dirtiest of the urchins. He was a skinny towheaded child with bare feet and ragged clothing, but he was the obvious leader as he stood in front of the captives and held his stick aloft.

"Dost thou surrender, villains?" he demanded of Eric.

Eric did his best to look truly captured. "Aye, we surrender, Sir Knight."

"Really, Eric, this is—" Jaufre began while gently trying to disengage his legs from the sticky mass of hands that clung to him. He received a light jab in the side for his interruption.

"Silence!" yelled the leader. He fixed Eric with a steely glare. "Dost know why thou hast been captured, villain?"

"For passing secrets to the traitor, Owain Glendower?" Eric suggested.

The leader thought that sounded good. "Aye! Thou'rt spies and must pay the penalty! What say thee, men? What shall be the penalty?"

"Death, death, death!" they all replied enthusiastically.

"Death?!" Aleric repeated incredulously. "That's a bit drastic for—ouch!" He received a jab.

"Silence!" the leader ordered. "Villains are not allowed to speak!"

"Eric!" Jaufre said in exasperation.

"All right, all right." Eric gave in. "We shall bargain with thee, Sir Knight, if thou'rt willing."

"What be this bargain?" the leader asked in a voice full of distrust.

"If thy men and thee will let us go, I shall bring to thee this eve, after all of thee have had thy meals, the finest tansy cakes to be had in the land. I'll meet thee at this very spot."

A murmur of approval met this offer.

The leader stared at Eric for a long moment, then shouted, "What say thee, men? Do we accept this offer?"

"Aye, aye, aye!" they chorused.

"Release the prisoners, then," he commanded and was obeyed.

Eric laughed with delight as the fierce attackers turned into joyful greeters who immediately abandoned Jaufre and Aleric to throw themselves at him with hugs and yells.

He knelt to receive better this rough show of affection, and he tousled heads, gently pulled ears, and generally did his best to hug them in return.

"Didst miss me, lads?" he asked and received cries of affirmation.

"And hast thou been good, lads, while I've been gone?" Again they answered in the affirmative.

"Now let me look at all of thee. Aye, aye thou'rt a fine set of knaves, I vow." He stood to look for the leader, who made a point of standing aloof.

"And here's my Thomas," he said fondly as he made his way to the boy. "What, no greeting for me, Tom lad?"

Thomas folded his arms across his thin chest and held his head high. "I'll not greet thee like a girl!"

Eric threw his head back and laughed. "By the Rood, thou'rt one and a kind, i'faith! Now then, give me thy arm and greet me like a man." He extended his own huge arm and Thomas clasped it firmly with his small, bony one. It would have been an amusing sight had not Thomas carried it out so solemnly, staring unmovably at Eric as he did so.

"Eric, Eric, Eric!" a small voice cried behind him. He turned to see a tiny girl running toward him with as much speed as she could manage on her bare feet. She was a remarkably pretty child, with long golden hair and bright blue eyes.

"Why, it's my Molly!" Eric cried with delight, sweeping her into his arms. "My pretty Molly, come to greet me. Give me a kiss, sweetling!"

Molly was all too happy to comply with this request.

"Eric, Father's waiting," Aleric admonished. "Come play with thy brats later." He tugged gently on one of Molly's bare feet as they dangled around Eric's waist. "Good day, pretty Molly," he added pleasantly, kissing her cheek before he started toward the castle again.

Jaufre was more gallant. "Hello, Molly, my love." He greeted her with a kiss as well.

"'Lo, Jafee," she returned with a toothy grin.

Jaufre smiled at her. "Molly, sweet, someday when thou hast grown into the most beautiful lady in the world, and I come to beg thee to marry me, I expect thee to be able to say 'Jaufre,'" he informed the delighted toddler.

Eric shook his head. "Nay, Jaufre. It is I whom she shall marry. She can already say 'Eric.'"

"That," Jaufre declared as Eric carried Molly toward her nearby home, "is not saying much."

Eric ignored this remark and placed Molly in a little chair by the door. "I'll bring thee something special tonight, sweetling," he whispered. "Now give me one more kiss. There's a good lass." He hugged her and left with Jaufre, waving and shouting good-bye to the boys who had returned to their games.

"Poor little Molly," Jaufre said as they made their way. "I wonder what will happen to her when her grandmother dies. Such a pretty child!"

"I do not know," Eric said. He shouted and waved at another one of the villagers, then added, "I'll adopt her, mayhap."

Jaufre was shocked. "Thou? Adopt Molly without a wife to play mother? And I suppose thou'lt take in that brat Thomas as well?"

"Mayhap. He and I are one of a kind, and his father beats him. I'll take him under my care someday, one way or another."

"That I believe." Jaufre shook his head. "Good lack, man, thou'lt be turning Belhaven into an orphanage yet, I vow!"

4

"*Be damned!*" Eric slammed a huge fist on the long table in the great hall, causing it to shake with a resounding rattle. "Sir Walter was right all along about Terent of Ravinet." He handed the missive he had been reading to Jaufre. His eyes met Garin's.

"What do we now, Father? Without the proof of his servant's word we have naught with which to convince the nobles of the man's guilt. With thy blessing I will gladly ride for Ravinet this eve and deal with the man myself."

Garin's face fairly shone with pride at his son's bold words, but he shook his head. "Calm thyself, Eric. I'll not let thee go anywhere in such a state. 'Twould be foolish by half." He reached for the wine decanter just delivered by a servant and filled his goblet.

Jaufre's long blond hair swept the table as he bent his head over the document. He swore under his breath when he finished reading Sir Walter's words. Aleric held out a hand, indicating that he would like to read it as well, and was ignored.

Jaufre spoke angrily. "Something must be done, Father. We cannot let Ravinet commit treason and we know of it."

Aleric gently tried to tug the missive out of Jaufre's firm grasp, but to no avail.

Eric began to pace, hitting the palm of one hand with the fist of another. "Damn! We should have stayed at Shrewsbury 'til Sir Walter returned. The king believed he was right all along."

"We should have gone with him!" Jaufre countered heatedly. "That servant would be alive today had we been there."

"Or thou might have been killed, boasting popinjay," Garin stated bluntly. "Walter le Brun and Allyn De Arge are two of the finest knights in this land. Dost think thou art as skilled as they? Yet they barely escaped alive. Nay, nay. Terent of Ravinet and his are none to be played with, boy."

Jaufre scowled.

"Excuse me, please. Why am I here?" Aleric spoke politely, standing by the table with his hands behind his back.

"Son?"

"Why am I here if I am not allowed to read the missive?" Aleric repeated peevishly. "'Tis a most interesting conversation, sir, but if I cannot join I'd rather retire to my chambers, if't please thee. I've a translation of *Plutus* to complete, after all."

Garin frowned at Jaufre, who still held the missive. "Let the boy read it," he demanded.

Reluctantly, Jaufre handed the document over.

"'Tis all right, lad," Garin reassured him. "Aleric needs to know what we're about. He'll join thy brother and thee on thy journey to Reed to fetch the lady Margot. 'Tis time and since he got away from Belhaven after being cloistered here like a monk so long."

Eric stopped pacing and stared at his father in shock. "Reed! Sir, how canst thou say such a thing!? Wouldst have us play nursemaid to a lady whilst Ravinet plots against Henry? I say nay!"

"Nay?" Garin bellowed loudly, shooting off the bench on which he sat and overturning it. "Thou darest naysay me? Dost thou? Speak thusly to me again, froward whelp, and I'll turn thee over my knee and break thee in two! I say thou wilt ride to Reed!"

The hall, filled with people engaged in various and noisy activities, including Lady Elaine and her ladies, grew still at Garin's raised voice. Every eye turned in the direction of the lord and his sons.

Eric drew in a breath to calm the fury raging within him. His own dark eyes stared into Garin's challenging blue ones. When he finally spoke his tone was quiet, tight, and fully respectful.

"Dost say we go to Reed, Father, to Reed we will go."

Jaufre had righted his father's bench, and now Garin sat once more and drank deeply from his goblet. Noise and activity slowly resumed in the hall.

"Thou wilt go tomorrow, the three of thee and as many men as thou wilt need. The lady Margot is in grave danger, as thou canst see from Walter's letter. If 'tis a fight thou'rt seeking, lads," Garin said, staring meaningfully at the still-fuming Eric, "thou wilt most like find it at Reed. Terent's men may e'en now be in hiding there to secret the lady away. 'Twill be fortunate indeed if you arrive ere any mischief occurs."

Aleric, having read the document and dropped it on the table, seemed pleased about this unexpected adventure. "Why is Sir Walter's daughter in danger? I cannot think she'd make a good hostage."

Eric, his temper finally cooled, sat at the table opposite his father and accepted from him a goblet of wine.

"She is an only child, Aleric," he explained. "If Sir Walter dies, she inherits all that is his, including some border lands which he holds."

Aleric shrugged. "So?"

"So," Jaufre said, "those border lands, if they were held by someone like Terent of Ravinet, would allow an easier invasion for the earl of Northumberland and his cohorts. If Terent were to force the lady Margot into marriage, and should Sir Walter have a—a fatal accident, the control of those lands would pass into Terent's hands through the lady Margot's inheritance."

Aleric shook his head. "It seems unlikely that the king would accept such a marriage as binding, especially without a marriage contract. 'Twould be easier to reclaim the lands and gift them to another."

"Aye, lad, that it would," Eric agreed, "but the difficulty is that without proof of Terent's treason, many of the nobles would view such an action by the king as heavy-handed. Too many already waver in their loyalty, waiting to see what the outcome of the trouble with Northumberland and Worcester will be. Thou'rt forgetting that Henry of Bolingbroke hath been on the throne only a few years. Many are unsure of him as yet. If he began taking away rightfully held lands without good cause, other nobles might think him capable of doing the same to them, and they might flock to the rebellion."

Aleric considered this a moment, then asked, "How many days' ride is Reed?"

"With thy camp it may take a little more than five days," Garin answered. "Reed is far south of Belhaven. Thou must make all haste to reach it in good speed, and having arrived waste no time in returning. The return to Belhaven may be dangerous if Terent and his men are aware that the lady is in thy hands. Terent will stop at naught, I daresay. He was ever a determined knave."

His sons looked at Garin with surprise.

"Thou hast met Terent, Father?" Jaufre asked.

Garin smiled wanly. "Oh, aye, I know him and well, as doth Walter. We trained for knighthood together, the three of us, under Montfiort. Terent was violent and ill mannered even as a young man, determined to have his own way in all things. A man who would rather torture and maim an opponent than kill him outright, and a man who would rather beat a servant for a slight than let it go with a word. 'Tis rumored that he murdered his own parents in their beds and blamed the matter on angry vassals whom he publicly hanged in the village." Garin rubbed his chin. "He never was knighted," he added as an afterthought.

Jaufre and Eric glanced at each other, passing an unspoken communication.

"How old is the lady Margot, Father?" Aleric was asking, drawing their attention back to the table.

"I believe she has lived ten and eight years."

"So old!" Aleric was surprised. "Why hath she not yet wed? Is she ugly?"

Garin laughed. "Nay, lad, that she is not. King Henry told me to my face that she is the loveliest maid he hath e'er set eyes on. And old! God's wounds! I'd not let thy sister hear thee say that ten and eight is old. She would ring a peal over thee thou wouldst carry to thy grave, I vow!"

His father and brothers laughed, but Aleric ignored them and held his head high. "I never said Liliore is old."

"Lovely, is she?" Jaufre queried, still chuckling. "I shall be most happy to meet this lovely, unmarried Margot."

"Thou hast met her, son," Garin said with a smile. "And turned her from thee most cruelly. I daresay she'll have naught to do with thee."

"I? Turn away a lovely maid? Not by my life would I!"

"She was not a lovely maid when thou turned her away, lad," Eric told him. "She was a pretty little child at court. Father found her hiding in his chamber, remember? Thou wouldst not play with her."

Jaufre looked repulsed. "Not the girl with the halting speech! *That* is Lady Margot le Brun? God's pity! I had no idea during all the times we discussed her with Sir Walter."

"She was delightful!" Eric returned hotly. "Bright and well mannered. The stammer nearly disappeared once she relaxed, though I found it to be rather pretty even when she did speak it."

Garin smiled into his goblet at these words.

"Thou'rt welcome to her, Eric," Jaufre assured him.

"Not I." Eric looked at his father knowingly. "Methinks she is for our brother James, is that not so, Father?"

Garin had not planned on telling Eric that Margot was to marry either himself or one of his brothers. That was something Walter and he had discussed in private. Somehow Eric had found out and, as Garin had feared, had already discounted himself as the potential bridegroom.

"Mayhap," he replied with a shrug, deciding it best to let Eric think what he would. Let him fetch the girl and spend some time with her; if they were meant to fall in love, they would, if not, not. "Thou wilt be in command of this journey, Eric. Thy brothers will obey thee, I am sure." He stared meaningfully at both Jaufre and Aleric, who returned his look with appropriate meekness. "We'll have much to do this eve in preparation, for I want thee gone by daybreak. After our evening meal we'll choose the men thou wilt need and have the supplies readied." He reached across the table and grasped Eric's hand. "I know thou wilt make me proud, son, as thou hast always done."

Eric returned the grasp with affection. He loved and honored his father, just as he knew his brothers and sister did. But for Eric, the affection of his parents meant something more. He knew he was not their natural child, knew he was not born a Stavelot, though they had never, by word or deed, treated him as otherwise. If he had not discovered the truth about himself from the loose tongue of a villager, he never would have guessed.

He could remember vividly the day he had heard the truth, and how it had devastated him. He had been ten years old. When he confronted his mother about what he had heard in the village, her reaction had confirmed the truth. He hadn't cried, though his sister and brothers, even James, had burst into tears and protestations. No, he hadn't cried. He had sat silently, staring ahead of himself, feeling as if he was going to die. He was ashamed and frightened and horrified. Even his beautiful mother, the bravest woman he had ever known, had started to weep as she put her arms around his stiff body. None of the servants had dared to come near the table, he remembered, but had stood by with downcast eyes.

Father had walked in then, returning with some of his men from hunting. Eric could remember his father staring in shock at the scene and bellowing.

"Why in God's name are all my children crying, woman!?" he had demanded furiously, trying to hide his concern. His men had stood back from the table. Mother had told Father, crying through the whole of it, and Father had gone silent.

Eric could remember standing to face his father. He remembered how his heart had pounded in his ears, remembered how every muscle strained with tension in his body. "Is it true, sir?" he had whispered, not able to make his voice any louder.

Father had placed his giant hands on his shoulders in a strong grip. It had probably been the only thing that held him up, Eric thought in hindsight. The strong, reassuring hands of the man who had always been his father.

Father had firmly looked into his eyes. He had bent over Eric and his long blond hair had fallen forward, caressing Eric's forehead. The words he'd said were spoken slowly and quietly. Eric would never forget them.

"I am thy father, Eric; Lady Elaine is thy mother; and thou'rt our son. Thou hast never known other parents. We have loved thee and raised thee as our own. This shall not change. Ever. I will kill any other man who lays a claim to thee."

Eric had thought he would faint with relief, or cry maybe, except that Father had said a man should not cry, so that he would not do. Instead, he'd found his voice.

"I am thy son, Father, if thou wilt have me, on this condition. I will swear eternal fealty to thee and repay with my life what thou hast given me."

Father had been shaken. Mother had come from behind and placed her soft, cool hands on his arms.

"Nay, son. Thy mother and I give freely to thee. I'll not have such fealty from a child of mine."

But Eric had held firm and refused to be swayed in the matter.

At some point Mother had gone onto her knees and begun to weep once more. Father had sworn aloud.

"By the Rood, here's a stubborn child to make his mother and brothers and sister weep like babes! Very well, obstinate lad, I'll have thee swear fealty if thou'lt promise to ne'er again say thou'rt not my son. And to keep the villagers' tongues from wagging and the children from crying we'll have a formal cere- mony, tomorrow day, to do the deed. I shall accept thy fealty and thou wilt accept thy mother and me as thy true and only parents. Give me thy man's hand on it."

Father had held out his arm and Eric had clasped it, much as he was doing now.

"Aye, Father," he answered as he had answered him then. "I shall make thee proud."

Jaufre caught up with Eric later in the day, just as he was coming from the kitchens.

"Well, Eric," said Jaufre, striding beside him, "hast

thou charmed Cook into giving thee cakes for thy brats?"

Eric nodded. "'Tis a shame that we must forego Dortha and Alois this eve, but I'll not go back on my word to the children."

"I should say not!" exclaimed Jaufre, shocked. "That brat Thomas would organize them all to scale the castle walls seeking revenge, I daresay."

They laughed and turned up the stairwell toward their chambers.

"Aye, Thomas is a rare lad," Eric said. "I'll put him to squire someday and then to knighthood. He'll make me proud and thou'lt no longer call him brat." He walked into his chambers and Jaufre followed. Geoff, who was busy with Eric's armor in the antechamber, dutifully jumped up to see if there was anything his master needed.

"Good lad, Geoff. Thou'rt making mine armor shine as new. Wilt take a moment to fetch some wine?"

Geoff was only too happy to do so and ran off immediately.

Jaufre casually reclined on the large bed in the middle of the room and Eric crossed to one of his clothing chests. He opened it and began searching for something.

"What dost thou think of the task ahead, Eric?" Jaufre asked.

Eric glanced back at him. "I cannot like it. If Terent is as determined as Father says, we will certes run into danger. Could we somehow keep the lady

Margot safe at Reed 'twould be better, for I'll not feel easy having her on the open road and prey to Terent's attack. We needs must keep our wits about us, brother."

"S'truth," Jaufre agreed. "And I like it not that Father sends Aleric with us. He's bright as any ever born, but a more worthless man in a fight I have never met."

Eric chuckled heartily at that. "My sight, that is true enough! Were our good brother to find himself at a stand he might verily try to talk his way out of it. And succeed yet! Ah, here it is." He held a small, dull brooch up for inspection and let the chest lid close with a sound thump.

"What?" Jaufre asked, lifting his head to look. "Oh, 'tis thy brooch."

"Aye." Standing, Eric turned the small, plain pin around in his large fingers, being careful not to drop it. It was solid, made of brass and with no stones to ornament it, only a filigreed design. Cheap and old, it was certainly worthless, but it was the only identification Eric had with his physical parents. Mother had found it in his swaddling on the night he was brought home, and had kept it and given it to him on the day he had sworn fealty to Father. It revealed no clue as to who he was, only that his parents had, indeed, been poor.

He looked at it a moment longer, then tossed it onto his dressing table.

Geoff returned with a decanter of wine and two goblets. He set them down and made to leave.

"Geoff." Eric stopped him.

Geoff obediently turned.

Eric walked to him and placed a large heavy hand on one of his shoulders. "Lad, thou'lt not be going with us to Reed."

Geoff gave a start. "Not—!"

"Easy, lad, and hear me out. Thou hast given me more than good service as squire this past year, especially at Shrewsbury. Never did I see thee afeared during battle, and always didst thou put my needs and safety ahead of thine. A better squire a man could not ask for. But thou canst not remain my squire forever, much as I would like it. 'Tis time for thee to train for knighthood, and I have asked my father to attend to thy training, under my sponsorship. Thou wilt begin in two days' time."

Geoff's eyes lit at the thought of knighthood, yet he knew he could not let his lord go on a long journey without his squire to aid him. It was unthought of!

"I thank thee, Sir Eric," Geoff replied gratefully. "Truly, I would be most happy to train for the knighthood, and indeed I am not unaware of the honor thou'rt placing upon me. But I'll not let thee go to Reed unattended."

Eric's eyebrows rose. "Not let me?" he repeated. "I do not give thee a choice, Geoff."

"But, sir," Geoff protested, "who will help thee to dress? And who will care for thy belongings and thine armor? And who knows better than I how to care for Bram? Why, there will be no one to bring

thee dinner, or to fill thy cup, or to prepare thy tent!"
The more he spoke the more upset he became at the
thought of his lord being so utterly helpless.

"Geoff, Geoff," Eric soothed. "Indeed I shall miss
thine excellent services and ministrations, but I am
not a babe. I shall do perfectly well, I vow, and
methinks my good brother may lend me a hand ere I
need one."

Geoff looked skeptically at Jaufre, who was still
sitting on the bed and who cheerfully held his hands
out, palm up. At Shrewsbury Geoff had squired both
Eric and Jaufre, though he belonged to Eric, and he
had some doubts as to Jaufre's ability to do much of
anything except fight well and get into scrapes.

"I'll take care of him as though he wert a babe,"
Jaufre vowed. "I give thee my troth!"

That didn't make Geoff feel any better at all. He
had visions of his lord's armor coming back to
Belhaven as a pile of rust.

"My lord," he pleaded, looking at Eric.

"Now Geoff, thou'rt being foolish as a silly maid.
I've dressed and taken care of myself before, i'faith,
so I'll have no more of this. I want thee to pack all I
will need and assist me to dress in the morn. Those
shall be thy last duties to me. Ere long thou wilt have
a squire of thine own."

"Yes, m'lord," Geoff replied miserably, returning
to the outer chamber with his head hung low.

Eric watched him go and shook his head. "One
would think I had told him he was going to be
executed."

Jaufre laughed and stood to pour himself some wine. "Bah! The lad loves thee and is a good squire. He's a little sad now but in two days' time he'll not give thee a second thought. I'd put a wager on't."

"Mayhap. I shall hope it is so." Eric took his own goblet to an ornately carved table set by a window. He secured the window covering against the wall so that sunlight and fresh air spilled into the room, then settled himself into one of two large velvet-covered chairs.

"Come then, Jaufre, let's get to mapping the task ahead. Bring the wine to the table."

Eric was full weary as he made his way into the castle several hours later. He had been to see the children and had made certain as well that everything was ready for an early departure in the morning. It was late, and the great hall was lit with candles and fireplaces, one of which he stopped by to warm himself. His mother and sister were still up, he could see, and sitting across the hall, in the glow of candlelight, conversing as they bent over needlework. Servants worked at clearing the tables of the sumptuous meal that had taken place a few hours earlier. Another going-away feast, Eric thought glumly.

He had missed his home in the past eight months; had missed his mother and brother and sister. He'd even missed the village brats and Thomas, and little Molly. Now he was leaving again. If he'd had his way, he would be riding full speed to Terent of Ravinet's abode with a full complement of men. He would make short work of Terent and return to Belhaven in time to enjoy the rest of the summer season at home. It wasn't to be, however, and he knew that he must make the best of things. In truth, it might not be such an unpleasant matter to renew his acquaintance with Margot le Brun. She'd been a lovely child and had most like grown even lovelier. A man could certainly ask for worse duty than escorting a beautiful woman through England, even in the face of such danger as Terent of Ravinet presented.

But, damn! He was still leaving Belhaven when he most needed and wanted to be here. He thought of how he'd found Thomas when he met the children at the square earlier. Even in the dim light of evening he had seen the bruises, and the lip that was bleeding. Eric had washed the boy's face carefully by the village well, knowing full well that it had to hurt, yet Thomas had neither flinched nor cried. No. Not Thomas. He had stared defiantly into Eric's eyes, making it clear that he was not a child to be treated thus. It was all Eric could do to keep from going to Thomas's dwelling and mutilating the boy's drunken sod of a father. There would be no time to deal with the man properly before he had to leave. He could only ask Father to keep an eye out for the boy until he could return, and would have to trust that all would be well.

The sound of giggling came from across the hall, gaining Eric's attention, and he turned to see his mother and sister looking at him and laughing like two children. Shaking his head dolefully at their unladylike behavior, he moved toward them.

"Eric," Liliore said as he bent to kiss her in greeting, and she grasped fistfuls of his hair to hold him still for her kiss in return, "I thought thou wouldst stay brooding by the fire all eve and not come to say hello. I do wish thou wast not leaving in the morn. It hardly seems right when thou hast been gone such a long time."

He kissed her again. "I would not leave could I not, Liliore," he told her, smiling as he stood, "but go we must, and so we shall."

He crossed to the waiting arms of his mother and knelt before her, letting her draw him close and hug him tightly. He was weary, so weary from the many months of fighting, and it felt good to be like a child again, held close in his mother's grasp. He rested his head against her shoulder, closed his eyes, and let himself enjoy the feeling for several minutes.

Lady Elaine stroked her son's dark hair and felt him press against her, seeking love and comfort. She was a petite woman and Eric dwarfed her, but she rocked him to and fro as though he were a little child. After a time he pulled away and kissed her cheek with a loud, loving smack.

"'Tis not fair that thou shouldst leave us after only a few days, Eric," she said, picking up a skein of colored wool. "I've worried enough o'er thee and thy brothers and father these many months, and I shall worry all the while thou'rt gone to Reed. Hold out thy hands, son."

Eric was still kneeling before her, a position that put their heads at about the same height, and he dutifully held out both hands, fingers sticking straight up.

"I am sorry for it too, Mother," he said as she began to loop the fine yarn around his giant hands, "for I have missed thee and Liliore and Aleric as well. And I am weary of traveling about the country."

"Thou dost indeed seem weary, Eric," Liliore commented, looking at him closely. "But mayhap this journey will not prove so tiring. Mother says thou'rt to escort the lady Margot le Brun to Belhaven, and if she is as beautiful as 'tis rumored, she may make thy journey most pleasant."

"That may be as it is."

"Thou'rt not eager to see this beautiful lady?" Liliore seemed shocked. "Jaufre is, I vow. He is forever chasing after pretty maids."

"Aye, that he is, but methinks he'll keep this one at a distance."

His mother looked at him strangely. "Why should he do that, Eric?"

"The lady Margot is to marry James, is she not? Jaufre overheard thee telling thy ladies to prepare for a wedding feast shortly."

Liliore nearly dropped her needlework, and Lady Elaine shook her head.

"James is to marry the lady Margot?!" Liliore cried. "Why am I the last to know of it?"

"Jaufre was mistaken," Lady Elaine answered calmly, concentrating on her yarn. Eric's hands were now fully wrapped with the material. "I make no plans for James's wedding."

"Whose, then?" Eric asked, bewildered.

"Thine, perhaps," she answered with a grin, and saw Eric's mouth drop open for the brief moment before she laughed.

"Tease," he chided as she carefully drew the yarn off his hands, folded it, and placed it with her other materials. "Thou knowest full well I'll ne'er wed."

She smiled sadly and put a hand to his cheek. "Oh, thou sayest such now, my dear one, but someday thou wilt meet a fine and lovely maid who will steal thine heart and take thee from me. And that is as it should be."

Eric hugged his mother ferociously. "Do I ever meet a maid as beautiful as thee, Mother, I shall consider it!" He kissed her cheek once more and stood.

"I'm for bed." He stretched full height. "By my life, I am tired." He bid them good night and went to his chambers.

They watched him go in silence until he had disappeared up the stairs, then Liliore turned to look at her mother.

"What dost thou think, Mother? Would it not be wonderful if Eric and Lady Margot fell in love? 'Twould be of all things the most romantic!"

Lady Elaine nodded, gazing at the staircase where Eric had gone. "Aye, 'twould be wonderful indeed. He is worn and weary and needs to rest. But 'tis neither travel nor battle that wears on him, methinks, and neither sleep nor days of leisure will give him ease."

Liliore seemed to understand and nodded in agreement.

"Please, God, he may soon find what he needs to give him peace," said her mother.

5

They left for Reed at the break of day. Eric led the way, followed by his brothers, thirty men-at-arms, three wagons carrying tents and supplies, and four servants to cook and look after them.

The first few miles were easily completed and at good speed, and Eric's spirits lifted as the sun rose higher and made promise of a beautiful day for the beginning of their journey. With the woods to his left and the valley to his right, he stopped a moment to look back on Belhaven. It was surely the most beautiful place in all of Britain. The land was fertile and well maintained, the valley floor was level and wide, the fields were neatly lined with dry stone walls. In the morning light he could see workers dotting the land, and horses and cows pulling rough ploughs. A wide, lazy river flowed beyond the town and castle, and the forest swept lush and green around the fields and nearly down to the town walls. In all his life he had never seen any place as lovely as his home.

"Who follows us there?" Jaufre reined his horse in next to Eric's. He pointed to a small moving dot of white and gray.

Eric shrugged. They were on the main road leading out of the valley, and it wouldn't be unusual for one of the villagers to be following behind, probably going on some errand in a neighboring township.

"Do not find danger where there is none, brother," Eric advised. "Save thy fears for when they are needed." He turned Bram sharply and headed for the front of the company, leaving his brother staring after him.

At nightfall the men camped by a stream. They had covered many miles that first day, Eric having pushed them as much as he dared, and they were full weary. Camp had been pitched and fires lit. Aleric and two of the men-at-arms had gone hunting as soon as Eric had called the halt, and they had returned with several fresh rabbits for dinner. Servants were busy preparing the meal, the smell of which scented the camp. A guard had been selected for rotation and sent out to strategic points. The horses had been fed and rubbed down and secured for the night, and now the men relaxed around the fires, drinking wine and ale and telling stories, waiting for their meal to be ready.

Eric stood at the edge of the stream, listening to the men laughing and joking in the camp behind him. He was far enough away from the fires to be able to see the stars above. The night was cool and still, and the fresh air mingled with the sultry smoke of the fires. It was a blessing there were no clouds in the sky, for another summer rainstorm such as Belhaven had suffered two nights before would make their trip miserable indeed. He would pray in the morning that God would continue to aid them with such good weather.

He strolled along the bank, farther from the noise of the camp and into the welcome darkness of the forest. It was peaceful and quiet, and he leaned against the hard trunk of a tree and relaxed. With one hand he absently fingered the plain brooch that he'd dug from his clothing chest the day before. He didn't know why, but for some reason that morning, after Geoff had finished helping him to dress, he had picked up the brooch and pinned it to the tunic inside his hauberk. Now that his armor had been removed, his fingers found it and ran over its filigreed design. He hadn't taken his brooch to Shrewsbury, though he had been in the habit of wearing it inside his tunic since Mother gave it to him, and he had disliked not having it. He'd been afraid of losing it then, either in battle or in the endless months of tent living, so he had left it at Belhaven, hoping he would come back alive to wear it again. He probably should have left it home this time as well, since he couldn't be sure what manner of danger he might meet along the way to Reed and back home to Belhaven. But he hadn't left it; he had brought it and was wearing it, and it felt good to touch again.

It wasn't much, this brooch, and yet he clung to it. The ache within him to know about his own people never went away. Somewhere in England he had another family, maybe brothers and sisters and a whole swarm of relatives. For all he knew he had passed by them somewhere, had joked with them in a tavern, or had unknowingly killed them in battle. The ache grew strong and he drew in a breath to try and push it away. He put his hands to his eyes and covered them, rubbing gently as if to keep himself from thinking. And took another breath.

A scuffling in the leaves startled him, and he instinctively withdrew the dagger from its sheath at his waist. It was only Jaufre, he realized with relief, who was strolling toward him as languidly as though he were strolling from his bedchamber to the great hall at home.

"What art thou about, Eric?" he greeted. "Out making sonnets to the moon?"

Eric grinned and sheathed his dagger. "About to cut thy throat, more like, thinking thee a stranger."

Jaufre clasped his hands behind his back and feigned shock. "What an unfriendly fellow thou art, brother. I shall have to remember never to surprise thee in thy sleep. 'Twould be most deadly, methinks."

"Most," Eric agreed. "What dost thou here?"

"Come to fetch thee, lad. We've captured a wily creature who was skirting the camp. Thou wilt find him most interesting, I vow."

Eric started for camp without further explanation. Jaufre had to pick up speed to keep up with his brother's lengthy strides.

"A creature, thou sayest? What manner of creature?"

"A human creature," Jaufre replied pleasantly.

"A man? Was he trying to steal the horses? Was he armed?"

"Thou wilt see, and I said not he was a man," Jaufre said, though it was unnecessary. Eric had walked into the clearing and was met by the sight of two of his men holding, with all their strength, a struggling, cursing boy.

Thomas.

"What in God's name—!" Eric began, then stopped. He strode forward to where Thomas fought and bit at the two men holding him, and with one strong, steel arm snatched him up into the air. He held him up until they were face-to-face, Thomas's thin, bare legs dangling a long way from the ground. The child had ceased to struggle the moment Eric came into his view, and now he stared at the knight with utter defiance.

"Thomas, what is the meaning of this?!" Eric thundered, his voice full of fury and his face tight with anger. "How hast thou come here?!"

Thomas neither flinched nor withered beneath Eric's scalding tone. "I have followed behind since thou left this morn!" he shouted in return. "I am going with thee!"

"Going with me?!" Eric repeated in a rage, staring

with disbelief into Thomas's insolent eyes. "What maggot has taken to thy brain to make thee do such an empty-headed thing!? I should knock thee sense-less three times over!" He began to shake him so violently that the boy's head nearly snapped. "How didst thou follow? Hast stolen one of the villager's horses? A white one, mayhap?"

Thomas steadied himself against Eric's violence by gripping his captor's massive shoulders with his thin, bony hands and holding on with all his might. He gritted his teeth to keep them from clattering and fixed Eric with a steely glare. "Aye!" he managed to yell into Eric's face. "I took my father's mare—I stole it! If thou takest it from me I will follow thee still! Thou wilt have to kill me to stop me!"

The shaking stopped as suddenly as it had begun and they stared at each other for a long, hard moment. Finally, Eric set Thomas on his feet and released him. The boy stumbled to the ground, took a deep breath and stood again, lifting his head. He tilted his chin defiantly.

Eric looked at the child, working to control his anger. Thomas's face was still swollen with the bruises of last eve, his clothes were ragged and dirty, his feet were bare. He looked worn and exhausted and hungry, but his expression was strong and determined. Eric believed the lad truly would rather die than turn back, though he couldn't understand why he'd followed in the first place. He was thoroughly repulsed with himself for losing his temper as he had. The rage he'd felt was wrought by shock and fear, for

Thomas had no idea of the danger he'd brought himself to, but for all that there was no excuse for such a lack of control. Sighing, he let his anger drain away. He'd always loved Thomas as though the boy were his own. The fact that he had refused to back down made Eric love him all the more.

"Thomas." Eric's voice was serious. "Thou hast displeased me, and I should full well send thee back to Belhaven, but I will not. However, if thou dost not wish to be left here to thine own devices, thou wilt swear complete obedience to my will. I'll take thee alongside of me as squire, for thou must work for thy keep if thou wilt come with us, but do I hear one word of complaint from thee, or one word of defiance, I will punish thee harshly. Dost understand me, Thomas?"

Thomas nodded and said quietly, "I swear to be obedient to thee in all things, Sir Eric."

Eric looked at Jaufre, who stood behind him with folded arms. Aleric and the rest of the men in the camp had grown silent during his confrontation with the boy.

"It seems we have a squire," Eric announced, and put one hand gently on Thomas's thin shoulder. He could feel the bones protruding beneath the boy's skin.

"How old art thou, Thomas?" Jaufre asked.

"I have lived ten and two years," Thomas replied evenly.

Jaufre nodded. "Thou'rt rather frail for a squire. I doubt thou wilt be able to do much, but we shall see."

In truth he doubted the child would do more than eat a great deal of much-needed food and be a pest, but he wasn't about to enrage Eric again after the display his brother had just shown. For one frightening moment he had thought Eric was going to break the boy's neck. He'd never before seen him so angry.

"He'll need decent clothes, and some shoes," Aleric pointed out. He had been as stunned as Jaufre by Eric's uncontrolled fury, and was glad that the moment had passed. "I'll see if I can find aught to suit him 'til we reach Reed."

Eric nodded his appreciation. "'Tis well. He needs must make due with whatever thou canst find, Aleric. Methinks the lady Margot will clothe him properly once we are there."

He looked at Thomas again. "Hast eaten today?"

The boy shook his head.

"Were the cakes I gave thee yestereve thy last meal?"

Thomas nodded.

Eric exerted enough pressure on Thomas's shoulder to guide him toward his tent. "Come with me now, lad, and rest 'til dinner is ready. Wilt have food brought to us there, Jaufre?"

"Aye," Jaufre replied soberly as Eric and Thomas disappeared into the tent.

Eric was silent as he made Thomas lie down on his own pallet. The boy was silent in return, though he watched Sir Eric's every move out of his great dark eyes. He had worshiped Sir Eric since the first day he'd known him, which seemed to be all of his life.

His father beat him regularly; his mother had died when he was a baby. Sir Eric was the only brightness in his life. The only good things he had ever received had come from him. The only gentle touches, the only kind words, the only concern. Sir Eric had cared for him when he was hungry, and had fed him; when he was ill Sir Eric had made certain that he had care; when his feet were bare he had provided him with shoes. His father sold the shoes faster than Thomas could break them in, but Sir Eric always brought more. The past eight months when he had been gone to Shrewsbury had been hell for Thomas. There had been no care, no concern, no kindness. He had waited and waited for Sir Eric to come home, and when he finally had it was only to turn around and leave again. Thomas could not bear it, would not bear it. If he had to follow Sir Eric around the world to be with him, he would do it, but he would no longer be separated from him, no matter what hardships befell him.

Eric sat beside the boy and began to examine his bare feet. They were calloused and held some few sores on them, as well as cuts, but he could see no infections to worry over. He rubbed them gently for a few minutes, and felt Thomas relax as he did so. What was he going to do with the boy? he wondered. What could he possibly be thinking to take him so far away from Belhaven, to expose him to such danger? If anything were to happen to him, Eric would never forgive himself. And yet, he was glad to have Thomas away from his brute of a father.

"I'll be a good squire to thee, my lord," Thomas said quietly.

"Wilt thou, lad?" Eric asked, still rubbing his feet.

"Aye, thou wilt see. I shall take care of thee."

Eric chuckled. He couldn't see how such a thin, frail child could possibly take care of him, but he wouldn't say so. At the moment Thomas seemed to need more looking after than he did.

Jaufre entered the tent with a tray of food and a decanter of wine. It was his tent as well as Eric's, for they always shared lodgings away from home, and he had brought enough food and wine for himself as well as for Eric and Thomas.

"Here we go, lads." He set the tray on a stool. "Let's eat our fill." He sliced portions of roasted rabbit and broke a round of parsley bread into chunks.

Thomas sat up eagerly and reached for the plate offered him, gobbling down the food as soon as he got it. Jaufre laughed at the boy's healthy appetite and poured him a goblet of wine.

"Here, lad, do not drink it all down at once," he admonished, handing it to him.

Thomas lifted grateful eyes to Sir Jaufre and was careful not to swallow too much of the deep red liquid. Then he concentrated on his food again, eating as though he had never tasted anything so good in his life.

"He'll be quite fat at this rate, Eric."

"The cooks are to be commended," Eric said. "Or Aleric, mayhap. This is better fare than ever we had at Shrewsbury. Thank God our youngest brother is so skilled with his bow."

Jaufre, seated on his own sleeping platform, nodded between bites. "Please God, it may last throughout the journey."

Thomas reclined on the pallet as soon as he finished his meal, barely aware that he did so. He was shortly sound asleep. Eric pried the empty plate and cup out of his hands and placed them back on the tray.

"And where wilt thou sleep, brother, now that thy brat has taken thy bed?" Jaufre asked, still eating.

Eric surveyed the cramped quarters. "I've no intention of relinquishing my bed to my squire," he said, thoughtfully considering a clear area at the foot of his pallet. He rolled up the one sturdy rug that had been placed on the tent's dirt floor and set it over the area. Thomas never felt Eric lifting and placing him on the rug, or covering him with a blanket. That being done Eric sat down on his pallet and took up his plate to finish his meal.

"Well done." Jaufre refilled Eric's goblet. "Thy wish to adopt one of thy brats hath come true, hath it not? Sooner than thou expected, but still come true."

Eric made a grunting noise in reply. "I cannot believe Thomas hath done such an idiotish deed, and 'tis certain I am that I'll regret not returning him to Belhaven. As if we did not have enough to worry o'er without keeping an eye on a disobedient, mischievous child. He'll plague us every step of the way, most like."

Jaufre smiled at the ill-concealed affection in Eric's rough words.

"Thou knowest not, Eric. Mayhap his coming is a godsend. He may prove yet to be a blessing in disguise."

Eric didn't think that very likely. He considered the sleeping form at the foot of his bed, noting again how small and thin Thomas was. The boy had grit, though, and determination. And something that Eric couldn't quite put his finger on, a rare quality of some kind.

"Mayhap, Jaufre," he said. "I will hope it is so."

6

"*And that one looks* like a giant squirrel eating a mushroom because he was too busy courting his lady when he should have been collecting nuts," Jace said informatively, lying on his back in the soft grass of the inner bailey and pointing at one of many clouds moving slowly above him in the blue afternoon sky. "And that one looks like a knight come home from the hunt with only one rabbit and two pheasants to show for it. Poor knight!" he said with sympathy.

Margot giggled from where she lay beside him, looking up at the clouds as well. "They look like no such thing, J-Jace. How s-silly thou art! Poor knight, indeed!"

"That is what it is, I tell thee!" Jace insisted. They had been lying in the grass looking at clouds for almost a quarter of an hour, relaxing between contests of archery. Margot was a much better archer than he, but she regularly insisted that he match his skills against hers for practice. It was something she had done since she was eight years old.

Margot closed her eyes and felt the cool breeze caress her face. It felt so good, so relaxing. She tentatively touched her fingers to her lips in order to reassure herself that the bruises and cuts were completely healed. It had taken days for the pain of them to go away, and she thought of her encounter with that hunter in the forest with a shiver. She hadn't gone outside the castle walls since that day and, in fact, hadn't gone outside the castle itself for the first three days following the incident.

Today was the first day that she had spent so much time outdoors, and it felt wonderful. The weather was not too hot and the blue sky was filled with giant white clouds. She had horrified her ladies-in-waiting by donning a loose, unadorned outfit and going out of doors with her hair completely unbound and uncovered. She had wanted to feel the breeze in her hair, to let it flow loose and free. It was a rather shocking thing to do, but no one outside the castle would see her and that was all that mattered. In an hour or so she would let Minna dress her in finery and tightly braid and cover her hair. For now she only wanted to relax and feel free. She opened her eyes again to look at the clouds while Jace chatted on about nothing in particular; neither of them noticed the three men who stood on the nearby terrace and watched them.

*   *   *

"Who in God's name is that perfect creature?" Jaufre asked in an awed whisper.

"She looks like an angel," Aleric added, as visibly impressed as his elder brother.

Eric, standing beside them, was so stunned by the sight of the beautiful girl lying in the grass-covered bailey that he couldn't even speak.

Was she an angel? he wondered. She certainly looked like one as she lay there, her arms askew and her golden hair shining against the blanket of green. She was smiling up into the sky and laughing, the sound both feminine and soft. Even from this distance he could see how perfect her features were, how white her skin, the cornflower blue of her eyes. He became aware of the young man lying next to her, who was laughing with her, and he felt a momentary desire to kill him, whoever he was, for being so close to her, whoever she was.

The girl jumped up and said something to the boy, who complained and rolled over onto his stomach. She didn't give up though, and knelt to tug his hair playfully, laughing and tugging and beating his back with a tiny, perfect fist until he grudgingly gave in and got up as well. Eric watched with fascination as they picked up crossbows and strapped on leather quivers. In a moment they were aiming at a target set several feet away, and his memory began to stir. His eyes were drawn to her unbound hair. It fell like some sort of silken material as it cascaded about her waist and arms, shooting off golden highlights where the sun touched it. When she pulled her arm back to draw the string of her bow her hair stirred and shimmered from the movement. He wondered if it felt as soft as it looked.

She was an excellent shot, almost hitting the bullseye. Her companion was not nearly as accurate. Eric watched as the girl shot arrow after arrow into the target, and his memory kept stirring. If she hadn't been dressed so simply, and if the hair flowing down her back had been bound, he almost would have been tempted to think she was the lady Margot. He recalled the day he'd spent with her when she was a little girl and tried to remember her coloring. Yes, she did have golden hair and unusually colored eyes. They were a misty color. Cornflower blue. Definitely cornflower blue.

Jaufre sighed worshipfully. "She is magnificent."

"Aye, beautiful indeed," agreed Eric.

"Good shot," Aleric pointed out practically.

"I've ne'er seen such beauty. For a moment I thought I was seeing a divine vision," Jaufre said, still gaping.

"She hath grown to be as lovely as I've heard tell," Eric said. "I wonder if she will remember me."

Jaufre and Aleric turned their heads to stare at him. Jaufre looked more shocked than Eric had ever seen him before.

"Never tell me that that perfect creature is Margot le Brun!" His eyes were wide with disbelief.

Eric chuckled and nodded. "I do believe that is she."

Jaufre slapped a hand to his forehead in distress.

"Good lack!" he cried. "And I turned her away ten years past! What a fool I was! What an idiot! If I'd ever known she'd grow to such perfection I would have spent my every waking moment entertaining her!"

"My lords!" a soft voice interrupted them. They turned to see a petite young lady curtsying before them. She was more of a girl than a lady, Eric guessed, being probably closer to Aleric's age. Her face and coloring were plain and honest, and she had a very wholesome look about her. She finished her curtsy and straightened, offering a timid smile. "I am Lady Minna D'Sevanett, and I welcome thee to Reed. Please accept my most humble apologies for the absence of Lady Margot in greeting thee formally at thy arrival. We—we did not expect thee so soon." Her voice trembled, and she glanced nervously from one brother to the next as though expecting one of them to pounce on her. She seemed especially frightened of Eric, whose size obviously alarmed her.

Eric made a slight bow and smiled encouragingly at her. He was used to people, especially women, being apprehensive of him until they knew him better. "We thank thee for thy welcome, my lady. I am Eric Stavelot of Belhaven, and these are my brothers, Sir Jaufre Stavelot and Aleric Stavelot." His brothers bowed politely. "Forgive us for wandering about Castle Reed without leave to do so," Eric added, somewhat chagrined. "I fear we grew rather curious after being left alone in the great hall so long and sought the fresh air the terrace offered."

Minna didn't hear this last part of his speech. Indeed, she didn't hear a word he said past his own name. Utterly forgetting her manners, she gaped openly at the giant standing before her. "*Thou* art Sir Eric?" she whispered, shaking her head in horrified disbelief. No. He couldn't be. This terrible monster *couldn't* be her mistress's beloved! Sir Eric Stavelot was the handsomest, noblest, most favored man on God's own earth! He was as a prince compared to other men! Margot had said so over and over again. She had recited the litany of Sir Eric's virtues so many hundreds of times that Minna herself could repeat it perfectly, backward, forward, and in her sleep. No, no! There was some mistake. This man could never be the beautiful, brave Sir Eric. This man was hideous! He was ugly, and unkempt, and *huge!*

Eric tilted his head questioningly at this response to his introduction. "I am sorry, my lady. I perceive thou didst not expect my father's sons to be sent to fetch the lady Margot. There is no need for fear, I assure thee. We are well manned and well armed. She will be kept perfectly safe, I vow."

He *was* Sir Eric.

When the realization struck her, Minna thought she might swoon.

Oh, it was terrible! So incredibly terrible! Something awful had happened to Lady Margot's beloved during the past ten years, and he had some-

how grown into a dreadful creature. There was nothing at all about him that could even remotely be
called attractive. His dark, rugged complexion was
scarred, his nose was overlarge and misshapen, his
black eyes, topped by shaggy black brows, were small
and completely undistinguished. Long, thick, unruly
black hair crowned his head and flowed unkempt to
his massive shoulders. The rest of him was one big
muscle from top to toe, and he seemed to want to
burst from the clothing that covered him. He was,
without a doubt, the biggest, tallest, brawniest man
Minna had ever set eyes on.

Looking at him, Minna felt a deep, wretched sadness for her mistress. For ten years Margot had loved
and worshiped a man who didn't exist. When she
saw the truth of Eric Stavelot she was going to be
utterly devastated.

With difficulty, Minna collected herself. "Please
forgive me, my lord." She cast a quick glance at his
brothers. "My lords," she amended with a blush.
"If—if thou wilt follow me into the hall I shall make
thee comfortable. Wine hath been set out, and I am
sure thou'rt very tired from thy long journey."

"But what of the lady Margot?" Eric asked.

Minna turned bright red. "She will join thee
shortly, my lord. She is presently detained with an
important matter."

To her surprise the ugly giant laughed, not at her,
but just laughed. She was further surprised to find
that the sound was quite pleasant.

Eric turned and walked to the edge of the terrace,

looking to where Margot and Jace were shooting arrows.

"Aye, my lady, a most important matter indeed," he said.

Minna picked up her skirts and demurely brushed past Jaufre and Aleric to look out on the carefully manicured lawn and gardens of the inner bailey. She gasped audibly at the sight she saw there, and when she realized Margot's state of dress she dropped her skirts and pressed her hands against her cheeks in horror.

Eric glanced at the little lady and saw with some concern that all the color had drained from her face. Without thinking he set a hand around her waist to keep her from fainting.

"Art thou unwell, my lady?"

"Oh!" Minna replied weakly. "Oh! I—I hardly know what to tell thee, my lord. I have been in the village all day and did not know—I only returned after thou hadst arrived and John the Steward bade me look to thee."

Eric didn't pretend to understand what this strange speech meant, save that Lady Minna hadn't realized where the lady Margot had been, what she had been doing, or in what state her person had been while she was doing it. He led the trembling girl to a nearby bench and sat her down gently.

"Aleric," he commanded, "come and chafe Lady Minna's hands."

Aleric did as he was bade without question.

"Nay, I am well," Minna protested, but she allowed

Aleric to kneel beside her and rub her hands anyway. "This is terrible!" she continued, speaking to no one in particular. "I do not know what I should do! My lady will be mortified to receive thee thus attired." She was going to be mortified, regardless, Minna thought, but kept those thoughts unvoiced.

Jaufre chuckled and stood beside Eric to gaze out on the lawn.

"I suppose we should do the mannerly thing and discreetly return indoors," he said.

"Aye," Eric replied, "we should do so. But I think 'tis too late for that. The lady and her companion have seen us."

It took Margot several long moments to realize where she was. She had finished shooting all of her arrows and had merely turned around to wait for Jace to shoot his last one when her gaze naturally wandered up toward the long terrace that ran the width of the great hall. That was all she remembered. When she came to herself she was standing at the bottom of the terrace steps, staring up at her Eric. She didn't know how she had gotten there, since she didn't remember walking across the bailey. She didn't know what had happened to her crossbow, which she knew she had been carrying. And worst of all, she didn't know how long she'd been standing there, trancelike, staring up at the one who had stolen all her wits from her.

He was staring back at her just as intensely, and

Margot thought for a moment that she was going to start crying. She could feel the tears welling up in her eyes and she drew in a sharp breath, forcing her emotions under control.

Ten years.

It had been ten long weary years since she had last seen him, and she had only been a child. He had grown so tall and strong, though she remembered that he had been both these things long ago. And his face was so beautiful, so beloved to her. His black hair was longer than it had been then, feathering softly around his shoulders. He was perfect. Unbelievably perfect. She had dreamed of him so often and for so long that he almost didn't seem real, but she knew that he was there. Her Eric was there, finally there, standing only a few feet away from her.

Sir Garin had sent his son to fetch her. She had never considered the possibility and had fully expected to see the lord of Belhaven himself or one of his knights riding up to the castle gates any day now. But her father had written that Sir Garin would send his finest men, and of course that would be her Eric. She only wondered that she'd not realized as much at once.

They had come sooner than expected, as well, and she had not been waiting to greet them properly. Somehow she was going to have to collect herself enough to traverse the steps before her and go to greet her guests. She knew she had to do it. She'd been standing there sufficiently long enough to be embarrassed about it. For the first time she noticed that there were others on the terrace as well, and that they were all staring down at her, including Minna, whom she had never seen quite so pale.

Jace was standing behind her—she had no idea if he'd been there the whole time or not—and he began to poke her inconspicuously in the back. She turned to look at him and he gave her a reassuring smile. She saw that he had gathered her crossbow and now held it with his.

"My lady," he said, using words he never used in a voice that wasn't his, "with thy permission I shall put these away while thou art looking to the comfort of thy guests."

Margot stared at him blankly. Jace shouldered both crossbows on one arm and held his free arm out to her. She instinctively set her hand on it and allowed him to lead her, step by step, slowly up to the terrace. She kept her eyes cast downward so that she wouldn't meet Eric's, and she wondered how she would be able to hear any introductions with her heart pounding so loudly in her ears.

Once the terrace was attained, however, Margot found that her reeling brain had cleared and that she remembered her protocol. Jace disappeared, and Minna made introductions. Margot graced her guests with a deep curtsy, then lifted her face to theirs with a charming smile.

"My l-lords, I w-welcome thee to Reed and pray thy forgiveness for our l-lack of courtesy in meeting thee upon thy arrival," she began, hearing the words coming out of her mouth as if someone else were saying them, as if this were not the moment she had been waiting for and dreaming of for so many years— for all of her life, it seemed. He stood just an arm's length away from her now. *Him. There.* So close that she could reach and grab hold of him, touch him, feel the warmth of his being at last. "We have n-not expected to s-see thee so soon," she went on by rote, quite coolly, "though 'tis an honor indeed to receive thee at this earlier time. I am most grateful that th-thou hast made this journey for the sake of my f-father, Sir Walter le Brun."

Heart pounding, hands shaking badly, she looked tentatively at Eric and saw that he had ceased to look as discomposed as he had from the bottom of the stairs. In fact, he seemed to be giving her only the polite attention due her. The other two men were staring at her openly, something she was well used to when first meeting men. It was because of the way she spoke. For some reason it always seemed to bother men more than women, so that they could not keep from gaping at her as though she were some kind of amazing spectacle. It was an uncomfortable circumstance, initially, but in time they would grow used to her manner of speech, and would be more relaxed.

Eric was a little stiff doing it, but he responded by kneeling on one knee and taking her right hand in his to kiss it gently. He then set his forehead against her hand.

"We are honored to escort thee, my lady. Our lives are thine to command," he vowed.

He should have hopped back up immediately after that, he knew, but he continued to press her hand a moment longer. Her soft, delicate fingers were trembling almost as badly as his rough, callused ones were.

Jaufre followed suit once Eric stood, though he seemed barely able to get the words out. Aleric bowed politely, unable to make such a knightly declaration and glad of it for the first time in his life.

"I thank thee, my l-lords," Margot managed quite pleasantly regardless of her strong desire to collapse. He had *touched* her, and the heat of his flesh had burned stunningly against hers. "I will have chambers prepared for th-thee and quarters for thy men. If thou wilt j-just tell me how many—?" She looked questioningly at Eric.

He spoke very slowly, very carefully, his expression perfectly collected. "My men await us at the castle gates, my lady. There are thirty men-at-arms, four servants, and one squire. The servants will assist in our care and in preparation of meals. The squire may be quartered with me."

Margot nodded her understanding and suddenly realized how she looked. She could feel her face brightening with heat.

"I shall s-see to it immediately," she assured him quickly. "Thou must be weary from thy journey. If thou wilt please to bring thy men to the hall and refresh them th-there, I shall send s-servants to see to thee as s-soon as m-may be."

Eric voiced his approval of this and thanked her.

"I m-must change my attire." Margot curtsied. "I have j-just remembered how inappropriate it is. Please forgive m-me for greeting thee thusly." And without another word she swept herself through the door and into the castle. Minna bobbed a brief curtsy and followed her.

The brothers stared for a long silent while at the open terrace door through which the ladies had disappeared.

"Well," Eric finally said, wishing his hands would stop trembling. "We needs must see to the men."

"And the horses," Jaufre added.

"Aye," Aleric said with a sigh.

They continued to stand and stare.

"James is a lucky man," Aleric said almost wistfully. He had never been awed by a beautiful lady before and was rather stunned by the experience. "I suppose we shall soon be able to say that the lady Margot is our sister."

"Thou wouldst say something like that to brighten our day, Aleric," Jaufre snapped with disgust.

"Leave the lad be, Jaufre," Eric reprimanded. "Canst not see he is smitten with the lovely lady?"

"I am not!" Aleric cried indignantly.

"Oh, come now," said Jaufre. "We are all behaving like fools. Lady Margot is as beautiful as can be and what man would not fall in love with her at first sight?"

"But Aleric hath the right of it, Jaufre," Eric cautioned. "She is for James and that we must not forget. We are only to make certain she gets to Belhaven alive and well. There will be no wooing of the lady on the journey. Now let's to the men and horses."

He led his brothers inside and felt thoroughly convinced of his own words. As soon as his heart stopped thrashing and his hands stopped shaking he knew he would be perfectly able to banish the lady Margot's image from his mind and keep his thoughts on the task ahead. And he would stop wondering when he would see her next. Would that be at the evening meal? Or would she return to the great hall sooner? Truly it would be most easy to think of nothing but returning to Belhaven. He wondered if she would permit him a private audience this afternoon. He was sure that he had a great many details regarding their journey to discuss with her. Faith, it was going to be simple indeed to think of naught save going home. He felt very pleased with himself.

7

Eric's wish to see the lady Margot again was granted sooner than he expected. He had only enough time to see the horses stabled and his men comfortably settled in the great hall before she made her way down the stairs and toward him.

Every man in the room stood, including Eric, who was so startled by her sudden appearance that he spilt ale down the front of his tunic. If it was possible, she looked even lovelier than she had earlier, wearing a rich blue surcoat trimmed with gold braid over fine white silk undergarments that were shot through with gold embroidery. A thick gold chain adorned with rubies girdled her waist, and her hair was braided down her back. On the crown of her head sat a simple circlet of gold and pearls and nothing more, of which Eric was glad. To cover such exquisite hair would be a crime, indeed.

The quietness of the men was palpable, and Eric felt himself drowning in the silence as she approached. He was painfully aware of his own physical state, of being sweaty and dirty from the morning's ride. How he wished he were bathed and dressed in his finest tunic and leggings so that he might draw her attention away from the plainness of his face and the blackness of his coloring.

The silence in the hall meant nothing to Margot: Her every thought was centered upon Eric. He was hers, she thought with a fierceness that surprised even herself. Yet it was the truth. He had *always* been hers and she had every right to set her claim to him. God help any other female who so much as looked at him with even a grain of interest.

How very handsome he was, she thought as she drew nearer to him. How strong and masculine and godlike. Did he find her attractive, as well? Their first meeting had been unfortunate, for she had surely looked unladylike, but perhaps he would not remember it long or hold it against her. She would be most careful never again to give him a reason to take her in disgust.

Margot stopped before him and curtsied, lavishing Eric with a smile that just about sent him reeling.

"My lord," she greeted.

"My lady," he replied weakly.

"Has all been made well with thy m-men and thee?"

"Aye. We have been well looked to, I thank thee."

He looked somewhat discomposed, and Margot's

heart sank. It was her speech, of course. He was disgusted, just as he should be, just as she had always known he might be, just as she had always prayed he wouldn't be. With an effort she softened her tone, and went on.

"I have m-much to discuss with thee, Sir Eric, regarding our journey. Wilt thou c-come to the garden and speak privately with me?"

Eric smiled so suddenly and so charmingly at this suggestion that Margot had to draw breath in. The room suddenly felt quite warm.

"Aye, my lady, I would be most pleased to speak with thee away from all this noise." He realized too late that the room was deathly quiet. The men, and especially Jaufre and Aleric, were staring at the lady Margot and himself most intently. "I mean," he amended, "in the garden."

She put her hand lightly on the arm he held out to her and they turned and walked toward the terrace without further comment, leaving Eric's two brothers fuming and the rest of the men wondering.

"I have b-been remembering the day we spent together t-ten years ago, my lord," Margot commented conversationally as they traversed the terrace steps toward the well-kept gardens of the inner bailey. "I wondered if thou w-wouldst recall it as well."

Eric heard her words but had difficulty responding. He was trying to stop seeing visions of Margot as she had been earlier that day, in the same garden, lying on the grass and looking ethereal.

"I remember that day very well, my lady," he managed. "We spent a very pleasant afternoon together, did we not? 'Twould be poor of me, indeed, to forget having been in the company of such a lovely young lady, though I am amazed that thou shouldst remember me."

"Oh, but I have remembered th-thee most well, Sir Eric!" she insisted, a little too quickly she realized at once.

"I'm honored by thy remembrance, my lady, and am glad to see that thou hast learned to shoot so well. If the skill I saw this afternoon is to be believed, thou'rt as fine a shot as any I've e'er seen." Eric led her to a bench in the midst of a scented herb garden.

Once seated, Eric made the mistake of looking into his companion's beautiful face and all conversation died away. Margot was gazing at him in a thoroughly intimate way, almost as though he were her lover, and he felt every limb in his body turn to water. Those cornflower blue eyes seemed hot as they caressed him, taking in his face and chest and arms, and he vaguely wondered if she was trying to burn a hole in him to see through his armor. Their eyes locked and, to his dismay and wonder, Eric saw Margot's face coming closer and closer to his own.

He was off the bench before he knew it, leaving Margot falling over the place he had vacated. He walked a few steps away, then quickly turned and walked back, not daring to look at her.

It was just his imagination, he thought. He was tired and probably hungry, and certainly overawed by the extraordinary beauty of the perfect creature who had been sitting so close to him. She had not been about to kiss him. The idea was absurd. Ladies did not go about kissing strange men to whom they had just been reintroduced after ten years and with whom they had spent less than five minutes conversing. And they certainly didn't go around trying to kiss someone like him! Jaufre, maybe, with his handsome good looks, but never him.

"This is a very—nice garden," he said stupidly, striving to look interested in his surroundings.

Margot watched him pace back and forth in front of the bench and sighed. She had lost her restraint, being so close to him in such a private place. She had been unable to stop looking at him, taking all of him in and trying to see all of the ways in which he had changed. Her ten long years of pining had welled up inside her all of a sudden and burst like a dam. Before she knew it she'd accosted him as though she were the village whore, and he had been understandably shocked. She had to remind herself that he couldn't possibly know what her feelings for him were, and he obviously didn't realize that he was to be her future husband.

"Yes, it is very nice," she agreed demurely, determined to behave herself. "My m-mother planted it many years ago. Our cook was m-most grateful."

Eric finally looked at Margot and found that she was sitting very primly and properly, her perfect hands clasped together in her lap and her face schooled into an innocent, maidenly countenance. He drew in a deep breath and sat on the bench once more, as far from her as he could manage. His hands were trembling again and he firmly clamped them on his knees.

"Lady Margot," he began shakily, "there is much to settle between us regarding our journey, and then I've a request to make of thee regarding my squire."

Margot nodded in compliance.

"If thy household can be made ready by tomorrow morn, I'd like to leave by the break of day. The sooner we return to Belhaven, the better." He neglected to say what his hurry was, knowing that she was unaware of the danger she was in. It had been decided between his father and himself that she was merely to think that Sir Walter wished assurance of her safety, and nothing more. She was not to be allowed to worry and fret.

Margot shook her head. "I d-doubt that all can be m-made ready by then. Perhaps the next morn?"

Eric frowned but realized this wasn't an unreasonable request, especially since he and his men had arrived earlier than expected.

"'Twill have to do, my lady, but I do beseech thee to make all ready by no later than then. My men and I shall be at thy disposal to help in any way we can. As to the supplies we shall need for the journey," he began and continued to list his requirements.

An hour passed without either of them knowing it. They spoke about the journey, and of what the countryside would be like as they passed through it, and of whether it would rain on them or be dreadfully hot, and of the various funny incidents that had occurred to Eric and his men while they'd journeyed toward Reed. Margot laughed with delight when he told her about Thomas.

"My g-goodness!" she exclaimed. "What a m-most unusual child!"

"Oh, aye, that he is, my lady," Eric said, thinking that if he could spend the rest of his life sitting on this very bench with this beautiful woman he would be the most contented man alive. "When he woke the next morn to find himself sleeping at the foot of my bed he was most pleased with himself and announced that he should henceforth sleep thusly in order to protect me during my slumbers. His good mood remained until I took him to the nearby stream and bade him wash, and then he did naught but complain 'til I threatened to leave him behind. He came out of that stream better scrubbed than a cooking pot!" They both laughed again and after a moment Eric was able to continue. "I hope thou wilt be able to clothe him properly, my lady, for all this way he hath made due with the clothing of a man and 'tis all he can do to move about without tripping. I fear he is a rather small lad."

Margot instinctively reached out to place her hand reassuringly over one of his huge ones, not considering what she did.

"Do not worry, my l-lord. I shall find suitable clothing for the boy. He will be well satisfied, I v-vow."

Eric didn't hear anything she said, so completely distracted was he by the touch of her cool hand. His laughter vanished and he gazed at their hands together, feeling a shiver of sensation go through him such as he had never before experienced. He couldn't keep himself from turning his hand under hers until it was palm up, and he watched in amazement as his fingers, of their own volition, gently curled over her small, delicate ones.

Neither of them spoke, both were staring at their hands as though they had never seen them before.

"How small thy hand is in mine," Eric whispered at last.

"Eric—"

"So, this is where the two of thee have been hiding!" Jaufre exclaimed as he strode through the bushes toward them. They snatched their hands away as though caught in some crime. "Wilt thou keep the lady Margot out all eve, brother? Canst not see 'tis growing dark? The evening meal will be upon us soon and thou'rt not fit to eat in the stables, let alone with such a beautiful lady."

Eric and Margot rose hastily and realized, for the first time since they'd begun their conversation, that the day was indeed approaching sunset.

Feeling very much in the need of a cold bath at the moment, anyhow, Eric nodded toward his brother and made a quick bow to Margot.

"Thou'rt quite right, Jaufre. Please forgive me, my lady, for keeping thee so long. I fear we let the time fly from us, though we accomplished much, and I thank thee. Wilt thou not forget to look to Thomas for me? I am most grateful for any care thou might givest him. If thou wilt excuse me, I'll go prepare for the evening meal." Eric spoke this string of sentences so quickly that Margot didn't have time to respond. He was already on his way out of the garden, making long, fast strides toward the terrace stairs. In another moment he had disappeared altogether.

Jaufre beamed at Margot and offered her an arm. "May I have the honor of escorting thee through the gardens, my lady?" he asked politely.

Looking at him, Margot was more inclined to give him a scold for causing Eric to run off so suddenly, but Jaufre was soon going to be her brother and she wanted to get along well with her new family.

He had bathed and changed into a fine blue tunic trimmed at the collar and skirt with rich brown ermine. Long open-cut sleeves trimmed in brown ermine as well revealed muscular arms clothed in pale yellow silk undergarments. His tight leggings were of the same color, and on his feet were the customary soft, pointed shoes. The tunic was belted at his slim waist with a gold chain and dagger; another chain, with a medallion, adorned his neck and chest. He presented a most handsome figure, Margot thought, surveying him in his finery. His long blond hair reached to just beyond his shoulders, his features were strong and fine, his blue eyes devastating.

Resigning herself to be pleasant, Margot placed her hand upon the proffered arm. "Only until the evening meal, my lord."

His smile was charming. "Of course, my lady. I thank thee."

*   *   *

In his chambers Eric sat in a tub of cold water and tried to think of anything save Margot. Thomas scurried busily in the background, setting out clothes and shaving preparations, occasionally returning to the bathtub to scrub Eric's back or hair with the soap his master had left lying neglected on the floor. He was assisted in these labors, surprisingly enough, by the companion who had been with Margot earlier in the day. Eric had learned that his name was Jace and that he was the castle troubadour. He was somewhat amazed that the jester of Reed should wish to serve him so, but he accepted the boy's presence without a word, totally unaware that Jace, knowing of his lady's love for the giant knight, had already accepted Eric as his master.

The castle at Reed was large and modern, causing Eric's beloved Belhaven to seem almost old-fashioned in comparison. There were two residential floors above the great hall, and all of the chambers were large and airy, with both balconies and windows. Eric's room was more opulent than his own at home, with expensive tapestries on every wall. Convenient garderobes were located on each floor, built directly over the river that ran alongside the castle. The great hall, expensively furnished and fastidiously maintained, was several times larger than the one at Belhaven, though he preferred the homeyness and comfort that his mother had achieved at the latter. Even the stables for the horses and the quarters for his men were beyond compare. When they returned home the men who had come with them would probably present his father with a petition that similar lodgings be built for them at Belhaven.

Ah, but James was a lucky man, Eric thought ruefully. He would inherit not only Belhaven one day, but Reed as well. Reed was a prize, indeed, as good in land as Belhaven, only larger, and its village was nearly a town, so large and populated it was. Eric was duly impressed when he had ridden through it that morn and seen the many merchants, an indication of wealth and prosperity. What wouldn't he give to be the lord of such a land? Especially if the lady Margot came with it? She alone was a treasure worth all a man had. All, indeed.

He sat up quickly and shook his wet hair, sending drops of water flying onto the floor. He was not going to allow himself to think such thoughts. He was not going to think about sitting beside her in the gardens for the space of an hour and feeling as though he were in heaven. He was not going to allow himself to remember the beauty of her face or the music of her laugh or the soft feeling of her hand in his. He was not. It would be unfair to James, and Eric would not betray his eldest brother, not even in his mind.

And he would not dress in his finery, as Jaufre had, to impress her. No. Absolutely not. He would wear a simple tunic and leggings, just as he did at home, and that was that.

With these thoughts firmly in mind he called Thomas over to rinse him, and marveled for the tenth time in as many days at what a wonder the boy was. He had made himself undeniably useful since forcing his way into the camp, and had amazed not only Eric but Jaufre and Aleric as well with his ability to play squire. Thomas seemed so frail, yet he had strength enough to assist in drawing Eric's heavy armor off, and he had ridden ahead with the servants each day to make the camp ready for their arrival. Eric had gone to his tent each night to find his sleeping pallet ready to receive him, as well as clean clothing, warm water, and soap awaiting him. Each mealtime found the boy fighting his way to the front of the line to secure the choicest victuals for his master, which he refused to share, insisting that he would eat whatever was left over later with the servants. Indeed, Eric was beginning to wonder how he had ever gotten along without the boy. Thomas seemed to realize what his needs were before even he knew them.

As the boy helped his master to dry, a knock was given at the antechamber door. Jace answered it and returned with a pile of shoes and clothing.

"These have been sent by my lady and with her compliments. They are for Thomas." He set the pile on a nearby chair.

Eric was pleased to see Thomas's eyes light up as the boy surveyed the clothing, which looked to be made of the finest cloth, and the two pairs of shoes, one sturdy leather pair for traveling and one soft pair for wearing at the castle. Jace held the clothing up piece by piece for inspection.

"Now thou must bathe thyself as well, lad," Eric instructed, smiling as he watched the excited expressions that passed over the boy's face. "Once thou'rt dressed in thy fine new clothes we shall make a noble sight, indeed, on our entry to the great hall."

8

Thus it was, half an hour later, that Sir Eric Stavelot of Belhaven and his well-dressed squire made their grand entrance to the hall, looking for all the world as regal as the king himself would had he entered with his squire. Eric, against his better judgment, had allowed Thomas and Jace to dress him in the finest outfit he had brought with him. He should have kept his resolve to dress simply, he knew, but they had already laid the finery out and it would have been wasteful to make them put it away. And, truth be told, the look of approval on Margot's face as she surveyed him gave him a great deal of pleasure.

Margot, at the moment, was wondering if her heart was ever going to beat normally again. It seemed to take up the most erratic thumpings whenever she saw Eric, and now the sight of him dressed so handsomely set it to rattling away. He wore a green velvet tunic, pleated across his wide chest and trimmed, like Jaufre's, with brown ermine at the collar and the edge of the skirt. The sleeves were lined with yellow and were pendant, opening just above the elbow and falling in a feathered pattern almost to his knees. His muscular arms were encased in silk undergarments of a light orange color, and his equally muscular legs were covered by darker orange leggings. Around his neck were two simple gold chains, and around his waist was a thin leather belt upon which hung the obligatory dagger. His long black hair had been brushed until it hung silky and straight, and his skin was smooth and shaven, Thomas having earlier scraped it unmercifully with a sharp blade.

Margot knew she stared, but she consoled herself with the knowledge that all the other women in the room were staring, too. He was magnificently and powerfully built, like some great and fabled beast: surely no other man on God's earth compared. He moved with the grace of a cat, with the controlled strength of a destrier, every line of every muscle straining against the taut material of his garments. She thought she heard several feminine sighs as he made his approach, and she gripped at her chair to master the jealous anger that rose within her. Eric made a perfect bow and gave her a devastating smile when he straightened. Margot rose and offered him her hand.

"My l-lord, we have awaited thy arrival," she told him with a smile, gazing past him to Thomas, who was standing behind his master with a typical scowl set on his face. Margot held out one of her hands and drew the boy forward to look at him better. "And this is thy T-Thomas. Well, thou'rt a very f-fine l-lad indeed, sir, and how well thou d-dost look in thy new clothing. How do you d-do, Thomas?"

Thomas, being young, was not stricken by the lady Margot's beauty as older males were, but he had never heard such stammering before and that intrigued him. He also had no idea of how to respond properly to such a grand lady, having spent his entire life among women of a much lower class. Therefore he turned to the one person he did understand and addressed himself.

"She makes a funny sound when she speaks," he informed his master simply.

Eric's face reddened and he placed one heavy hand on Thomas's shoulder to turn him back to Margot, who was smiling with delight at the boy's artless honesty.

"Thomas, make a bow to the lady Margot and beg her pardon for thy rudeness," Eric instructed, pressing his hand on the child's shoulder in an effort to aid him in this task.

Thomas gave Margot a look of confusion as he obeyed his lord and made a rather unelegant bow.

"I beg thy pardon, lady," he said dutifully.

Margot surprised both Thomas and Eric by laughing pleasantly. She put an arm around Thomas's thin shoulders and led him toward the high table at the end of the great hall, leaving Eric to follow behind.

"Do not apologize, Thomas," Margot told the boy

gently. "Thou wilt g-grow used to my speech. It takes a little time, but people g-get used t-to it. Canst thou understand m-me when I speak?"

Thomas could not remember anything about his mother, since she had died when he was very young, but he suddenly thought that if he could have known her, she would have been very much like the lady Margot. She would not have been insulted because of his ignorance, and she would have put her soft arm around his shoulders just so, and she would have smiled at him in just such a way.

"Oh, aye, lady, I understand thee. It's just that I never heard anyone speak like that before," he replied, thinking that she smelled nice, like flowers.

"That is fine, then. We shall be g-good friends, shall we n-not?"

"I would like that, my lady. I'll serve thee at table, if thou wilt have me."

Margot told him that indeed she would like that very much, and as his master and she were going to sit together he would be able to serve them both easily, instead of having to run from one to the other.

The meal was sumptuous, a small miracle considering the amount of time Margot had had to order her cooks to prepare a feast in honor of her guests. There were four courses with as many as twelve dishes per course, including several different kinds of fish and meats, both roasted and prepared with herbs, sauces and vegetables, as well as stewed fruits, colored jellies, baked and fried breads, and cakes with creams. French and Italian wines and dark ale were put out for drinking, and well-trained servants made certain that all at the tables were sated with both food and drink.

Margot had instructed one of the servers to help Thomas, and Eric watched with approval as the boy dutifully followed every instruction given him.

"He is wonderfully quick, is he n-not, my lord?" Margot said.

Smiling, Eric nodded. "That he is, my lady. Only see how serious and stern he is as he goes about his duties."

Jace made an appearance and walked from table to table with his lute, singing one ballad after another to entertain the feasters. When the meal was over and the guests had washed their hands and left the tables to relax in front of the fires and at gaming tables, which had been set out, he announced that he would proceed to perform great and daring feats that would amaze and amuse them. These feats consisted mainly of juggling, acrobatics, and storytelling, but as he performed them with both ease and showmanship the company was indeed charmed and entertained. Margot clapped her hands when Jace finished an especially difficult juggling demonstration.

"N-now thou must sing again, J-Jace," she requested.

Jace bowed and took up his lute. "Thy wish is my command, Margot lady," he said, and strummed thoughtfully on his instrument. He strolled around the hall and winked lecherously at some of the ladies present. "Now, let me see if I can think of a song which will please. Ah, here is one." He began to play a rather boisterous tune and lifted his head to sing loudly:

"Sir William enjoying his damsel one night,

He tickled and pleased her to so great a height—"

"Jace!" Margot reprimanded in a shocked tone that made the men laugh. "Shame on th-thee! Save thy bawdy s-songs for when ladies are n-not present!" She blushed and glanced at Eric, who only grinned at her ladylike embarrassment.

Jace sighed and bowed to her again. "Very well. Mayhap the ladies will like this one better." He embarked on a love song.

Sir Basil, who had made the acquaintance of the Stavelot brothers earlier in the day, approached Eric as he sat with Jaufre and Margot.

"Good eve, my lady." He bowed to Margot and then nodded to Eric. "Sir Eric."

Eric returned his greeting and smiled at the man whom Sir Walter had left in charge of Reed during his absence. Sir Basil was an unlikely knight and protector, as short and thin as Eric himself was tall and muscular, but he was both sharp and intelligent, qualities that Eric knew not to underrate in a man of war.

"Wilt do me the honor of a game, my lord?" Sir Basil asked. "Backgammon, perhaps? Or chess?"

Eric stood, towering over the small man. "'Twould be an honor, sir, to match thee at whatever game is thy pleasure. My lady, wilt thou excuse us, please?"

Sir Basil led Eric to a small table set in a private corner of the room, and with some unease, Margot watched them go. She had thought to keep Eric by her side that evening and continue her efforts to woo him, but Sir Basil had innocently outwitted her. Jace continued to sing and entertain the company as they relaxed around the great hall, and servants brought out mugs of ale for the men and hot spiced wine for the ladies. Margot was satisfied to see that Eric's men were enjoying themselves and that her ladies were putting themselves out to charm and entertain.

Aleric and Minna sat on one side of her, deep in discussion over some Latin writing or other, and Jaufre sat on her other side, conversing pleasantly enough yet unable to draw her interest away from the table where Eric and Sir Basil sat. Bent over a game of backgammon, the two men seemed strangely serious, and she couldn't help but wonder what it was they discussed. While she watched, Eric suddenly stiffened, and in another moment he turned to look in her direction. Their eyes met only briefly and she saw with some surprise that his face was grim. His eyes passed from hers and went to Jaufre's.

"Wilt thou excuse us, please, Lady Margot?" Jaufre said, rising and placing a hand on Aleric's shoulder to bring him to attention. Aleric looked up from his discussion with Minna and saw the direction of Jaufre's gaze, which he followed. Upon seeing Eric's face he stood as well and made his apologies to Minna.

"I wonder what that is all about," Minna mused as she drew closer to Margot.

Jaufre and Aleric had drawn chairs up to the table

where Sir Basil and Eric sat, and soon the four of them were huddled in private conversation.

"I do not know, M-Minna," Margot replied. "They seem very s-serious, though, do they n-not?"

"And this huntsman was never found?" Jaufre asked incredulously. "Not even a sign of him?"

Sir Basil shook his head. "Nay, not a sign of one man, but of many. After I escorted the lady Margot back to the safety of Reed I returned with several of my men to have another look at the spot where she had been accosted. In their rush to find the huntsman my soldiers overlooked several sets of hoofprints left in the muddy ground, or perhaps they had not thought they were of consequence at the time, as many do hunt in the forests for their livelihood. Sir Walter hath long been considerate of his villeins in this manner. But we had suffered a great storm the night before and the ground would have been washed of any existing marks that might have been there. Yet I found several, indicating that not one, but many men had recently been at the sight where Lady Margot's basket was dropped."

"Didst thou never find these men who had been in the forest?"

"We did not, though we found the remains of what looked to be a camp of sorts."

Eric's eyebrows rose. "What is this? When didst thou find this? And how?"

"Having found the hoofprints in the forest I returned to Reed and gave strict orders for the lady Margot's protection, and made sure that she would neither be left alone nor allowed to leave the castle walls. On the following morn my men and I rode through the immediate lands surrounding Reed in search of any odd activities or strangers. 'Twas midafternoon when we rode through the hills to the north and found the camp. There were signs of hasty activity, as of a sudden leaving, and two small fires were still warm and smoking, but those were all the signs of life we found. Those and more prints on the ground, both of men and horses. I have sent men out each day since finding the camp to make certain no one has returned to it, and no one has."

"Could it have been a hunting party?" asked Jaufre.

Sir Basil straightened and looked seriously from one brother to the other. "I cannot think so. I fear the spot was not meet for hunting, though it gives a very good view of both the castle and the lands of Reed. Such a vantage point would give anyone there a plain sight of those who come and go from the village walls." His meaning was very plain.

"Ravinet's men," Eric said solemnly, and looked at Jaufre. "Watching for the lady Margot and waiting for their chance. If they saw us ride into Reed this day they will be waiting for us to leave, and they will follow, hoping for an opportunity on the open road. Damn!" His hands clenched into fists. He looked back at Sir Basil.

"Is it possible for a group of armed men to remain well hidden in those hills, regardless of thy men searching daily?"

"Very likely," replied Sir Basil. "The hills of Reed are tricky, and there are many caverns in which to hide. Very likely, indeed."

"I would see this camp which thou found, first thing in the morn, Sir Basil."

Sir Basil said that he would show him the place.

"Good." Eric nodded toward Jaufre and Aleric. "My brothers will accompany us and mayhap we'll have a look at these northern hills of Reed." He rose from where he sat. "We've much ahead of us on the morrow and needs be we must rest while we may. Wilt see to the men, Jaufre, and make certain they are secured for the eve? Aleric, I'd have thee look after the Belhaven servants and see that they are comfortable as well, and send Thomas to me as soon as may be. I'll take our leave of the lady Margot. Be ready to ride at the break of dawn."

Margot saw Eric at once as he rose and left the table where he had been sitting with Sir Basil and his brothers. She smiled as he walked toward her, though he did not return the smile. He made his bow and took Margot's hand in his when she rose to greet him.

"My apologies, Lady Minna," he said politely to that lady, "I must speak with thy mistress, if I may?"

Minna excused herself and left. Margot turned an inquiring face toward Eric. She was taken aback by how set and firm his features were, and by how stern he seemed to be. He placed her hand on his arm, led her from the company to a more private corner of the great hall, and turned to her as soon as they were alone.

"My lady, I wish not to speak in front of the others, but I must request that thou waste no time preparing to leave on the day after next."

"I have already t-told th-thee that all shall be ready by then."

Eric nodded. "That is well, my lady. I regret that my brothers and I shall not be here to aid thee in the morn, but my men and the servants are at thy disposal. Please do not hesitate to make use of them."

"Thou wilt not be here in the morn—?" she began in confusion, but Eric disconcerted her by taking both of her hands in his and pressing them against his lips.

"I thank thee for a most pleasant eve, Lady Margot." His voice was quiet and earnest. "And I shall take leave to ask thy permission for my brothers and me to retire to our chambers. I fear we are rather worn from our journey."

"Of—of c-course," she replied, rather stunned that they should be leaving the company so early but unable to keep them from doing so. He stared at her intently, and she murmured, "Sleep well, Eric."

Eric was surprised to hear her use his name thus, and the casual, gentle sound of it coming from her lips made him feel warm and slightly dangerous. He felt an unbidden, overwhelming desire to pull her into the shadows and kiss her, though he realized that doing such a thing would both sicken and disgust her. Still, she was gazing at him with those cornflower blue eyes in a most unusual manner. He found that his hands were trembling again, and he tightened the grip he had on hers.

"My lady," he whispered, "promise me thou wilt stay inside the castle walls on the morrow."

"W-what?" she asked, and smiled as though he were jesting.

"Promise me," he insisted and pulled her even closer so that their faces were near one another.

"I promise," she said in a small voice, and he could feel her warm breath on his face.

He released her quickly and made a short bow.

"Good night, then, my lady."

In mere moments he had bounded up the stairs, leaving a thoroughly bewildered Margot staring after him.

9

The sun had barely made an appearance the next day when Eric and his brothers stood with Sir Basil overlooking the valley of Reed from the spot where Black Donal's camp had been.

"'Tis a perfect view, indeed," Jaufre said tersely, the cool morning air steaming around his mouth as he spoke.

Eric nodded. "And a well-hidden vantage point." He indicated the campsite with a wave of one gloved hand. "'Twould be impossible to see that a camp was here from the valley floor, while all below is easily seen. It is understandable that whoever was here was able to see any approach and therefore able to make a hasty departure. That is surely what happened when thy men and thee came so nearly upon them that day, Sir Basil."

"I wonder where they are now," Aleric pondered nervously.

"Where and how many of them are there," Jaufre added.

Eric walked along the edge of the viewpoint and scanned the surrounding hills. "These hills must provide a hundred safe hiding places for a small band of men and horses. If they are here somewhere they have the added advantage of having seen us heading north this morn. A skilled man could have followed our path here without alerting us to his presence. We may even now be watched by such a one." Eric turned and strolled in the opposite direction. "If we spent weeks trying to find them there is every chance we would not be able to."

"A true game of cat and mouse, my lord," Sir Basil agreed. "My men and I have searched every inch of Reed many times over in the past few days, but to no avail. Ofttimes I am tempted to think we are chasing ghosts, save that we come across signs of human presence every now and again."

"Not ghosts, nay," Eric said, "but men well trained and well led."

"Making them all the more dangerous and deadly," Aleric stated.

"What dost thou think, Eric?" Jaufre asked. "We needs must get the lady Margot to Belhaven as soon as possible. We cannot stay here and wait for Ravinet to bring all his men down about our heads. No offense, Sir Basil," he addressed that man, "but Reed is not presently as well manned as Belhaven, since most of thine army is with Sir Walter at Shrewsbury. 'Twould not be difficult for Ravinet to make a quick and successful siege here had he the men and resources to do so."

Aleric spoke before Eric could reply. "We could send a messenger to Father and have him bring the army of Belhaven here," he suggested hopefully. "Then we would not have to take the lady outside the castle walls."

Eric shook his head. "That would be well, lad, if Ravinet did not get here first. We've no way of knowing where he is; how close or how far. We cannot take the risk of waiting to find out. Aside from that, any messenger sent might not make it to Belhaven alive were Terent or his men to waylay him on the road. Do not worry, Aleric, we'll think of a way."

"I would send some of my men with thee, my lord," Sir Basil told him, "if thou wilt have them. They may be able to provide greater protection for the lady Margot, and I think her father would wish it."

Eric shook his head once more. "I thank thee, Sir Basil, but nay. Thou hast not enough now to spare and I'll not leave Reed so unguarded." He looked out over the scenic valley again. The sun was rising higher in the sky and light spread across the valley floor. "I do not wish to discuss this further here," he finally said. "We may have unwelcome ears listening to our words. Let us return to Castle Reed. Methinks I've a plan."

*   *   *

"They are returning to Reed, sir," Eamon announced from his position of lookout. Black Donal came up immediately and peered over his shoulder.

"Who in the Fiend's name are they, I wonder?" Black Donal said softly, a contrast to the day before when he had soundly cursed as he watched an unexpected contingency of fighting men ride into Reed, led by two knights wearing the colors and coats of arms of a castle he didn't recognize. This was something he hadn't counted on. Reed had been nicely undermanned, the lord being away at the wars, and could be easily taken if need be. This additional group of men would not make the castle much harder to take, being, by his count, only thirty-seven, some of whom were certainly servants and squires. The fact that they were there at all was what bothered him, and not knowing who they were bothered him even more.

He had spent the night trying to convince himself that they were only men on their way to Shrewsbury who had decided to stop at Reed for the night; and that would have made sense had they not stopped so early in the day. No fighting man would waste more than half a day relaxing when he could be making good time in his travels. No. These men were at Reed for some reason, some purpose. He would have to keep a close watch on them until he knew what it was.

Already he had taken overlong in fulfilling his charge to capture the lady Margot, and as each day passed, he grew angrier and more tense. The arrival of these unknown men made him even worse. Terent of Ravinet was a hard master, and did Black Donal not deliver up the lady soon, he would receive unwelcome punishment from his lord. But get her he would, even if he had to scale the castle walls at midnight and carry her off in her night shift.

Some hours later, while she continued to work toward finishing the plans for her journey, Margot looked up to find Eric watching her from across the great hall. He looked away quickly, as though embarrassed that she should catch him watching her, but their eyes had met briefly and she could see the fascination in them.

It was a good sign, she thought. At least he was beginning to have some sort of interest in her. Soon enough he would realize he loved her. She gazed at him affectionately for a few moments before returning her attention to John the Steward.

Across the room Eric was trying to concentrate on a list of supplies for the return journey to Belhaven. He felt angry with himself for not being able to give more attention to his task, which needed to be completed soon so that the wagons could be packed. What was wrong with him? Why couldn't he keep his eyes off her? The way she had looked at him when she had seen him watching her—it had made him feel the way no other woman ever had. But he must stop thinking of her. She was for James, whom he loved and revered. James, who was smart and kind and handsome and—legitimate; the sort of man a lady such as she deserved.

The sheets of parchment before him seemed to waver, and he looked toward her again, from the corners of his eyes, so that she would not see him. She had returned her attention to the steward, and Eric let himself stare at her openly. She was so beautiful, so perfect in every way.

Too perfect for him.

Reluctantly he looked back at the list.

Eric dressed casually for the evening meal that night, as he had promised himself he would. Thomas had railed at him mightily in an effort to make him dress more finely, but Eric had refused. There was no reason to play the peacock when his casual clothes were perfectly suitable for the occasion. Besides, it was time to begin thinking of the lady Margot as no one more than his sister, though this he did not share with Thomas.

He was sitting alone in a private chamber located just off the great hall, going over the final plans for the next day and looking at a rough map of England when the lady Margot found him. He looked up as she walked in and closed the door behind herself, his face betraying both pleasure and discomfort.

"Good eve, Sir Eric," she said in a very pleasant voice, leaning against the door. "I hope I d-do n-not disturb thee?"

Eric stood quickly. "Not at all, my lady," he responded courteously, wishing she would go away. "I am always at thy disposal."

Margot pushed away from the thick wooden door and drew closer to him. She was dressed in a surcoat of lavishly embroidered burgundy, which made her golden hair seem more luminous than ever. Eric stepped behind the chair he had been sitting in, to force a space between them.

Margot stopped on the other side of the chair. "I wished to t-tell thee that all has been made ready and that we shall be ready to l-leave in the morn." She lowered her eyes. "I d-did hope thou wouldst be pleased."

"Yes, indeed, I am," said Eric, much stirred by the sweetness of her manner. "Well pleased. And grateful. 'Twas want of me to demand such speed with thy preparations, and I pray thou'lt forgive me, my lady."

She gazed up at him with great, wide eyes that nearly knocked him over.

"There is n-no n-need to ask forgiveness, my lord. I should be happy to do anything thou d-didst ask of me, Eric. Anything at all, I promise thee."

He believed her. She spoke the words as though she were repeating a wedding vow, and Eric's heart responded with a furious beat. His palms began to sweat and his mouth felt suddenly dry.

"Thou—thou'rt most kind, Lady Margot. Again, I am grateful. But I shall hope to have no need to make any more such requests of thee, other than that thou wilt harbor no fears regarding the coming journey. I know 'tis strange for thee to leave thy home in such a way, but, in sooth, I'd have this be a most pleasant time for thee."

"Oh, I am n-not afraid when I am with th-thee, Eric," Margot assured him with a look that made him take a step farther away. "I know I am always safe with thee." She followed him around the chair.

"Aye." Eric gulped nervously. "I would surely protect thee with my life, Lady Margot. Always will I keep thee safe." He wondered as he backed away from her if he were the same supposedly brave man who had faced entire armies before.

She was smiling at him now. "I am l-looking f-forward to living at Belhaven with thy family and thee. Is it a very pretty p-place?"

"Very pretty," Eric replied before he ran into another chair and had to change directions. Margot changed courses with him. "Though 'tis different from Reed. I think thou wilt find it pleasant enough." He had never been pursued around a room by a beautiful lady before, and the experience, though highly complimentary, was rather unsettling, especially since the lady in question looked as if she were about to leap upon him as a hungry beast might leap upon its next meal.

"I remember thy f-father and mother a little from my d-days at court," Margot continued. "Thy mother is accounted t-to be one of the most beautiful w-women in England. Is this not so?"

Eric took a step around the table at which he had been working. "Indeed she is most beautiful, my lady, but I would be lying were I to say she was more beautiful than thee. I fear thy beauty will cast both her and my lovely sister into the shade."

Margot laughed delightfully, a soft musical sound that made him stumble as he continued his circumference of the table. "My, what a flatterer th-thou art, Sir Eric! Dost t-truly think me pretty?"

She asked this so sincerely that Eric wondered whether she was honestly unaware of her beauty. It had been said that Sir Walter kept his daughter fairly cloistered at Reed after his wife had died, save for a few visits to court, where he likely had kept a close eye on her. Eric found it hard to believe that Margot did not know how amazingly beautiful she was, though her unaffected manners did seem to bear the idea out.

"Aye," he replied quietly, his retreat halted as the backs of his legs came up against the chair he had been sitting in earlier. Margot stopped closely in front of him, effectively trapping him, and lifted her face to his inquiringly. He knew in that instant that his battle was lost. "Thou art . . . the loveliest lady I have ever set eyes on . . . Margot."

It was the first time he had ever said her name without attaching her title to it, and Margot felt a tingle run through her. She wanted to kiss him so badly, to feel his lips against hers as she had dreamed of all these years, to touch his face and hair, to feel his arms around her. The distance between them seemed to close without either of them moving.

Eric couldn't stop himself. He wanted to, knew he

had to, but he couldn't. She was a magnet whose draw he couldn't resist, no matter how hard he might try, and as he lowered his head to kiss her he consoled himself with vague thoughts of inviolable scientific facts.

"Margot," he breathed against her mouth before touching his lips to hers. Soft, warm, moist. *God's mercy, she's sweet,* he thought as he went down and down and down.

The kiss lasted only a moment, and Eric had only just felt the warmth of her body as his hands circled her waist, before a loud knock sounded on the closed door, causing them to jump apart.

"Ah, I've found thee at last," Jaufre said cheerily as he strolled into the room unbidden. "I've been searching for thee nigh on an hour, brother. My lady." He bowed to Margot and smiled knowingly. "Have I come at a bad time?"

Margot could have screamed. What a nuisance the man was! This was the second time he had intruded upon a promising encounter between Eric and herself. And his timing! She had only felt Eric's kiss for a mere second before Jaufre knocked. Disappointment raged through her.

"Nay, Jaufre," Eric said quickly, truly relieved for the interruption. He didn't like to think about what might have happened if his brother hadn't walked in when he had. "The lady Margot and I were just going over the map of England, discussing the route we shall take on our return to Belhaven." He indicated the map with the wave of a hand.

"Ah, yes." Jaufre gazed casually at the map. "I was going to have a look at this myself earlier. Mayhap we should go over it together before the evening meal?"

Margot's face was flushed and she glared at Jaufre rather pointedly. "I have seen all that I n-need to," she said stiffly. "If thou wilt excuse me, p-please, I m-must see that the meal has been p-properly p-pre-pared." She didn't bother making a curtsy before storming out of the room.

Jaufre watched the lady go, then turned a disbe-lieving look upon his red-faced brother. "*Going over the map of England?* God's toes, but thou art a romantic knave! Aleric has naught on thee, i'faith!"

Eric cleared his throat and started to roll the map up. "Thou dost not know what thou sayest. There is no need to speak of romance."

"Nay?" Jaufre's eyebrows went up in mock sur-prise. "I hate to be the one to tell thee, Eric, but that lovely creature is in love with thee."

Eric gave a shout of laughter. "Very good, Jaufre, very good. Hast been receiving thy training from Jace? Thou wouldst make a fine court jester, indeed. Never have I heard anything so outrageous in my entire life."

Jaufre shook his head. "I tell thee the truth, lad. Art thou the only one in this castle who is blind to it? 'Tis plain as the nose on thy face. That lady is in love with thee."

"That lady is soon to be our sister." Eric was fast losing his sense of humor. "And a vision such as she would ne'er love an ugly devil like me. Thou'rt imagining things." He tucked the map under one arm and pushed the chair aside to leave.

Jaufre stepped in front of him. "I did not say I understood why she loves thee, man, only that she does. Mayhap thou dost not believe it. I did not either, at first. But what if 'tis true, Eric? What if the lady does love thee? What then?"

Eric drew in a shaky breath and stared past his brother at the door through which Margot had just departed. He could still feel the warmth and softness of the lips that had touched his. She had lifted her face to receive his kiss, indeed, had seemed eager to receive it. The memory made his knees weak. Yet he could not believe that she could want him, *him* of all people. They hardly knew each other. Surely he had misinterpreted her actions of this afternoon and of last eve and of the day before. She had only been making an effort to be friendly and to make them feel welcome; this afternoon she had simply been conversing, not chasing him around the room as he had imagined. And the kiss—the kiss had been a simple mistake, and she'd been too well bred to push him away as she had probably wanted to. He looked at Jaufre.

"It would not make a difference, even if 'twere true. She is to be James's wife and I'd not stand in the way of that. Still I say thou art imagining things. She loves me not."

Jaufre stayed alone in the room after Eric left and mulled the situation over. The lady Margot was in love with his brother and of that he was certain. Her feelings for him were written plainly all over her face whenever Eric was near her. Only a blind man, or his thick-headed brother, wouldn't see it. Everyone in the castle knew and talked of it. Jaufre had even heard a few of the kitchen servants referring to Eric as the future lord of Reed. All he could surmise from the little bits and pieces he'd heard was that Margot le Brun had been in love with Eric since she spent that one day with him so long ago at court.

Jaufre sighed and leaned against the table.

Of all the rotten luck. It could have been he she fell in love with if he hadn't been quite so stubborn all those many years ago. What a crime! The lady Margot was a prize beauty, a woman any man would love. There probably wasn't anything he wouldn't do to win her hand and heart, and the devil take James, who hadn't even met her yet! But there wasn't any getting around the fact that the lady had already made her choice in Eric and, no matter how much his brother denied the fact, or how much Jaufre himself would have liked to gain Margot's attentions, she seemed bound and determined to have her choice.

10

"Anything to report, Eamon?"

Eamon jumped in surprise when Jason spoke so suddenly behind him, though he had been neither dozing nor daydreaming.

"Thou gavest me a start, Jason!" He grinned sheepishly and with a little embarrassment. "Give me more warning, next time."

"Sorry, lad." His yawning friend peered over Eamon's shoulder to look at the valley below. "Anything to report?" he repeated.

Eamon shook his head. "Only the villeins going to work this morn. The same as every morn. Is he asleep?" He knew he didn't have to explain who "he" was.

"Aye. Well for us, eh?"

"Aye," Eamon agreed heartily, wanting to get some sleep himself. Black Donal was as hard a taskmaster as Terent of Ravinet, and there was no relaxing when the man was awake.

"Get some food, man, and some rest," Jason advised as Eamon moved out of his watch position and stretched. "Methinks he hath something for today. Best to be sharp. Hey now, what's this?" He was looking intently at the valley.

"What?" Eamon looked toward Reed again and blinked several times. The early morning sun made things difficult to see.

Jason pointed toward the main road that led into and out of Reed, where several groups of workers made their respective ways toward their fields to begin the morning's work.

"There." He motioned toward a small cart drawn by a donkey. A driver sat at the front of the cart while another person, looking from that distance to be a girl, though they could not be certain as she had her back to them, sat inside the cart atop some hay. Two other figures walked behind, each leading a goat.

"What of them?" Eamon asked tiredly.

"They are not field workers. What are they about, dost thou think?"

Eamon almost laughed at his friend, who was obviously taking his task too seriously. "What dost *thou* think, Jason?" he said with a hint of ridicule. "They are peasants on their way to the next village to sell some stupid goats."

"I do not know," Jason replied thoughtfully, watching the cart and its people make their way along the road. It seemed normal enough, but he had never seen any farmers from the village taking their animals elsewhere for sale. Reed was a large estate where people from neighboring villages usually brought their stock to sell, not the other way around. "Mayhap we should alert Black Donal. He said to tell him of any unusual activities."

Eamon laughed aloud. "Wake Black Donal to show him a few goats? God's mercy, man, dost want thy head served on a platter? Here, give me thy sword and I'll run thee through now to save him the trouble."

"Very well." Jason gave Eamon a look of disgust. "Thou hast made thyself plain. Go along and get thee to bed. I only hope thou'rt right or 'twill by thy head on that platter, jesterman."

"Are we not past sight now, Jace?" Minna complained from behind the cart as she dragged an unhappy and unwilling goat along. "I would dearly love to kill this beast." It was bad enough to have to dress as a peasant and hold on to a goat, but realizing that Thomas, a small, thin boy, was able to handle his charge so easily made everything that much worse.

Margot smiled at her sympathetically from her perch on the cart. "I will trade with thee, M-Minna, and thou shalt ride on the cart. 'Tis somewhat uncomfortable, b-but 'tis better than pulling a g-goat along, I vow."

"Not yet, Margot lady," said Jace from the front of

the cart. "There will be no changes 'til we are well past the hills."

"Oh," Margot replied, offering Minna an apologetic smile. She was a treasure indeed to go through so much for her. If everyone hadn't made such a fuss over her face and blond hair, Margot would gladly have walked alongside the cart with her friend and Thomas, but Sir Basil and Eric had impressed upon her the importance of sitting in the back of the cart with her back turned to the northern hills of Reed until they were well out of sight.

The need for all this trickery hadn't been explained to her, of course. Oh, no! She'd been rudely awakened in the middle of the night and expected to accept fully, without question, this strange plan for leaving Reed. If Eric hadn't been the one to ask it of her, Margot never would have gone along with it. But he had asked it of her and had also asked her not to question him. She'd been absolutely furious, but one look into those beautiful brown eyes of his and she'd folded up like a dressing screen and given in to the man. She could still hardly believe it.

As it was she had been dressed in the worst of peasant clothing, with her hair pinned tightly to her head and then covered with a shawl. She had protested the shawl, which was made of coarse wool and consequently was hot and scratchy, until Eric himself had taken the ugly thing in his own hands and placed it gently atop her head, pronouncing her both brave and beautiful. That was all the attention he had given her since their half kiss, and for only that she was willing to submit.

"Just like a d-dog," she muttered, thinking of it, "waiting for any l-little crumb."

She grasped the shawl with both hands and tucked it closely under her chin. The horrid thing was valuable to her since his hands had touched it. He'd hardly spoken to her the night before, though she had tried and tried to gain his attention. Indeed, he had seemed almost angry with her and had repeatedly ignored her in favor of one or the other of her ladies, openly flirting with them until every wretched one of them had succumbed to his charms and practically thrown themselves at his feet. Margot had wanted to commit murder. Directly after the meal Eric had excused himself and gone to his chambers, taking Thomas with him and leaving her feeling both lonely and frightened.

Damn him for being so unfeeling when she faced leaving the home and friends she had known all her life! Her only reason for being glad to go to Belhaven was that it was Eric's home. She'd spent the night crying instead of sleeping, thinking of both her father and Eric, the two people she loved most in the world. She didn't know if she would ever see her father alive again, and she wasn't at all certain she could ever cause Eric to fall in love with her. Indeed, last eve he had seemed as far away as he had been for the past ten years.

Everything had happened so quickly that morn; one moment she was standing in the cold, dark stables, unable to think about what she was doing, and the next she was lifted off her feet by Eric's strong hands and being placed, surprisingly gently, on top of the piles of fresh straw in the cart.

She could barely recall what words had passed between Eric and Jace, something about not stopping until they were well out of Reed and of taking all possible care. She smiled when she remembered Thomas reassuring his master that he would "guard the lady Margot with my life." Eric had solemnly clasped the boy's hand and told him that he had all faith in him.

Sir Basil had kissed both Margot and Minna farewell and had given them God's blessing. Jaufre had kissed them as well, but with his usual merry charm, as though he were handing out wedding kisses instead of wishing them safe passage on a long journey.

Eric had said very little to Margot before giving Jace the leave to start, other than admonishing her to keep the shawl upon her head after he had carefully arranged it to his satisfaction.

"We shall see thee ere long, my lady," he'd assured her. "There is naught for thee to fear. Did I not promise yesterday that I would always keep thee safe?" He kissed her hand very briefly, nothing more than a knightly tribute, but Margot could remember the warmth of his lips upon her morning-chilled skin, and the way his dark, disordered hair had tumbled forward as he bent and then fallen back when he straightened and moved away.

Nothing to fear, she thought over again, watching the home she had known all her life falling farther and farther into the distance. Nothing at all to fear.

"There, sir, thou canst see them well now."

Black Donal shoved Jason aside, even as that man made to point at what he was speaking of. He leaned slowly into the lookout point, his eyes squinting to view better the column of men riding out of Reed.

"So," he murmured to himself thoughtfully, "they go as they came. All in a hurry and all of a sudden. So." He straightened and contemplated the sight before him. "Jason," he said, not looking at him, "count along with me the number there are."

Jason counted, then reported, "I count seven and thirty, sir."

"Seven and thirty," Black Donal repeated. He drew his hands behind his back and stood quietly, staring, watching. "Aye, seven and thirty, just as there were when they came. None left behind, none added. Very good. Very, very good." He watched the horses and their riders progress along the main road out of Reed until they were nearly out of sight. "And all the banners with their colors, just right, though whose colors they are I do not know. But 'tis just right. Just as it should be. Exactly," he said, finally turning to pin his gaze on Jason, "as it should be."

*   *   *

Jaufre had never ridden so stiffly in all his life. His lower back was hurting even before they were halfway out of Reed, and he tried to keep from glancing at Eric, who, if possible, looked even more rigid.

"If thou dost not stop looking toward the hills every three seconds," Eric warned between his teeth, not looking at him, "I am going to beat thee senseless at the very next opportunity."

Forcing his eyes frontward, with difficulty, Jaufre replied, "I was not looking at the hills. I was looking at thee and wondering how much longer thou'lt be able to keep this slow and steady pace before giving way and letting us ride full speed."

"We'll keep this pace," Eric replied, "'til we are well and out of Reed. Dost wish to make Terent's men curious?"

"Nay, 'tis only our fair burden I am thinking of. Jace seems a fine enough fellow, and I know thou dost think highly of thy Thomas, but I cannot like leaving two ladies in their sole protection."

Eric was silent a moment, then said, quietly, "Nor can I, Jaufre. Still, we keep this pace. Slow and steady. We'll be riding hard soon enough."

"Oh, my aching back!" Margot complained, throwing off her shawl and stretching. "Please God I n-never have to ride in s-such a contraption again!" She gave the cart beside her a hateful look.

Minna, next to her, heartily agreed. "Please God, I

never have to set eyes on another goat! What stupid, stubborn creatures!"

"Please God, I never have to travel with two such females again!" Jace whispered fiercely. "Wilt the two of thee keep quiet, for God's own sake!"

Margot and Minna scowled at him but obediently fell quiet. They were hiding in the dense roadside shrubbery, waiting until Eric and his men arrived to take them up and onward.

Another ten silent minutes passed and Margot became unsettled. "Did we take the r-right r-road, Jace?" she whispered. "What if we are l-lost? Wh-what if we are—"

"Hush!" Jace commanded, putting up one hand and listening.

They all heard it soon: the sound of many horses riding toward them full speed. A few seconds passed and the sound drew closer; they stood still, a little afraid, waiting and wondering. Another second, then another, and finally came the sound they had been waiting for—Thomas's sharp whistle signaling that all was well. With relief they bounded toward the road, leaving the cart and the donkey and the goats behind.

Eric, Jaufre, and Aleric were at the forefront of their men, mounted on horseback, anxiously awaiting them. Margot smiled at her beloved as she struggled out of the bushes, and she instinctively started toward him.

"Eric—" she began, relieved.

His own expression softened when he saw her,

then resumed its solemnity as he bent and lowered one massive hand toward her.

"Come, Lady Margot. Thou wilt ride with me. Hurry now."

Gladly Margot grasped his hand, felt him put his other arm around her waist, and allowed herself to be weightlessly lifted and placed in front of Eric's warm, hard body. He gently settled her into his saddle, then secured her there with one muscular arm about her waist.

"Jaufre, thou wilt take up the lady Minna, and Aleric, thou wilt take up Thomas. Jace, thou wilt find an extra horse saddled and ready at the end of the column. Waste no time!" he thundered, so that Margot could feel his words rumbling through her own body. His arm around her tightened and he took up the reins of his destrier. "Now, Jaufre," he addressed his brother, and Margot could hear the smile in his voice, even if she could not see it, "thou didst pine for hard riding, so hard riding we shall have." He pulled his horse around, until Margot could see every man behind them, and Eric lifted a little in his saddle, pulling her up with him. "Let every man understand!" he shouted so all could hear, "We've a long road ahead this day, and a fast pace to endure for many miles. I know full well thou'rt men and not babes. I'll have no complaining from thee, nor will I, for any reason, accept any. So forward men, and follow me well! We're toward Belhaven this very hour! Let us set our mark for't!"

Eric's men responded with a loud cheer, and

Margot's heart swelled with pride. She smiled and pressed against his chest, thinking how wonderful her Eric was and of how romantic this ride with him was going to be. Perhaps, during the next few hours, she would even be able to tell him of her love, and of the fact that they were going to be married. It was important that he know about that soon. Certainly he should have a chance to get used to the idea before they reached Belhaven.

And then Eric turned his horse around and set off.

Shortly they were riding at a full gallop and it was all Margot could do to hold on. Eric held her tight and eventually slowed the pace to a fast trot, but still she was jarred and rattled over every hard-ridden mile, her teeth clattering in her mouth like skeleton bones and her bottom growing more tender and sore with each bump and jolt.

Hours seemed to pass—miserable, awful, painful hours—before Margot had finally had enough. She elbowed Eric in the side as hard as she could, but he either ignored her or didn't feel it. She tried again with the same result and almost felt like crying. They rode on and on without respite and she began to think her head was going to part ways with her neck. Finally, in desperation, she dug her fingernails into his thick arm, harder and harder, until he bent his head forward and shouted into her ear.

"Is aught amiss, my lady?"

"I—" she began, feeling foolish as well as miserable. "Can we n-not stop for a few minutes? Please?" She had to shout, too.

He seemed not to hear her, so she repeated herself until he nodded that he understood.

Then he shouted in her ear again. "Nay, I am sorry. Art beginning to feel unwell?"

Unwell? Margot thought. Decidedly so. "Aye," she managed.

Eric fell quiet, as though considering, then she felt him nodding again. Without slowing his steed, he turned Margot so that she faced him. He slid one leg up onto his saddle, then pulled her onto his knee and held her tighter against himself. Understanding, Margot gratefully put her arms around his neck and hugged tight, pressing her face against his warm, slightly moist skin. She felt his other hand tuck her knees in around his waist, where they rested against his other drawn-in leg, and almost immediately the pain she had been suffering subsided. There was still the up-and-down jarring of the destrier's trot to rattle her, but now, at least, she was cushioned against Eric's body, and now, at least, she could be close to him and be held by him as she had dreamed of during many nights in the past several years.

He was so much bigger and so much more muscular than she had thought, and it was so good to be close to him like this, body to body and heart to heart. Without thinking, Margot hugged him in a loving embrace, and without thinking, Eric returned the hug, though only for a moment before he went stiff again. She smiled and thought that he must have felt the movement against his neck, for he lowered his mouth until it was against her ear, and when he spoke, the warmth and movement sent shivers down her spine.

"Is that better, my lady?"

She didn't answer, but nodded, still smiling. Eric went back to the business of guiding his horse and leading his men, and Margot, with a yawn, unwittingly fell asleep.

It was madness, Eric thought later when he finally felt that it was safe enough to slow the pace he'd set for himself and his men. Complete and utter madness. The woman in his arms who lay sleeping as sweetly and innocently as a babe was as powerful and seductive as any sorceress. He held her and felt as though he were holding his whole life, his heart, everything, and it did not do good to tell himself that the feeling was ridiculous and worse, wrong.

He slowed Bram, and heard his men slowing as well. They had made good speed thus far and Eric was pleased. Soon it would be prudent to dismount and walk their horses a mile or so, and then they would need to find a water source for the beasts and themselves. Soon, but not yet.

As Bram gentled his pace, Eric allowed himself to feel the wonder of his closeness with Margot. Mindful of Jaufre's watchful eye, he was careful not to betray any of what he was feeling, but oh, God's mercy, how good she felt to hold! Her face was pressed against his neck, her breasts against his chest, her arms were all around him, one around his shoulders and one wedged between her body and his. He gazed for a brief moment at her pale, beautiful face and he thought, with some wonder, that he loved her. But what was there to wonder at in that? he asked himself. Every man who saw her must love her. There was no help for it.

With a slow, gentle hand, and being careful not to waken her, Eric tucked the wretched shawl she still carried up around her shoulders and a little over her tightly bound hair. That beautiful hair! It was dreadful to keep it locked away thus. He itched to touch it, to touch her, just for a moment and told himself once again that this was madness.

He loved her. Yes. It was foolish to deny it and even more foolish to indulge it. He'd been foolish the night before, trying to keep away from her, trying to ignore her. He had flirted with some of her attendant ladies in a purposeful effort to make her give up her pursuit of him, or whatever it was she had been doing when she had followed him around that room yesterday afternoon. He still could not believe that she loved him, as Jaufre had said, but he could believe that perhaps she had developed some kind of misguided infatuation for him. After all, he had been kind to her when she was a little girl, and it was obvious that she had not had much contact with other men during her life. Perhaps what she saw in him was a kind of elder brother. He hoped so. Yes, he truly hoped so.

Margot muttered a little in her sleep. She squirmed and resettled, hugging him more tightly.

Her face moved against his neck, and then, as Eric
froze, Margot pressed her lips softly against his jaw
and kissed him. The kiss lasted only a moment, and
then she turned her face back into his neck, sighed
and whispered, "Eric," before dozing off again.

Never in all his life had a simple caress so thoroughly jolted Eric. His whole body responded to
Margot's brief, unlikely kiss as though they had been,
or rather, were about to make love to each another,
and the overwhelming feeling panicked him. He
brought Bram to a sharp halt and pushed Margot
upright.

"My lady!" He shook her. "My lady, 'tis time for
thee to awaken!"

"Wh-what?" Margot replied, yawning. Muddled
and still sleepy, she found herself being handed down
to the ground before she could fully waken. The next
thing she knew she was at arm's length from Eric. He
didn't release her until her feet were steady, and by
that time Margot had rubbed her face and yawned
again. "Where are we?" she asked, gazing about in a
stupor at the others who had stopped and were dis-
mounting. "Are we there already?"

Eric didn't reply. He turned away and took hold of
Bram's reins.

"So, my brother the slave driver!" Jaufre strolled
up to them, leading his horse. Minna scurried to
Margot's side. "Thou hast finally decided to give us a
rest, thank a merciful God!"

Eric managed a grim smile in Jaufre's direction.
"Thou must make up thy mind, lad, as to whether

thou dost wish to ride fast or slow, so I will know better next time. I distinctly remember thy impatience of this morn. But here," he pulled Bram along, leaving Margot and Minna behind, "we'll walk the horses for half an hour's time and then we shall set our goodly pace again."

Fully awake now, though still confused as to why her nap had been brought to such a sudden end, Margot stared after the retreating figures of Eric and Jaufre.

"Sir Eric!" she shouted. He stopped and turned and Margot suddenly felt foolish standing there in the middle of the road, dressed as she was in the ugliest of peasant's clothing. "What—what shall we d-do?"

In the most unfriendly manner possible, her beloved Eric frowned at her for no reason Margot could think of and replied, "Dost thou not have two feet, my lady? Use them!" And then he turned and started walking again, engaging a shocked Jaufre in conversation as that individual haltingly followed after him.

"My dear Lady Margot," Aleric said, coming up behind them, his face reddening, "forgive him, please. I think perhaps my brother is . . . a little tired and perhaps . . . overworried." His words were sincere, but Aleric looked as surprised as Margot was.

"Here, she don't mind," Thomas said, edging smoothly around Aleric to get to Margot. "I've two good arms, my lady." He stuck an elbow at her by way of offering his arm to prove his point. "I'll give thee escort, if thou'lt have it."

Although stung by Eric's sharp words, Margot looked into Thomas's proud and eager face and smiled. He was *not* going to make any apologies for his master's behavior, of that she was certain, but he would do whatever he could to make up for it. She put out an open hand.

"I'll t-take thy hand, Squire T-Thomas, if thou dost not mind, rather than thy arm, and I would be m-most honored to have thee l-lead me."

If it was possible, Margot thought she saw Thomas blush a little. Then his grim, set expression became dutifully serious and he opened up his small, bony hand to grasp hers. They set off, leaving Aleric behind to escort Minna.

"What maggot has taken to thy brain to make thee speak thusly to that beautiful creature?" Jaufre inquired pleasantly, strolling beside Eric. His older brother was stomping along as though he were carrying a twelve stone weight on his shoulders, and Jaufre couldn't resist teasing him. "If Mother or Father should e'er hear thee speak so crudely to a lady they would call for the priest, i'faith! I feel a mite afeared for thy heretofore pure soul myself. And thy wretched behavior of last eve! Shocking! Truly, truly shocking. Flirting so openly with all the lady's maids and breaking their innocent hearts. Scoundrel!"

Eric shook his head and grunted something indistinguishable.

"Well," Jaufre pursued, "thou'rt verily a fool ten

times over. I tried to tell thee last eve that the lady Margot loves thee, and thou wouldst have none of it. Wilt bark and howl at her the rest of our journey just to keep her at bay? Or wilt thou give up this foolish notion about James and accept the inevitable like a man?"

Eric scowled. "The inevitable?"

"Aye, the inevitable. Dost not know that a woman who wants a man badly enough will always get him? One way or another? That woman wants thee, Eric, lad, and she'll have thee, too, one way or another. Thou'lt see."

Eric was still fighting a battle with his stunned physical responses to the lady in question, and he was not amused. "What I see, Jaufre, is that thou'rt crazed. Since thou dost find the lady so lovely, thou shalt henceforth have the pleasure of riding with her."

"Gladly!" Jaufre exclaimed, grinning fully.

"And if thou dost so much as to touch her, thou lecherous fiend," Eric warned, feeling quickly murderous at his brother's eagerness, "I shall break every bone in thy body with my bare hands!"

11

Love does strange things to people, Minna reflected as she brushed her hair in preparation for bed. She was sitting on her sleeping pallet in the tent she was to share with her lady, and she was all alone, Margot having decided to take a walk in the cool night air before turning in. All in all their quarters were amazingly comfortable, she thought gratefully, especially considering that Sir Eric had not stopped until very late in the day, so that there had been neither much time nor sunlight in which to pitch the camp.

Minna smiled when she thought of Sir Eric, and she wondered why she had ever been frightened or repulsed by him. Faith, he could never be called a handsome man, though there was no denying that his physique was unmercifully fine, yet what a good man he was, and how kind and gentle! She was beginning to see why her mistress loved him so. It had been quite pleasant to ride with him that afternoon when their walking break was through, and to be held so intimately in the arms of such a strong, giant man. She had enjoyed that, indeed, though she had been constantly aware of her mistress's hot eyes burning into her from where that lady had ridden with Sir Jaufre.

But there had been so much more to enjoy during her ride with Sir Eric than just his delightful body. He was a very pleasant, knightly man who had made every effort to entertain her as they rode. Shy by nature, and painfully conscious of her own unattractiveness, Minna had been reluctant to do more than stare at the road ahead, but Sir Eric, with friendly conversation and gentle questions, had soon put her at ease. Minna could not remember when she had ever spoken so freely or laughed so much with any person other than her own dear Lady Margot. By the end of the day she was half in love with Sir Eric herself, and it was with regret that she'd seen their ride come to an end. Only Margot's angry behavior had brought her to her senses and had made her remember that Sir Eric was already spoken for.

Now *there* was a dreadful problem, Minna considered, stroking her hair to a silky sheen. For some reason Sir Eric and her lady were at odds instead of rejoicing at their reunion. Margot had always feared that when she finally saw her Eric again he would find her wanting and, though Minna found it hard to believe, this did seem to be so. It broke her heart to see Margot so sad, for she had loved Sir Eric faithfully for so many, many years. Whatever could trouble the man to keep him from loving such a sweet person as her lady?

"Minna?" she heard suddenly, a low, soft whisper. It was Aleric, and Minna stopped brushing in midair. What was he doing there? She cast a glance at herself, dressed only in her night shift, her hair completely unbound.

"Minna?" he repeated more loudly.

"Y-yes?" she answered, too high-pitched she realized.

"It is . . . Aleric," he said softly, speaking against the cloth of the tent so that Minna felt a shiver of intimacy pass through her body. He might as well have been whispering in her ear, for mercy's sake!

"Yes, Aleric?"

"May I, that is, Eric sent me to ask if the lady Margot has sought her bed yet. He wishes to speak with her."

Was that all? Minna thought, disappointed as well as a little irate. How stupid of her to think that any man, even a young, unseemly man such as Aleric Stavelot, should ever come to seek *her* out at night.

"My lady has gone out, sir, and is not here. You may tell your brother that he may speak with her on the morrow—"

The tent opening was flung aside and Eric himself stormed in, crowding the tent with his large person. "My God! Can this be true?" he shouted at

Minna, who sat paralyzed in complete stupefaction. "That wretched female has gone into the forest alone?! What kind of idiot is she, for God's own sake?" He reached down and grabbed Minna by the shoulders, pulling her off the pallet and shaking her and generally treating her to a display she would not have thought him capable of. "Speak, woman! Where has thy mistress gone?! In which direction?"

"To—to the stream," Minna stammered, shocked and frightened.

He set her aside and strode out of the tent as suddenly as he had come, leaving Minna staring wide-eyed at Aleric, who filled the tent opening his brother had exited.

"Minna—" Aleric began, concerned, his own eyes wide. Without warning his gaze took in Minna's shapely form, covered only by the thin cotton of her night shift, as well as her long, beautiful, unbound hair cascading all the way to her hips, and he gulped loudly. This was not at all a proper circumstance in which to be alone with a lady, he told himself. His parents would never approve. Yet, at the same time, he had an overwhelming desire to move farther into the room and take Minna into his arms. She was distraught, he could tell, and badly in need of support. As an aspirant to knighthood, he argued, he should surely do his utmost to lend comfort; on the other hand, as a good Christian he ought to walk away immediately. He wanted to walk away, truly he did. But even as he stared at her, Minna's dainty shoulders began to shake, and she began to cry, and the next thing Aleric knew he was across the space that had separated them and had folded her into his embrace.

Though not a profane man by nature, Eric was surprised to find, as he crashed through the forest shouting Margot's name, that he was possessed of a fairly large vocabulary of amazing words such as he had never before suspected he'd even known. He had obviously picked them up somewhere, however, for in a short space of time, as he continued his frantic search, he variously cursed every physical aspect of his surroundings, from the moon to the trees to the brisk breeze, in a remarkably detailed manner. He thrashed his way to the stream at last and, disentangling himself agitatedly from a particularly pertinacious sheaf of branches, informed his creator aloud that, in his opinion, trees ought to lead the way of all other such evil beings into perdition.

"Damned nuisances!" he swore, actually ripping the offending branches from the tree and throwing them down. He turned toward the stream and looked in all directions. Margot was nowhere in sight, and he swore again. "Damn it all! Margot!" he shouted, then shouted her name again. Nothing. Now what was he going to do? God's mercy! What was he going to do? If she had come to any harm, if one of Terent's men had gotten to her, he would—

"Eric!" he heard her call out and his heart fell to

his feet. She sounded panicked, frightened. "Eric!" she wailed again, closer this time. He started running alongside the stream in the direction of her voice.

"I am here, Margot! Here!"

Just as Eric was about to plunge back into the forest again, Margot came stumbling out of it, lunging at him with a cry.

"Margot, thank God!" He caught her in his arms and hugged her hard against his chest. "Thank God!" he repeated, kissing the top of her head, her hair, and her tear-stained face when she turned it up to him.

She clung to him tenaciously, as a child frightened from a bad dream might cling to her parent. "I w-was c-coming back to th-the c-camp and I s-saw s-s-something!" Her stutter was painfully magnified by her fear.

"'Tis all right," Eric soothed, kissing her wet cheeks, hugging her trembling body tighter. "Thou'rt safe now."

"It w-was an a-a-a— a b-b-big a-a-a—"

"Animal," Eric provided, stroking her hair.

"A-aye, and I d-d-did not know wh-what it w-w-was b-b-but it l-looked so b-b-big and I w-was so f-f-f . . . so f-f-f—"

"Frightened?"

She swallowed loudly and nodded. "I s-s-started to r-run b-b-but I did n-not know where I w-was going and I thought I w-would b-b-be lost all n-night!"

"Margot, please do not cry so," he pleaded as she broke into fresh tears. "Thou'rt safe now. I'll let no harm come to thee. Do not cry, dear heart, please."

"I w-was s-so glad," she sobbed against his neck, "s-so g-glad to hear th-thy v-v-voice."

"Hush," he whispered. "Hush, now. Always will I keep thee safe, Margot."

"I th-thought thou w-wouldst be very angry w-with me for g-g-going off by m-m-myself." She looked up at him again. "Please d-do not be angry w-with me, Eric. I c-could not bear it."

Eric gazed into her beautiful, stricken face and was almost frightened by the strength of the emotions that flooded him. He lifted a hand to wipe the tears from one of her cheeks, and at his touch Margot closed her eyes and pressed her face into his palm, like a cat craving a human touch. A short, shuddering sob racked her body and then she stilled. When finally she opened her eyes again and looked at him, Eric knew that he was completely lost.

"I am angry with thee," he whispered, sliding his fingers slowly around the back of her head and into her soft, warm hair. "I am very, very angry. I should beat thee. I should—I should chain thee up." His eyes were on her lips, which were parted and moist and inviting. With the slightest pull of his hand he drew them upward, closer and closer, while his own lips lowered to meet them. "I should punish thee. I should surely punish thee," he whispered before finally kissing her.

It was a gentle meeting at first, soft and slow and very tentative. Eric kept her head still with his hand while his lips caressed hers with tender kisses, one after another, giving both of them time to learn the taste and feel of each other. She made a low, whimpering sound in the back of her throat and slid one soft, cool hand up to touch his cheek while her other hand lost itself in his hair.

Hesitantly she returned Eric's kisses, imitating him in such an innocent manner that Eric thought, with what little presence of mind he had left, that perhaps this was the first time she had ever been kissed. The thought maddened him even more. He didn't want to frighten her or give her a disgust of himself, but she tasted so good, was so soft and sweet and willing, that he could not stop himself.

Gently, though insistently, he turned her head until their mouths fit one against the other completely, and he proceeded to kiss her with all the pent-up desire he'd fought against since setting eyes on her three days before. She was surprised, he knew, for she made a sound of distress at this greater intimacy and briefly struggled, but Eric only held her that much more tightly, subduing her with his mouth and hands and body until she finally gave way, relaxing against him again and giving him free rein.

How long the kiss, or rather kisses, continued, Eric could never later remember. All he knew was that at some point he managed to bring the embrace to an end, and that when his reeling brain had finally begun to function again with some semblance of order it was to find Margot gazing up at him with an exceptionally tender expression. She stroked his cheek and smiled.

"I never knew how w-wonderful it w-would be,"

she whispered, then lowered her face to his chest and sighed. "I love thee so, my Eric."

To hear her actually say the words aloud stunned him, and he stared at her bowed head in wonder. Eric knew himself to be a man with an unusual need to be loved and accepted, especially by those whom he loved, such as his family. He had recognized long ago that this seemingly bottomless need had been born out of his lack of identity, and from his depleted sense of self. Just as a starving man might crave food to satiate his hunger, so Eric craved the love and affection of his friends and family to satiate his hunger, the hunger to be accepted, to be made worthy. He did not believe that the beautiful Lady Margot truly loved him, for he could see no reason why she should do so, but hearing those very words, "I love thee so, my Eric," flooded him with an incredible warmth that, for the few moments he allowed himself to believe them, filled the void within him such as nothing before ever had.

Pressed tightly in the embrace of her beloved's arms, Margot realized a happiness she had waited many years to know. At last she had arrived at the place she wanted to be.

Had it only been an hour or two earlier that she had stood beside this very stream, determining that she had had enough and deciding that she was going to march right back to the camp and find Eric and tell him that she would no longer put up with such unkind treatment from her future bridegroom? How very foolish of her! And what a dreadful scene she would have made, to be sure, by informing him that she refused to be ignored any longer or to be spoken to as though she were a naughty child.

Yes, how perfectly foolish she had been, because now, now everything was going to be just as it should be.

Eric loved her. Why had she ever questioned it? Of course, he would have to love her just as she loved him. And he had kissed her. It had been a little frightening at first, because momentarily she felt caught in something she couldn't control, rather like what one would imagine drowning to be, and she had struggled to keep from going under, only to discover, when she had finally given up the fight, that her Eric was able to keep her safe even as he carried her further and further into that unexplored realm.

How very gentle he was, and how—skilled. Never had she imagined that such intimacy with any man, even her own Eric, could be so wonderful. Especially not after that dreadful encounter with the huntsman. But it *was* wonderful, incredibly so, and Margot was filled with curiosity about the rest of a physical relationship between a man and a woman. She didn't have much of a chance to think on this, however, as her future husband had decided to set her down.

Actually, it was more like being dropped than being set down, for he put her on the ground so suddenly that she nearly collapsed from the abruptness, and the warmth of her happiness was chilled by the absence of him.

"Eric—" she began, only to stop when she saw how pale he was and how distressed.

"My lady," he said unhappily, stepping away from her even as she advanced, "I hardly know how to begin begging thy pardon. What I have done is . . . unforgivable. My only excuse is that I was so—so relieved to find thee safe and unharmed."

"My Eric," she said soothingly, "there is no n-need to apologize. I am g-glad."

He only took another step away and shook his head.

"I love thee so, Eric. I w-wish thou wouldst kiss m-me again." She put her arms out toward him, and Eric practically jumped away.

"Oh, God." He groaned. "Do not—"

"Please," she pleaded.

"Margot—*Lady* Margot." He put his own arms out to keep her away. "This is wrong. Very, very wrong."

She laughed, that beautiful sound that sent shivers of desire through him. "It is only wrong in thy m-mind because thou dost n-not know the full of it." She stopped in front of him and smiled broadly. "I did not w-want to tell thee 'til thou hadst had a little time t-to think on't, but now I know thou dost l-love me as well as I love thee, so 'twill be well to give thee the truth. We are to be m-married, thee and I, when we have reached thy home of Belhaven. M-married, my Eric." She stepped forward and took hold of his hands. "So thou m-must see that what we have j-just shared is not wrong at all. Wilt thou not k-kiss m-me again?" She turned her face up to his with lips puckered.

Eric dropped her hands and walked even farther away. "My lady, thou'rt mistaken." His tone was cold, chilled, even angry.

"Mistaken? Nay, I am n-not—"

"Mistaken, I say!" he thundered, looking full at her. "Somehow thou hast heard wrong, or thought wrong, or something! 'Tis my brother, my own brother James thou'rt to wed, not I. God's wounds, woman! Thou'rt to be my sister! What I have just done—what thou'rt asking—'tis base and vile! God's body! I must be possessed to have touched thee so!"

"'Twas not b-base and v-vile!" Margot insisted, growing angry as well as frustrated. *This* was not at all the way he was supposed to respond to the news of their impending marriage. "And 'tis thou who art m-mistaken! I know n-n-naught of this brother of thine, of this J-J-J . . . this J-J-J—"

"James," Eric supplied.

Margot nodded. "I kn-know only of thee, and that I l-love thee, and have l-loved thee since the very day I m-met thee, and that I have waited and waited 'til n-now, 'til we could be t-t-together again, and that n-now that we are, thou'rt being exceedingly s-s-stubborn and art m-making me crazed!"

By the end of this speech she was actually shouting, but Eric didn't notice. He hadn't gotten past the part where she said she'd loved him since that day they'd met so long ago.

"So, I was right," he whispered, somehow strangely hurt. "'Tis naught but childish infatuation which drives thee."

Margot gasped as though he'd struck her, and Eric inwardly recoiled as though, indeed, he had.

"Ch-ch-childish inf-f-fatuation!" she repeated incredulously, fury tumbling her speech almost more than her fear. "I have l-loved thee f-f-faithfully for t-t-ten long years and thou d-darest to s-stand there and call it a ch-ch-childish infatuation?! Oh! I'll n-not stay and l-listen to s-s-such cruel and f-f-false insults!"

She turned to stride away, but Eric caught her by the shoulders and sharply spun her to face him.

"What thou'lt do, my lady," he informed her tightly, "is behave thyself. I am sorry if I have offended thee, and more than sorry that I kissed thee, but what passed between us this night has not left me unscathed, either. Thou speakest of my cruelty, but thou'rt more cruel than I could ever have imagined." He dragged her closer until he was able to look into her beautiful eyes, and his fingers dug possessively into the soft flesh of her arms. "I know that I am not a comely man, but I am a man, nonetheless, and thou art a beautiful, desirable woman. If thou dost indeed bear any gentle feelings toward me thou'lt cease this unkind teasing and leave me be. 'Tis pitiless as well as cruel, for 'twould be an outright falsehood were I to pretend I felt no desire for thee, yet must I keep my distance, knowing thou'rt spoken for. If thou dost not wish to torment me, lady, then leave me be. For God's own sake, leave me be."

"Teasing?" she whispered, her eyes welling with hurt and disbelief. "Is that what thou d-dost think?

That I am t-teasing when I speak of my l-love for thee?"

"What else am I to think?" he returned, exasperated. "Look at me, Margot, and look at thee. What else *could* I think? Thou'rt beautiful as a new dawn, nay, more beautiful even than that, for such a fleeting moment could ne'er compare to thy loveliness, while I am ugly as a stray mongrel, and illegitimate besides."

Margot fought back her tears and shook her head furiously. "Thou'rt not ugly! Thou art the m-most beautiful m-man in the w-w-w . . . in the whole w-w-w—"

"World? Nay! How canst thou look at me so surely and lie to me so well? Dost enjoy making jest of me? Dost think I know not how I look? Or art thou blind as well as deaf? Didst not hear what I said, my lady? I am base-born. A bastard. The people who are my parents fostered me, but did not give me birth. Dost not understand, Margot?"

"Nay. I d-didst not kn-know of thy birth, but it matters n-not. I l-love thee. Dost th-thou not understand, Eric?"

Eric shook his head at her words. She could not love him. She *could* not. It just wasn't possible. Compared to James—compared to any other man— he was nothing, or worse than nothing. But her eyes, God's mercy! Her beautiful eyes were gazing into his openly and honestly, daring him to believe that what she said was true.

"Margot," he murmured, squeezing her arms as

though trying to squeeze some sense into her, "I can hardly think what to say to thee, my brain is so rattled by thy sweetest of all professions. But I do know that this is wro—"

"I know, my love," Margot interrupted, putting fingers up to touch his lips. Her voice was gentler now, her anger abating as she sought to make him understand. "I know 'twas n-not what thou expected. I never th-thought thou wouldst think of m-me, or l-love me, these p-p-past many years as I have loved and th-thought of thee. Thou'rt the finest man alive, and I am the m-merest of women. I kn-know that I am neither talented n-nor clever, and of course, there is my w-wretched stammer. But I think thou m-might grow used to it in t-time." She smiled and lightly touched his chin with her fingertips, noting with pleasure the way his eyes closed as though in ecstasy. "I do not expect thee to l-love me yet, though thy kiss did truly hearten me. I shall m-make thee love me. I'll be a fine wife to thee, I vow, as b-b-best I can, and never will I give thee cause to regret w-wedding me."

Eric kept his eyes closed and groaned. He vaguely thought of Satan's temptation of Christ in the desert and wondered if this was how the Lord had felt. Her hand, so soft on his face, on his cheek, made him tremble with wanting, and he was sorely tempted to give in. Instead, he remembered himself. "Nay, Margot," he said softly, opening his eyes to look at her with real misery, begging her to understand. "I know not what this is, other than madness. Thou must never speak thusly again. 'Tis my brother thou'rt to wed. My eldest brother, James. He is a handsome, well-born man, and will make a worthy husband for thee. He will make thee so happy thou'lt quickly forget this infatuation of thine, and then thou shalt laugh to think thou couldst ever have loved such a one as I. Indeed, we shall both laugh and think it a merry jest to share as we grow older."

"Ohhh!" Margot raged, her frustration returning full force. "Why art th-thou so s-s-stubborn?! Hast n-not l-listened to me? 'Tis thou I shall w-wed and no other! And if thou dost s-s-speak of thy brother to m-me once more I shall scream!" She pushed out of his grasp and glared up at him, her hands clenched into tiny fists, looking very much as though she would like to hit him.

Eric straightened and huffed out a breath of air, running one hand tensely through his thick hair. "Very well, my lady. This exchange is upsetting to thee and we'll speak of it no more, which would be well for both of us. I sought thee out this night to apologize for my rude behavior earlier this day. 'Twas want of me to speak harshly to thee as I did, especially so in front of so many, and I do beg thy pardon."

Margot made no reply to this sincere apology; she was still too upset with him. An awkward moment passed while Eric uncomfortably wondered why he should feel like the worst knave alive. When he spoke next his tone was purposefully gentle.

"Come, I'll carry thee back to the camp so thou'lt not muddy thy feet any further."

Margot petulantly folded her arms across her chest and turned away from him. "I d-do n-not wish to return as yet. I believe I'll remain beside the s-stream for a t-time and think. Alone. I shall f-f-follow thee later."

Without a word Eric scooped her up into his arms and started for the forest, ignoring her cry of protest. "Thou'lt return to the camp now, my lady," he told her as he carried her through the trees, "and shouldst thou ever again wander off by thyself before we have reached Belhaven, I shall beat thee."

Margot gasped. "Thou wouldst n-not d-dare!"

"Nay, I would not," Eric agreed truthfully, with a very slight grin. "Even so, while thou'rt under my care thou'lt do as I say or take the consequences. I've no desire to waste my time chasing after thee each eve."

She was quiet for a time, until finally she relaxed and put her arms around his neck. "I hope thou'lt not be such a t-tyrant when we are wed," she whispered.

"I'll not be," he returned, quickening his pace to match the racing of his heart, "for we shall never be wed."

She sighed heavily at this but said nothing, for at that moment they were passing the camp guards. When they arrived at her tent, however, she bade him wait until she could fetch something. Impatient though he was to be as far away from her alluring person as possible, Eric waited as Margot disappeared inside. She returned quickly, bearing a scroll that she pressed into his hands.

"Here, my Eric. I know 'tis t-too d-dark for thee to read it now, but take it with thee and read it when thou m-may. It will explain all to thee."

Eric gazed at the scroll curiously, then looked back at Margot's childishly happy expression. "My lady—" he began, but Margot stopped him.

"Just read it," she insisted. And then, without warning, she stretched up as far as she could and grasped Eric's shoulders, pulling his face down to hers. He tried to push her away, but Margot insistently pressed her lips against his, ending the kiss with a great, loud, hard smack. Then she let him go. "Good night, my l-love," she whispered, and disappeared into the tent again.

Eric, very aware that every eye in the camp had witnessed this kiss and was upon him still, was loath to turn around, so he stood where he was, staring at Margot's tent and fingering his lips where she had so ferociously kissed him. His mouth still tingled from her unskilled touch, but, truthfully, he thought perhaps he didn't really mind. He had never been kissed thus by a lady, so fresh and true, and the experience was far from unpleasant, just as the kisses they had shared earlier had been far from unpleasant. Far, far from it.

Oh, Lord, he thought miserably, what am I going to do?

With a sigh he turned at last, and resolutely headed for his own quarters, avoiding the smiling faces of the men he passed, and absolutely ignoring the hearty laughter of his damned impertinent brothers.

12

The following morn was dark and overcast, and Eric, who'd already suffered a sleepless night, gazed out at the gloomy sky with something less than enthusiasm.

"My lord," Thomas said, stirring him from his stupor a little. He pressed a tankard of ale into Eric's hands and tossed a warm blanket over his master's bare shoulders before turning away to continue his packing.

Jaufre, scratching his broad, hairless chest, yawned and sat beside Eric on the pallet. He took the ale from his brother's hands, drained half of it and gave it back, then rubbed his eyes and followed Eric's gaze out the tent opening to the lady Margot's tent across the way.

"Didst dream of thy lady love last eve?" he asked sleepily.

Eric drank his ale before answering. The truth was that he had dreamed of Margot the night before, of Margot and of the missive she had given him to read.

"She said that she loves me."

"Ah," said Jaufre, satisfactorily, "I told thee so, did I not?"

"Aye."

Jaufre stretched and yawned again, making a great deal of noise about it. "Well, brother, thou'rt the luckiest man on God's own earth, to be sure. Margot le Brun is the loveliest creature I've e'er set eyes on. More lovely even than Jannis de Chaumperre, whom thou knowest well I loved as I have loved no other."

"Aye." Eric chuckled. "And she loved thee in return with a candlestick applied to thy head. Had I not followed behind thee that night when thou didst steal into her chamber she would have beaten thee to death, i'faith, and with good cause. God's mercy! I never did see such a righteous female."

"Mmmm," Jaufre replied. "At least my righteous female did not keep me awake at night, as thine did last eve. Thou never tossed in bed at Shrewsbury as thou didst last night. I wast nigh on throttling thee."

Eric sighed. "I wish thou hadst throttled me. Never have I been so miserable." He took another long drink of ale and continued to stare at Margot's quiet tent.

The jester of Reed, Jace, came into his view, mincing his way across the muddy ground toward Margot's tent as delicately as a highly bred she-dog, his face bearing a look of disgust at having to dirty his feet, which were softly booted. Eric watched, half-fascinated and half-jealous, as the troubadour spoke against the tent door, then entered a moment later, evidently beckoned.

"I cannot decide what that creature is," he muttered, "either man or boy. He seems man enough when needs be, but boy at all other times."

Jaufre yawned again. "He is both, methinks. He was brave as any man I e'er knew yesterday, when he had his mistress's life in his hands, but last eve, when thou wast out courting this same lady, he kept the rest of us at camp with the most amusing entertainments."

"I wondered why thou didst not make thy usual appearance," Eric chided. "I must have shouted as loudly as God last eve when I sought the lady Margot. I was certain thou wouldst hear me."

Jaufre grinned, a little abashed. "I would have, Eric, truly, had I not been distracted. The moment thou left camp Jace started his performance, and I swear, brother, 'twas most thoroughly entertaining. I'd dare any man to have pulled himself away from't."

"It matters not, lad. It matters not now, at any rate." He turned back to Margot's tent and felt helpless again. "God help me, Jaufre, what am I to do?"

"Why, what dost thou mean, Eric?" Jaufre asked, surprised.

Eric hung his head. "She told me she loves me."

"So?"

"So? How am I to meet that? What must I do?"

Jaufre gave out a shout of laughter. "What must thou do? Thou must marry her, of course, and do thy best not to gloat too much to the rest of us poor fellows, that is what thou must do. What else could there be?"

Eric lifted his eyes and gazed at his brother in disbelief. "Do not tease me, Jaufre. I am asking thy help."

Jaufre lost his grin. "I tease thee not, Eric. Why art thou so downcast? It cannot be thou dost not wish to marry the lady Margot, or that thou dost not love her."

Eric made no reply to this.

"What is it then, lad?" Jaufre asked in confusion and concern. He'd never seen Eric like this. His elder brother was a man who solved problems, not one who was beset by them. "Never tell me 'tis that ridiculous vow of fealty thou made Father which holds thee back." He laughed. "I've heard of sacrifices, Eric, but that is beyond anything!" He laughed again and waited for his brother to join him, but instead Eric stood and walked to the corner of the tent where his clothing chest was. On top of the chest sat the valueless brass brooch. With slow, careful fingers Eric picked it up, turned it round a bit, and gazed at it.

"Eric," Jaufre entreated, shaken by his brother's strange mood.

Eric shook his head and said quietly, "'Tis not only the vow, Jaufre. Always before 'twas the vow, for I hold it dear as my own life, but, truth be told, I'd break every vow I've ever spoken to make her mine."

"Well, then," Jaufre replied with relief, "if 'tis not the vow, then naught else can stand in the way of thy happiness. 'Tis more than plain that the lady wishes to wed thee . . ." His cheery voice died off. Eric still stood where he was, staring at the brooch, except that now he was shaking his head disconsolately.

A great silence filled the tent, broken only by the shuffling sounds of Thomas packing and by the waking sounds of the camp. Jaufre stared at his brother's wide back as the truth grew in his mind, and when finally the whole force of what was troubling Eric hit him, he was furious. "My God," he whispered with thinly veiled anger.

Eric cringed at the tone of his brother's voice. "Jaufre—"

"Do not," Jaufre warned seriously, his whole body shaking with his rage. "Do not ever speak such things aloud in my hearing."

They were quiet again and Thomas stopped his packing to watch the confrontation between the two brothers. Sir Eric stayed where he was, back turned and head bowed, and Sir Jaufre stood and stared at him for what seemed like an eternity, his chest rising and falling heavily with the effort to control himself.

"If ever I heard any man say such things about thee, Eric" he whispered, "I would readily kill him!"

Sir Jaufre looked as though he had more to say,

Thomas thought, watching him, but the man's voice seemed suddenly caught in his throat, and his eyes began to look bright. He gazed at Sir Eric's back another moment, swallowed hard a couple of times, and finally strode out of the tent and into the day without another word, evidently unconcerned that he was both half-naked and barefoot.

"Thou'lt never catch him that way, my lady," Jaufre advised Margot later that day as they rode together atop Jaufre's horse. "My brother is a strong-willed and stubborn fellow. 'Twill take more than jealous glances to turn his mind."

"I am only n-now discovering how very right thou art, my l-lord," Margot returned, giving Eric one last good glare before finally turning her eyes away. "Thy brother is the m-most s-stubborn man I've e'er known. I'll n-not even remark on Lady M-Minna's shocking behavior, save to s-say 'tis m-most unlady-like."

Jaufre chuckled with amusement. "Really? I'd not noticed that fair lady lacking any of the finer quali-ties. In sooth, I feel most sorry for her. Truly I do. Between my idiot brother's efforts to flirt with her and thine own angry eyes shooting daggers at her, the poor creature is like a frightened rabbit caught on the battlefield betwixt two hell-bent foes, if thou'lt par-don my language, my lady."

"I have n-not n-noticed her s-suffering because of Sir Eric Stavelot's advances," Margot said huffily.

"Faith, she seems right pleased with herself. The wr-wr-wretched traitor!"

"Ah!" said Jaufre, grinning from ear to ear. "Now this is love indeed if't can so easily make one jealous when there is no cause. Poor Lady Minna! I shall have to see what I can do to rescue her from the dreadful plight of being tormented by two such love-sickened beings."

Margot stubbornly crossed her arms over her chest and kept quiet, refusing to absolve Minna of her obvious sins. After a few moments, however, she softened and cast her gaze to where Minna rode with Eric some few feet ahead. They were laughing together at something he'd just said. "D-dost think he is enamored of her?" she asked pitifully.

"Nay, of course not." Jaufre comfortingly tucked the wool cloak that was meant to protect Margot from the cold more firmly around her shivering form. "I believe Eric loves thee, regardless that he may not yet know it. Thou hast no need to be jealous of Lady Minna. My half-brained brother is only behaving like an ass in order to drive thee away." Jaufre didn't add that successfully flirting with women was a skill his elder brother had long since perfected, by necessity, having learned at an early age that his looks and person frightened the softer sex out of their wits. Having learned to do it so well, charming females had become something of a hobby with Eric, so that now he often did it simply by rote.

"But why?!" Margot wailed. "If he l-loves me, why dost he w-wish to drive me away? I love him so! How can he h-h-hurt me as he does? This morn he would not even speak g-good d-day to me, and n-now he fawns all over M-Minna as though she were a g-goddess!"

Jaufre sighed and shook his head. "I wish I could explain it to thee, my lady, save I hardly understand it myself. I have already admitted 'tis foolish of my brother, yet he thinks his cause is just. More just, I think, because he doth love thee and thus wishes to save thee from what he thinks will be a terrible fate. Perhaps thou art not aware of his birth—"

"I am aware of it. He told me l-last eve that he wast not l-l-legitimately born and th-that th-thy parents had fostered him. Indeed, I am sorry if the circumstances of his birth make him unhappy, but I cannot see how s-such a thing should s-signify."

Margot suddenly found herself being very heartily hugged by her future brother-in-law, who, after he finished squeezing her, kissed her cheek and said, "Thou'rt a fine and very beautiful lady, Margot le Brun. I hope my worthless brother realizes what a lucky man he is to have such a one as thee love him. And thou'rt quite right. His birth signifies naught, save perhaps to him."

Margot turned to look at him. "But why doth it m-matter to him?"

Jaufre gazed at her contemplatively, then turned his eyes back to the road and began to speak. "When Eric and I were children, around the ages of seven and five, I thought that my older brother was the finest person in the world. I worshiped Eric as only a younger brother can, and I followed him everywhere and was constantly under his feet. Even at night I would seek him out, and would sneak into his room and crawl into bed with him. Every morn my mother knew just where to find me." He shook his head at the memory and smiled. "Thou wouldst think he'd have hated such a bothersome shadow, wouldst thou not? But he did not. Always he was patient with me, always kind. At age seven, Eric was big as a young man, and I less than half his size. It took me three steps to make up for every one of his, and I used to fear I'd lose sight of him whene'er I followed him about." Jaufre's voice grew wistful, as though he were seeing what he was speaking of. "Dost know, my lady, that he would wait for me? He knew I could not easily keep up with him, so he made himself walk slower, no matter what he was about, and he would stop often to make sure I was not too far behind. He ne'er coddled me, nor treated me as less than he, but he would wait nonetheless."

Jaufre was thoughtful for a moment, then he spoke again. "There was an understanding in our family, unspoken but true, that Eric was the best among us. That doth not sound quite right," he said, struggling to explain it correctly. "'Tis not easily put into words. 'Twas not that the rest of us felt less or worse, only that Eric was so good and strong and—and sure of himself. Yes, I suppose that might be right. He was very sure of himself, and of us, too. My parents loved us all equally and never favored one child over another, but 'twould be false to say that they did not appreciate Eric's good qualities. He was not perfect, certes, and still is not, as thou knowest full well, having had a taste of his hardheadedness. When a child he possessed a stubborness which continually enraged my father." Jaufre chuckled. "And still does from time to time." His laughter drew down to a sigh. "But certainly not as it did when he was a child. On the day Eric learned of his birth he changed. Everything changed."

"That m-must have b-been a terrible day," Margot murmured, clutching her cloak more tightly.

"Aye," Jaufre agreed soberly. He settled one arm more securely about Margot's waist and hugged her a little closer in an effort to keep her warm, though he knew it was probably in vain. It was damned cold for September, and windy as well. Any moment now the dark sky looked as though it would open upon them. "'Twas terrible indeed. I was eight years old and had no understanding of what was happening. From the way my parents and older brothers behaved I thought someone was going to take Eric away from us, and I cried and cried and cried. God! What a dreadful day! I was ne'er so relieved in all my life as when I realized Eric was staying. And as terrible as that time was for me, I can only guess at how much worse it was for Eric. As I said, he changed after that. He became painfully obedient to my parents and was e'er busy making himself useful around Belhaven. It seemed as though he tried to earn his keep, if thou canst understand such a thing. And he was very aware of the difference between himself and the rest of us, as if we were permanent and he only temporary, like a visitor or some such. It took years before he relaxed into the family again." He sighed. "And then, of course, there is the vow of fealty he made our father when he learned of his birth."

"Vow?" Margot repeated. "What v-vow is this?"

"When Father and Mother told Eric that he was adopted and not their natural-born child, Eric insisted that he must make a vow of fealty to our father. Of course my parents would have none of this, but Eric insisted he would only stay if he could make this vow, and repay what had been given him with his life's service."

"But that is most foolish!"

"Most," Jaufre readily agreed. "And so thought our father, but Eric stood firm and Father finally gave way, just to keep the peace, I think, and to make everyone stop crying. Certes he did not take the vow seriously, but Eric did and always has. I tell thee, my lady, my dear brother has determined that he shall spend all the days of his life at Belhaven, denying himself and doing our parent's bidding. When we were at Shrewsbury, Eric was greatly honored by the king and was offered a place by his side in London. But Eric refused His Majesty's offer, explaining that he could not leave our father's service because he had vowed eternal fealty. He asked instead that the honor be given our eldest brother, James, who finally agreed to accept it only when none of us could persuade Eric to change his mind."

"Oh, d-dear," Margot murmured.

Jaufre laughed. "Aye, that is just how we felt, too. Father's rage lasted the night, I vow! Never have I seen him so furious, but naught could change Eric's mind."

"V-verily, he is s-stubborn," said Margot. "Is that why he d-does n-not wish to wed me? Because of his vow?"

"Not the vow, entirely, though because of it he has sworn he'll ne'er marry. 'Tis a little of everything, methinks, dear lady. I was ready to strike him this morn when we spoke of the matter, for I'll tolerate no one, least of all *him*, saying he is not worthy because he happened to be found in a forest. Such words make me feel as I did when I was eight years old, when I thought someone was going to take him away. My brother possesses the finest and noblest soul I've e'er known, and I love him well, but he's as obstinate and thick-headed a fool as God ever made. He has it in his mind that he is not worthy of thee, Margot le Brun, because of his birth and because of his person and because of his vow. Thou'rt a beautiful, highborn lady who will bring her husband a coveted title and great riches when she marries. Eric cannot see that he might be worthy of these things, all he can think is that thou must have a better man than he, a man who is legitimately born and—worthier."

"Like J-James?"

"Like James."

They fell quiet for a time. Margot gazed thoughtfully at Eric's back as he rode ahead of them, and she gave way to the soothing, rhythmic *clop, clop, clop* of the horses' hooves as they rode. Today's pace was slower and steadier than yesterday's, though Eric had earlier announced his intention that they would cover as great a distance before stopping.

"My Eric will be a challenge," she informed Jaufre after a while.

"Aye," Jaufre agreed with a smile in his voice. "A true challenge, but a worthwhile one."

She nodded. "I am determined to b-be his wife, my l-lord. I can b-be just as stubborn as he, I vow."

"Thou'lt needs be. My brother is a fierce opponent. I've yet to see him bested."

"There is always a f-first t-time, and if I have learned one thing over the p-past t-ten years, 'tis how to b-be patient. I'll wed no other, certes."

"Thou'rt well matched then, for he swears he'll have none of thee. 'Tis a shame to be disloyal to mine own brother, but I do believe, dear lady, that I'll place my wager on thee."

Margot laughed, but her merriment was short lived by the sound of Minna's keen, spine-tingling scream.

Eric brought the entire column to an abrupt halt and turned his destrier sharply, roaring at Jaufre as he did so, "Cover her eyes! *Now!*"

"God's mercy!" Jaufre swore fervently, and the next thing Margot knew he clapped one of his hands over her eyes. But he was too late. Margot had already seen what he was trying to keep from her: the body of a man hanging from a tree.

The man, lately called by the name of Eamon, although those who now gazed at him would not know that, had not been dead long. His still-warm body swung gently back and forth, back and forth across the road, entirely impeding their progress.

13

"*Jaufre,*" *Margot mumbled* beneath Jaufre's ever-tightening grip, while she tried to peel his hand off her face, "I am not the l-least bit squeamish, I assure thee. I already kn-know there is a d-dead man in the road. Now, p-please."

Jaufre released her. "I am sorry, my lady," he muttered absently, his eyes on the dead man's body as he rode closer to where Eric sat on his horse, doing his best to soothe a hysterical Minna. Aleric and Jace joined them in a few moments.

"Eric," Jaufre said, but his brother wasn't paying any attention to him; he was too busy trying to calm Minna, though to little avail. The unhappy girl in his arms was shaking violently and screaming, her hands covering her face.

Aleric sidled his horse up on Eric's other side and said, or rather, commanded, "Give her to me."

Without waiting to discuss the matter, he put his arms out and pulled Minna to his own saddle. Minna readily went to him and Aleric hugged her securely. He turned a sober expression to the three looking at him in surprise before guiding his horse around and heading for the back of the column.

"Well!" said Margot, much impressed, "I had n-no idea that those t-two were—"

"Jace," Eric said, "take the lady Margot to the back of the column as well. Make certain that she and Lady Minna are well guarded. *Well* guarded," he repeated emphatically.

Jace nodded his understanding.

"But I wish to stay—" Margot protested, even as Jaufre handed her into her friend's waiting arms.

"Now!" Eric thundered.

Jace and Margot quickly disappeared into the safety of the column.

Some minutes later the two brothers knelt over the stiffening body, their faces grim and their thoughts grimmer.

"What dost thou think, Eric?" Jaufre asked, intently regarding the bluish countenance of the corpse.

Eric, with surprising gentleness, smoothed a bit of hair off the dead man's face. "I do not know, lad. Perchance this is the work of thieves, though this poor fellow doth not seem a very worthwhile victim. Perchance 'tis the work of Ravinet or his men. If the latter be true, we are in grave trouble, I fear." He gazed at the dark, quiet forest that lined both sides of the road. "They may be watching us even now, and listening. We do not know how many there might be, or how well armed. This man's body may have been placed here to stop us exactly so, to trap us."

"What a happy thought!" Jaufre let out a breath. "But we've not been set on yet, so we must hope there are more of us than there are of them. Indeed, this would be an ideal spot to wrest the lady Margot from us, so something holds them back if they are there."

"Aye," Eric agreed quietly, "and stopping us gives them the advantage of assessing our size and strength, whilst we learn naught of them. But we'll take no chances." He looked at Jaufre. "If memory serves, there is a monastery close by, is there not?"

"Down this road a distance," Jaufre replied, nodding. "'Twould take a few hours riding to reach it, and from the looks of it we may be in for rain soon."

Eric gazed at the sky. "That may be, but 'tis a discomfort we'll needs must endure, for we must achieve that monastery this night. I'll not have the lady Margot open to a threat 'til we're more sure of ourselves."

"Then we must start at once, lad."

Eric contemplated the corpse for a few seconds, seeing, as he always did, someone who might have been an unknown relative.

"Aye," he agreed quietly, "and take this poor fellow along with us. Whether his death was just or no, he deserves a decent burial, at least, and we've no time for that now. Mayhap the monks will put the creature to rest, please God."

*   *   *

The monastery at Linsett was an ominous, ancient pile. It had originally served as a fortified keep some two hundred years or more previously, so it came as no surprise to either Eric or his companions that the personality of the place was as stern as those of the monks who lived there. For their present purpose, the less approachable it was, the better. If Terent or his men were truly on their trail, perhaps the foreboding nature of this structure would keep them at bay. At least until something could be thought of to get the lady Margot safely to Belhaven.

And if the abode they had found refuge in for the night was not entirely welcoming, Eric mused as he looked out a window in the main hall, at least it was dry. And at least they were now dry, though Eric had begun to think he would never be so again after riding for four long hours in the downpour that commenced immediately after they had secured the dead man's body onto a cart.

It was still raining, though now it was more of a drizzle than a downpour, and Eric gazed at the whole wet mess and wondered what to do. He wished, for perhaps the thousandth time, that his father was there to guide him, but as he was not, and as Eric was, if nothing else, extremely practical, he did not dwell upon his wishing too long. It was very late at night and everyone else, including the monks, had sought their beds. But Eric could not sleep. He was restless, and about more than the danger of Terent of Ravinet. He was restless about Margot.

She had stayed with him for the remainder of their ride to this place, a circumstance Eric had very much wanted to avoid. It was bad enough being within a mile of her lovely person; it was sheer torture to hold her warm body next to his, to have his arms tight about her, and worse, to have her holding him just as tightly. There had been no choice in the matter, however, he told himself, because had there been any danger on the way he would have been the one best able to protect her. Had there been an attack he would have kept her safe, for there was nothing he would not do, no man he would not kill, no—

"Lord," he murmured, touching the thick green windowpane with one finger, "who am I fooling?"

He had insisted she ride with him only because he'd wanted a suitable excuse to have her in his arms. That was all, and that was the truth. Indeed, he *was* the best man to keep her safe merely because he was the man who best loved her.

"Loves her," he corrected aloud, softly, running his finger down the pane to make a clear line in the condensation.

How strange it was to be in love. And how it had happened to him he simply did not know. The only thing he did know was that the thought of her made his heart pump rapidly, the sight of her made him perspire, and the close proximity of her person made him unfit for public viewing. There was something about her. God. *Something.* When she looked at him, when she looked into his eyes, he felt as though he had already loved her for hundreds or thousands of years. She was his. *His.* But *not* his, he forced himself to remember, rubbing his eyes with one hand as though to rub his desires away. *Why* couldn't he make himself stop thinking of her? And if he could not master his thoughts, then he'd better get used to keeping his feelings regarding Margot to himself. He had a whole lifetime to look forward to that, after all.

It was quite late, and Eric had not expected anyone else to be up and about as he was, yet he was not entirely surprised when the movement of something white upon the stairs caught his eye and revealed that the object of his thoughts was descending.

Margot saw him standing by the window and turned her steps toward him. She came slowly, not smilingly, not seductively, yet looking undeniably beautiful and desirable nonetheless. She was wearing a white robe that seemed much too large for her slender person, for it fluttered and danced as she moved, creating the illusion of otherworldliness. Her long, golden hair was unbound as it had been on that first day he'd seen her at Reed, and it shimmered in the firelight that lit the hall like something newly gilded.

A fine trembling coursed over him as she drew near, for he knew, he *knew* that if he held out his hand to her she would place her own in it and would come into his arms and would willingly press herself against him and receive his kiss; his kiss and anything else he might wish to visit upon her person. He knew these things as surely as he knew his own name, and, God help him, he wanted to stretch out his hand.

Instead, he forced his sweating palms behind his back, pressed them flat against the wall, then leaned upon them with his full weight to keep them there.

Margot came to a stop closely in front of him, and, copying him, put her hands behind her back as well and pressed them into the other wall which bordered the window's alcove.

"Good eve, my l-lord," she greeted coolly, disconcerting Eric with her calm, casual tone. How was it possible that anyone, especially she, could stand so near him and not be caught up in the raging storm that was his emotions?

"Good eve, my lady," he replied with admirable indifference. "'Tis late for thee to be from thy bed. Wast not able to sleep?"

She shook her head. "Nay, though n-not for l-lack of trying. Thou'rt unable to f-find thy rest as well?"

"As thou seest."

"Aye."

He nodded. "Aye."

They fell uncomfortably quiet. Margot stared at her slippered feet and Eric thought it would be a miracle if she wasn't able to hear the thundering of his heart over the silence. Hopefully she would think it was the rain.

"Didst have a chance to read the m-missive I gave thee last eve?" she asked almost shyly.

Strange that his shaking hands should so quickly turn to stone, Eric thought. "Aye. I read it last eve, by the light of a candle. 'Twas most interesting. I thank thee for giving it me."

Her head shot up, revealing wary eyes. "'Twas m-most interesting? That is all thou d-didst find it? Interesting?"

"Aye."

"But wilt thou n-now admit that we shall be wed?"

"Nay."

"But—my father's m-missive! Didst not see that I am f-free to have my choice?"

Eric was twenty-three years old. He felt, though he knew it was not entirely true, that he had had a lifetime filled with longing and disappointment. Longing to be other than what he was and disappointment that he never could be. It had been thirteen years since he learned the truth about himself, and Eric had begun to think that, after all this time, there was nothing left that could hurt him regarding his birth.

But he'd been wrong.

"Thou'rt to have thy choice from amongst my father's eligible sons."

At least she didn't try to feign ignorance of what he meant, Eric thought gratefully.

"Thou art eligible," she whispered.

Eric couldn't speak. He shook his head and looked away, out the window again. He felt threatened by his emotions, anger and humiliation and impotence. Margot was silent for a full minute, giving him time to master himself, and again he was grateful.

"My f-father m-meant thee as well as thy brothers," she said finally. "He knows how I have l-loved thee all these years. That is what he m-meant when he said I would be w-well pleased."

Eric looked at her in disbelief. "I have known thy father well these past many months at Shrewsbury, and never did he speak of any—affection—thou might bear me."

She gave a tiny shrug. "Why should he speak of it? He, l-like thee, thought it a childish inf-fatuation which w-would one day pass."

"Mayhap he was right."

"Never!" Margot returned emphatically, smiling for the first time and dispelling some of the tension. "I shall l-love thee my whole l-life, Eric Stavelot. I shall g-go to my grave l-loving thee." For some reason she laughed after this and Eric, surprised at himself, laughed a little, too.

"Thou'rt obstinate, then, my lady."

She grinned mischievously. "As art thou, sir. We are w-well matched in one another. I wonder how our children shall m-manage us."

Eric's smile faded. "My lady, thou'rt fanciful as well as obstinate. Even should I believe thou couldst truly want to wed such a one as I, and should I myself also desire such a match, thy father would never sanction it. Thou'rt his only child. I cannot think he would see thee wed to one base-born."

"He d-did not find thee unsuitable any t-time these past ten years," Margot countered. "Indeed, when I w-would speak of my l-love for thee he seemed pleased to think of being related to his g-good friend, Sir Garin, through our m-marriage."

"Then he knew not of my birth," Eric insisted. "Had he known I am a bastard he would have quelled thy infatuation right quick."

Margot was becoming angry, he could tell. Her expression grew stubborn and her stammer became worse. "Thou d-dost n-not know if thou'rt indeed a b-b-bastard! Thou d-d-dost not kn-know who thine p-p-parents might b-be!"

"And that, dear lady, makes me even less eligible to be thy husband," he returned bitterly, making an impatient gesture. "'Tis true, I know not what I am, or from what stock. Dost think I have not wondered time and again these many years? The happiest truth I can presume is that my parents were peasants who could not afford to feed yet another hungry mouth and thus decided to abandon me to whatever fate God might hand me. From there all other possibilities become worse and worse."

Agitated now, Eric pushed away from the wall and paced toward the window, looking out of it. He had pondered these things so many times, but each seemed like the first, and just as terrible and torturous. "Perhaps my mother was a simple village girl, perhaps a serving maid, or perhaps a whore. Perhaps my father was a goodly knight, a field worker, or a town baker. He could have been a murderer, a thief, or a great nobleman who took his pleasure of my mother and abandoned her as she abandoned me." He turned and impaled Margot with his hurt and anger. "I am very dark and was found in my father's forest, so mayhap my people were gypsies. Hast ever

considered that, grand lady? Would thou be so anxious to mix thy pure, noble blood with mine were I
gypsy born? My nose is overlarge, thus one or both of
my fine parents might have been a Jew. Is that what
thou dost wish for thine children? To gift them with
the heritage of infidels?"

He hadn't realized how upset he'd become, or how
loud and agonized, until Margot pitched toward him
and threw her arms around his waist, hugging him
tight and burrowing her face against his chest.

"Do not, my Eric," she pleaded. "Do not t-torment
thyself s-so."

This sudden physical contact unleashed a torrent
of desire in Eric and that, coupled with his feelings of
utter helplessness and frustration, undid him. His
arms went around her and he lifted her up until their
mouths met, hungrily. This was no slow and gentle
kiss but urgent, demanding, needing. He *needed* to
soothe the raging pain inside him, needed to soothe it
with *her*, with her body and mouth and love.
Margot's arms went about his neck, her body pressed
against his and her lips met his willingly. Only when
he swathed her lips with his tongue, trying to press
through to the heat beyond, did she stiffen and try to
pull back. He kissed her more gently, then, wooing
her to trust him, but she would have none of it. She
was panicked and struggled, and Eric finally released
her.

Shaking a little, and breathing just as heavily as
she, he picked her up fully and collapsed on the
bench beneath the window, cradling her in his lap.

"I cannot imagine why I keep doing that," he said stupidly, trying to marshal his reeling brain.

"What w-wast thou t-trying to do?" Margot accused, sounding as though he'd tried to kill her.

"What?"

"That—that—" She struggled for the right words. "Is that n-normal?"

He laughed, realizing what she meant. "God! Thou'rt still a child."

She stiffened and Eric hugged her. "Forgive me. 'Tis bad enough I insult thee with my kisses; I should not insult thy good upbringing as well."

"I do n-not m-mind thy kisses, my Eric. Indeed, I w-wish thou wouldst kiss me night and day. 'Twas that other, th-that . . . lip licking."

Eric grinned and was tempted to demonstrate further just what that "lip licking" was all about, but she was so ignorant of men, so innocent about the ways of a man and a woman, that he was certain she would only panic again and run away. He sighed. "I should not be kissing thee at all. Margot, this is madness! Why canst thou not understand?"

"Understand what?"

"That I am not fit for thee! That never can I be thy husband."

She stroked his cheek with a gentle hand. "That, my Eric, I shall n-never understand. Thou couldst be half-b-bear and half-cat and still I would l-love thee. Nothing thou hast said this n-night has m-made a difference to that."

The feeling that swam over Eric at her words was

foreign to him. He felt happy, relieved, and, most of all, frightened. He didn't understand it, didn't understand *her,* for that matter, and realized that arguing with her would prove to be a great waste of time. Instead he dropped a loving kiss on her forehead, then fell quiet, closing his eyes and resting his cheek against the top of her head again. They sat thus for several long minutes. Margot continued to stroke his cheek and Eric finally drew his own hand up to touch the soft warmth of her face. He ran his thumb over her eyes, her lips, her nose. When she lifted her eyes to look at him he knew she was asking for another kiss, but he purposefully refrained from giving her one.

Instead he gave her a slow smile. "If one of the monks finds us thus," he said, "we shall be thrown out into the rain."

In response she lowered her head and snuggled up against him. Margot was simply content to be held in her love's arms, but Eric was pondering what he must do.

He had never been in love before and had never expected to be. Of course, there had been certain women in his life who had meant a great deal to him and whom he had loved, such as his mother and sister, his two grandmothers, his aunt Meredith and his cousins, Katelyn and Elizabeth, but he had never loved a woman as he now loved Margot. Even his youthful loves, the loves he had felt for the women who had variously warmed his bed since he was ten and three years old had never come close to engendering what he felt now. He knew he could never marry Margot, but he must make certain that she was happy. It was a duty, much like the duty he owed his father.

He cleared his throat. "My brothers, James and Jaufre, are very fine men. They are both knights, of course, and both educated. James has been greatly honored by the king of late and will likely make a name for himself in his days. I do not think thou shouldst consider Aleric, for he is younger than thee and will not be ready to wed for a few years yet. Thou dost seem easy with Jaufre, but, though I love him well, he is still a bit wild and might not make the best of—"

Margot sat up straight, pushing Eric's hands away. She took his face between both her hands and looked sternly into his eyes. "Make no m-mistake, my Eric. 'Tis th-thou I shall wed and n-none other. Speak n-no more to me of thy brothers."

She kissed him as unskillfully and painfully as she had done the night before, though this time she pulled back, hesitated a moment, then planted her mouth over his again and flicked her tongue shyly across his lips. When she finally pulled away she looked very pleased with herself.

"Good night, my love," she murmured, sliding off his lap.

Rubbing lightly at his bruised lips, Eric watched her climb the stairs, torn between regret and relief.

"Someone," he said quietly, "*must* teach that woman how to kiss."

14

The next two days were, for Margot, like a siege. She'd found the object of her desire, studied him, and determined her method of capture.

For Eric the days were like a hunt, and he the game pursued.

He was wary from the moment he saw her on the morning they left Linsett. He hadn't felt this leery even when he'd been on the battlefield at Shrewsbury, where at least his foes had had the decency to meet him headlong. But Margot, Margot knew just how to bait him, was in every way as cunning and skilled as any warrior he'd ever come across. If she'd only come charging at him with a readied sword, he might have been able to defend himself, as it was he felt fortunate at the end of each day simply to have his wits about him.

She had greeted him that first morn in a calm, sure

manner that had put Eric forcibly in mind of the way his parents greeted each other, which was to say, possessively. He'd done his best to be indifferent and merely polite, for he had become even more determined during his sleepless night that he would have to save Margot from herself, but she hadn't been the least bit unsettled by his stern and proper behavior. She'd simply ignored him and continued to act as though they were already an old, married couple and long used to each other's odd mood swings.

And she'd concealed her hair that morning, tightly covering it so that Eric had not had even a glimpse of the gold-spun treasure. It was a cruel tactic on Margot's part, and one he never would have thought her capable of. They rode together, for Eric refused to trust her safety to any other man now, and the sight of her pale, beautiful face without its natural halo made him nearly mad, mile after tortured mile.

"I wish thou wouldst uncover thy hair, my lady," he'd complained on the second morning.

Margot, sitting primly forward, cocked her head back to glance at him. "I am sorry, my l-lord. Doth my mantle disturb thy view? I shall tuck it in a little m-more tightly so thou'lt have no further n-need to worry."

"Nay." He sighed heavily. "It disturbs not my view. 'Tis only my peace of mind it disturbs."

"Thou speakest in riddles, sir." She laughed. "If thou wilt only b-bid me do it, I shall remove my covering, and gladly. Thou knowest f-full well I wish to please thee in all things."

"Not—not to please me," he faltered.

"If not to p-please thee, and if thy v-view is n-not disturbed, then why shouldst thou w-wish it removed?"

He was pleased with himself when he thought of his answer. "Because thy hair is beautiful, and beautiful things should not be hidden."

She'd only laughed again, as lightly as doves cooing, and rested her head against his shoulder. "Thy logic is f-flawed, my Eric, for there are many beautiful things b-best left covered, or so I believe. But that, my l-lord, I shall leave for thee to think on. However, this much I promise, that when we are m-married and have become one, I shall n-not c-cover any part of myself which thou dost think b-b-beautiful, when thou shalt ask it of me."

Eric had groaned aloud and shifted uncomfortably in his saddle, wishing she wouldn't speak to him in such intimate and impossible terms. It was worse than torture, and he still wasn't convinced that her protestations of love weren't some form of cruel amusement at his expense.

"My brother James will be grateful to wed such a dutiful bride, I vow," he'd muttered testily.

Margot had stiffened and made no reply to this, and Eric had felt as though he'd made some headway on their field of battle, though why he should feel miserable about it he could not understand. Her hair remained covered, however, as tightly as a locked cellar, and his discontent over it continued to grow, so that he could never be certain whether he had won this particular skirmish or not.

Her next line of attack had been to make all normal conversation completely impossible. Circumstances forced them to ride together, but Margot openly took advantage of the situation. She lost no opportunity to remind him of her opinion regarding their foregone marriage, so that Eric was forced to take the offensive at every turn.

"What d-didst thou think of Reed, my Eric?" she asked one day.

"I think it a fine, rich land, my lady," he replied, fully aware of what she was leading up to. "My brother James shall find it thus as well."

"How f-fortunate!" she exclaimed without a pause. "Then there will b-be no reason why he cannot visit us often when we are w-wed and thou art l-lord there."

Eric had clamped his teeth together and gone silent.

The most provoking maneuver of her onslaught, however, occurred at the end of each day, just before it was time for all in camp save those on watch to seek their beds, when Eric went to make certain the ladies were well and comfortable. He fulfilled this task unwillingly, of course, but as the leader of this expedition it was his duty, his sacred duty, to make certain all was well with his charges each night, regardless of how unpleasant it might be to do so.

Having approached the lady Margot with what he was sure were the most proper and formal of manners, Eric's reward was Margot's unique brand of torture. She would kiss him, pulling him quite

against his will into shadows where she would caress
and madden him, whispering words of love and longing so that he could barely pull himself away.
Fortunately for him, Margot still suffered from
extreme inexperience, so that she imparted more pain
than pleasure during most of these trysts. Her
embraces were hot and passionate and totally naive.
She strangled rather than hugged him in her ardor,
and between her steel-tightened lips and alternately
lapping tongue, her kisses threatened to disfigure his
overabused mouth.

"Margot—*Lady* Margot," he gasped on the second
night, putting her forcibly away from his aching body,
"that is *not* how 'tis done!"

She stamped her foot. "But thou'rt the one who
d-d-did it to me first!" she insisted. "I would n-never
have conceived of such strange l-lip licking if thou
hadst not introduced it!"

"Oh, God!" he said miserably, barely constrained.
"Margot, if ever I have an enemy I wish vanquished,
I'll be sure to turn thy lips on him first. By my troth,
thou dost kiss like a full assembly of wasps!"

But he was sorry, sorrier than he ever knew he
could be for speaking these words, because Margot's
beautiful eyes grew large and pained and wet, and her
bottom lip puckered out, quivering, so that he was
forced to draw her close against his body and hold
her as tightly as his love for her permitted.

"I'm sorry," he whispered. "Forgive me."

"T-teach me then," she begged just as miserably,
clutching him with desperate hands. "I kn-know that

I am ignorant and rep-p-pulsive, but I wish to please thee, my Eric. Teach me what to d-do."

"Margot," he pleaded, half-groaning with his longing, "nay. Nay. Thou must cease speaking such things to me. I am not made of stone. Thou must wait for thy husband to school thee. 'Tis his God-given right. And do not," he said, his voice lapsing into a hoarse whisper as he gently nudged her chin up so that he could look at her, "do not say that I shall be thy husband someday, for I shall not, and 'tis well and time that thou didst give up thine infatuation and accept this truth."

She only looked at him, her eyes shining with unshed tears, and Eric knew he could not go on. He cursed himself as a fool. A weak, blundering, lost fool.

"Eric," she whispered, supplicating.

"Hush." He stroked her cheek with one thumb. "Hush now, Margot."

He placed one hand gently on either side of her face to hold her still, then slowly, tenderly lowered his mouth to hers. When she made to put her arms around him he stopped her.

"No, love, be still," he whispered against her mouth. "I'll teach thee." He kissed her again, lightly, only a breath of touching. He pulled away only slightly. "Relax, dearest heart." His lips caressed hers more lingeringly before adding, "'Tis meant to be a gentle joining. Soft and loving and—" He kissed her thoroughly to demonstrate his meaning. When he lifted his head again to look at her he was pleased to see her half-shut eyes gazing back in a dazed manner. He slid one hand under her mantle to the nape of her neck and gently massaged the silky skin there, his other hand he slipped around her waist.

"Dost trust me, Margot?"

"Mmmm," she replied, finally putting her arms around his neck and smiling limply at him. "With all m-my heart, my Eric. I l-love thee so."

He lifted his hand from her neck and pulled her mantle from her head, at last exposing that golden mane of hair that even in the moonlight among the trees shone like new wheat in the sun. He dropped the white cloth on the ground without care and pleasured himself with the feeling of her hair's cool silk in his bare hand. The slightest pressure drew her mouth closer to his again.

"Then open thy mouth for me, love, and trust me."

He smiled when she so readily obeyed him, opening her mouth wide as though to let him examine her throat.

"Nay, love, only a little." He chuckled. "I only wish to kiss thee, not weigh the soundness of thy teeth."

She closed her mouth again, but left her lips slightly parted, and looked at him wonderingly. Before she could question him Eric kissed her again, with all the love and desire running through his veins. This would be the only time, he told himself as he persuaded her lips to open a little more beneath his. He would taste her fully this one time and then he would never, ever touch her again.

Her whole body tensed when she realized his

intent, when his tongue licked at her lips and teeth, finally slipping all the way inside the heat of her to graze her tongue. He held her firm, moving his mouth over hers surely and steadily, stroking and exploring in a manner intended to make her cave in.

She did, and all at once. With a low, husky moan she collapsed so that he had to hold her up, and her hands moved over his face and into his hair as her mouth widened to accommodate his growing demands, and her own tongue finally met his, timid and trembling and unsure.

And Eric moaned in return. He felt her melt into him like wax under a flame and completely lost his head. He crushed her against his body, burning with the need to take her into himself. He buried his fingers deep in her hair and savagely twisted her head so that he could possess every mystery of her sweet mouth with his own seeking one, so that he could taste and explore and remember.

She whimpered beneath the ferocity of his attack, yet still struggled to be closer, answering his need with her newly awakened one. His hands began to find her then, in the first step to making her ready for more, because Eric knew that he was going to have her, right then and right there, else he'd surely die of want.

His fingers found and were tantalized by the curvaceous side of one warm breast, and he began to slide his hand around the delicate mound, his progress impeded only by the fact that their two bodies were so tightly pressed together.

"In sooth, I always feel that doing one's own translation is the best way in which to understand such complex works. I, myself, am currently working on a translation of *Plutus*, which, please God, I hope to have finished by Saint Martin's Day. I've been working on it now for what seems like forever!"

This, followed by two young voices laughing, caused Eric to draw away from Margot, for he realized who it was. He held her, though, just as tightly, and drew her into the deep shadows of a tree where their labored breathing only seemed magnified.

"Oh, Aleric, how clever thou art! And how I envy thee! Never should I even dream of being able to read such a work as *Plutus*, though I did have the good fortune to read Gervase of Melcheley's *Ars poetica* last year, which was so wonderful."

Eric persuaded Margot's head gently down to rest against his chest because he could no longer bear the feel of her warm, moist breath against his chin. She complied readily, as though also relieved, and Eric stroked his fingers through her now-unbound hair.

Aleric and Minna walked right by them, though neither seemed to notice the couple so mightily straining for self-control beneath the sheltering branches of the maple tree. Both Margot and Eric turned their heads to watch the young couple pass, strolling hand in hand in the shade of the moonlit night, their heads together, laughing and talking and obviously very intent.

"Aye, that is a fine work, indeed. And if thou didst enjoy *Ars poetica*, Minna, thou'lt be interested in my collection of Horace, methinks. When we reach Belhaven I'd be most pleased if thou wouldst . . ." His voice drifted in the distance.

Eric and Margot stayed as they were, feeling the warmth of each other, not speaking. He continued to stroke her hair in a calming caress, and she relaxed into him completely, so that even their breathing took on the same rhythm.

Eric finally caused Margot to look at him, and was stunned. Her face, her expression, was transformed by the open desire he saw there. She had tasted real passion for the very first time, and she knew, or at least had an idea of, what a man and a woman could share. For one odd moment he vaguely wondered if this was what his own expression had been like on the occasion when he discovered what Margot was now discovering. But his first open-mouthed kiss had come from the village whore, who had lured him into her dwelling when he was thirteen with the promise of something sweet, while Margot's had come from the man who was destined one day to be her brother by marriage.

He sobered and pushed her away. "Go," he ordered tightly. "Now."

She looked at him with pure confusion. "B-but, my Eric."

He was furious. "*Never* call me that again. I'll not cuckold my brother, whichever one thou dost marry, and I'll not shame him more than I already have. For God's sake, go away from me now! Now, Margot! Go!" And he shoved her in the direction of her tent, because he knew that if she stayed even a moment longer he would have her, fully, and would never after know what to say to his brother.

Margot was thankful to find her tent empty when she finally stumbled into it. Minna was still out with Aleric, and Margot hoped she would stay with him a while longer.

She needed time, she thought as she sat heavily on her pallet, some time to absorb all that had occurred within the last hour, though she wondered if all the time in the world would ever be enough to make her heart stop pounding so erratically, or to soothe the sensations that tingled over her entire body.

Never in her wildest imaginings had she ever considered that a man and woman might kiss in such a way! How naive she had been, and how foolish she must have appeared to Eric, licking at him as though he were a sugar candy and believing herself to be so knowledgeable. Why, she had even boasted to Minna of her accomplishment as though she were already a long-married, experienced lady. She could now only hope that Minna would not make the same, embarrassing mistake she had.

But how wonderful it had been! How wonderful and how . . . intimate. She could still feel his mouth, so warm and soft. And his hands! They were large hands, hands capable of meting out a great deal of punishment and pain, hands capable of killing a man with ease, but this night they had been sure and gentle as they stroked and touched her in places where no man had ever touched her before. She almost felt as though she could have drowned in the touch of those hands, indeed, in all of him. Just thinking of it made her shiver.

She sat thinking for a while before rising to ready herself for bed, and she came to the conclusion that love was an insatiable need. Only minutes before she had discovered a way of kissing that had fully surprised her, yet she was far from satisfied. She wanted more of her Eric, more and more and more, until she knew all of him, completely.

Eric stayed beneath the tree after Margot ran away, leaning against the trunk of it and gulping in great breaths of the cool night air to calm himself.

God! What a muddle he'd made of things! All his determination to keep Margot at bay, all his vows to love her from afar and never to give in to her sweet persuasions, all of it gone to ruin because of his own damned weakness and uncontrollable desire. He shuddered once, then closed his eyes and rested his head against the tree.

It was no good. No good at all. As long as Margot continued the game they'd joined in these past two days he would never be able to stay away from her.

She had to stop.

She had to, because he couldn't, and if one of them didn't keep away from the other, they were going to find themselves in deep trouble right quick.

Tonight even—Lord! If Aleric and Minna hadn't walked by when they had, Eric knew without a doubt that he would even now be lying with Margot, right there on the ground, their bodies united and his seed deep inside her, and only after they had both come to their senses would either of them have realized what they'd done. She would have been irrevocably ruined, and he, the man who claimed to love her so well, would have been the one responsible for it.

But he did love her and seemed to love her more and better each day. When she wasn't driving him crazy with her determined pursuit of him, she was making him laugh at some ridiculous story, or making him thoughtful with a comment, or even coaxing him, amazingly enough, to speak about himself, something he rarely if ever did. How could he ever bring her harm? He could not do it, would not do it. He must find a way to save her from herself, to protect her from her own misguided feelings.

He would find a way, he vowed, his eyes falling upon the mantle lying so white against the dark ground. He stooped to pick it up, bringing it to his face to rub its softness against his skin, to smell Margot's scent on it.

"I love thee," he murmured into the silk, kissing it softly as though it were Margot herself. "I'll live to see thy happiness one day. I swear it."

He tucked the mantle into his tunic, then stepped away from the tree so that he could gaze up at the early fall stars. Fall already, and only a few days of riding to reach Belhaven. Perhaps only two. God's mercy, but he would be glad to reach home again! There had been no sign of trouble from either Terent of Ravinet or any of his men, but Eric would not rest easy until he had ridden Margot into the safety of Belhaven and seen the gates shutting behind them. Aye, he would be able to stop worrying about Terent then, only to start worrying about how he was going to live through watching one of his brothers take Margot to wife. God! The idea made him ache with misery, so much so that he pushed all thoughts of it from his mind. He would think about that when the time came, and he would find a way to deal with his misery then, too. For now he must keep his thoughts on Terent of Ravinet and on getting Margot to safety. And on one more thing, he reminded himself. The most important thing of all.

One way or another, he must make Margot hate him.

15

"*Thou'rt riding alone today,* Jaufre? Where is the lady Minna?"

Eric reined in his destrier to ride more closely to his brother, his arm tightening about Margot's waist only slightly to help her keep her balance. Her hair was uncovered this day, and it shimmered in the early morning sunlight as she too turned her head to look at Jaufre.

"She deserted me to ride with Aleric," Jaufre said sadly, falling into a comfortable rhythm beside them. "Our little brother insisted that they had much to speak of and thus should be allowed to ride together. He vowed to take good care of her." He winked at Margot. "And so I believe he shall."

Margot smiled at him in return. "They do seem to get along m-most readily," she said. "And M-Minna certainly enjoys discussing literature with him."

Jaufre laughed out loud. "Poor Lady Minna! She'll regret the day she e'er set eyes on our little brother, I vow, when he's wearied her to tears with his learned prattling. 'Tis one thing to talk, but well another to prate endlessly on and on and on, as our Aleric does."

"Nay, Sir Jaufre!" Margot countered. "And shame on thee for speaking th-thusly of thine own brother! Minna told me last eve how v-very g-glad she is to have Aleric's c-company and c-conversation. She hath never m-met another who loves b-books as well as she, and is grateful to have a fellow admirer to t-talk to."

Jaufre shook his head. "But talk, I'd wager, my lovely lady, is not all those two have on their minds. Ah, to be young and innocent again," he said jokingly, turning his grin on his brother, "eh, Eric?"

"Thou wert never innocent, lad. On the day thou wast born Father and Mother drew in one glance of thee and called for the priest to begin thy moral reformation forthwith. As to age, why, thou'rt still wet behind the ears, puppy."

"Puppy!?" Jaufre laughed heartily. "I'd challenge thee for that, save thou'rt so old and decrepit thou wouldst fall down just from standing up, Grandfather! Puppy, indeed!"

They all laughed and Eric felt himself relax for the first time that day. Thank God for Jaufre. He could always be counted on to lighten an uneasy situation. And Eric was more than uneasy at the moment.

Margot had looked so beautiful that morning

when she finally walked out of her tent, even more beautiful than the day before, if such a thing were possible. Her hair was uncovered, but that was not what had made such a difference. There was something about her this morn that seemed more alive, more alight, more womanly, and Eric had recognized what it was, one of the most powerful forces in the world: knowledge. She knew something now, a couple of things, actually, knew more about them than she had the day before, and had experienced them and thus felt more sure about both them and herself.

Passion and desire were no longer strangers to Margot le Brun, though her acquaintance with them was still slight. Her whole person glowed with the change, and Eric was thoroughly shaken. Still, he'd made his resolve and would not move from it. Tonight he would do what he must, and tomorrow she would love him no longer.

"Hey now, what's this?"

Jaufre's remark brought Eric out of his reverie, and he saw that a wagon with a broken wheel lay across the road just ahead of them, impeding their progress. Instinctively he pulled back on the reins, bringing Bram and the men behind them to an abrupt halt.

"Ride ahead and make certain that this accident is an accident in truth, Jaufre," he commanded quietly, his arm tightening about Margot's waist and his hand moving to find the hilt of his sword. "One word from thee will tell me, brother."

Jaufre nodded and started his steed slowly forward.

"I'll speak it loudly, then," he promised, approaching the seemingly deserted wreck with caution.

"B-but Eric," Margot said, bewildered, "'tis only a broken wheel some p-poor people have suffered. There c-can b-be no reason for worry."

"We'll hope not, my lady," replied Eric, backing Bram a few steps closer to the safety of the column.

"What's amiss, Eric?" Aleric and Minna rode up beside them, and behind them came Jace, also curious.

"I know not," Eric told his little brother, keeping an eye on the spot where Jaufre had disappeared around the side of the large, tented wagon.

"A broken wheel!" Aleric said. "We'll needs must lend aid to these poor folk, whomever they may be." He made to dismount, but Eric stopped him with a severe glance.

"Stay where thou art, lad, and wait 'til Jaufre gives word."

"But look!" Margot exclaimed, causing Eric to look back. "Why, they're d-d-d— a whole family of d-d-d—"

"Dwarfs," Eric provided, gazing wonderingly at the five small people who came rambling into view with Jaufre in tow. They were brightly dressed, all of them, in the same manner that Jace was, and they were smiling at Eric and his men with great relief.

"Why, 'tis my own people!" Jace shouted with joy, sliding off his horse without delay.

Eric dismounted as well, pulling Margot along with him.

"I do believe thou'rt right, J-Jace," Margot agreed. "They m-must be traveling m-minstrels, or actors, mayhap."

"It seems we've come just in time, Eric," Jaufre announced as they drew closer. "These fine people lost their wheel more than two hours ago, and have not been able to get the new one in't's place. They were just about to hang their heads and cry before we arrived." He proceeded to make introductions. "Bogo of Brantwell, I make known to thee the lady Margot le Brun of Reed, and also my brother, Sir Eric Stavelot of Belhaven."

Bogo of Brantwell was a middle-aged man, dark-haired and long-bearded, with a red, cheery countenance that made him appear elflike. In height he barely reached a little above Eric's kneecap, but he approached the giant man with undaunted enthusiasm.

"My lord! My lady!" He bowed rapidly to both of them, then held out one small, childlike hand to Eric. "Thank God thou hast come! We were nigh on misery, indeed we were, kind sir, and so again will I thank God! I am most, most pleased to make thine excellent acquaintances!"

Eric had to bend to shake the proffered hand.

"As are we to make thine, Bogo of Brantwell," he assured the excited man.

"My lady!" Bogo of Brantwell exclaimed, kissing the hand Margot extended him and bowing over it grandly. "'Tis a fine, great honor to meet such a beautiful, regal lady. I thank thee!"

Margot laughed and exchanged looks with Eric. "Thou'rt m-most kind, sir. Indeed, the honor is m-mine."

"May I make known to thee my wife, Katrene?" Bogo turned and pulled forward a tiny auburn-haired lady who blushed and curtsied. "And this is our daughter Neysa and her husband, Josko." He indicated a young couple standing together, the girl auburn-haired and blushing like her mother, the man taller than the rest by a few inches with dark, handsome features. "And our son, Loyce." He waved toward a boy standing behind the others, his dark head and brown eyes all that were visible of him.

Eric bowed. "'Tis an honor," he said, and introduced Aleric, Minna, and Jace to them in return. When all the introductions were through he asked, "What happened to waylay thee thus, Bogo of Brantwell? Didst meet a rut in the road? And the cattle, are they well?"

"'Twas not a rut in the road, my lord," Bogo explained as everyone began to wander toward the wrecked vehicle. "We were on our way to Wickham where a fair is to be held, and where we are meant to perform, God help us, if ever we get there. We are acrobats, i'faith, and widely known if truth be told. The lord of Wickham himself requested our presence at the fair, for he wished to have only the best performers entertain."

"I see," said Eric. "Then I am sorry we'll not be able to see thee performing, for it verily sounds a treat." He squatted down to have a closer look at the broken wheel. "Check the horses, Aleric," he said, "and Jaufre, tell the men to dismount. We'll have a few minutes rest 'til this is fixed." He examined the wheel and axle carefully, then shook his head. "Thou'rt right, Bogo, 'twas not caused by unevenness of the road. What happened to drive thee aside so suddenly?"

Now that Eric was squatted down, Bogo's head was almost level with his shoulders, so that they were able to look at each other eye to eye.

"'Twas just after we'd gotten started this morn, my lord, when a horde of devils came swooping down upon us like a very swarm of bees."

"Men on horseback?" Eric asked with a frown.

"Aye, and they gave us no choice but to swerve out of their path. The road was not wide enough for all of us!"

"'Twas either that or risk charging the horses, sir," Josko put in, somewhat shyly, "and they were startled enough, as thou canst tell."

Eric nodded. "Thou'rt lucky and more to be alive, it seems. The poor beasts must have been thoroughly rattled to have swung thus sharply. A little more and the whole cart had been overturned."

Margot, who was standing behind Eric, put both of her hands on his shoulders. "But we d-did not pass any m-men on horseback earlier. How can this b-be?"

Eric absently covered one of her hands with his own, squeezing lightly.

"I know not, my lady," answered Bogo with hands

held palm up. "They came from the same direction that thou didst. 'Twas only two hours past, perhaps a little longer."

"How very strange," she murmured, and Eric squeezed her hand again.

Jaufre returned and squatted beside Eric. "The men were pleased to rest early," he said, craning his neck to have a better look beneath the vehicle. "And I set guards out," he added casually. "Shall we set to repairing this, then? Bogo and Josko have unlatched the new wheel."

"Aye, the axle looks well enough. Let's fix it."

"I'll call for a few of the men—"

"Nay, nay," Eric said, standing. "I'll do it. Get the wheel ready."

And then, to the amazement of all save his two brothers, Eric stooped, secured one corner of the wagon beneath one massive shoulder, and lifted the vehicle from the ground so that Josko, Aleric, and Jaufre could replace the shattered wheel. He grunted a little when he set the wagon back down, but that was his only sign of discomfort.

"Eric, how w-wonderful thou art!" Margot exclaimed, smiling up at him with admiration.

Eric returned the smile and looked a little embarrassed. "'Twas naught, but thy praise is better than gold, my lady."

"Sir Eric," said Bogo, happily, "if thou dost ever wish to take up performing, let me know! I could make a fortune from such a giant as thee!"

Eric laughed and looked at Jaufre, who was wiping

his hands. "There, brother. My fame and fortune are made!"

"God's mercy!" Jaufre laughed. "Only a fool would pay good money to watch thee perform, thou pompous ass!"

"Oh, I'd not say that, Jaufre," Aleric joined in. "I might pay as much as two pennies to see Eric stand on his head or some such."

"Two pennies!" Eric said with a laugh. "My career is over before 'tis begun, it seems. I'd best stick to playing knight and dutiful son."

Everyone laughed but Thomas, who, having come to make certain his master was well, glared openly at Aleric. "I'd give everything I had to see Sir Eric," he declared loyally, earning a grateful hand on his shoulder from his lord.

"Thank the good Lord for faithful squires who'll ne'er let their masters starve!" Eric turned his smile on the grateful family. "Thou'rt welcome to join our train, if't please thee, Bogo of Brantwell. We needs must pass through Wickham on our way home to Belhaven and would be glad to see thee safely there in time for the fair."

"Good sir," said Bogo, coming forward to shake Eric's hand again, "we should be honored, as well as grateful to accompany thee. Mayhap we shall find a way to repay thee for thy kindness on the way."

"Mayhap." Eric nodded. "A private performance for my men and the ladies would be payment enough, I vow."

"Done!" said Bogo, and his family murmured

their approval behind him. "We'll perform tonight, my lord, and tonight shall be a night thou'lt never forget!"

How right the man was, Eric thought later as he sat beside Margot in the cool, early evening, watching the family of dwarfs performing the most marvelous of feats, sometimes aided by Jace, who'd made quick friends with his fellow entertainers. No, he would never forget this night, or these last few minutes when he could feel Margot sitting beside him, warm and happy, smiling and laughing and so very beautiful.

He put the inevitable off as long as he could, but when she reached over and squeezed his hand he knew the time had come.

"Margot," he said close by her ear so that no others would hear him, "come with me."

"Yes," she whispered in reply, smiling up at him trustingly.

They did not walk very far, only to the other end of the camp where Margot's tent was located. Eric stopped in front of one of the fires and gazed into the flames. Margot stood beside him.

"My Eric," she said softly, touching his hand.

"I told thee last eve never to call me that."

She was surprised by the terseness of his tone, and drew back her hand. "I kn-know, Eric, but I d-did not think thou m-meant it. I know thou w-wast angry last eve, but 'tis time thou d-didst accept the truth."

He stiffened. "The truth? What truth is this, my lady?"

"Oh, Eric, must I say even th-that? Wilt thou not say it freely?"

He forced a brief glance at her. "I do not wish to appear stupid, my lady, but I know not of what thou dost speak."

"Aye, thou dost," she replied gently, "but I'll not f-force thee. One day thou wilt tell me of thy l-love, and 'twill be the s-s-sweetest day of my life. 'Til then I w-will l-love thee unfailingly, and will n-never cease to t-tell thee of't."

The light of the fire flickered across the hopeful expression on her face and danced shadows on her motionless figure. She stood there, smiling serenely, so certain of herself and of him and not caring that they were surrounded by an entire camp of people, and Eric wanted to cross the two-step distance that separated them and fold her into his arms and love her until neither one of them would ever be able to pull away again. Being so much bigger than she, he thought he might hurt her if he held her as tightly as he wanted to, might crush her like a new rose so that he could inhale the fragrance of her. But he knew instinctively that Margot would not let him harm her; she would open for him willingly. She would give herself to him willingly. The knowledge made him ache with his longing, so that he had to turn away.

"Eric," she pleaded behind him.

He shook his head. "It matters not, my lady," he said into the darkness. He hated himself for what he was about to do, for what he had to do, and he cursed God and life and everything simultaneously for forcing him to do it. Somehow, he realized, he was going to have to look her in the eye.

"Does it n-not, my Eric?" she replied, and he could hear the smile in her voice when she spoke.

"Nay," he replied slowly, trying desperately to think of anything that might make him angry enough to face her. He did his best to conjure up memories of battles he had been in, of the different injustices he had seen in his life, of all the people he had loved who had died, even of the day on which he had learned the truth about his birth, but all he could think of, the only images that would form in his brain, were visions of Margot and James being wed in the midst of a great and royal celebration, of James taking Margot to his bed, of Margot bearing James's children. He turned and looked at her.

"It matters not, Lady Margot, if thou sayest thou love me. I have tried time and again to turn thee from this foolishness, and I have striven to be gentle in the doing so as not to hurt thee, for we are soon to be brother and sister and I'll not cherish any strife between us. But it seems thou'lt not be dissuaded with gentleness, so now I must speak plainly. I love thee not, Margot le Brun, and I would have thee cease this childish prattling about whatever feelings thou dost fancy thou hast for me."

Stunned momentarily, Margot quickly recovered. "I d-do love thee, Eric," she insisted, her hands forming small, determined fists at her sides, "and have always d-done so. 'Tis neither fancy nor inf-f-fatua-tion or whatever thou wilt call it next. 'Tis l-love and love alone. And I know that thou d-dost l-love me, also. Thou'lt not admit it, but thou dost l-love me."

Before Eric could answer, Jaufre strolled into the circular light of the campfire as calmly and casually as though he were strolling through the gardens at Belhaven. His direction was toward Eric, but he cast a friendly nod toward Margot as he made his way.

"Eric, man," he greeted with a clap of one hand on his larger brother's tense shoulder, "I know not of what the lovely Margot and thou art speaking, but it might be a good idea to keep that rasping voice of thine down. The whole camp can hear thee. Bogo and his family will think thou'rt trying to upstage them."

Eric stared at Jaufre, knowing full well that his tactful brother was doing his best to diffuse the situa-tion. It occurred to him that it would be a good idea if everyone in the camp could hear the lie he was about to give Margot. Saying it in front of witnesses would make it harder for him to take it back. With an angry gesture he shoved Jaufre's hand away and looked back at Margot.

"All can hear? That is well," he declared loudly. "Well, indeed. Now wilt thou believe me, woman, if I state my feelings so openly? I love thee not, not now and not ever."

"Eric!" Jaufre said in nervous surprise, grabbing his brother's arm as if to hold him back. "What is this?"

Lady Minna came into the light now, closely followed by Aleric, Jace, and Thomas.

Taking one look at her mistress's pale face, Minna rushed to Margot's side. "My lady! What is amiss?" She put an arm around Margot's waist and turned to look at Eric, questioning him with her eyes.

Margot ignored her. "Eric . . . thou d-dost . . . thou *dost* love me," she persevered shakily.

"Nay. I do not."

"Oh!" Minna ejaculated, much shocked. "Oh!"

"Damn thee, Eric!" whispered Jaufre, his fingers biting into Eric's arm. "Thou'rt acting the fool!"

"Please, Margot, let us go to our tent," Minna pleaded, pulling at Margot. "Sir Eric requires a little solitude, perhaps—" She cast Eric a hateful look.

Margot would not be budged, neither would she turn her eyes away from Eric. "Nay, Minna, he is only f-frightened of admitting the t-truth. For once he admits it he m-must also admit he was w-wrong." To Eric she said, "The times thou kissed me, thou d-didst l-love me, Eric."

"The times he *kissed* thee!" Jace roared.

"Oh, God!" Jaufre groaned, shutting his eyes.

Aleric's quick arm shot out to hold Jace back. "Steady, lad," he advised seriously. The difference in size between his older brother and the jester was laughable, not unlike the difference between a mountain and a pebble. "Delay a moment before doing anything so foolish."

"The times I kissed thee were pleasant, indeed, my lady," Eric admitted readily, "and I thank thee for them, but 'twould be false to let thee think that no other man would have enjoyed such." He shoved Jaufre toward her. "Surely thou hast been aware that even mine own brother has coveted the sweet taste of thy lips."

Jaufre righted himself from Eric's push and stared at Margot in horror. Never in all his life would he have imagined that his overly courteous brother could speak so crudely to any woman, let alone to Margot.

"I—" he began, but stopped when he saw the strange, pained expression on Margot's face. She wouldn't look at him, anyway. Her eyes were intent on Eric.

Margot was stunned and embarrassed all at the same time, though more for Eric than for herself. Why did he have to make this so difficult? She had tried to understand and, indeed, wanted to understand. This cruelty in him was false. She would not accept it. Cruelty could not exist in her Eric. Ever. Mustering a sort of smile as best she could, she said simply, with a fluttering of both hands, "I l-love thee, Eric."

He seemed to tighten all around the edges and then replied, as if only the two of them were present and as if every word he said did not feel like a knife to his heart, "It matters not, Margot. Even if I did bear thee love, which I do not, how canst thou think I would want a wife such as thee? One who stammers with every other word? I would be ashamed to be seen with thee, would be ashamed to have thy name on mine. Thine own parents could not bear to take thee to court, or even abroad. How canst thou think I should wish to do more than they? Canst imagine I would ever want to come home to a woman whose voice grates on me with every word she speaks, whose speech I could not bear to have imprinted on my children? Nay, Margot, nay. Take thy love and keep it. Save it for a man who'll not mind such sputtering. I want it not, just as I do not want thee."

Margot stood paralyzed in the stunned silence that followed, like one turned to stone. Only her eyes, shocked and wide, gave any indication of how she received these harsh words. Finally her mouth opened, gasping, and she pressed one hand over her stomach. When she closed her eyes tears spilled from them freely, running down her cheeks like overswollen rivers.

"My God, Eric—" Aleric whispered.

Eric had killed more men than he could ever remember on the field of battle, and those deaths had left him stunned and depressed. But this, this was beyond comprehension. Unable even to think on what he had done, and certainly unable to watch, he simply turned and walked away.

"Eric," Jaufre called after him. "Eric!"

Heedless, he began to run, and kept running, burying himself deep in the dark blanket of the forest.

Thomas found him sometime later, though how he had done so Eric would never know. He came shuffling quietly through the trees, his thin arms loaded down with blankets. When he saw his master he sighed wearily and set the blankets down.

The boy was a wonder. Eric had already decided that it would be best if he stayed away from the camp until morning, until he could deal with his own misery and self-reproach, and with his loss. But Thomas could not have known that.

"Thou'rt a good boy, Tom, lad," he said softly, watching as Thomas began to lay the blankets out, "and more than a good squire. I thank thee."

Thomas said nothing but continued with his task, carefully positioning his master's blankets just so.

Eric gazed with an aching heart at the boy's stubbornly bowed head. "I know thou dost not understand all that has taken place this night, Thomas, but I cannot blame thee for hating me. In sooth," he whispered softly, "I think I hate myself."

Like a branch pulled in too many conflicting directions, Thomas snapped, flying off the ground and throwing himself full-force at Eric, his bony hands and arms hugging him around the waist and holding tight, his face buried against his hard chest.

"Thomas," Eric said, thoroughly taken aback. Gingerly he placed his hands on the boy's thin shoulders. He was crying. God! Thomas was crying, sobbing and shuddering against him like a tiny child with a broken heart. Eric hugged him close and gently stroked his hair. "Forgive me. Forgive me, lad."

Thomas shook his head violently and clung to Eric all the more tightly. "Never," he sobbed, "never will I hate thee!"

Eric held the boy warmly and rocked him from side to side. "Hush, lad. Do not take on so."

"N-n-never—"

"Aye, lad, I understand. And 'tis glad I am to know it, for thy good opinion means much to me. Never will I hate thee, either, Tom, no matter what evils befall either of us. Now, here, I cannot bear to see thee so unhappy. Always will I love thee, Thomas, and always will I take care of thee."

These words seemed to work a miracle on Thomas, though it took a few moments for his tears to cease. Slowly he relaxed against Eric, his body rising and falling in great heaves. Eric continued to rock him back and forth.

Finally Thomas asked, with a sniffle, "Dost thou love the lady Margot?"

"Aye."

A few more sniffles. "Why wast thou so mean to her?"

"Because I do love her so well. Because I love her more than my own life, or more than anyone or anything else in life."

Thomas nodded against his chest to indicate that he understood these sentiments, then he pushed from Eric, gazing up at him with red eyes and wiping his nose with one forearm. He took a whole step away and met Eric's eyes with a daring look.

"Thou'lt think me a girl for bawling."

Eric didn't dare to smile at him. "Was that what thou wast doing? I thought thou wast comforting me in my misery, as a good squire should do."

Thomas surveyed him with some disbelief, then wiped at his eyes with his other forearm. "I *was* bawling," he stated defiantly, daring Eric to contradict him.

Eric nodded. "Very well, if thou dost insist. But if thou thinkest I know not the difference between a boy and a girl, thou'rt in error, and most gravely." And then he smiled.

Thomas shook his head as if to say he would never understand his master's odd sense of humor and returned to his task of setting out the blankets. When he had finished making Eric's bed he took a few blankets and made his own, at the foot of where his master would sleep.

"Nay, lad, I'll not have thee suffer out here with me," Eric insisted when he understood the boy's intent. "Go back to the camp and sleep in thy place there. I'll see thee in the morn."

Thomas pointedly ignored his master's words and lay down for the night. "I'll sleep here," he said, then yawned and closed his eyes.

"Stubborn whelp!" Eric muttered. But he was too tired and too miserable to argue. He lay on the bed Thomas had made for him, careful not to kick the boy where he insisted on lying, and pulled a blanket up to cover himself.

He did not sleep, however. He lay awake, picturing over and over again Margot's face as he said all those damned, *damned* lies. Sometime during the night Thomas turned over in his sleep and put an arm around one of Eric's legs, hugging it in his slumbers as a child might hug a doll. The simple touch, so evocative of the boy's pure love, set Eric's tightly controlled emotions free. In the cool safety of darkness, his heart dying of misery while Thomas's hand warmly attached itself to one foot, Eric let his grief have its way.

16

"*God, she's a beauty.* I never seen a prettier maid in all my days."

The man leaning over Margot was the ugliest creature she had ever set eyes on. His nose was broken in three places, his eyes were bulging like a frog's, and he was actually drooling all over one side of his face. His breath, as he came closer to her, was so foul it threatened to make her swoon, and his teeth, which he bared in gross semblance of a smile or grimace, were mostly black and rotting. He placed one filthy hand on her face and petted her.

"I'd like to mount her up for a nice, long ride, by God. What a journey we could have together, sweeting, thee and me, bound up together as cozy as two rabbits in the making, eh?" He chuckled loudly and pinched her cheek so hard that tears came to her eyes.

"Leave her be," said her other captor, a tall, thin, nervous man who did nothing but pace the tent they were in, stopping to look out the opening every few seconds. "Thou knowest full well Black Donal said she wast to be kept untouched, *or else.* Dost wish to end up like Eamon?"

"Eamon was an idiot!" the other replied, his hand straying from Margot's face to her breasts, one of which he squeezed while Margot writhed in disgust. "Ohhh, God! She's soft and round as a baby's bottom. There's no reason why we cannot see a little more." He began to unlace the front of Margot's surcoat, but was shoved away by the tall man.

"Damn thee, John, I'll not risk my head because thou'rt a lecherous fool! Now keep away from her, else I'll kill thee with mine own hands! Better yet," he practically picked John up and threw him out of the tent, "cool thy lust by watching for Black Donal. He'll be here any moment now, and I've no desire that he catch us unawares."

The tall man took up his pacing again, never sparing Margot a glance in his worry, and, relieved, she turned flat on her back and gazed up at the roof of the tent. She could not speak, having had a rag tied tightly around her mouth and head, but it was just as well. When first captured she had screamed and railed at them, yet had been totally incomprehensible in her rage, so that one of them, the ugly one, had gagged her, saying he could no longer bear listening to her demon's tongue.

"Thy parents should have cut thy tongue from thy

head when thou wast a tiny child," he'd told her, tying the gag so tightly that she cried. "'Twould have been a just favor to thee, i'faith, and a mercy to the rest of us."

She'd been too frightened at that moment to think on the man's words, for she'd been in the midst of being abducted, having been pounced upon all of a sudden as she searched the dark forest for Eric. Her two captors had carried her some distance away, until they had ridden into their own camp, where they were enthusiastically greeted by many more men, and where she had been picked off her mount and carried, forthwith, into the tent where she now lay, evidently waiting for the man named Black Donal to arrive.

But now as she lay helpless and frightened, she turned her mind back to the man's cruel words, and beyond them to the more painful words that her Eric had spoken. Even as she thought of them tears came to her eyes and she cried freely and without remorse. All her life she had struggled with the pain of knowing that she was deformed, and that the deformity made her repulsive in the eyes of others. This much she had learned to accept and to live with. But never had she believed that her own beloved Eric would find her thus, at least not after he'd had a chance to grow used to her speech. In all her dreams he had come to love her as she loved him, and had always treated her with the same kind gentleness with which he had treated her the day they first had met. But now she knew the truth. Oh, God! Now she knew.

He had only been as kind to her that day as he ever was to anyone. He was kind to Thomas, kind to shy, eight-year-old girls, kind to people he met stranded on forest roads. She closed her eyes against the pain. Eric Stavelot was kind to everybody, and she had spent ten long years loving the man simply because he'd been kind to her for a few hours one warm spring day. What a fool she'd been! And how much more than foolish to think that a man like that could ever love a stammering creature like herself! He could have any woman in the entire world. Why should he spare so much as a glance for a freak like her? She could look back now and see that he had only been kind during this journey, even during those times when he had kissed her, those precious times she thought so special. To him they'd probably been dreadful occurrences, and he'd merely forced himself to be dutiful in order not to offend her.

The tent flap opened and Margot opened her eyes.

The thin man was suddenly angry. "Get out! Thou hast no business here! I am waiting for Black Donal."

"Calm thyself, man," a new voice commanded, both strong and sure. "'Tis Black Donal himself has sent me, to make certain the lady is kept well 'til he arrives. He'll be here any moment now. Thou canst keep an eye out for him."

Margot turned her head to see who this new man was, though her interest was only the mildest sort of curiosity. Every one of these criminals seemed alike to her, and one no better or worse than the other. But when she finally saw who this man was she gasped, even through the barrier of her gag.

Oh, dear God! No!

No! No! No! No!

It was *he*. That wretched hunter from the forest who had so brutally assaulted her.

She began to struggle against the ropes that bound her hands and feet, staring at him with pure horror. As if feeling her gaze upon him he turned, his eyes meeting hers, and he smiled.

"My, my, she is a pretty one, is she not?" he commented easily. Strolling closer to where Margot lay, he added, "I have heard rumors of the lady Margot's beauty before, but never have I believed them. Now I can see 'twas all truth, and even less than truth." He knelt beside the cot. "She is a very vision of beauty. But look," he said sadly, placing two gentle fingers on her cheek and causing Margot to jerk her face away, "she has been crying. Now that is verily a crime, for such a lady should ne'er know tears and sadness. She is too lovely for that."

"Aye," the man behind him said tightly, "and she'll stay that way, at least 'til Black Donal arrives. What he does with her then I do not care, but thou'lt keep thy hands to thyself, or taste my wrath, otherwise. And I'll not regard that Black Donal has taken such a fancy to thee, either, marksman. I've been with my lord more than ten years now, while thou hast only a few days to thy credit."

The hunter chuckled but never took his eyes from Margot, who glared at him with all the hatred and anger she could muster. "Never fear, Talbot. Thou'lt have thy reward for capturing this pretty doe, I vow. She'll come to no harm by my hand, and Black Donal will be here soon enough. Now be a good man and go outside to wait for him."

Talbot barked a sarcastic laugh. "Not by my life will I! She is well, as thou canst see, so thou may take thine own leave, ere I throw thee out, bastard of Sorenthill!"

Margot watched, both frightened and fascinated, as the hunter's face first hardened, then took on a strange, powerful kind of smile. His eyes grew far-away, as though he saw nothing before him, and all his fingers relaxed and opened.

"Talbot," he said quietly, "wouldst thou like to accompany me on the morrow when I go to fetch our dinner? Black Donal has said that I might choose any helper I wish this time, and thou dost seem a likely man to face the tensions of hunting. A good helper, Talbot, is a great necessity when a man hunts. Philip was the last to assist me thus, as thou'lt remember. Black Donal himself asked me to take him along, and to take good care of him while we were about our task. A pity he got in the way of that last arrow, was it not? Thou wouldst like to retrieve my arrows for me as well, I am sure. Wouldst thou not, Talbot?"

Margot groaned more loudly than Talbot did at these words, for as much as she disliked the thought of being alone with the thin, nervous man, so much more did she dread being left with the hunter, whom she hated more than any of the others. She writhed and wiggled, emitting as much noisy distress as she could to tell Talbot of her fear, but that man had only grown pale and silent. He stared at the hunter's stiff back for a second or two longer, then said, "I'll go," and left.

"Mmmmmmmm!" Margot screamed into the cloth in her mouth. The hunter reached out a hand and touched her bound hands and she violently pulled from him, screaming again and again to alert anyone who might hear.

"Hush!" the hunter hissed at her. "Lady Margot, be quiet! I mean thee no harm, foolish woman! Now, be quiet!"

Margot met his eyes openly and shot all her fury at him, continuing to scream until he put one hand up to her chin and gently squeezed, forcing her to be quiet.

He leaned closer and whispered his next words. "I am not a foe, Margot le Brun, and I've no time to explain so thou must believe me. Now be still and listen well. There is not much time 'til Black Donal comes, and if I'm ever to get thee out of here we must both understand our parts. No, I cannot untie thee now, so stop struggling and be quiet."

Margot did as he bid her, though she both distrusted and disbelieved the man. He was a liar as well as a fiend, evidently, but all the screaming and writhing in the world weren't going to do her any good now. It seemed a better idea to at least save her strength and hear the man out. When he saw that she was going to behave he slowly removed his hand.

"There, that's much better, my lady." He shook his head. "How Eric Stavelot, of all people, managed to let thee get captured is beyond me. Thou wouldst think at least one of those Stavelot boys would have kept an eye on such a beautiful lady at all times. The lack-wits!"

Eric! This man knew Eric! Hope dawned in Margot's breast as she heard the familiar way in which he spoke the Stavelot name.

"And if I know Garin's sons, they are on their way here e'en as we speak, most like, ready to rescue thee in some reckless, heroic manner. God's bones!" He ran a hand through his thick brown hair in agitation. "With my fortune they'll arrive just as Black Donal has come. I'll needs must keep one eye open for them and one eye trained on thee. Please God Eric will use stealth rather than force to make his rescue. That will be our only hope. One way or another, my lady, someone shall come to take thee from here within the next few hours, whether it be I or another, and thou must play this game well 'til then, and be ready when the time comes. I'll let no harm come to thee, and that I promise by God Himself, but 'twould be best could we avoid danger altogether.

"Listen well, now. The leader of these men is coming to make certain of thee, for he is to take thee forthwith to his master and can make no mistakes, and when he arrives thou must never look at me. Dost understand, Lady Margot? Regardless of any and all, do not look at me, nor even in my direction, lest Black Donal's suspicions be roused. He is a

sharp and cunning man, and one glance is sufficient
to tell him all that he desires to know. Say naught to
him, if thou can keep from doing so, but if thou must
speak, say little. And do not struggle or rail at him,
for his temper is hot and painful and he'll not with-
hold his fist even from such a delicate one as thee."
The sound of horses hooves and men's voices
approaching made the hunter stand quickly. "Forget
not all that I have said, Margot le Brun," he whispered urgently, "and as thou dost trust thine own
father, so also trust me."

He stood, put his hands behind his back, and
assumed a stance of relaxed boredom just as three
men, dressed in full armor, stormed into the tent.

"Well met, Allyn of Sorenthill," one of them said,
his voice dark and cool as an unexplored cave.
Margot turned her eyes to look at this new man, and
she became afraid again. He was remarkably dark,
much as Eric was, though he had neither Eric's height
nor breadth. Indeed, he was not much above average
height and his round stomach indicated that he was
given to eating and drinking well. The rest of him, as
solid and stout as a tree stump, appeared to be a com-
pact mass of muscle.

Black Donal, thought Margot, and the name fit
him well. Everything about him was black, from his
clothing and armor to his hair and wide beard. His
expression, even, was dark, almost evil in its sure and
penetrating character. His eyes shocked her. They
were blue, or, rather, white-blue, the same color as
clear spring water iced over in winter.

"She is here, as you see," replied the hunter, "and is well."

Black Donal's gaze passed from the hunter to Margot, stunning her with those eyes as they washed greedily over her. Fear rose up in her throat as he drew closer, and her body stiffened. He knelt and Margot instinctively pressed away.

"Aye," he whispered softly, "that she is. My prize. My prey. Thou hast run me a merry chase, Lady Margot le Brun, and for that I will gladly see thee broken." He did not touch her or come any closer, but she felt the power in him as though he had laid a knife to her throat. "Thou didst think to outwit me, thee and thy protectors, but never shall Black Donal be outdone. And all the trouble and time thou hast cost me, my lady, thou shall regret. When thou'rt under my master's hand I shall make thine life a misery. And thus I give thee my solemn vow, with this warning—cross me not again, lady, lest thou dost wish thy misery to be made a very hell. On this journey, and for the rest of thine days, however few or many they may be, give me no trouble. Thou wouldst not like the feel of my taming, I promise."

Margot stared at him blankly, her only movement the slow, singular blinking of her eyes. Her mind had emptied while Black Donal had spoken, and now she stupidly wondered if perhaps she were only having a very bad nightmare from which she would surely waken. What did these men want her for? Was it for ransom? extortion? what?

"Ah, she is so calm and still," Black Donal murmured, then looked at the hunter and laughed. "Were that all women as sensible as this one, eh, Allyn?" The hunter grinned in agreement and the other two men present chuckled. Black Donal turned back to Margot. "This one knows how to give way to a man's will. Thy new master will be pleased with such complacency, Margot le Brun, as thou wilt soon learn. Very well." He labored up to a standing position. "Jason, thou and Talbot will guard our captive 'til we leave at dawn. I'll post men without all around the tent, but make certain that none is allowed inside to glimpse our prize. 'Twill be hard enough to keep the rutting hounds at bay 'til we've reached Ravinet. Allyn, good man." He placed a heavy hand on the hunter's shoulder. "Tonight we celebrate, e'en as we keep watch against those fools who tried to take our prize from us. I'd have thee use thine most excellent skills to bring us a goodly feast, eh? I've a taste for venison, lad. Rich and sweet." He patted his round stomach and Margot dully thought that every man, every person, has at least one weakness in this world.

The hunter half bowed. "Venison it shall be, my lord. I'll have a fine doe to the cook before the sun has set, I vow."

They left together, Black Donal and the hunter, with one of the other men in tow. The one left behind, a young pale man with a mop of straight brown hair, collapsed on a chair the moment he was alone. Margot stared at him thoughtfully, rotating her numb hands and wrists around the ropes that bound them. Her feet, bare and equally bound, ached, as did her whole body. Her mouth, so long gagged now, was as dry as sun-caked mortar.

The young man set his elbows on his knees, then cradled his head in his hands as though distraught. He stayed thus for some time, occasionally rubbing his fingers through those finely straight strands of hair and sometimes massaging his eyes. He sighed several times and muttered to himself. Finally he looked at Margot and met her steady gaze.

He was on his feet in a second.

"I am sorry, my lady," he apologized, flushing. "Thou'rt so quiet, one could almost forget thou wast here." He quickly moved to a far corner of the tent and turned his back to her. "Wouldst like some water, Lady Margot? I am sure thou must be thirsty." When he turned around he held a goblet in one hand. "Here, this will comfort thee." He knelt beside her and set the goblet down. With surprising gentleness he reached his hands behind her neck and undid the silencing cloth. She gasped when it finally came away, and gulped in air as though she'd been suffocating.

"There, now," he said soothingly, stroking the back of her neck as she coughed with relief. With one hand he held the goblet, with the stroking hand he helped her to sit. "Here, drink some of this." He set the water to her lips. "'Twill make thee feel better, i'faith."

Margot drank the cool, stale water thankfully, feeling as thirsty as though she'd not tasted water in a year.

"Slower, my lady," the young man cautioned. "Do not make thyself ill for want. Thou mayest have all thou dost wish. See, now, I shall fill the goblet once more. Wait a moment."

It took two more goblets to quench Margot's thirst, and when she was through she fell back on the cot with relief, breathing easily now that she was sated and without the gag.

The young man smiled down at her. "My name is Jason. Jason of Welshore. I already know that thou'rt the lady Margot le Brun of Reed."

Margot only returned his stare and brought her bound hands up to wipe at her wet mouth. She sighed and turned her eyes heavenward. The touch of his fingers on her chin brought her around sharply, and she twisted away. He insistently put his hand on her cheek and she glared at him.

"Thou'rt indeed lovely," he whispered, as though awed. "Thine eyes, my lady, are so pretty. . ." He trailed off and struggled with himself, then shook his head and removed his hand. "But thou hast no need to fear me. I have a wife—a pretty, beautiful, sweet wife." For a moment he sounded as though he were going to cry, and Margot watched him with something close to horror. He bit his lower lip and was quiet a moment. "She is waiting for me in Welshore. My sweet Jenny. Waiting for me." He nodded. "And I'm going back to her soon as I have my pay. As quick as I can. We'll have a chance then." He kept nodding as though to convince her. "Aye, we'll have a chance." He fell quiet. Margot closed her eyes.

It seemed a long time before he spoke again.

"I have heard much about thy devil's tongue, my lady. Wilt thou not speak some of it for me?"

She didn't even bother opening her eyes. She shook her head. No. Never.

He stood. "I'll not gag thee again, then. If thou'lt not speak there is no need."

No, there was no need, Margot thought. She would never speak again. Never make anyone suffer the wretchedness of her speech. From that moment in her youth when she could understand, she had known that the sound of her speaking was intolerable, and she had lived with that knowledge, always speaking as little as possible. At the age of eight she had been set free. She had begun to live as fully as any other child, and she had learned that her deformity could be defeated. Perseverance was all it had taken. A little perseverance and every man, woman, and child who'd been uncomfortable in her presence soon overcame their discomfort. But Margot had no perseverance left in her, and it would be useless even if she did. It did not matter whether anyone else ever again grew used to her speech. Without Eric it just didn't matter.

Jason of Welshore shuffled around the tent restlessly, humming to himself. The sound filled Margot's ears, so soft and resonant and rhythmic it was. She did not know what the tune was that he hummed, but it was pleasant to listen to, and Margot, giving herself over to the odd, simple pleasure, listened until she finally drifted into sleep.

It was dark when she woke. The tent was illumined by candlelight, and two men sat nearby, chatting in low voices. Margot's eyes were gummy when she opened them, and she rubbed them with numb, swollen fingers. Her feet, and most of her body now, were almost completely deadened from lack of circulation, and she tried to wiggle around without success. Giving up she lifted her hands again and stretched, yawning, then turned her head and squinted through the dim light at the men sitting there.

"Well, mayhap 'tis want of me, but I say the man is a damned crafty fox! Black Donal may believe him a godsend, but I'll not be surprised if he turns out a vile curse instead. God! He gives me the shivers, he does."

Jason of Welshore shook his head and laughed. "Thou'rt overwrought, Talbot. 'Tis this bad task has done it to thee, making thee see enemies in every man. Once we've returned to Ravinet all will be meet again. Wait and see if 'tis not. Allyn of Sorenthill seems well enough to me, and he is certes skilled with a bow."

"True enough," Talbot agreed grudgingly, "but still I say the man is not to be trusted. He's a bad habit of smiling far too much, and that is a sure sign of deviltry if ever I've seen one."

As if beckoned by the words spoken about him, Allyn of Sorenthill entered the tent, strolling in casually and, just as Talbot had said, smiling.

"I've come to relieve Talbot," he said cheerily, stopping in front of that man. "Black Donal says thou'rt to have thy dinner first, and when thou hast finished Jason can have his turn."

The two men exchanged looks.

"But," Jason said uneasily, "Black Donal bade us strictly not to leave the tent. For any reason."

Allyn of Sorenthill shrugged. "I only know what he told me. No more, no less."

"Then bid him come tell us himself," Talbot demanded. "Otherwise we stay where we are."

"He cannot come to thee now," the hunter explained lazily, strolling over to gaze at Margot. "A wagon has recently passed nearby, and he has gone with some of the men to make certain of it. 'Twas that wagon we forced to the side yesterday morn." He looked back at them again. "The one with the dwarfs in it. It seems like naught to me, but Black Donal takes no chances, as thou knowest full well. Now go and have thy meal, Talbot. We'll break camp soon and every man must needs be strong and ready for the long ride ahead. Go and eat. Jason and I shall make certain no harm comes to the precious captive."

"Nay," Talbot replied, unsure. "I'll not."

"Very well. Then Jason shall go. Go ahead, Jason. Thou dost not also wish to incur Black Donal's wrath by starving thyself, dost thou?"

Jason stood but was uncertain. "But, Black Donal did say—"

"Aye, aye, I know full well what he said!" the hunter broke in impatiently. "But he also bade thee eat, and eat thou shalt, if thou dost not wish to anger him. Come now, men, what can be the problem?" His tone grew reasonable, soothing. "There shall still be two within to guard the girl, and many more without guarding as well. Can you truly think any harm will befall her in the short time in which each of thee dost take his rest and nourishment? God's wounds! Thou'rt as worrying as nettlesome old ladies. I say, cease this foolishness and get thee hence, else I've no choice but to inform Black Donal of thine obstinacy."

Jason sighed unhappily. He hung his head and started for the tent door. "Very well, I'll go."

"Nay, damn it all!" Talbot shot out of his chair and grasped Jason by the shoulder, pulling him back. "I'll go first, God's teeth!" He turned a snarling expression on the hunter. "And I'll be back in ten minutes' time, man. Make certain all is well, or I'll see thee pay dearly!" He stormed from the tent in a fury, leaving Jason rather stunned and Allyn of Sorenthill shaking his head.

The hunter patted Jason on the shoulder and said somewhat overloudly, "Well enough, then, Jason. Well enough. And how has our fair lady been?" He peered over at Margot as he asked this, smiling warmly.

Jason glanced at her, too. "She slept for a time. Art hungry now, my lady? Wouldst like more water?"

Margot shook her head slowly, dully.

The hunter regarded her. "Thou hast removed the cloth, yet she speaks not?"

"Nay, she speaks not," Jason replied sadly.

"A true virtue in a woman." Allyn of Sorenthill

patted Jason's shoulders again, taking hold of them and turning him more fully toward Margot. "She is very beautiful, is she not? Look at those eyes, Jason! Never have I seen eyes such a color! Dost not agree?"

"Aye. They are most beautiful." Jason nodded and gazed deeply into Margot's eyes, while Margot herself watched with interest as the hunter, standing behind Jason, stealthily slipped a hand into one pocket and unsheathed a large hunting knife. With the other hand he kept Jason turned toward her, and all the while he continued to speak, loudly, smoothly, hypnotically.

"They are blue as cornflowers, are they not, Jason? As blue and lovely as a whole field of cornflowers. A man could lose himself in such eyes, Jason lad. He could verily lose himself."

"That he could, Allyn of—"

The heavy handle of the knife came down on Jason's head with a dull thunk, and Jason crumpled accordingly into a limp mass.

Although Margot could not help drawing in a sharp gasp, she managed to keep from screaming, and stared in silent horror as the hunter dragged Jason's body to one corner of the tent. Still he kept talking, loud and cheerfully.

"She appears distressed by our attentions, lad, so we needs must let her be. Come, sit with me and let me tell thee of my home at Sorenthill. I've never told thee of it before, have I?"

A quiet ripping at the back of the tent was the reply, and Margot pulled her eyes from the terrible spectacle of the hunter's machinations with Jason to see what this new sound meant. A knife had rent the back tent wall apart, from top to bottom, a quick and sudden slashing. A huge man, cloaked and hooded, stepped through the opening, sheathing his knife as he did so.

Eric.

He and Allyn of Sorenthill nodded to each other while the hunter continued his monologue.

"Ah, lad, Sorenthill is every man's dream of heaven, I tell thee. I'faith, I doubt there is another part of England so fair as that."

Eric lost no time in crossing to the cot on which she lay. His eyes, so dark beneath the hood, stared into hers as he took her up in his powerful embrace.

"In the summer 'tis warm and tender," boomed Allyn of Sorenthill. "In the fall 'tis golden as the king's very crown. In the winter 'tis mild, yet pure and white as the Blessed Virgin herself."

Eric carried her into the cool, dark night without delay, waiting for the hunter only long enough so that Margot could see the bodies of four guards lying on the ground.

"And in the spring, why, Jason, in the spring 'tis as though God Himself had come down from the heavens to bless the land."

He started for the dense shadows of the trees nearby and Margot heard Allyn of Sorenthill sliding through the tent opening to follow them. Eric held her safe and tight as he stealthily traversed the forest, and Margot allowed herself to feel relief at being in

his arms again. She would have hugged him if she
could, if her hands had not been tied. As it was she
pressed her face against the familiar hardness of his
chest, feeling at once the rapid pounding of his heart.
He hugged her more tightly and kissed the top of her
head, but said nothing. Allyn of Sorenthill, running
beside them to keep up with Eric's long strides, was
silent as well.

In a few minutes they reached a clearing, where
Jaufre waited with three horses. No words broke the
silence as they mounted, Eric pulling Margot up
into the saddle in front of him without assistance.
He turned her securely into his arms, so that he cradled her against himself, and they set off without
delay, riding as hard and fast as the horses could be
persuaded.

17

Minna cried out with relief when Eric finally carried Margot into their tent.

"Margot! Oh, thank God! Margot!" She threw her arms around her mistress, whom Eric had set on her sleeping pallet.

Exhausted and still tied, Margot raised her swollen hands and gently touched Minna's hair. Minna sobbed and sobbed, and Eric took the opportunity to remove his hooded cloak, heedlessly dropping it to the ground. He knelt before the women and placed one large hand on Minna's shoulders.

"'Tis all right, Lady Minna. Thy lady is with thee again, safe and well. 'Tis all right."

Minna threw herself at him. "I thank thee, my lord. I thank thee with all my heart!"

Eric returned the unexpected embrace with one arm, and Margot watched the display taking place over her lap with detachment, as though she were not present. Eric's other hand, his free one, snaked its way to her hip, and rested there warmly, squeezing slightly. Margot only stared at it.

"F-forgive me, Sir Eric," Minna stammered, wiping her tear-stained face. "I was overcome to see my lady safe again."

"I understand," Eric assured her. "I am likewise relieved to have the lady Margot safe again." He glanced at Margot, then returned his gaze to Minna. "My lady, I know 'tis much to ask of thee, as thou wilt be anxious to tend thy mistress, but wouldst leave us for a moment?"

Margot clutched Minna's arm as best she could and shook her head violently. Minna stared at her with wide eyes. Eric forcibly turned Minna to look at him.

"Only for a moment." His own fingers unlatched Margot's from Minna's arm as he lifted the latter to her feet. "Please, Minna," he whispered, practically carrying her to the door.

"But," Minna protested, as Eric set her through the opening.

"I'll keep her safe. I swear I shall," Eric vowed, pushing Minna all the way out. "And I think Aleric might be happy to see thee for a few minutes, as well."

Minna evidently went away, for Eric alone turned back within the tent. He approached Margot slowly and knelt before her once more. With a gentle hand he drew forward her bound wrists, pulled his knife out and cut away her bonds.

"I should beat thee, as I promised," he said quietly, not looking at her, "for leaving thy tent unescorted last eve."

It was true that she had left her tent alone. But she had left it in order to find him, something which she could not now understand.

When the ropes finally fell from her wrists, Margot gasped, much as she had when her gag had been removed. Overwhelmed with relief, she closed her eyes and let her head fall back, bringing her wrists out of Eric's grasp to turn them freely. Only a moment passed before he grabbed them again, pulling them ferociously up to his mouth.

"God, Margot!" he whispered fiercely, pressing her sore wrists against his lips. "Thou canst never know what I went through, knowing thou wast gone!" He kissed every inch of the red lines that swelled around her hands, and when he had finished he soothed them with his tongue.

With difficulty, making no reply, Margot pulled from his tender ministrations and met his questioning gaze with her own direct one. Eric lowered his eyes and picked up his knife again to cut the ropes from her feet. She felt the same rush of release, but this time made no show of it. He tossed the rope aside, and then his strong fingers came back to massage away the pain. She turned her head.

"Margot," he said, his hands and fingers loving her with tenderness as they continued massaging. "Wilt thou not even speak to me?"

She did not look at him, did not speak to him, did not acknowledge him in any way.

Everything about him stilled, and Margot could feel the tension within him. Then his hands left her ankles and his fingers began to run, softly, up and down the calves of her legs. Up and down they went, several times, finally resting beneath her knees, squeezing lightly. They stayed thus only a few seconds, and then he pulled away, standing up and away from her entirely.

"'Tis well," he announced with sudden coldness. "I'd just as soon not hear thy stammering. Thou knowest full well how I hate the sound of it."

She looked at him then and saw that he was standing rigidly, his hands clenching and unclenching into fists. Their eyes met and held, hers filled with angry tears, his with remorse. Finally he turned and left, plunging through the tent opening as though escaping a raging fire.

Later, as Margot sat and spoke quietly with Minna, who had returned as soon as Eric had left, Thomas entered the tent.

"Thomas," Margot said, surprised and pleased by the sight of the boy. She held out one hand and Thomas moved toward her, coming into her embrace willingly. "'Tis glad I am to s-see thee."

His bony arms refused to return the embrace, though he readily leaned into her. He tucked his face into the space between her neck and shoulder and he stayed thus, all his weight pressed into her.

"My master brought thee back safe," the boy stated matter-of-factly.

Margot smiled and replied, "Aye, that he d-did, Thomas."

He pushed away and studied her. "Dost thou love Sir Eric?" he asked.

Margot was shocked, but nodded and answered honestly, "Aye, I do love him."

"Then why wilt thou not speak with him?"

Her heart lurched, and she put a gentle hand on the boy's solemn cheek. "He does not l-love me in return, Thomas, and 'tis n-not easy to speak w-w-with him when I kn-know this."

Thomas shook his head. "Thou'rt wrong, my lady. He does love thee."

"Nay, he does not, Thomas. He t-told me s-so."

"Thomas, the lady Margot is very tired now," Minna admonished. "Thou must not tease her."

"I tease thee not!" Thomas replied sternly, pulling from Margot's grasp. "Sir Eric loves thee!" He was angry, nearly shouting. "He told me so, and if thou dost call him a liar I'll ne'er—I'll ne'er speak to thee again!"

"B-but, Thomas," Margot countered, reaching out to pull him gently close again, "thou didst hear him with th-thine own ears! Thou wast present when he t-told me of his distaste for my speech."

"He meant not what he said to thee then," Thomas insisted, letting Margot put her arms around him. In an unusual show of affection, the boy took one hand and placed it on Margot's hair, stroking clumsily to express his distress and love. "He told me afterward that he loves thee, that he loves thee more than his own life, and more than anyone or anything else."

Margot stiffened. Her hands, arms, legs, everything, became paralyzed. Yet Thomas continued his stroking. His skinny hand and fingers tangled through her hair while his other hand clutched her arm.

"Please believe me," he pleaded. "He *did* tell me he loved thee. He said he was only mean to thee because he loved thee so well."

"Oh, dear!" Minna exclaimed, flushing and looking a little embarrassed. "Aleric remarked something very similar after Sir Eric said those awful things to thee. He said his brother was only trying to drive thee from him so thou wouldst wed one of his brothers, Sir Jaufre or the eldest, Sir James."

Margot stared at her.

"And when Sir Eric returned this morn and found thee missing, he was in such a state," Minna rushed on. "He and Sir Jaufre had the most dreadful fight!"

Thomas nodded in earnest agreement. "Aye, that they did, my lady. Almost came to blows, they did. Sir Jaufre was full angry with my master, and shouted all manner of insults at him."

"Thomas, he did not shout insults," Minna admonished. "He merely called Sir Eric some—names."

Margot's eyebrows rose. "Names?" she repeated.

Minna cleared her throat uncomfortably. "Well," she began, "they were rather harsh names, 'tis true, but Sir Jaufre was most angry."

"What d-did Sir Jaufre call his b-brother, exactly?" Margot inquired.

"Cursed idiot. Damned fool. Godforsaken liar." Thomas listed them eagerly.

Margot looked at Minna for confirmation, and her maid only blushed more hotly and nodded.

The implications of these words took a full minute to hit Margot, but when they did she was stunned. Torn between relief and fury, her whole body began to tremble.

"Why that cruel, w-w-wicked, wretched m-man! Ooooohh!" She shot up off the cot and paced toward the tent opening, shaking with rage. "I'll g-get even w-with him f-for this! I w-will. I will!" She turned sharply and fixed Minna with intense, angry eyes. When she spoke again her voice was tightly contained. "Thomas, th-thou m-must leave. I w-wish t-to dress for b-bed."

"I tell thee, Eric, 'twas only the most blessed luck that let us find one another in the forest this afternoon. Canst imagine the confusion had we met trying to rescue the lady Margot at the same time?"

Eric grinned a little sheepishly and rubbed the back of his tired neck with one hand. "We probably would have killed each other right off and only waited to see who the other was 'til too late."

"Aye," said Jaufre, standing beside Aleric, "and what a pretty sight that would have been for Terent's men." He clapped Allyn of Sorenthill on one shoulder and grinned fully at him. "But, by the Rood, man, 'tis glad we are to see thee. I care not if thou wast sent by Sir Walter to keep an eye on the lady Margot and on us. Thou'rt the most welcome of spies."

"Aye, that is true enough," Eric added, chuckling. "So happy was I to see that ugly face of thine I near forgot myself and kissed thee."

"God's bones!" Allyn of Sorenthill grimaced. "Is that the sum of thy gratitude? I'll thank thee to keep thy lips to thyself or to the ladies, more like."

"Amen!" Eric laughed, then turned back to the table at which they had all been standing, looking at the unscrolled map of England. "Come now, enough foolery. Let us have a final understanding of our plan, and let us make certain all know their part."

The men in the crowded tent drew closer, straining to see the map. Three of Eric's most reliable men were present, as well as Jaufre, Aleric, Allyn of Sorenthill, and himself.

"Dost think well of this plan, Sir Allyn?" Eric asked.

"Not as well as I'd like," Allyn admitted honestly, "but we've not time enough to do much else. Black Donal is cunning as a fox, and clever as a sure-footed weasel. Never have I met a man so well sensed as he. Did I not know it to be impossible, I'd swear by God's own teeth that the man had eyes in the back of his head. He'll not be long confused by the false step we gave him, and will shortly reason that we rode back rather than forward."

Eric nodded soberly. "Then Lady Margot and I had best set off without delay."

"Aye. We'll do our best to keep Black Donal confused, but 'twill verily be a miracle if thou'rt indeed able to reach Belhaven without mishap. Thou must take every care, Eric. The slightest slip and all might be lost. I cannot say enough how crafty the man is, or how powerful Terent of Ravinet himself is, and thou must never forget this." Allyn tapped a hard finger on the map. "His eyes are everywhere, man. Everywhere. And his methods are ruthless and dishonorable, as are those of his men, especially Black Donal, whose godless cruelty I have witnessed with my own eyes."

Eric drew in a breath and expelled it slowly through whistling lips. He nodded again. "I understand. I'll not forget."

"Good. Now, we'll meet thee in two days' time at Wickham, to make certain all is well. The confusion of the fair should serve us well, please God, and help to keep the lovely lady and thyself hidden. Stay safe at the Lamb's Head Inn, if thou can. Otherwise leave a message there with Old Mac, the proprietor, to let us know where and how thou art. Old Mac can well be trusted to lend thee aid in any cause, for he once served under my father and proved himself a valuable man. I'll send Thomas to thee if we get there safe, and he'll give thee word on our next direction."

"But Belhaven is only a day's ride from Wickham," Jaufre put in. "Surely once we leave there 'twill be but simple to merely ride hard and make for home."

Allyn of Sorenthill gravely shook his head. "Nay, not at all, Jaufre. From Wickham all our difficulties become worse. Ravinet is also a day's ride from Wickham, though in the opposite direction. 'Twould be an easy thing for Black Donal and his men to way-lay us on that open road leading to Belhaven, for like a cat toying with a mouse, he'll know he has us cornered and that we've no place to go but forward. And 'twould be ideal as well, for he'd not have to carry the lady Margot very far himself, if he can capture her again."

"What can we do then, once we've reached Wickham—*if* we reach Wickham—safely?" Aleric asked, his voice tinged with the nervousness of youth.

"Verily, I haven't a clue, lad," answered Sir Allyn, glancing at Aleric with a comforting grin. "We'll needs must achieve Wickham first, and then think of our next move. Please God to give us one."

"Please God, may Bogo of Brantwell and his family make Wickham safely," Eric murmured, his eyes scanning the map of England. He shook his head and stretched up full height, so much taller than the other men in the tent. "'Twas brave and kind of them to offer to do so much for us."

"Indeed it was," Jaufre agreed. "But they'll make it safe, Eric, never fear. Jace will take good care of them and will find a way to assuage Black Donal's wrath should he stop them and find not the rescued Margot. He's a clever lad, that Jace. More clever than he lets on, i'faith."

"I pray thou'rt right, lad. Indeed, I do pray thou'rt—"

The tent flap swooshed open and someone entered hastily, causing the head of every man present to snap up and see who dared intrude. A general gasp went up, and then all were still and quiet, as though hardly breathing.

The lady Margot stood there, her long golden hair unbound and free, her feet bare, her body covered only by a thin, white robe, and her expression a very fury. She stood with her hands defiantly on her hips and with her feet set apart, causing her robe to fall open in the front and expose her long slender legs from the knees down.

Seven masculine mouths gaped open, and seven pairs of eyes rode over Margot's curvaceous form from top to toe, then back up again, as though they had never seen a woman before and couldn't quite believe it.

With something between a groan and a curse, Eric lunged through the group. Realizing his intent, Margot tried to sidestep him, but Eric easily scooped her up, ignoring her struggles.

"No!" she shouted, hitting his shoulders and chest with her two tiny fists. "P-p-put me d-down!"

He carried her out of the tent.

"Put me d-down!" she insisted angrily.

Eric merely gritted his teeth and strode purposefully toward her tent, walking inside and setting her down roughly on the dirt floor. Before she could escape him he had her by the shoulders, his taut fingers biting into the soft flesh there.

"Art thou crazed?!" he shouted into her face, bending to do it. "Art mad?! What in God's name has taken over thy senses to make thee do such a stupid, foolish, wayward thing?"

Margot faced him down. "W-w-wayward!" she repeated incredulously.

"Aye, wayward! Or wouldst thou prefer sluttish? Whorelike?" He cast about for something particularly good. "Wanton?"

She gasped. "How d-d-dare thee!"

He loosed her. "I dare, my lady," he assured her angrily. "I dare very well, indeed. Dost think men are made of stone? My men are well enough under my command, but even they have a breaking point. Thou'rt beautiful enough to tempt any man to savagery, regardless that he may die for't."

"Every m-man but thee, my l-l-lord," she spat out. "Shoudst thou ever f-feel a d-desire for me, all I should have to d-do would be speak my d-d-devil's tongue and thou wouldst l-leave me b-be!"

"That is more than untrue!" He took hold of her arms again as though to shake her, though all he did was pull her close.

She shook him off furiously, shoving at him. "I c-c-care not!" she shouted. "And I want n-not to hear thine p-p-p, thine p-p-p—"

"Pleadings?" Eric asked.

She shook her head vigorously. "Nay, thine pr-pr-pr—"

Bewildered, he tried, "Prayers?"

"Nay!" She nearly screamed, then hit her thigh

with a fist and said, "Ooooohhhh!" in frustration. Finally, having taken a deep breath and concentrated, she said, slowly and carefully, "Thine protestations. I do n-not wish to hear them. In sooth, I d-do n-not wish to speak to thee at all! I only w-went to thy t-tent to ask thee about m-my father."

He straightened, a little surprised. "About thy father?"

She fixed her steely gaze on him, unwavering. "I w-want the t-truth, Eric. After all that has h-happened, I d-deserve to kn-know. Is my father in d-d-danger?"

He swallowed hard and felt uncomfortable, wishing his anger would come back so that he might hide behind it. He had promised his own father that he would not tell the lady Margot of either the danger in which she stood or of her father's precarious circumstances. Yet he didn't want to lie to her, for surely she would see a lie for what it was, having already been in Black Donal's clutches.

"Aye, Margot," he admitted. "Thy father is in danger, as well art thou." Briefly he explained about Terent's plot, and of how both she and her father figured into it.

When all was said Margot paled and covered her mouth with one shaking hand. "Oh, merciful God! My f-father!"

He tried to take her in his arms but she stubbornly pushed him away. "Thou hast s-said thou dost n-not l-love me," she stated, as though that explained why.

He grappled with the painful urge to contradict her.

"Margot, thy father will be safe as long as thou art safe," he soothed as best he could from a distance, trying to keep his eyes from wandering all over her half-naked body. "If Terent is unable to capture and marry thee, there will be no need for him to harm Sir Walter. Now thou canst understand why 'tis so needful that we get thee to Belhaven as soon as may be."

"Indeed," she agreed heartily. "But why d-do we w-wait? Should we n-not even n-now be riding?"

He nodded, staring helplessly at her impertinent nipples as they peaked through the thin cotton of her robe. He ached just to touch her. "Aye, and we shall be very soon, my lady. In sooth, thou shalt needs prepare thyself right quick, for thou and I shall take our leave of this good company before the hour is out, and shall make our way alone for Wickham."

Very aware of his hot gaze, Margot self-consciously folded her robe a little more tightly around herself, covering her breasts with her forearms.

"As thou c-canst not abide my speech, s-sir," she stated coldly, "I would prefer that S-Sir Jaufre, or even th-that wretched hunter who accosted m-me in my father's forest, accompany me."

"That man whom thou dost say accosted thee is Sir Allyn de Arge, one of the finest knights under the king's command. By thy father's request he agreed to follow behind us, unnoticed, to keep an eye out for thine safety. As to the other," he said, clenching both fists and teeth together, "thou shalt make do with me, my lady, for I'll not trust thy safety to another."

"Bold man! Thou'lt m-make us both suffer for thy v-vanity!"

That was enough, he thought, just before he snapped. The next moment he had Margot wrapped captive in his arms and had forced her mouth back to receive his ungentle, hungry kiss. He did not wait for her acquiescence this time, and he would not go slow but forced his tongue inside the warmth of her mouth to claim what he knew would always be his, regardless whom she wed. He kissed her long and hard, waiting and waiting for the submission which never came.

Unbelievably, she fought him, and it hurt more than his pride to know that she could resist him so.

When finally he let her go, she stumbled back, breathing hard and shaking. She stared at him in disbelief, as though he had raped her, and pointed a trembling finger toward the door.

"G-g-go!" she stammered.

He wiped his mouth with the back of his hand and nodded. "Get thee ready to leave, Lady Margot. I'll come for thee in a half hour's time." Then he started for the opening, only to be stopped by Margot's tight voice.

"One m-more thing, Sir Eric S-Stavelot of Belhaven!" she said angrily. "If thou hast th-thought to r-rid thyself of me with th-thine insults, thou'rt f-fully wrong!"

He turned at the tent flap and looked at her, standing

there so beautiful in her fury, as beautiful as a new
blazing fire. "I l-love thee s-still," she announced
loudly, wiping the back of her own mouth for good
measure and because he had done it, and adding, "G-
God help me. And I'll m-marry thee one d-day, t-too!
Best set thy m-mind to that, m-man, for 'tis certain as
the s-sun rising in the m-morning sky!"

For many years to come, indeed, for all of his life,
Eric was to remember this vision of Margot, standing
so beautifully righteous in her state of half-undress,
her golden hair falling all around her like a shining
curtained halo and her sweet face so ridiculously set.

"Just get thee ready," he whispered, which was not
at all what he wanted to say.

She answered nothing in return, only looked at
him with her fists clenched, and, unable to say anything else, Eric turned himself around and walked
away.

18

They left a few hours before dawn, riding cautiously until the first glimmer of sunlight encouraged them to pick up their pace. The forested countryside gave way to mostly open fields by midday, and Margot felt thoroughly exposed and vulnerable, but Eric, riding beside her, seemed so sure and at ease that she tried to put the feelings aside.

They did not speak as they rode, except for the few instructions Eric gave her regarding course and speed. When they took a few minutes to water and rest their steeds, they were both on a constant lookout, too aware of the danger of their situation to engage in conversation. Not that Margot would have talked to him anyway. In fact, she was sure that, regardless of their circumstances, she would not do so. She was still much too angry to talk to him. Yet.

That night, exhausted and hungry, when the darkness made it impossible for them to continue, Eric took her horse by the reins and led them toward a small group of half-timbered buildings, just off the main road, which looked to Margot like the dwellings and outbuildings of some local lord's vassals, for they were similar to the dwellings of her own father's vassals.

Several stout men came out of the main dwelling to meet them or to scare them off; Margot could not be sure. When Eric dismounted they all took one glance at his height and breadth and grew amazingly meek. Eric took pains to be polite and soft-spoken with these men and with the women and children who soon filed out into the yard to see the giant. He explained that he and his wife required lodging for the night. They were full weary, he said, having ridden so hard all day, and could go no farther in the darkness in search of a nearby town. They had money and would pay whatever price was asked, even if they should be required to sleep in the stables.

The leader of this clan approached Eric and stared steadily up at him. "My name is Michael of Dunleavy," the man stated in a harsh, gravelly voice. "And this is my family, and my family's family." With a jerk of his chin he indicated the crowd of onlookers standing behind him. "Our overlord is Vincent of Calvelroy. What is thy name, sir?"

Eric made a half-bow first to Michael of Dunleavy and then one in the direction of his family. "I am pleased to meet thee, Michael of Dunleavy, and also thy family, and thy family's family. I am Eric of Belhaven, and this is my wife, Margot." He nodded toward Margot, who submissively pulled the hood from her head to expose her face and was greeted with low whistles and expressions of awe.

Michael of Dunleavy considered Eric for a full, hard minute, then turned his piercing gaze on Margot, who shifted uncomfortably beneath his scrutiny. In the end he returned his gaze to Eric, settling it on him stonily. His face tipped down as he took in Eric's finely made suit of chain mail, as well as the coat of arms embroidered on his wide tunic.

"Thou'rt a knight of the realm, then, Eric of Belhaven?"

"I am."

"Didst fight on the side of King Henry at Shrewsbury, of late?"

"Aye, I did so."

Michael of Dunleavy nodded curtly. "'Tis well enough. Thy wife and thee art welcome in my home. Come inside and sit at table with us. We'll be honored to break bread with thee." He turned and spoke gruffly into the crowd of relatives. "John! Simon! Take their horses and stable them."

Eric reached up to lift Margot down, and she was so relieved at being able to rest and eat that she nearly cried. Eric put one warm arm around her waist to lead her into the dwelling.

"And make certain to feed and water the beasts!" Michael of Dunleavy shouted at the two boys who led the horses away. "And rub them down well before blanketing them!" He fell in beside Eric and Margot as they walked toward the two-story manse where the rest of the family had already returned to make preparations. "Young fools!" he muttered as he strode beside them.

Eric smiled down at the man and hugged Margot's waist. "We are most grateful to thee, Michael of Dunleavy, for opening thy home to us. In sooth, we are bone weary."

They stopped at the entrance to the house, and Michael of Dunleavy turned to look at them, causing them to stop as well. He studied mostly Margot, who was so tired that her head seemed only to be capable of falling complacently against Eric's hard chest. First Michael of Dunleavy nodded, then he snorted and shook his head, and finally he gave Eric a hard look. "Aye, thou'rt both well and weary, lad. Though what maggot has taken to thy brain to make thee drag thy good lady so far out at night I cannot say. But come in, children, and make thyselves warm and full, for thou'rt as welcome here as in thine own homes."

"God b-bless thee, M-Michael of Dunleavy." Margot yawned as Eric led her in.

What passed after that was like a blur to Margot. The family of Michael of Dunleavy, and his family's family, other than Dunleavy himself, were a very happy, warm group of people. There seemed to be more than thirty in all, between sons and their wives, and daughters and their husbands, and the children and grandchildren. They all sat down together, more

or less, at a large oak table in the midst of the main
hall, and feasted on herb-roasted pheasant and goose,
boiled fish smothered in an onion wine sauce, lemon
rice with almonds, fried squash, sallet mixed with
mustard and sugar, good carob bread, and finally
lentil-and-berry-filled pears. All this was washed
down with plenty of ale and wine, and as the dinner
progressed all those present grew merrier and merrier, including Eric, who refused nothing and ate and
drank everything. Within a short time he was fully
inducted into the Dunleavy family and seemed as
comfortable with them as he would with his own people. Margot, too tired and too self-conscious of her
speech, didn't join in quite as much. She gratefully
ate her fill of the delicious food, however, and drank
two glasses of wine, after which she felt so relaxed
that she threatened to drift into slumber at any
moment.

"Come, my dear," a soft voice came beside her,
causing her to look up and find Leatie, the wife of
Michael of Dunleavy, standing next to her chair,
"thou dost look most weary. Come and I shall draw a
nice, hot bath for thee to soothe thyself in."

That sounded wonderful to Margot, who hadn't
had a bath since leaving Reed, other than the cloth
baths she and Minna had taken each morn. She
glanced at Eric, who grinned at her and squeezed her
hand.

"Go on," he insisted. "I'll join thee later."

Two of Leatie's daughters had joined their mother
and Margot rose and went with them willingly. Soon

enough she found herself in one of the comfortable upstairs chambers and sitting in a wonderful, hot, towel-lined tub of water. She almost fell asleep in the tub, but Leatie and her girls came to help her dress for bed before that happened.

"Thou'rt s-saints," Margot declared sincerely, "or angels, even, for thou hast treated s-strangers as k-kindly as friends. May God bless thee all thy d-days!"

Leatie patted her shoulders in a motherly fashion. "There, my dear, thou must not thank us so. 'Tis glad we are to give thy fine husband and thee a place for the night. 'Tis an honor."

They left after that, leaving the tub filled for Eric to use should he wish it, and Margot, exhausted, crawled into the soft feather bed.

She did not know she had been asleep until she was awakened by the sounds of water lapping, as though someone were gently dipping a hand in and out of a still forest pond. She stretched, taking a moment to remember where she was and why, and then she turned toward the source of the sound to peer through the dim room, now lit only by one feeble candle.

She squinted through the darkness, first, at what she thought she saw, then rubbed her eyes to make certain. Eric was there, sitting in the tub, the majority of his naked body hanging out of it. His massive chest was thoroughly exposed, as were his muscular arms, and his long, firm legs were clumsily set so far out of the tub that his feet actually touched the floor.

Shocked, Margot pushed into a sitting position, staring at Eric with wide, fully awake eyes. Eric stared back, totally horrified, his deep blush of embarrassment visible even in the dim light.

"Margot I—I did not mean to wake thee," he said, croaking. "Forgive me." He cleared his throat and self-consciously tried to cover some of his chest by crossing his arms. The hand that held the washing cloth surreptitiously dropped into his lap. "I shall take care to be, uh, more quiet, and I'll be finished in only another moment so—so thou canst go back to sleep—Margot." This last came out as pleading.

Margot ignored him. Strangely, the more she surveyed him the shorter she felt of breath and, in an effort to relieve the tightness in her chest and throat, she loosened the laces at the neck of her night shift.

"Thou'rt s-so beautiful, Eric," she whispered, wondering why she should feel warmer and warmer even though she had loosened her laces.

"Margot," he said, begging now, "please, get thee back to bed."

She shook her head. "I do not th-think I could s-sleep."

He sighed with exasperation. "Well, if thou canst not sleep, at least lie down and keep thy back turned. This water is cold. Wilt make me stay here the whole night?"

She grinned wickedly. "When we are w-wed, my Eric, I shall t-take the greatest of p-pleasure in helping thee to b-bathe."

The sound of her calling him 'my Eric' again, after

so much hurt and anger had passed betwen them made Eric tremble with relief and joy. And her meaningful promise of helping him to bathe made his already excited body only spring that much more to life. But, stranded as he was in the tub, his need to repel her seemed doubly important, at least at the moment.

"We shall never wed, Margot," he returned testily. "Hast already forgotten my dislike of thy speech?"

Her expression momentarily saddened, but she didn't become angered as he thought she would. She did, however, lie down and turn away from him.

"We shall be w-wed, my Eric, and if thou d-dost truly hate my speech then th-thine l-life shall be a misery, I suppose."

He rose from the bath carefully, covering himself with a drying cloth as quickly as he could in case she should change her mind and suddenly turn. It wasn't so much that he minded being seen naked, but to be seen naked in such an aroused state was beyond endurance.

"And thou hast already t-told these fine p-people that I am thy w-wife," she pointed out, speaking to the wall she faced.

That was true enough, Eric thought, rapidly pulling his chausses on. The worst part was, not only had he lied to Michael of Dunleavy and his family about Margot being his wife, he had gloried in the lie, letting himself believe and enjoy it for as long as he could. It had been a wonderful, amazing thing, to boast on his beautiful wife after she had retired to bed, to answer all of the exclamations over her beauty with calm, possessive agreement. Boasted! By the Rood, he'd done more than that! He'd bragged on and on about her excellent qualities, about her charm and faithfulness, and of her exquisite, unbounding love.

"Some lies are necessary, my lady," he countered, running his fingers through his still wet hair, "though never desired." He contemplated the bed for a moment, thinking how small it was. His own bed at home had been specially made for him, his father having ordered Belhaven's best carpenters and craftsmen to fit it to his unusual size and length, and his mother and sister having sewn the extra long and wide mattress for it. But this bed was barely big enough for two regular sized people, let alone one of him, and Margot already occupied her rightful half of it.

"I s-suppose thou'rt r-right, Eric," she agreed wistfully, yawning a little. "Though 'twas n-nice indeed to hear thee n-name me thy wife. Still, I d-do think I should m-make an honest m-man of thee, and so, one day, I shall."

He said nothing to this, but blew out the candle, throwing the room into darkness. In another moment Margot unexpectedly felt the bed dip beneath his weight, and she turned over and sat up again.

"Eric! Wh-what art thou d-doing?!"

"Preparing to sleep," he replied sheepishly, drawing the covers over himself. "There is no place for me on the floor, and no extra covers with which to keep myself warm. And there is every chance that Michael of Dunleavy or one of his might come to fetch us in the morn. Wouldst wish to expose our lie by letting them find one of us asleep in the bed and the other on the floor? Besides," he added, "I'll not touch thee during the night, Margot. Thou hast no need to worry o'er that."

He took up so much of the bed, and his weight dipped the mattress so heavily, that Margot had long since rolled helplessly against the warmth of his half-naked body, her mouth plastered against his ribcage while he said these words. She struggled against the force of gravity, having to place one hand on his chest to do so, until she could speak more directly toward his face.

"When we are w-wed, my Eric, I shall more than w-willingly sleep with thee, but I c-cannot think it a good idea at the m-moment."

Realizing the discomfort of her position, Eric reached one hand down to grasp her beneath the arm, inadvertently brushing the curve of one full breast as he did so. Finally finding the port he sought, he deftly pulled her upward until she was tucked beneath his arm, her head on his shoulder. He hugged her like that, one arm around her waist, his large hand carefully finding a resting place above her hip.

"I'll not touch thee," he repeated emphatically, "and no one else shall ever hear of our spending the night together in this same room and bed."

She lay stiff as a board against him for several long, silent minutes, while her conscience struggled with her desires. There was no doubt whatsoever in her mind that it was wrong, very, very wrong to sleep in the same bed with a man before one was married to him, yet at the same time it was undeniably pleasant to lie thus against her beloved, to feel the warmth of his naked skin beneath her face and hands, to be able to feel that warmth burning all the way through the thin cotton of her night shift, so that she could almost imagine what it might be like to lie equally naked with him.

He turned his head and sniffed her still-damp hair.

"We both smell like roses," he whispered, and she could feel him smile against the top of her head.

Helplessly, she giggled. "Leatie put oil of roses in the b-bathwater. I only w-wish Jaufre was here to t-tease thee for it."

He chuckled out loud. "God be thanked he's not! He would tease, too, e'en when I could not possibly be blamed for wanting to rid myself of more than four-days' filth!"

"Nay, thou c-couldst not," she agreed, running one gentle hand slowly over the breadth of his chest, her fingers feeling the tickle of the black, curling hair upon it. He grasped her hand quickly.

"Stop that," he whispered, trembling a little.

They were silent again, their uneven breathing the only audible sounds in the room, and they lay perfectly still, unwilling to risk an inadvertent caress.

Margot broke the silence at last.

"Eric? D-dost think we m-may have drawn M-Michael of Dunleavy and his f-family into our t-troubles?"

He squeezed her hand slightly and sighed. "I hope not, Margot. Indeed, I have wondered the same thing o'er and o'er since we arrived. 'Twould be unwant repayment of their kindess should Black Donal or any of his seek us here. Please God all will be well 'til we leave this place."

"Aye, indeed," Margot agreed, then added, "Does every person c-come to love thee so w-well, my Eric? Is there n-no one whom thou hast n-not befriended?"

"Why, what dost thou mean, my lady?"

"Everyone, all whom w-we have m-met since leaving Reed, all c-come to love thee so well. We were strangers t-to these f-fine people who hath so k-kindly taken us in, yet at table this eve they d-did quickly come to l-love thee, as though thou wast their own s-son and brother."

He shrugged slightly, jostling her head a little with the movement. "They are good people, that is all. They would be inclined to love any poor, hungry soul, I vow. Their kindness to me has been no more nor less than their kindness to thee."

"True, b-but they did l-look at thee most longingly, my Eric, as though they w-would like to keep thee for their own." She sighed. "I s-suppose I needs m-must grow used to such admiration as thou w-wilt have from thy fellow b-beings, as thou'lt no d-doubt continue such c-conquests once we are wed."

"Margot," he said soberly, "never shall we be wed. Thou must cease saying so. What has happened to thy fury of yesterday, and even of today? Hast forgotten that I love thee not?"

She shook her head against his chest. "I forget n-nothing thou didst s-speak to me that night, for thou d-didst hurt me m-more then than any other has ever done. Black D-Donal himself could never hurt m-me so badly. But thou d-dost love me, my Eric, even if thou wilt n-not admit it. One d-day thou shalt tell me s-so, though I d-do hope 'twill be s-sooner than later. I should hate to b-befall an accident and d-die before hearing those sweet words."

His hand moved up to bury itself in her hair. "Never speak of thy death to me," he whispered fiercely.

Margot ignored him. "As to my f-fury, why, I am still m-most angered with thee. Faith, I intend to be angry for s-sometime. At l-least 'til we reach Belhaven. And I am s-so angered with thee that I'll n-not e'en let thee kiss me good eve."

His hand dropped from her hair. "I was not planning on kissing thee good eve," he lied. In fact, while she spoke he'd been wondering whether he might be able to maneuver her into a kissable position and still be able to make it appear a complete accident. "Or at any other time. Thou'rt vain as well as fanciful, my lady, to think I should wish to kiss such a one as thee."

"Well, thou m-mayest not do so even if thou d-didst wish it," she replied without offense, yawning. She closed her eyes and snuggled against him to get more comfortable, causing him to groan. Her ear rested upon his chest. "How thy heart doth b-beat, my Eric! It pounds as r-rapidly as a falcon's wings in f-flight."

Good Lord! he thought, wondering what madness had ever possessed him to think that he could possibly sleep in the same bed with such a soft, sweet woman without making love to her. His heart wasn't the only part of his body that was pounding away at present, or, more accurately, throbbing away. Never in his life had he wanted to love a woman more than he wanted to love Margot now, and he wondered if he dared to fall asleep lest he fulfill his desires in a weakened, half-conscious state.

"Get thee to sleep, Margot," he commanded gruffly.

"Aye," she murmured, half-asleep already, "that I shall. I am m-most weary. Good night, my Eric. I l-love thee so."

"Good night, Margot," he whispered, grateful when the room fell into silence.

Her breath soon fell steady and even on his neck like soft, tender caresses, and her body relaxed into his, molding against him. Only when he was certain she was fully asleep did he let his own body relax.

A few long, deep breaths helped to steady him, to slow the pace of his still rapidly beating heart. God, how he loved her! He never could have believed it possible, but the wretched feeling seemed to get worse and worse every day, growing as a tiny seed grows into a mighty tree. It was as a sickness, a terrible, all-consuming sickness that ate and ate at him until he felt weak and powerless as a babe. He wondered if there weren't some potion he might take to cure himself. Perhaps when he got back to Belhaven he would visit the local leech and see what could be done. *Something* must be done, and quickly, for at the rate he was going he would soon be reduced to a slavering mass at Margot's beautiful feet.

And, hopefully, if all went well, they would be at Belhaven soon. Soon. Aye. And soon Margot would be wedding one of his brothers. What a wretched thought. What would he do, he wondered, when that day finally came? Perhaps he would not be able to bear it; perhaps he would have to leave. Yes. That was what he would do. He would leave. He would tell his father that he had decided to do some journeying and would ask to be released from his vow of service for a few months' time. Father would make him wait until at least the wedding day, most like, but if he could somehow make it through that he would be able to leave directly after the ceremony was over. He would never be able to sit through the wedding feast and watch as one of his brothers was carried up to Margot's chamber for the consummation of the marriage. No. That was asking too much. He would not be able to do it.

Just thinking of another man, even one of his own brothers, touching Margot made him grip her more possessively. But he was unaware of how his anger made his hold on her a painful one, until she sleepily whimpered in protest and squirmed in his grasp. He loosened it immediately and turned his head so that he could place a gentle kiss on her forehead.

"I am sorry," he whispered. "Go back to sleep now."

She sighed and cuddled against him again, this time pulling one knee up over his legs. Eric smiled and started rubbing her hip again.

What an odd thing it was to sleep with a woman without making love to her. In sooth, he had never done it before, for even on those occasions when he had taken a woman to his bed she had only stayed long enough for the pleasure, and then left. At Belhaven it was because the serving maids who usually sought him out didn't want to be caught out of the servants' quarters in the middle of the night. Away from home, with whores or willing village girls, it was either because there was the potential for more money to be made that night or out of fear of being found out by a strict father. However it was, he had never slept a full night with a woman in his arms, and it was a strange, oddly comfortable thing. Margot's body was soft and warm pressed up against his. She felt good to touch and to hold; he didn't even want to let himself start thinking about how good it would feel to be able to turn her over onto her back, cover her with his own body, and come inside her.

With a slight shake of his head, he forced that particularly stunning image from his mind.

He should have sent Jaufre with her. That's what he should have done. Jaufre was a good man and a well-trained fighter, both stealthy and sharp-witted when danger arose. He surely would have been able to keep Margot as safe as he, himself, could. Perhaps better, even, for he did seem to bear tender feelings for the lady.

He *should* have sent Jaufre. All would have been well had he done so, and even now it would have been Jaufre lying here with Margot, his arm snug around her tiny waist, his hand caressing the soft swell of her hips—

In his fury, Eric started gripping Margot too tightly again.

"Eric!" she cried out sleepily.

"Forgive me, sweet babe," he whispered. "I'll not do't again. Hush now, and get thee back to sleep."

She muttered something indistinguishable, but eventually relaxed. Eric let out a breath and stared into the darkness. No, he shouldn't have sent Jaufre, and he was damned glad he hadn't. Soon enough, in no more than two days' time, he would be parted forever from this woman whom he would love all his days. Two short days he would have in which to enjoy her, in which to have her all to himself. Two days which must last him a whole, long lifetime.

"I do love thee, Margot," he whispered into the still, cool air.

She neither responded nor moved but only continued to breathe against him, slowly, deeply, steadily.

Eric pressed his lips against the silken fall of hair on her forehead once more before finally closing his own eyes.

It was hardly light enough to see by when they were abruptly wakened the next morning. Two loud raps at the door and a whole group of women barged in on them.

"Up! Up! My lord and lady! Up, I say!"

It was Leatie shouting at them, her tone filled with urgency and fear. She strode directly to the one set of shutters in the room and flung them wide, letting what little light there was come into the room along with the dawn chill.

A long-hardened soldier, Eric opened his eyes and sat up as though the call to arms had been sounded. Along the way he unceremoniously dumped Margot onto the mattress, whom he had only moments before been cuddling as closely and tenderly as a child might cuddle a doll. Having been thus rudely tossed aside, Margot woke, too.

Eric rubbed his eyes while Margot struggled into a sitting position. What they saw stunned them.

Several of Leatie's daughters were gathering up all of their belongings and throwing them out the open window, while Leatie herself approached them, wringing her hands.

"I am so sorry, my lady, my lord, for having disturbed thee thusly, but there are several men outside, on horseback, who have only just arrived. They demand to know whether we have seen a beautiful, fair-haired lady of late, and if so, when and in what direction. My husband has told them naught, my lord, and is doing his best below to keep them at bay. But I fear they mean to search the place, and will find thee lest we hide thee right quick."

In a swift, fluid movement Eric threw the covers

aside and stepped out of the bed, pulling Margot along with him. She stumbled out, hardly awake enough to realize anything except that Black Donal had finally arrived to take them away.

"Leatie," he began, but she cut him off.

"There is no time to waste, my lord! Thou must come with me. Now!"

One of her daughters tossed Eric his tunic and he slipped into it, grateful that he'd had the forethought to wear his chausses to bed. Margot was covered only by her thin night shift and they were both barefoot, but that could not be helped now.

"Michael, get undressed and into the tub!" one of the daughters instructed her little son, who obediently began pulling his clothing off. Two other daughters continued throwing things out the window, including Eric's heavy chain mail.

"My armor!" he objected with horror.

"The devil take thine armor!" Leatie nearly screamed at him. "'Tis thine lives thou must think of now!"

He knew she was right and began to follow her, grabbing Margot's hand and pulling her along, but he could not keep from giving a whimper of dismay when he saw his beloved sword go the way of his armor.

Leatie ran down the stairs toward the main hall, with Eric and Margot behind her. When Margot stumbled Eric pulled back and lifted her into his arms, then raced after Leatie again. She stopped in the middle of the room, where two of her sons had pulled the rushes back to reveal a small cellar opening in the dirt floor. The whole Dunleavy family, save Michael of Dunleavy and his remaining sons, stood in a circle, watching with wide, nervous eyes.

"Here!" Leatie motioned frantically into the cellar. "In here! There is not much space, but enough, please God!"

Eric stepped into the opening, holding Margot tight in his arms. Indeed there was not much space. Four laddered steps were all there were to this earthen cellar, and he quickly crouched into it, squatting so that Margot sat in his lap, then he squashed his overlarge body and head into what remained of the cramped space. He was crushing Margot with his weight, he knew, but she said nothing, only put her arms about his neck and hugged tight. Soon enough a wooden board was set over their heads and the rushes were put back in place, covering them with complete darkness.

"Be thou not afraid," he whispered to Margot, wishing the harsh sounds of his own excited breathing would lessen. "Try to stay calm and breathe slowly." His mouth was against her cheek, while hers was against his neck.

"I sh-shall, my Eric," she murmured in return, and he felt her heart respond to the the erratic thrashing of his. "I am n-never afraid wh-when I am w-with thee." Her worsened stammer gave proof to the lie, but he was glad to hear the words.

"Shoud aught befall us, Margot. Whatever it may be," he said, then gulped so loudly that he thought everyone in the room must hear it, "I want thee to know that I love thee. I do love thee. With all my heart."

She gave a sudden sob and hugged him all the more tightly. "I kn-know, my Eric. I kn-know thou d-dost. J-just as I l-love thee."

He found her mouth with his own then, in that gravelike darkness, and kissed her ferociously.

"All that I spoke of thy speech—all those damnable words! 'Twas all lies! Lies!"

"Hush, love. I already kn-know thou d-didst not mean those things."

"Margot, I love thee. I love thee," he insisted before kissing her again. It was such a redemption to admit his love that he was overwhelmed by it, by the relief that swelled in him, and he wanted to break through the shroud that covered them and shout his joy to the world. Only the sounds of many men marching through the front door of the dwelling stopped him and pulled his deliriously happy mind back to reality.

Michael of Dunleavy's voice could be heard above the others, indignant and angry. "This is an outrage! I'll have my lord Calvelroy informed of't soon as thou hast gone, by God I shall!"

"Do that, old man," came a surly response, "and welcome. We'll not be here to answer thy lord's wrath. Search the dwelling!" the same voice commanded loudly, and a great scampering of feet came overhead.

"I'll not have it, I say!" Michael of Dunleavy announced, and a struggle ensued.

Enough time passed before the surly voice came again. "Thou'lt have it, old man, or see thy family suffer for thine obstinacy. Thou hast some pretty daughters here, I vow, and e'en thy lady-wife has much appeal, at least to such a one as I, and neither I nor my men have had the pleasure of a lady's company in a long, long while. Now." A chair was thrown aside with a great clattering. "We can either search thy abode in peace or enjoy thy women in distress. 'Tis neither one nor t'other to me." A silence followed, during which Eric could almost envision the expressions of the men hoping that Michael of Dunleavy would prove stubborn, but the next thing that Eric heard was, "Enough, then." And, more loudly, "Search well, men. Let no place be left uncovered."

They held their breaths as feet tramped above and directly over their heads, and they both began to sweat, heating up the small, damp earthen space almost more than they could bear.

"That horse in thy stable," said the surly voice, "it seems an unlikely steed for thee to own."

"There are many horses there," came Michael of Dunleavy's defeated voice, a terrible thing to hear. "Of which dost thou speak?"

"Of the giant roan. The destrier. 'Tis a fine steed for any vassal to possess. How camest thou by such a one as that?"

"Oh, God," Eric whispered in torment. "Bram."

Margot's hand crawled up to cover his lips. He gratefully pressed them against her trembling fingers, closing his eyes and willing himself not to react.

"My lord Calvelroy gave't us, for my son Harold," Michael of Dunleavy answered steadily. "Harold means to be a knight."

Harsh laughter followed this, joined by other masculine voices not of the Dunleavy family.

"A son of thine wishes to make himself a knight, does he?" the same voice taunted. "God help him, then, for no good man should wish to have fealty from such a pig as thou hast sown, farmer!" The laughter grew louder, but when this did not ellicit the obviously desired response, the voice added, "And Harold! An odd and Saxon name for a British subject."

"Aye," returned Michael of Dunleavy, suddenly emboldened. "A Saxon name. And what of it?"

"Naught, old man," was the leering reply, "save that no Harold I know of should be allowed such a steed. Mayhap we'll take the beast, as recompense for thy obstinacy. What say thee, men?"

Whatever men were in the room with the hateful voice cheered loudly, and Eric's miserable groan came unbidden from his lips.

"Thou'lt not take that horse," said Michael of Dunleavy, his tone a miracle of iron, "nor any other cattle of mine. If thou dost then thou may as well kill me now, and every member of my family, for not a one shall rest 'til we have thy heads for such evil. Is that not right, children of Dunleavy?"

A chorus of voices, from child to adult, both male and female, pronounced, "Aye."

The surly voice was deadly now. "Threaten me not, old man. I'd just as soon kill thee as not, save I've no time for't. So tempt me not, else I'll find the time."

The trampling of the men returning from their search halted this speech, and again Eric and Margot felt several pairs of heavy, booted feet clomping over them.

"We found naught, my lord," one man reported, "save a wench bathing her brat abovestairs."

"Then we're off. Tell me, old man, who else abides in these parts, southward?"

"None 'til thou hast reached Styne, a village two-hours' ride south. God save them if thou dost mean to have thy way there as thou hast done here!"

The surly man laughed aloud. "Come now, Dunleavy, thou'rt most ungrateful, i'faith! Thou hast thy home and wife and daughters intact, and thy life as well. We are but gentle men doing our duty. See? We shall go as we came, with none the wiser, and thou canst return to thy meal without delay."

The sounds of the men filing out of the house were welcome, indeed, and Margot and Eric sighed in unison.

"I'll still tell my overlord of this outrage!" Michael of Dunleavy promised as he followed the men out. "I'll go to the king himself if I have to!"

"Thou'rt welcome to do so, old man," came the reply along with the sounds of horses being mounted. "Just make certain to bar thy door each night in case of thieves. The next men who enter here may not be as longsuffering as we. Think on't, Michael of Dunleavy. Good day to thee, my lady Dunleavy. I'll see thee in my dreams."

They rode away, making enough noise about it that Eric thought there must have been at least ten men altogether.

A full, silent minute passed before the rushes and boards were lifted off their heads. They both gasped when the fresh, clean air hit them, and then Eric slowly uncrouched and lifted Margot into the waiting arms of the Dunleavy sons. They were both filthy from being in the dirt cellar, and Margot's night shift was more brown than white. One of the sisters put a woolen blanket around her shoulders and Margot clutched it gratefully, glad to cover herself more decently.

Eric hopped out of the space with ease, stood up straight, and began to brush himself off.

"Good friends!" he said with heartfelt gratitude. "How can we thank thee?" He went to Leatie, grasped her hands with both of his and kissed them soundly, then he turned to Michael of Dunleavy and solemnly clasped his arm. "We owe thee our lives, Michael of Dunleavy, and shall ne'er forget thy bravery this day, nor that of thine excellent lady and good family."

If it was possible, which Eric thought it probably was not, Michael of Dunleavy appeared to blush a little. He squeezed Eric's arm in return and reached up to pat him on the shoulder.

"We'll hear none of that, now, lad. 'Twas naught

but what any good Christian folk would have done. There's no need to thank us."

"But we do, most sincerely," Eric insisted, and Margot nodded vigorously from across the room, still clutching her blanket. "And we owe thee an explanation as well."

"Thou owest us naught, Sir Eric of Belhaven," Michael of Dunleavy replied firmly, his voice once again gravelly. "We know thou'rt not criminals, just as we know those men were evil as the Fiend himself."

"Verily, we are not criminals. Of that I give my most solemn vow. But surely thou dost wish some explanation."

Michael of Dunleavy held up his hand and shook his head. "Nay, I do not, and neither does my family, nor my family's family. For whatever reason those men do seek thee, 'tis only for thy lady and thee to know. All I do wish to know is what thou must do now, and how we may help thee to do't. Thou'rt welcome to stay here with us as long as it may please thee to do so."

"We should indeed be pleased to stay with thee, good sir," Eric assured him, "but we cannot. We needs must hie to Wickham and achieve it this eve, if we can. We've friends there who will help us further."

Michael of Dunleavy nodded his understanding. "Then we must waste no more time, lad. Leatie, get the lady Margot abovestairs and into some traveling clothes. Sir Eric," he said, turning his stern gaze on him, "we'd best go see what's left of thine armor."

19

It was a solemn, sad occasion which took place around the pigs' wallow just below the window of the room in which Eric and Margot had spent the night.

Eric stood in front of the deep, muddy wallow, surrounded by the adult Dunleavy males whilst the younger Dunleavy males prodded at the muck with long sticks, doing their best to retrieve everything which had been tossed into it earlier.

Troubled, and a little depressed, Eric stood quietly, one hand absently fingering his brooch. On one side of him stood Michael of Dunleavy, on the other the eldest Dunleavy son, each with one hand resting consolingly on his shoulders.

"'Tis a bad stroke of fate, son," Michael of Dunleavy said sympathetically. "No doubt about it."

His sons nodded in silent agreement.

Eric sighed sadly. A man's armor was a precious thing, but his was more valuable than most, having been specially fitted to his unusual size. He shook his head and turned his eyes upward, toward the window out of which everything had been thrown. Margot was in the room beyond the window at that very moment, being dressed in clothing borrowed from one of Dunleavy's daughters. It was no trouble for her to be fitted with another's clothes, of course, for she was of a regular size, but had Eric himself not already been dressed in his chausses at the time of that morning's intrusion he would have been forced to go naked. Proof of that was his bare feet. If his boots could not be retrieved he would have to go without, for only the cobbler at Belhaven knew how to fit his huge feet just right.

"'Twill be all right, Eric, lad," said Michael of Dunleavy, having heard his sigh. "Why, look there, Lawrence has been the first to find aught."

Sure enough, one of Michael of Dunleavy's young grandsons had hit something with his prod, and now struggled to push it to the mud's surface. When the first hint of what it might be showed, Eric started, then bent and swiftly pulled the object out, not caring that he muddied himself in the process.

"My sword," he breathed, fingering the sharp work lovingly. One of the Dunleavy sons produced a cloth, and Eric wiped the sword with tenderness. "My father gave it me when I was knighted," he explained, his eyes watering up. The Dunleavy men circled him, appreciating the sword and its meaning, their own eyes watering with masculine sympathy.

It took a while, but eventually Eric's boots and armor were retrieved as well, along with a few articles of Margot's clothing. The boots were washed out and Eric pulled them on without waiting for them to dry. The armor was too far gone to be able to take with them, but Michael of Dunleavy promised it would be cleaned and cared for with the greatest respect until Eric should be able to return and claim it.

Too soon, it seemed, their horses were saddled, and Margot and Eric were ready to leave.

As Margot made her way through each member of the Dunleavy family, bidding them good-bye, Eric, holding Bram's reins, stood aside with Michael of Dunleavy.

"There is no manner in which we could fully repay thee for thy kindness, Michael of Dunleavy, or for thy family's kindness. Yet," he said, tugging at a small bag he had fortunately left tied to Bram's saddle, which held all their money, "I should like to give thee something for all the trouble we have caused thee."

A hand came out to stop him, and when Eric looked up it was to find Michael of Dunleavy frowning at him. "Wouldst insult me, Eric of Belhaven?" the older man whispered in surprise.

Only a half second passed before Eric responded. "Nay," he said, retying the bag, "I'll not, though still I thank thee, and swear that someday I shall find a way to repay thy kindness."

The Dunleavy family stood and waved as they rode away, and Margot kept turning her head back to look at them until they had ridden out of sight.

They rode hard the first mile, and then Eric slowed and stopped their horses, taking hold of the reins on Margot's horse to keep it still while he spoke.

"We'll ride toward the river aspace, and then along't 'til we reach Wickham. There's no sense taking a chance whilst Black Donal seeks us."

Margot nodded her full agreement of this plan and readily followed as Eric turned his destrier and set off through the nearest field toward the trees again. The mare she rode was young and strong and easily able to keep pace with Bram.

They rode several hours before finally stopping, hidden deeply now in the dense thicket of trees and shrubs that lined the riverside. The earth beneath the horses' hooves had grown damp and soft, yet neither steed seemed to mind the extra effort required to keep their fast pace, for it was so much cooler near the running water.

Eric had stayed ahead of Margot, firmly refusing to ride either beside or behind her, yet when he finally brought them to a halt he did it so suddenly that Margot neary overshot their stopping place. Only because Eric swung Bram around and reached out to grab her reins was Margot's horse brought to a standstill, and then only for as long as it took Eric to dismount and pull Margot down to the ground as well. He set her down rather roughly, and quickly took care of tethering the horses, then he returned to Margot and grabbed her up as hungrily as a starving man might grab up a welcome meal.

He was so much bigger than she, and so much stronger, that Margot could only let him have his way. Her feet dangled far from the damp earth, her body was ground against his, and her lips and mouth were consumed by the heat and passion of his. The most she could do was wrap her own arms around his neck, holding on for dear life, and return the fervent kisses her beloved gifted her with.

He pulled from her with a groan, finally.

"Oh, God," he whispered as though in agony. "God. I've been wanting to do that all these hours, yet I've been telling myself I should not."

"My Eric," she soothed, kissing his damp neck where her lips rested. "I l-love thee. There is no wrong in it."

"I love thee, Margot," he said softly, moving his head down so that he could brush her lips with his, "but it is wrong. 'Tis most wrong."

She replied by kissing him again, long and thoroughly, and Eric responded in kind. Only when her gentle fingers moved into his hair did he pull away again, breathing as heavily as though he'd just run a great distance.

"Nay, my love, do not. Do not touch me thus or I am all undone. 'Tis bad enough to hold thee and kiss thee, but the feel of thy hands on me . . ." A great shudder racked his body. Slowly he lowered her to the ground, then took her face between his hands, tenderly kissing her eyes, nose, and cheeks. Finally he put his arms around her and simply held her close.

"We must not stop long, Margot, else we give our pursuers an advantage. But there is much I would tell thee ere we go on."

Margot smiled at him lovingly. She reached a hand up to stroke his cheek and murmured, "Yes, my Eric?"

He kissed her once quickly, then rested his cheek on the top of her head. "I want thee to know, to understand, how truly and deeply I love thee, and that 'tis not a passing matter for me. Not now, not ever. I shall love thee 'til the day I die."

"I kn-know, Eric—" Margot began, but Eric gently placed two fingers over her lips to keep her quiet. There was a smile in his voice when he spoke.

"Please, love, let me speak all that is in my heart. We've not much time and I wish to say it all. Wilt keep still 'til I have finished?"

Margot lowered her head and rested it against Eric's massive chest. "Aye," she whispered, and was quiet.

Eric drew in a breath and hugged her a little more tightly. The things he wanted to tell her weren't difficult to say, but all the same he felt slightly nervous. He'd never made a declaration of love to a woman before and had not expected that he ever would, yet here he stood feeling awkward and clumsy and amazingly inept, ready to lay his virgin heart at her feet.

"At first—when I first saw thee again—I thought perhaps I loved thee because thou art so very lovely.

Indeed, I think any man who sees thee must instantly
admire thee and feel himself in love, for thou art
more fair than any maid I've e'er set eyes on. Even
Jaufre and Aleric loved thee that first day, or so I
believe. 'Twas easy to tell myself that my reaction to
thee was no more nor no less than theirs, and that
'twould pass with the days like any other half love.
But it did not go away." He shook his head and
sighed. "It grew only worse each day, like some kind
of dread illness which can ne'er be healed, but which
consumes the bearer of it like a slow burning flame,
and all the while I told myself 'twas not love, but only
desire of thy beauty, or admiration of thy sweet
nature, or gratitude for the kindness thou didst show
in favoring such a one as I, regardless that the favoring was naught but a desire on thy part to make me
feel welcome at Reed. Nay, love," he put a hand up to
stroke her hair when she started, "thou didst promise
to stay still 'til I've finished. Only a few moments
more."

Margot obediently settled against him again and,
slowly stroking her hair, Eric continued. "On that
first night when we left Reed, when thou said thou
didst love me, I could not believe 'twas true. I *would*
not believe it. Thou art so beautiful and fine. It
seemed impossible that such a one as thee could ever
love such a one as I. And yet, though I did not believe
thou truly loved me, the very thought that thou
shouldst bear any affection for me, even the smallest
affection, made me feel as nothing in my life has.
Thou didst make me feel strong and full and com-

plete, Margot, and when I finally believed thou didst truly love me I felt almost reborn, as though thy love had redeemed me from—from the emptiness inside me, and had filled me instead with all the goodness and worthiness of thyself. I love thee, Margot," he took her head between both hands and caused her to look up at him, while he himself gazed into her beautiful face with renewed wonder, "and shall always love thee. I wanted thee to understand and believe this, so that no matter where thou shalt be in all the years to come thou wilt always know there is one who loves thee as I do, with all his heart and soul and being."

Margot's eyes were filled with tears and she smiled a little tremulously. "I have w-waited a l-long time to hear those words, Eric Stavelot. A long, l-long time."

Their mouths met halfway, sealing without words the acceptance of their love.

Eric pulled away first, smiling at Margot and touching her cheek with gentle fingers.

"Black Donal would be most happy to find us thus, i'faith," he said teasingly. "'Twould be an easy way to catch one's prey, methinks."

Margot giggled. "He would think us mad."

"We *are* mad," Eric replied, kissing her nose, "delaying so long. My father would have my head for doing such a foolish thing, should he ever know of it. And yet will I delay us a few moments more, for this may be the last chance we have to be alone together, and there is one thing further I wish to do."

"What is it, m-my Eric?"

He searched her eyes deeply. When he spoke his words were solemn.

"I wish to make thee a lover's homage."

The change in Margot was amazing. Her warm, willing body immediately pushed away from his. Her eyes, so loving and happy only moments before, gazed at him in shock. "A *what!?*"

Eric grasped her hands and tried to pull her back into his embrace, to no avail. "A lover's homage. I wish to vow my lifelong love to thee so thou may always be certain of it."

Margot was so stunned she barely knew what to think. "But, Eric, there is n-no n-need! I shall accept thy pledge of l-love on the d-day we wed, just as thou shalt accept m-mine."

"Sweetest heart," he said gently, still tugging her closer to himself, "thou knowest full well we shall never wed. The fact that we love each other does not change that."

With one sharp movement Margot jerked her hands out of Eric's grasp. Keen disappointment shot through her as she matched Eric's bewildered look. "We shall be wed! Thou sayest thou l-love me, yet still thou dost insist thou shalt s-see me w-wed to another? Thou w-wouldst insult me with a l-lover's homage? How canst thou b-be so cruel, my Eric?!"

To his horror, Margot looked as if she would cry, and his whole heart felt as though it were falling into his feet. He stepped forward to try and take her into his arms, but she moved away, staring at him with open pain and disbelief.

"I do love thee!" he insisted. "Margot, please, thou must give up this foolishness and accept what can never be. I would give all I have to be able to make thee mine, yet even that would not make me an acceptable husband for thee. I am bastard-born, without knowledge of either of my true parents. Naught can make me acceptable for a lady born such as thee, and thou must accept it, just as I have."

Speechless, Margot shook her head and turned her back on him, putting her hands over her face to control her tears. It was cruel, so unbelievably cruel for him to have finally given her all that her heart had longed and waited for and then for him to snatch it away only moments later. She was still fighting for control when she felt Eric's gentle hands slide around her waist, slowly pulling her up against his hard chest.

"Sweet babe," he whispered, hugging her and placing a soft kiss over her ear, "do not cry. I love thee so. 'Tis torture to see thee so unhappy, especially at my hands."

"M-marry me, then!"

He hugged her even more tightly and pressed his face against the soft hair at her neck. "My love, thou knowest I cannot, though I would if I could. Margot, listen to me." He turned her around in his arms and caused her to look at him. "This is all we shall have. Our love for each other. 'Tis all I shall have to live on for the rest of my days, all I will have to cling to when thou art wed to one of mine own brothers, all that will keep me sane when thou hast presented him with a beautiful child, who shall be my niece or nephew, though I should wish that child to be mine. And thou wilt have this, also, and wilt know that I am loving thee with all my being even though I'll ne'er be able to show it. Please, Margot. Let us do this thing for each other. 'Tis all we shall ever be able to do to declare our love. Please."

Margot felt like giving up. The man was so incredibly dense! He just couldn't get it through his thick head that they were going to be together. Forever. She sighed and wiped her wet cheeks, staring at him and thinking that someday they would have a good, long laugh over all this.

"The l-lover's homage is an old custom," she retorted stubbornly. "'Tis not done these d-days. There will b-be no merit in it."

"Aye," he returned gently, "there shall be. 'Twill have merit for us, in our hearts. We shall make it so."

"There are n-no witnesses," she pointed out as a last effort.

"Nay, and we need none," Eric replied, slowly going down on his knees. "God shall be our witness. We shall be each other's witness. No other living person shall ever know of it. It shall be betwixt us alone."

He was kneeling before her now, and he lifted his hands in front of his face, pressing them flatly together as though he were going to pray.

"Come, Margot."

As though horrified, Margot shook her head and took a step away.

"Eric," she pleaded desperately, "'tis no courtly l-love I want from thee."

"But 'tis all I am able to give. Please, Margot, do not deny me this. 'Twill give my heart peace to have it done, and we've not much time to waste arguing the matter. Besides," he added, grinning at her, "the ground is wet and my knees are already gone cold. Come now, Margot."

Her feet felt as heavy as great stone blocks as she moved to stand before him. His hands were there before her and she stared at them.

"Thou must place thy hands over mine," he prodded.

"I kn-know!" she replied testily, clapping her hands over his to prove the point. Then she steadily fixed her eyes on his. "I've read the w-works of the c-countess of Champagne. I kn-know how the ceremony 'tis d-done!"

She was so childlike in her righteous indignation that Eric almost laughed out loud, but did not. Instead he smiled at her and said, "I do love thee, Margot le Brun, and shall do so 'til I last draw breath. Never have I known another woman like thee."

Blushing, Margot lowered her eyes. When she lifted them again she saw that his smile had faded, and that he was gazing at her solemnly. Their eyes met and Margot almost thought that she could see into the very depths of Eric's soul, for his gaze held nothing back. He had taken every barrier down and made himself utterly vulnerable, laying his whole heart open for her to see.

The forest around them was still and quiet, save

for the sounds of the water running in the stream nearby and the occasional chirping of a bird. The intensity of the moment stunned her, and Margot felt her heart beat more rapidly. She parted her lips to make breathing easier, and moistened them with the tip of her tongue.

At last Eric spoke.

"I, Eric Stavelot, do solemnly vow and promise by my faith that from this time forward I shall be faithful to the lady Margot le Brun, and shall maintain towards her my homage entirely against any other being, in good faith and without any deception. I shall serve her faithfully until death, and shall defend her against all assailants. I shall love her unceasingly with my whole heart. For as long as I live, I am bound to serve and love her by my own free troth, and during my lifetime I shall have no right to withdraw from her love and affection, but must, on the contrary, for the remainder of my days, remain under them."

It seemed as though an eternity passed before Margot remembered that she must say something too. She licked her lips again and tried to speak with a calmness she did not feel. "I, Margot le Brun, do acknowledge and accept the homage of Sir Eric S-Stavelot. I deliver and commend myself into his l-love and protection. In return for his promised devotion and services, I shall f-faithfully under-take to deserve well of him as far as lies in my p-power, and shall bestow upon him my t-tenderest affections."

She leaned down and kissed him very gently on the lips, then lifted her head and gazed at him.

"I have n-no ring to give thee," she whispered with slight embarrassment. "I should g-give thee a ring to complete the ceremony."

He smiled and kissed her again. "'Tis all right. There is no need for a ring. I have something I wish to give thee, however."

Margot straightened. "But thou'rt n-not supposed to give me anything. 'Tis n-not part of the homage."

"I know, but still I wish to give it to thee." He pulled one hand from her grasp and dug around inside his tunic. "We shall bend the rules of the ceremony just a little more."

In a moment he pulled out his valueless brooch and wished, as he surveyed it, that it looked better than it did.

"I know it does not look like much," he told Margot, showing it to her, "but in a strange way 'tis the most precious possession I have. 'Tis all I have of my real parents, my mother having pinned it to the swaddling I was left in. I have cherished it since I have had it." He met Margot's eyes. "I want thee to have it now."

"Oh, Eric." She shook her head. "I cannot t-take it from thee. 'Tis f-far too precious."

He nodded. "Aye, and that is why I want thee to have it. Thou art more precious to me than anything in the world now, and I would give thee that which is dear to my heart." With sure and steady hands he pinned the brooch to her surcoat, just above her breast. "I only wish it was more valuable. 'Tis a homely piece, I fear."

Margot covered the brooch with trembling fingers.

"'Tis m-more beautiful than any jewels I have e'er seen. I shall cherish it, t-too. And shall wear it always. I th-thank thee, my Eric." She kissed him again, then grasped his hands and tugged him upward and off his knees.

Once he was on his feet again, Eric lost no time in pulling Margot into his arms and kissing her as thoroughly as he wished to. By the time he was finished they were both out of breath, and he was in that aroused state to which he was becoming frustratingly accustomed.

"I wish we could stay here all day, my love," he whispered, "and verily I would like naught better, but we needs must continue to Wickham."

"But I've n-not yet made my homage to thee, Eric. We m-must d-do that before we leave."

Eric smiled at her. "Nay, love, I'll not have thee pay homage to me."

"But—!"

"Nay, sweet. I do not want thee bound by such a vow. If thou canst," he said, hesitating a moment, "I would have thee grow to . . . love . . . whichever of my brothers thou dost wed. If thou canst."

Margot shook her head. "I have l-loved no other before thee, Eric Stavelot, and shall love n-no other after. 'Tis t-too much a part of me to l-love thee."

"Thou dost not know. My brothers are good men and easy to love. When thou art wed to one of them thou couldst easily come to love him, and I'd not have a vow stand in the way of that. I'd have thee free to love whom and where thou shalt please."

She sighed loudly. "I see," she said. "Thou m-mayest m-make a vow to me, because thou art certain thy l-love for me shall n-never fail, but I may n-not make the same vow to thee, because m-my love for thee m-might not last, e'en though it has already survived these p-past ten years."

He nodded.

She sighed again. "Thou wilt m-make me old before my t-time, Eric Stavelot. I shall tell our grandchildren that all of m-my gray hairs c-came from thee." She reached both hands up and placed them on either side of his face. "I shall love no m-man but thee, my Eric, as l-long as I shall live, and if thou wilt not accept my vow I shall give it to thee anyway. I l-love thee and thee alone and shall always do so, I pledge this b-before God Himself."

The relief Eric felt was intense, but he didn't let himself show it. He kissed her again, instead, and afterward held her close.

"We shall never be wed," he whispered, "and we must needs continue on our way. If we travel hard we might reach Wickham by nightfall."

They had reached the horses before Margot put out a hand to stop him.

"Eric! I have j-just remembered! I d-do have something I m-might give thee in return for thy homage. 'Tis n-not truly m-mine, but that d-doth not matter, does it? Here."

Eric watched as she began to twist at one finger, eventually drawing off a plain, thin band of gold. She held it out to him.

"I know 'tis a l-lady's ring and that 'tis m-much too small for thee to wear, e'en if thou w-wouldst w-wear it, but perhaps thou couldst keep it in thy pocket 'til I can have a ring m-made for thee at B-Belhaven."

"Margot," he replied with some astonishment, taking the ring from her outstretched hand to examine it. He knew she had not brought any of her own fine jewelry with her, but had left it all in Minna's care. "Where didst thou get it?"

She grinned wickedly at him. "Leatie gave it to m-me. She said 'twas a shame my g-good husband hath n-not yet given me a w-wedded ring, and that perhaps I should b-borrow hers 'til we reached our d-destination. I p-promised to send a m-messenger b-back with it when I could."

"Oh, God," Eric said with a groan, passing one hand over his eyes. "They *knew*. They knew we were not wed. Oh, God."

Shamelessly, Margot giggled. "Aye. And so thou d-dost see that I m-must truly make an honest m-man of thee, Eric Stavelot, else M-Michael of Dunleavy and his family will be sorely disappointed in us."

He shook his head with disbelief. "His family and his family's family. God's mercy, Margot, what good people they are to have helped us so e'en when we lied to them. Someday we must repay the kindness they did show us."

"Indeed we m-must," she agreed readily. "Wilt accept the ring as m-my homage g-gift, then?"

He smiled and bent down to kiss her warmly on the lips. "I would be pleased to, my love, did I not think thou hast a greater need of it. We've one more night to pass in Wickham, and though I hope to secure separate chambers for us this eve, we may yet needs pose as man and wife. 'Til then thou shouldst wear the ring." He took her left hand in his and slowly slipped the ring on her finger. It felt strange and wonderful to him to do so and he held her hand a few moments longer to enjoy the sensation. Finally he shook himself and forced his wandering mind back to reality. He brought her hand to his lips and firmly kissed the ring where he had placed it.

"We needs must be on our way."

20

It was dark by the time they reached Wickham, and darker still because of the black clouds that had appeared in the sky sometime before sunset. The damp, cool wind that followed the clouds promised rain, and Eric silently hoped they'd quickly be able to find some kind of lodging for the night. It was his opinion that the rain would come sooner than later, and judging from the number of horses and wagons lining the dark streets of Wickham, the town seemed already full to capacity. He hadn't thought of such a circumstance before, being more concerned about simply getting Margot to safety than anything else, but he had to wonder whether he was losing, or had already lost, his ability to think clearly at all. Any idiot would have foreseen that a town the size of Wickham would be packed with visitors when a fair was about to take place there. Any idiot except himself, of course, who lately seemed only to be able to think of one thing and one person to the exclusion of everything else. His only comfort, and it was a thin comfort at that, was that no one else, including the great Allyn of Sorenthill, had thought of Wickham being so crowded as to keep them from finding shelter. If worse came to worst, he supposed he would simply have to rent a dry space beneath one of the pageant wagons and try to keep Margot from freezing to death in the wet, open elements.

It took half an hour's time to locate the Lamb's Head Inn, and the sight of it was far from encouraging. Like every other inn they had passed, it was bulging with revelers, most of them loud, drunk, and excessively energetic. The outside of the inn was already littered with sleeping drunks and unconscious losers of fights; the noise and activity level of the inside suggested that these unfortunate persons would soon be joined by several more such companions. The people and visitors of Wickham, it seemed, certainly knew how to celebrate a fair.

Eric gazed warily at the inn, then cast a glance at Margot, who sat very still in her saddle. She had certainly never been subject to such a place as this, he imagined, or to the kind of behavior she was about to see. He was loath to take her inside, yet there seemed to be no way around it. He couldn't leave her alone for a moment and believe that she would be safe. He would have to take her inside and hope that all would be well.

Leaning over, he took hold of her horse's reins.

"Come, my heart, we'll stable the horses and go inside to find Old Mac."

Margot nodded and Eric pulled her into the stable at the back of the inn. For the number of people inside the inn, the stable was amazingly empty. Only a few horses and cattle were stalled, contentedly munching hay. Eric easily found spaces for both their mounts and, having pulled Margot from her saddle, settled them for the night. When he finished he turned to Margot and began to pull her cloak more firmly about her. She had remained conspicuously quiet all the while he'd taken care of the horses, and he realized she was frightened. When he spoke he purposefully tried to make his tone light.

"All will be well, love, never fear. I've spent many and many a night in just such a tavern as this and have ne'er come to any harm." He bent and kissed her lingeringly, then smiled at her when he lifted his head. "I'll let no harm come to thee, sweet babe. Trust me?"

Margot nodded and looked more worried than ever. Eric chuckled and kissed her again, then pulled the hood of her cloak almost all the way down her face.

"Thou needs must keep thyself well covered, my love, if we're to avoid any mischief. One glance of thee and I'll have every man in the place down about my ears. Stay very close."

Eric's words were unneccesary, Margot thought as she allowed him to lead her out of the stables and toward the noisy inn. He was already holding on to her so tightly that she would have had to sever his arms in order to get loose of him. He carefully guided her around the limp bodies lying in the street, the sight of which made Margot feel even more frightened, and then led her through the doors of the inn. The smell of the place hit her like a slap in the face, and for one horrible moment she thought she might swoon. Never had she imagined that such a dreadful combination of odors, sights, and sounds might exist. It was beyond the imagination.

The smoke in the room made it impossible to see clearly, let alone breathe, but even so she could tell from the noise and movement that the inn was extremely crowded. There was a great deal of shouting and laughing, accentuated by the regular clattering of tankards and glasses. From somewhere in the smoky din a band of minstrels was playing a hearty tune accompanied by a painfully tuneless choir of drunken singers. Mixed into this confusion were the smells: strong ale, pipe and wood smoke, a variety of food smells and foul body odors of every kind. The stench of urine was so strong it was nearly overpowering, and Margot wondered nauseously how anyone could stand to stay in this place of their own free will for more than a few moments. She felt herself swaying and Eric's arm around her tightened.

"'Tis not usually bad as this," he whispered into her ear. "'Tis only the upcoming fair which makes it so wild."

That didn't make Margot feel any better, and she felt a surge of disappointment to think that her Eric should ever make a habit of visiting such places. The crowd was, in her opinion, very rough. The men were loud and raucous and seemed ready to fight one another at every moment, and the women were even worse. Many of them appeared to be only half-dressed, their large bosoms flopping freely beneath useless bodices as they trounced about the place.

No one noticed them until Eric took them a few steps forward into the smoke, and then the room began to hush by rapid degrees, as though the silence were a wave washing over those closest to them and finally reaching those farthest away. This reaction was a mystery to Margot, but Eric seemed not to notice. He continued to pull her along until they reached a long wooden plank on which tankards of ale were being served. A woman nearby, who'd been placing full tankards on a tray, glimpsed up as they neared and screamed sharply, dropping the tray and all the tankards. She ran away as though chased by demons, followed by two other women who'd started screaming as well.

"Whatever is the m-matter w-with them?" Margot whispered aloud, unaware of how her voice carried in the now silent room.

Eric sighed heavily and watched the screaming women flee. "Hush, love," he said.

"What in God's name is going on here?!" a loud, angry voice demanded. The man belonging to the voice came into sight, storming up to them full-speed until he got a good look at them. His steps faltered then, and his angry face displayed surprise. He was a large man, both round and tall, and well past middle age. His head was bald save for a halo of pure white hair, matched by a long, thin beard on his chin. He'd been in the midst of furiously drying his beefy hands with a rag, but that activity had faltered, too, along with his steps, and now his fingers slowly, almost idly, toyed back and forth with the cloth as he stared avidly upward at Eric. A full silent minute passed before the man cautiously took the few final steps to meet them, and Margot could see that his expression was wary.

"What can I do for thee, sir?" he asked in a low, careful tone. "If 'tis lodging thou seekest I've none to let, so thou'lt best be on thy way. If 'tis ale then welcome and seat thyselves, if a seat thou can find. I'll send a wench to see to thee."

"Thou art the proprietor here, sir?" Eric returned politely, almost gently it seemed to Margot, and she remembered how gentle he had been when they had first met Michael of Dunleavy and his family.

"I am," the man replied.

"Dost go by the name of Old Mac, then?"

The man's eyes widened slightly and he gazed at Eric with open suspicion. "Aye, those that know me call me that. But I disremember ever meeting thee before, sir."

Eric shook his head. "Nay, we've not met before this, Old Mac, though 'tis pleased I am to make thy acquaintance." He extended one large hand toward the man, who stared at it and made no move to take it. "I am Eric Stavelot of Belhaven, and my wife and I were given thy name by Sir Allyn de Arge of Sorenthill. Hê knew we were coming to Wickham and directed us to make thy acquaintance."

Another wave of shock crossed the man's features, exceeding by far his previous shock, and his mouth gaped wide. Finally he took Eric's hand and held it, though not shaking it, and he moved his head in disbelief while a slow grin lit his face.

"Sir Allyn," he whispered reverently, his smile growing. "'Tis many a year since I've laid eyes on that rascally pup, but if Sir Allyn has sent thee then thou'rt welcome indeed, sir, thou and thy good lady." He nodded in Margot's direction and began to shake Eric's hand vigorously. "Aye, welcome indeed, e'en if thou art a damned giant! Trust Allyn of Sorenthill to send me a giant and give me one of the worst scares of my life, I vow! That rascal!" He laughed heartily and continued to pump Eric's hand, evidently unwilling to let go of it now.

The sight and sound of the proprietor making the giant welcome worked a release on the other occupants of the tavern, and slowly but surely the silence relaxed until the noise was as it had been when they first walked in.

"But come!" Old Mac said happily, finally letting go of Eric and waving them toward the serving area. "Come and have a draught of ale and tell me how Sir Allyn is. Where didst thou last see him? How long hast thou known of him?"

Margot obediently let Eric lead her to the long board, but she itched to pull the heavy cowl from

her face so that she might see better and breathe
more easily. Old Mac slapped a heavy tankard of ale
before her and she reached up to inch the hood
back a tiny bit, only to see Eric's hand come in front
of her face and quickly yank it down. Old Mac
didn't seem to notice this, indeed, no one in the
place seemed to think it odd that a woman should
be in their midst blanketed as heavily as a monk.
Sighing, Margot picked up the tankard and took a
sip.

"I have known Sir Allyn these past many months,"
Eric was saying, "when we fought together at
Shrewsbury on the side of King Henry. We saw him
last but two days ago, when he bade us seek thee out
as one who might lend us aid in Wickham."

Old Mac set a tankard before Eric and tilted his
head with curiosity. "Only two days since? He is not
far, then. And he bade thee seek me out? Indeed, I
shall be happy to do all I can for thee, sir, if thou'lt
only tell me how."

Eric seemed to drain his ale all in one gulp,
Margot thought, for his tankard seemed very light
when he set it down and Old Mac hurried to refill it.

"'Twould be most kind if thou couldst help us find
lodging for the night," Eric replied, taking up the
fresh tankard, "and feed us. I fear we are half-starved
from our long journey this day."

"Food and drink I can provide," Old Mac said,
"but I lied not when I told thee there is no further
room to be let here, though thou'rt welcome to sleep
in the tavern, if 'twould please thee to do so."

Eric glanced at Margot, envisioning just how much rest either one of them would get if he had to spend the night fending off every curious man in the place. And they would get curious before long, curious to know why such an obviously female form was so completely covered from head to toe. He would be curious himself, if he were one of their number, to know whether it was beauty or horror being kept from his sight. He shook his head. "Nay, I fear my wife would not find that meet. Thy stable seems sound enough. If thou wouldst lend us blankets, we'd be pleased to sleep there this night and to pay whatever thou wouldst ask."

Old Mac grinned. "Speak not of money to me, lad, not when thou hast been put in my care by my late master's son. The stable it is, then, and thou'lt needs have no fears of getting wet, I vow. The horses stay drier than we do, by God!" He laughed. "But come. Thy good lady will not wish to stay in this rough place any longer. Hie thee out to the stables and I'll bring all to make thee comfortable there."

Old Mac was right. Margot did not wish to stay in the tavern any longer and was relieved to step back into the fresh night air. Even the guttering moans and groans of the drunks on the ground were preferable to being inside that disgusting place, and whatever animal smells the stable had to offer were better still. She yanked her hood off the moment they were back inside and breathed long and deeply of the clean scents of wood and hay.

Eric came up behind her, rubbing her arms. "There. 'Twas not so bad, was it?"

Margot whirled and looked at him in disbelief. "'Twas worse than b-bad! And f-for wh-what purpose hast thou ever b-been in such a-a—" she searched for just the right word, "*hovel?!*"

Eric was bewildered by her sudden anger.

"I—we—that is, my brothers and father and I have had need to spend the odd night or two in taverns when we were on our travels. 'Tis not uncommon for any traveler to do so."

Evidently unsatisfied by this answer, Margot placed her hands on her hips and glared at him. "And is that the only r-reason thou hast had to enter s-s-such an establishment?"

"Nay," Eric replied slowly. "I have drunk many a tankard of ale in taverns, certes, just as any other man has done."

"And is that all?"

"All?" he repeated, dumbfounded.

"Aye!" She stamped her foot angrily. "Is th-that all thou hast ever d-done in a t-t-t— in a t-t-t—"

"Tavern," Eric said helpfully.

"Aye!"

Eric shook his head, at a loss to understand what she wanted from him. Women were the strangest creatures. One moment they were soft and loving, the next hot and furious, and God help any man to understand why.

"I suppose I have done my share of gambling in them," he admitted at last, hoping to appease her.

It didn't seem to be what she was after, however, for her eyes narrowed dangerously. "And what of the w-w-women?"

"The . . . women?" he repeated incredulously.

She nodded. "Aye, the women. Hast ever g-gone to a t-tavern to seek the c-company of women?"

Eric was shocked, truly, truly shocked that his sweet, innocent little love could ask him such a question. He had gone wenching in taverns many and many a time, of course, but he wasn't about to tell her that.

"My love." He lightly placed his hands on her shoulders to draw her nearer. "Didst not see the way those women in the inn reacted to me this night? They screamed at the sight of my ugliness and ran away. 'Tis always thus, sweet babe, I swear it. Thou hast no need to be angered."

Those weren't exactly lies, he supposed. He hadn't actually made any denials, but it was true that women usually did react to him that way at first, though he had never yet run across a female whose initial reaction to him couldn't eventually be soothed with a little time and effort.

Margot didn't seem to believe him. In fact, if anything, she looked angrier than she had before and shoved away from him forcibly.

"Here we are!" One of the stable doors creaked open and Old Mac walked in with several wool blankets under one arm and a tray of food and drink supported with the other. Eric hurried to relieve the older man of the tray and Margot reached for the blankets.

"God's sweet mercy!" Old Mac exclaimed, gazing at Margot in awe. "I can see why thou didst wish to keep thy lady well hidden, Eric of Belhaven, and glad I am thou didst do so." He turned wide eyes on Eric. "Canst imagine the brawl if the fellows inside had seen her?"

Eric laughed and set the tray on a blanket that Margot had spread. "Indeed I can," he replied. "I'd like to make my wife known to thee, sir. Margot, this is Old Mac, Old Mac, this is my wife, Margot."

Old Mac bowed. "'Tis pleased—most pleased I am, my lady." He looked at Eric again and winked. "Thou'rt a lucky man, Eric of Belhaven."

"Aye, indeed I am." Eric beamed proudly.

Only barely holding on to her manners, Margot plunked down on the blanket and began to eat.

An hour later the rain began to fall, and the stable was pervaded by a deepening chill. Eric glanced at Margot, who lay huddled beneath several of the blankets, obviously trying to keep warm without much success. She muttered occasionally, flopping around and rearranging herself, then giving up and flopping around again.

With a sigh Eric finished checking the stable, making certain all was settled for the night, then he blew out the candles that Old Mac had loaned them and made his way through the horses and hay to the empty stall where Margot lay fighting with her blankets. He sat beside her, pulled the blankets up, got in next to her, and settled the blankets firmly around both of them.

"I d-did n-not say thou couldst s-sleep with me!" she informed him tightly, giving him her back.

"Nay, thou didst not," he agreed, snuggling her body against his chest and wrapping his arms around her waist, "but methinks we'll both sleep better and more warmly if I do."

He was miserably unhappy that Margot was still upset with him, especially since he didn't know the reason. This would be their last night alone together, and he had thought it would be one of love and unity. She had been so cold to him since coming out of the Lamb's Head Inn that he was beginning to wonder if perhaps she had fallen out of love with him already. It was a terrible, wretched thought, but his heart felt heavy with the possibility of it. Only that afternoon they had seemed in such accord, and he had pledged his love to her, but he knew so very little about matters of love that it would have been easy for him to do something between then and now that would have given her a disgust of him. But what? *What?* If only he knew he would do anything in his power to make it right, anything so long as she would forgive and smile at him again.

He knew he should ask what was making her so angry, but, in truth, he was afraid to. He was afraid to hear her say that she no longer loved him, or that whatever it was he had done was irrevocable. Worst of all was a dread gnawing in the pit of his belly that she might have seen him as he truly was through the eyes of those women in the tavern. Perhaps she had finally seen just how undesirable he was, how monstrous he appeared in the eyes of others, and if that were true, then she must have a great disgust of him, indeed. Perhaps she had been trying to let him know of her disgust through her anger. Her body was very stiff in his arms; perhaps the very touch of him sickened her. He began to slide his arms away. Her hands clasped him tight.

"Margot," he whispered.

A soft sob answered him.

"Margot—"

"I w-want the t-truth from thee!" she cried suddenly, flipping onto her back to look at him.

Eric pushed himself up on one elbow and gazed into the shadows of her face. "Anything. Anything, my love. Tell me what thou dost want and I shall do it." He wiped the tears from her cheeks with a trembling hand.

"I want the t-t-truth!" she repeated.

"About what?" he pleaded. "Only tell me what it is."

Her own trembling hand covered his, holding it tight. Her body shook with her tears and her words came out with great misery. "Thou—thou hast known other w-women, hast thou n-not?"

He shook his head, confused. "Aye, I have known many women. My mother, my sister, my cousins—"

"That is n-not what I m-meant! I m-meant that thou hast kn-known other women. That th-thou hast had kn-knowledge of them."

Her meaning suddenly became clear to Eric, painfully so, and for a moment he was robbed of breath. His whole body froze with surprise. "I—I am not a virgin, if that is what thou dost mean," he whispered, feeling as though he were confessing the crime of all centuries.

"Oh!" Margot wailed, covering her mouth with both hands. "Oh!"

His heart broke into a thousand pieces. "Please, Margot—"

"No w-wonder thou d-dost n-not wish to w-wed me!" she sobbed, turning from him. "N-no wonder thou d-dost wish to g-give me to one of thy b-brothers!"

"What?!" Eric was more bewildered than ever.

She turned back to face him. "I'm flat!" she wailed.

"Flat?" What in the world was she talking about?

"F-f-flat!" she repeated miserably. "And undesirable! And s-s-skinny! W-why shouldst thou w-want m-me when thou c-canst have one of those b-big b-breasted females at the inn?"

He had to bite his inner lip to keep from laughing out loud. "Margot." His voice shook with repressed laughter. "Where in God's name didst thou ever conceive such an idea?"

"'Tis t-true, is it n-not?" she cried. "Thou canst n-not deny it!"

She was *jealous* , Eric realized suddenly. It was unbelievable, but true. She was jealous! For the first time in his memory a woman was actually jealous over *him!*

"Margot, I love thee," he vowed fervently before kissing her, "and I have no desire whatsoever for any of those women at the inn. Or for any other woman on God's own earth, save thee."

She pushed at him. "B-but, Eric—"

Another kiss silenced her. "Margot," he said softly when he finished and had her full attention, "I am more sorry than I can ever say that there have been other women in my life. If I could go back and remove them I would readily do so, but I cannot. All I can do is ask thee to forgive me and to believe that from this day forward there shall be no other woman in my life but thee, e'en though thou shalt only ever be in my heart. But I shall never touch another woman or . . . know her. Did I not promise thee that much this day?"

"Aye." She nodded, her tears still flowing. "But I am s-still undesirable, and f-flat."

He shook his head. "Thou'rt not flat, my love."

"I am," she insisted. "Here, f-feel." She grasped his hand and pressed it firmly against her left breast.

Eric did feel, and gladly. He gently kneaded the soft mound beneath his palm, unable to suppress a groan as he did so, then ran his fingertips lightly over her to feel the hardened tip of her breast.

"Thou'rt not flat," he whispered.

"What?" she murmured, evidently having forgotten what they were talking about.

"Thou'rt not flat," he repeated, against her lips.

"Oh."

Her hands slid up into his hair, pulling his face

down to hers, and when he began to kiss her Eric completely lost his senses.

It seemed an eternity before he finally found them again, and when he did it was also to find that he was in the midst of unlacing her bodice, evidently about to prove to her that she wasn't anywhere near flat or undesirable.

"Good Lord," he muttered in agony, freezing his hand and dropping his forehead until it rested against hers. His warm, rapid breath mixed with hers, heating the space between them even more. He shuddered once, fighting a good battle with his baser instincts. Being composed of very strong forces, the baser instincts nearly won out, but in the end his better self overcame. All he had to do was think of James. Slowly he removed his hand.

"Eric," Margot whispered, pleading, taking hold of his hand and trying to pull it back.

"Nay, love." Instead of eluding her grasp he merely intertwined her fingers in his and pressed both their hands together into the cool hay.

He moved until his face was above hers, until he could gaze into the deep shadows of her eyes. "Thou'rt so beautiful," he murmured, bending to kiss her neck tenderly.

Margot shifted beneath him, stretching, trying to get closer to him. "Make l-love to me, Eric. Please."

"I want to. God, I want to."

"Please," she begged.

"Nay, I cannot. We cannot."

She shivered and he held her tight, pressing his

face against her hair. "I love thee so, Margot. How could I dishonor thee? I fear I have already done so, though I shall never be sorry for it. I shall carry the memories of this night with me forever. I shall live from them."

"B-but, Eric—"

"Hush, sweet. I would not do this to thee, not when thou dost deserve so much better. I'd have thee go to thy marriage bed a maiden, and thus have all the honor and love thou dost so fully deserve. Canst think I would shame thee so greatly only to appease my own weak flesh? Or that I would shame my own brother by cuckolding him?"

Margot smiled very slightly and bit her lower lip to keep from telling him that he wouldn't be cuckolding anyone but himself. She was growing weary of repeating herself about their marriage. If the man wanted to make a fool of himself by insisting that the inevitable would never happen, so be it.

"Why art thou smiling, little minx?" he asked, looking at her, grinning himself. "What art thou thinking?"

Margot lifted her free hand and stroked the hair out of Eric's eyes. "I w-was thinking that thy brothers are f-fortunate indeed to have thee for a brother."

He sighed and lay down, pulling her tightly into his arms and tucking the blankets up about them warmly. "'Tis I who am the fortunate one," he said, yawning. "My brothers are good, honorable men. Well, perhaps James is more so than Jaufre, but Jaufre will grow into those qualities a little better once he has decided to settle down. James, though, is one of the best men I've e'er known. Thou wilt come to love him as I do when thou hast had a chance to meet and know him."

Margot nodded against his chest and yawned as well. "I shall m-make an effort to l-love all my new family."

Eric ignored the implication behind her comment and purposefully declined from reminding her once again that they would never be married. The words would have fallen on deaf and stubborn ears, he knew, and he was growing weary with having to repeat a fact that only depressed him. Soon enough Margot would realize the truth of his words.

"James is one who seems only to have good in him," he said quietly, closing his eyes. "He thinks of others first and of himself last. And a gentler man I have never known. When we were at Shrewsbury I worried o'er him constantly, fearing he'd be unable to kill his opponent ere his opponent could kill him. His way is always to seek peace before death, though he is as fine a fighter as any I've ever seen." He laughed. "I think he was the only man on the field of battle who made to rescue every man he'd wounded. He spent more time dragging his victims back to safety for caretaking than he did fighting. And after each battle, no matter how weary he might be, James was always the first man searching amongst the bodies for any wounded who might be saved."

"He sounds l-like a saint," Margot murmured sleepily.

"Aye, that he does. He always seemed so to me, e'en when I was a child." He yawned loudly. "Everyone loves him, and thou shalt love him, too, I vow. And I'll not be sorry for't, Margot. I'd rather have thee marry James than any other man on this earth. He'll be a fine husband to thee."

Margot lay very still against him, not replying. He opened his eyes.

"Margot?"

Silence.

She was asleep, he realized, and he wondered how much of his last few words she had heard. It didn't matter if she hadn't heard any of it, of course. He'd be sure to use the rest of their time together tomorrow in telling her all about James and of how happy she would be with him.

He kissed her forehead lightly and snuggled against her more closely, then he closed his eyes again. There were only a few hours left; a few precious hours in which he could still consider her his own. It seemed a shame to waste them in sleep. A great shame indeed.

21

"Get the woman first."

Even deep in sleep the trained soldier in Eric heard the words, and his hand was on the dagger at his waist before his eyes even opened.

It was still dark inside the stable, but every sense told him that he was surrounded by many men, all armed. He was up in a half second and fighting by sheer instinct, uncaring of whom he felled or how he felled them. For several confused moments there was only a rash of sound and confusion as his surprised attackers first swore aloud and then crumpled beneath the ferocity of Eric's skilled and deadly movements. Swords clashed together loudly in the pandemonium, making it impossible to either hear anything or think of anything save the fight. It was too dark for Eric to see how many he was up against, but he didn't care. He'd kill every single one of the bastards now and spare time to think about it later, when he had Margot to safety. He hoped she'd have enough sense to stay out of the way until it was all over.

Somewhere in the darkness, in the midst of all the madness, Eric heard a powerful voice shouting for light. Seconds later he was blinded by the flaring of a torch that flooded the stable with its sudden light. All of the fighting subsided for that brief moment as every man took stock of the situation.

Eric looked about, too, to see where Margot was and to see how many more men he had to contend with. He was surrounded by at least six armed men, with that many or more already scattered on the stable floor, either dead or dying. Unlike his brother, it had never been Eric's way to merely wound his enemies. Any man foolish enough to meet his sword met it for all eternity. For him there were no half measures in fighting, as the remaining men would soon discover.

He could not find Margot anywhere inside the stable, though he only had a chance to look for her briefly. He prayed fervently that she had gotten out safely and he prepared to renew his fight.

The men surrounding him prepared to fall to fighting again as well, now that their eyes had had a few seconds to adjust to the welcome intrusion of the light, but when they looked at Eric for the first time in that light they all, to a man, lowered their swords and stepped back, gaping.

"Come on!" Eric shouted at them, impatient to

have done with them so that he could find Margot. "Art knaves in the darkness and cowards in the light?!"

The men continued to gape, a couple swore under their breath, but none of them moved a muscle.

God's mercy! he thought irately. He was going to have to attack them in order to finish this thing! Were they so overcome by the sight of his size that they were willing to go to their deaths so readily?

"Eric."

He stilled.

"Er-ric," she pleaded again.

Oh, God. "Margot, where art thou?" He wasn't able to afford the luxury of turning his eyes to where her voice came from.

But Margot didn't answer him. The voice that did sent chills down his spine. "She is here, Sir Knight, in good keeping, and if thou dost wish to see her live o'er the next few moments thou wilt give way. Thou hast killed enough of my men this morn, methinks."

It was a deep, methodical voice, so sure and calm that Eric somehow knew this man was the Black Donal of whom Sir Allyn had spoken. Only such a man could sound thus.

"I'll kill every last one if thou dost not release the lady Margot and go on thy way," Eric answered. "Now!"

"I think not," was the unconcerned reply. "For if thou dost move even a step I shall kill the lady, and gladly. She has caused me more trouble than any ten fighting men ever could do. E'en now my hand doth tremble to draw my knife across her pretty throat. The sight of her blood spilt there would be the loveliest sight I have e'er seen, I vow. Here, watch now and I shall pleasure myself with just a pinprick, with just a drop of her blood to prove the truth of my words."

"Nay!" Eric shouted, plunging toward the torchlight through the men who surrounded him. All six men jumped on him, struggling to hold him back. He was knocked to his knees, then shoved facedown into the hay as every one of them leapt upon his back, their swords jabbing at his sides and neck.

At the same time Eric heard Margot whimper, then cry out in pain. He was just able to squirm his head around so that he could see her, close enough now that he was no longer blinded by the flaming torch.

"Margot!" She was held tight in the grip of one vicious-looking man while another had his knife at her throat. She struggled and cried out again, louder this time, and when the man took his knife away Eric could see the line of blood run slowly down the side of her neck. The man chuckled in his low, methodical way as he first wiped, then sheathed his dagger.

"Ah, she hath fainted," he said. "'Tis well. We'll not have to listen to her whining all day, at least. And as to thee, sir—" He turned to look at Eric, who was glaring up at him, and the words died on his lips.

"Bastard!" Eric hissed. "I'll kill thee for that! I swear it by God and by all that is holy." And he meant it. Even if the men atop him were to push their swords through his flesh, somehow he would find the strength to live just long enough to fulfill his vow.

Black Donal had no reaction to these words whatsoever. He was staring at Eric as though he were seeing a ghost. His eyes were wide, and shock was written plainly on his face, the struggle to regain control of himself was a visible thing.

"Shall we kill him, my lord?" one man asked, though his voice trembled as badly as a windblown leaf.

Mute, Black Donal shook his head. An immense silence filled the stable until he finally found his voice, and even then his words came out as though forced.

"Gag him. Bind him."

He turned on his heel and left the stable, flinging the doors wide to reveal the fact that dawn had arrived. The man who still held Margot lifted her limp body into his arms and followed his master outside, and Eric, who was relieved to find himself still alive, began to make silent plans as the men in the stable carried out their orders.

A small crowd watched as Black Donal and his men rode away with their captives. It was obvious to Eric that the people standing in the street were too frightened to be of any help, though he supposed it wouldn't do any good if someone had tried to intervene. Black Donal and his men were killers. Anyone daring to get in their way would be dealt with quickly and remorselessly.

Margot's unconscious body had been placed in a hay-filled cart for their journey, but Eric, fortunately, had been placed on top of his own Bram after he had been bound and gagged, as Bram was the only mount large enough to accommodate his weight, and he had been placed sitting up so that he could ride, his legs then tied together beneath his steed's belly so he would have no chance of escaping. He looked around as they rode through the town, straining to find a familiar face in the crowds. If he didn't succeed in finding anyone, he would have to hope that Old Mac, who had stepped out of the Lamb's Head Inn just in time to watch them pass by, would at least be able to tell Sir Allyn in which direction they had been taken. The poor old man had looked shocked beyond belief at the spectacle before him, and Eric wished he had confided a little more in him so that at least he would know that he and Margot were not criminals of some kind, being taken away legally rather than illegally.

They neared the town gates at a gathering speed, and Eric had nearly lost hope of finding someone he knew. But just as Black Donal approached the gates Eric caught sight of Jace, standing atop Bogo of Brantwell's wagon between Bogo himself and Bogo's son-in-law, Josko. It was obvious they had only just wakened, probably due to all the commotion, and all three looked rather rumpled and unkempt. Jace, especially, was a sight, his dark hair sticking out from his head in every direction but down. His mouth gaped when he met Eric's eyes. Eric nodded slightly, meaningfully, and Jace nodded back, understanding.

But then his gaze dropped to watch as Margot's inert body went past in the cart, and he saw, as Eric did, the untended flow of blood still streaming down her neck.

Eric quickly searched out Bogo of Brantwell to warn him with a look. Bogo noted, as did Josko, and they jumped on Jace together, knocking him down onto the wagon seat just as he was about to shout out his rage. The scream of fury still came out, though it was muffled, and the three of them struggled on the seat heedlessly. Black Donal stopped and turned to watch the scuffle, his eyes narrowing at the strange outburst. He turned to gaze back at Eric, then, and Eric met his eyes blankly, having purposefully drawn his own gaze away from his friends. There was no reason for Black Donal to think that three men engaging in such a spontaneous fight had anything to do with them, especially if the men had been drinking all night or wenching or gambling, while in the midst of a fair. Eric hoped the man would attribute it to those factors, at any rate. He hoped it very fervently. Sir Allyn had warned him of Black Donal's ability at second sight. If he guessed this particular situation, however, all would be lost.

Black Donal stared at him for a long moment and Eric unflinchingly returned his gaze. Finally, Black Donal turned his horse and rode on. Bram was given a harsh tug by the man holding his reins and a moment later Eric said a silent good-bye to the town of Wickham.

*   *   *

It was a relief for Margot, several hours later, when they finally stopped to rest the horses. Although she had been on a not-uncomfortable bed of hay in the cart, being forced to lie in the same position for such a long time, bound and gagged, had made her whole body ache painfully. Jason of Welshore, who had been assigned her care again, had ridden in the cart beside her, but had not bothered to do much more than glance at her occasionally, being preoccupied with keeping a lookout for any trouble rather than with whether she was comfortable or not. And so Margot had resigned herself to burning muscles and aching bones, and she was grateful that the gag was in her mouth; at least it kept her from grinding her teeth together from discomfort.

When the cart finally rolled to a stop, Jason jumped down. "We'll stop for an hour or so, most like," he said, reaching into the cart to pull her into a sitting position.

He hadn't been entirely unkind to her, Margot thought as she watched him check the ropes on her hands and feet. When she had first come awake to find him sitting beside her it was also to find that he was gently dabbing at the wound on her neck. He hadn't spoken to her, but he had given her a reassuring smile and had lightly tied a cloth around her neck to make certain the bleeding didn't start up again.

Her bindings appeared to be solid, and Jason put

his arms beneath her knees and shoulders, lifting her out of the cart altogether.

"I imagine thou wouldst be glad of a chance to relieve thyself, my lady," he explained, carrying her in the direction of the trees.

Margot groaned. She would be glad of a chance to relieve herself and, in fact, had been wondering whether these men were going to be humane enough to allow her such an opportunity. They certainly didn't appear to possess much of that quality. But she wasn't going to be glad of the audience she was going to have. Four stout men silently fell into step behind Jason and followed them into the shade of the trees, until he finally set her down.

Jason made the men turn their backs, which they did in a circle, surrounding her, but he himself had to help her with the task. Black Donal had given strict orders that neither she nor Eric were to be unbound at any point, for any reason, until they reached their destination, and Jason obviously took the command seriously. Steadying her with one arm he lifted her skirts until they were up around her waist, then he slowly, carefully, unlaced her satin undergarments.

His face was flaming by the time he tugged the soft garments away from her skin, growing even redder as his fingers necessarily brushed against the curve of her hip and thigh, and Margot closed her eyes with shame and embarrassment and tried to keep from crying over such humiliation. Fortunately it was all over quickly and soon Jason was tying everything back up again, though his fingers were trembling badly.

He took off her gag and gave her a drink of water when they got back to the cart, just as he had done on the first occasion when she was taken captive and, just as on that first occasion, he didn't put it back afterward.

"Thou wouldst not be so foolish as to scream, wouldst thou, my lady?"

She shook her head. There certainly wouldn't be any point in screaming. It would only serve to anger Black Donal, and if there was one thing she didn't want, it was that.

"Nay, I'll n-not scream," she replied quietly.

Jason of Welshore smiled. "'Tis the first time I've heard thee speak. 'Tis pretty for a devil's voice."

Margot stared past him to the sky above, wishing he would go away. The sound of shuffling feet made her turn her head.

"Eric!" she cried, and a moment later he was lying beside her in the cart, dipping it heavily with his weight and twining his bound fingers with hers. He, too, was ungagged.

"My love," he whispered, reaching to kiss her. "Art all right? Thy neck has stopped bleeding. Hast not been treated ill?"

"Nay!" she sobbed, suddenly able to release the tears she'd held in so long. She nestled into the warmth of his body and trembled with the relief of seeing him again, of having him with her again.

His hands' being bound made it difficult for Eric

to soothe Margot. He pressed as close as he possibly could and kissed her forehead gently. "Sweet babe," he murmured, stroking her fingers with his own. "'Twill be all right, love. Everything will be all right. Do not be afraid." He was very aware of the audience they had. The cart was surrounded by half a dozen men who obviously didn't mind staring at them, as though Margot and he were some form of entertainment. Eric was almost getting used to being looked at. It seemed that every time he had glanced about him during their ride it was to meet the intense stares of the men riding with him. He couldn't begin to wonder why they found him so interesting. People generally noticed his size and height, but the reactions of these men were more pronounced than anything he had run across yet. They looked at him as though he were an unbelievable apparition.

Margot was still crying, her face pressed tight against his neck. "I'm s-s-s-so s-s-s-sorry, Eric."

"Hush, sweet," he murmured, touching her cheek with the backs of his fingers. "Hush, now. For what cause dost thou have to be sorry, when I am the one who has failed thee?"

"If-f-f 'twas n-n-not f-for m-m-me, thou w-wouldst n-n-not b-be here!"

"Nay, my love, that is not so. If 'twas not for me thou might even now be safe at Belhaven. 'Tis my own weakness has brought us to this place. I'll not have thee blaming thyself."

Her tears subsided a little until another dreadful

thought came into her mind. "M-m-my f-f-f-father! M-m-my f-f-father is in d-d-d, in d-d-d—"

"In danger now," Eric supplied. "Aye, that he is, love. And 'tis reason enough for us to be as brave as we can be, for all our fears will do naught to help either him or ourselves. Sweet love," he murmured, kissing her eyes and wet cheeks and finally her trembling mouth, "thou must not give way to thy fears. I know I have disappointed thee, but canst thou not have only a little more faith? If not in me, at least in those whom we know will come for us?"

Margot tried to calm herself. Reaching her fingertips up she touched his chin, then closed her eyes and rested her forehead wearily against his cheek. "I shall t-t-try, m-my Eric," she whispered.

"Well, well, a most touching scene, i'faith! The two besotted lovers clinging to each other in their hour of need."

Eric turned his head to look up at Black Donal. The man was standing on his side of the cart, gazing down at him in an unpleasant manner. Their eyes held for a long, silent moment, and then Eric turned away again, deeming it best simply to ignore his captor.

"Face me," Black Donal commanded quietly.

"To what purpose?"

"To *my* purpose."

Another silence stretched while Eric refused to comply. When Black Donal finally spoke again his tone was as sharp as a newly hewn blade.

"Thou wilt learn to obey me, Sir Knight, else thou

wilt live to regret thy stubbornness." He unsheathed the dagger at his side and handed it to the man standing next to him. "Cut off one of her fingers. The littlest one first, I think."

"God!" Eric spat out furiously. "Thou'rt verily the coward I thought thee! Thou wouldst rather fight a woman than a man, craven bastard!"

The sharp hiss of gasps that sounded beside the cart told him how incautiously he had spoken, and Eric waited to see if he had inspired any wrath in the ice-hearted devil.

"Her finger," Black Donal said calmly. "Do it now."

The man obediently began to walk around the cart.

"Nay!" Eric called out, releasing Margot's trembling hands and flopping over onto his back so suddenly that the cart creaked and the wheels threatened to shatter. He glared up at Black Donal with hot, angry eyes. "I give way."

Black Donal nodded but said nothing. He reached out a hand and took his knife back, sheathing it without taking his eyes from Eric's. And then he began a strange, thorough examination of Eric, taking in and silently studying every inch of him. When the man's eyes came up to meet his again Eric could see that they had changed. Amazingly, an odd softness had come into them, unfitting in such a chilling face.

"What is thy name?" Black Donal asked, his voice an uncertain whisper.

"Eric Stavelot," Eric replied slowly.

"Stavelot," Black Donal murmured. "Of what place?"

"Of Belhaven."

Black Donal's eyes closed briefly. He nodded and said, softly, "Belhaven. Aye, Belhaven," then opened his eyes again to gaze at Eric. The look Eric now saw there shocked him. The softness of a moment ago had been replaced by a deep, internal pain. He was even more shocked, and slightly repulsed, when Black Donal reached out a shaking hand to place it on his chest.

"Thou wouldst be three and twenty years of age this year," Black Donal said. "Thou wouldst be three and twenty this past May."

A thought so terrible welled up in Eric's mind that he instantly repelled it. "Aye. How dost thou know this?"

"I know," Black Donal whispered fervently, leaning forward. He made a fist out of his hand and thumped Eric on the chest with it, not hard, but hard enough to express his turmoil. "I *know*, Eric Stavelot, because thou wast once one of the greatest weaknesses, and regrets, of my life!"

He struck Eric on the chest again, harder this time, so that the sound of it could be heard. Then he pulled his hand back, turned sharply on his heel, and walked away without another word.

22

The chamber she was locked in was more like a small dungeon than a room, but at least she had a roof over her head to keep her dry from the downpour outside. And that, Margot thought, was just about all she had to be thankful for. She was still bound, hand and foot, and was lying on a filthy blanket on the chamber's hard, cold floor, which was bare even of rushes. The blanket had been the only concession to her comfort that Black Donal had allowed when she'd been brought into this place some hours earlier. He had assured her that he wouldn't waste any wood in building a fire to keep her warm, and he had reminded her, as if she had needed reminding, of his promise to make her life a very hell if she gave him any trouble. Well, she had given him trouble, and he was obviously not a man who broke his promises.

Jason of Welshore, who had carried her into the room, had asked permission to stay with her, but Black Donal's only response had been to cuff him soundly across the face, nearly felling him. He had followed his master obediently out the door, throwing Margot a regretful look as he did so. The door had been locked and bolted and no one had come since. As the sunlight had faded a chill had seeped into the room. When the rain started the chill had turned into a freeze, and now Margot lay on the floor shaking so badly that her teeth chattered uncontrollably in her head.

Worst of all, she didn't know what had happened to Eric, or where he had been taken once they had arrived. She had seen him being roughly dragged away before she had been carried inside the small fortified keep at which they had stopped. Wherever he was, she fervently hoped he was being kept more comfortably than she.

He had been in a dreadful state of shock after Black Donal spoke to him that afternoon. She had tried to speak with him, too, to soothe him, but he was so stunned that none of her words seemed to penetrate. The thought that Black Donal might be his father, or even one of his relatives, had immobilized him, so that when an hour had passed and some men had come to take him back to his horse, he had been able only to kiss her good-bye without saying any words. His dark eyes had held a kind of terror as he had dazedly allowed himself to be taken away.

Wherever he was, however he was, Margot prayed that he would be able to shake himself of the fears that so overwhelmed him. If she could only be with him, she would *make* him do so, for she understood enough about him now to know how tortured his thoughts must be.

Margot was shaking so badly that she didn't notice the door being unlocked and opened until someone entered the chamber with a torch, and even when she did realize that someone had come she didn't have enough control over her own limbs to be able to turn her head to see who it was. She could, however, hear perfectly well.

"God's mercy! Look at the child! And this chamber is cold as death! Bring the light hither, John, and let us see what can be done."

She had never thought to be so grateful for the small warmth afforded by a torch, but the faint breath of heat that caressed her body as the light drew nearer elicited an unbidden moan from her lips. Hands pulled her shaking body into a sitting position, a heavy cloak was thrown over her shoulders and a cup of something hot was pressed to her lips.

"Here, child, drink this wine. 'Tis still a bit hot, but 'twill soon have thee warm, i'faith."

The hot liquid burned her lips and mouth, but Margot didn't care. She drank it down greedily, savoring the heat as it scorched her frozen throat and chest and belly. She was gasping when she finished it and still shaking badly, but already she could feel the warmth beginning to radiate into her limbs. When the cup was pulled from her fingers she grasped the cloak about her more tightly and looked at the woman who sat beside her.

"Thou wilt feel better in a moment," the woman assured her kindly, though there was nothing in her expression to indicate that she was kind. She was tall, thin, and very dark, and her black hair was drawn up tightly upon her head and left uncovered, making her already weary face look even more taut. Margot couldn't decide what the woman was, either a servant or one of the ladies of this place, for although she was dressed in worn and ragged clothing her bearing indicated higher birth. Yet she appeared to be the very embodiment of defeat, the very soul of resignation, as though life held neither joy nor mystery for her. All these things were immediately visible on the face of this woman, whom Margot guessed could not be so very old, or, at least, certainly not old enough to have learned so much of life.

"I d-do f-f-feel b-better n-now, I th-thank th-thee," Margot replied after a moment, cringing at how pronounced her stammer was.

Hearing Margot's strange speech, the woman stared hard at her, and then she shook her head. "I cannot imagine why Donal hath not had one of the servants to build a fire in this chamber. I suppose he hath reason. Here." She reached down and picked a bowl up from a tray. One whiff told Margot that it was some kind of gruel, and a most unappealing one at that. However, the woman shoved it under her nose and Margot obediently took up a spoon and ate it, grateful for anything with which to fill her hungry belly.

"Is th-this p-p-place R-R-Ravinet?" she asked when she was finished.

The woman smiled faintly. "Nay, 'tis not Ravinet, though its master is the same. This place is called Beronhurst."

"B-b-but L-Lord Ravinet is h-h-here?"

"Nay, he is not here yet, though he shall arrive any hour I believe. Donal sent him word as soon as thou didst arrive."

"B-Black D-D-Donal is thy m-m-master? Thy h-husband?"

This time the woman chuckled. "Donal is my brother, though perhaps *master* suits him better." Her smile slowly faded. "Terent of Ravinet is our overlord."

Margot nodded her understanding of this. "S-S-Sir Eric, who w-w-was b-brought w-with m-m-me, h-he is b-b-being t-t-treated well?"

"I know not of whom thou dost speak," the woman answered with a frown. "Donal said naught of another prisoner." Her frown deepened.

"Oh," Margot said, disappointed.

"'Tis strange in Donal not to do so," muttered the woman. "I must go, now, else Donal will come to fetch me. I shall have to take my cloak back," she said, reaching her hands up to pull the garment out of Margot's tight grip, "but I shall send someone with a blanket . . ."

Her words died away as she drew the heavy cloak from Margot's shoulders.

"Where—" she whispered, then swallowed heavily. "Oh, dear God. Where didst thou find that brooch?"

Margot's fingers instinctively flew up to cover the precious brooch which Eric had given her, and she felt a sudden fear. The woman stared unwaveringly at the brooch, as though she were going to snatch it from her.

"P-please d-do n-n-not take it f-from m-me!" she pleaded. "P-please do n-not! 'Tis all I h-h-have f-from m-my bel-l-loved. He g-gave it m-me as a p-pledge of his l-love. 'Twould h-have n-no v-v-value to anyone s-s-save him and me. P-please d-do not t-take it!"

The woman reached up and yanked Margot's hands down. She stared at the brooch in amazement. "'Tis indeed the same one," she whispered, her voice trembling. "The very same one, after all these years." She tore her eyes away and looked up at Margot. "Where did this man come by this brooch? How did he come to have it?"

"'Twas h-his b-b-by right. He d-d-did n-not steal or t-take it. 'Twas l-left him at h-his b-birth." Margot wasn't sure how much she should tell this woman. If Black Donal was truly Eric's father, then this woman was his aunt, but what that might mean to Eric she couldn't even begin to imagine.

The woman raised a trembling hand to her lips. "Who—who is this man? What is his name?"

Margot bit her lip and shook her head slightly, wishing she could know what to do.

"Please!" the woman begged. "Please tell me. Please. Thou canst never know what it would mean to me only to know his name! To know only that he is alive and well!"

Against her better instincts, Margot gave way. "His n-name is Eric S-Stavelot, and h-he was b-b-brought to this p-place with m-me."

The woman gasped, straightened, and put her hand to her mouth again. "He is here?! *Here?!*"

Margot nodded. "Aye, though I d-do n-not know where."

Not another word was spoken. The woman took her cloak and placed it back around Margot's shoulders, securing it firmly with shaking hands. Then she stood, took up her tray, and signaled the guard. In another moment they had gone and Margot was shut within the darkness again, all alone.

She sat in the silence, wondering if she had done the right thing and hoping that Eric would not be angry with her. The cloak provided a little warmth and she was grateful for it. Presently she lay down, closed her eyes, and tried to sleep.

The warmth in the place was nearly suffocating, or perhaps it was only because he was tied so close to the fire that Eric felt so warm. He wasn't going to complain about it, of course, for he was certainly being kept more comfortably than he had expected when he was first brought into this oversized dungeon some hours earlier. The initial sight of it had been enough to bring him out of the state of shock he'd been in for most of the afternoon, and he had fully expected to be stretched out on one of the several instruments of torture scattered about the chamber. Instead, Black Donal had instructed that he be securely tied to some iron rings on one of the walls and then let be by the two guards who remained in the room with him. On his way out the door Black Donal had stopped and turned long enough to order that a fire be started and kept going until Terent of Ravinet arrived. He had stared at Eric broodingly for several long moments after that, a dark frown on his face. Finally he had turned and left, and Eric had felt more than relieved.

It was difficult, even now, to think on the words the man had spoken to him earlier. In sooth, he almost could not do it. Already he had experienced the full agony of what those words had implied and had found himself nearly incapable of battling that agony; now that he had shaken free of his stupor he would not so willingly give into it again. Later, when he had Margot safe at Belhaven, he would think on those words again. Until then he would devote his every thought and action only to having Margot safe, to somehow getting her out of this miserable, rotting pile they'd been brought to.

Margot. His beautiful, beloved Margot. He prayed that she was being kept comfortably wherever she was and that she was being treated well. He prayed that she wouldn't worry over him, or try to do anything foolish that might bring Black Donal's already abusive hand down upon her fair head. Mostly he prayed that Jaufre and Sir Allyn were close on their heels, ready and able with a plan to escape them from this place. Eric had perused the small keep closely before he was dragged inside, and had realized at once that it could not be Ravinet. Unless Terent of Ravinet brought a large contingency of men along, the place was not so well manned as to withstand a decently planned attack. His own men would be outnumbered, Eric knew, but a little ingenuity could easily make up for a lack of men, and if there was one quality for which Sir Allyn was famed other than for admirable fighting skills, it was ingenuity.

The room grew hotter by the second and Eric sweated freely. His hands, stretched out above his head, had long since gone numb and his body ached from lack of rest and from the strain of having to bear himself up in one position, hour after hour after hour. Worst of all, he was parched with an almost overwhelming thirst. The guards had refused to give him water earlier and Eric had given up asking for it. So he closed his eyes and leaned his head against the wall, thinking of Margot and trying to convince himself that a little thirst and discomfort were certainly preferable to a great many other discomforts he might even now be suffering.

The chamber door clicked, then squeaked on its hinges. Eric opened his eyes. A woman bearing a tray walked in, followed by two guards. He closed his eyes to rest again. He was going to be given something to eat, it seemed, and the good Lord knew he was ready.

Neither Margot nor he had been allowed even a piece of bread today, and his stomach had given way to grumbling long before the afternoon had passed.

The touch of a cool, wet cloth surprised him, so that he opened his eyes once more to see that the woman was standing before him, bathing his hot face very gently. She was a tall, weary-looking woman, dark and thin and very pale. He thought perhaps she must be one of the servants, for she had such a look of defeat about her, as though her very spirit had been carelessly trampled and broken. Any servant of Black Donal's must be thus, Eric thought, and how much more so would be the servants of Ravinet. He felt sorry for the woman, and he smiled at her.

"Thou'rt most kind, mistress," he said gently. "I thank thee."

Her hand shook and her dark eyes welled with sudden tears. The cloth that had been moving across one cheek stopped.

She's frightened of me, he thought. It was doubly cruel of Black Donal to send this poor, timid creature to tend a daunting giant like himself when the man could so easily have sent one of his men to do the task instead. He wished that his arms, at least, were free so that he could hunch down a little and make himself smaller. Perhaps she wouldn't have been so frightened if he hadn't been stretched out to his full height.

Tears were spilling freely down the woman's cheeks now, and her whole face was trembling with the restraint of not crying openly.

"Mistress," Eric pleaded, his tone as gentle and soothing as though he were speaking to a child, "there is no need to fear me. Thou canst see that I am tightly bound with no hope of escape, but e'en were I suddenly freed I would do thee no harm." He smiled again in the hope of putting her at ease. "Thou hast no need to be frightened."

She shook her head and began to mop at his face again.

"And I shall behave very well while thou'rt about thy task," Eric promised, still grinning. "I'll be no more trouble than a newborn babe, I vow."

She shut her eyes and turned sharply away, and Eric could see that her shoulders were shaking as she covered her face with her hands, the very opposite reaction to what he had hoped for. The two guards nearby watched the woman in fascination until she finally straightened and looked their way. They snapped to attention, but she ignored them and went to fetch the tray. With resolution she turned back to Eric and brought it to him.

"Thou must be thirsty," she whispered.

"Aye, that I am, mistress, though not for ale, if't please thee. I verily believe I would sell my soul for a cup of plain water."

She ordered the guards to bring water, and when they complied she held the cup to Eric's lips so that he could drink. When he had gulped down the first cup she gave him another, and then another, until his great thirst was quenched.

"Sweet mercy!" he gasped when he finally finished.

"If God e'er created a better thing than water, I should like to know what it is! I thank thee, mistress. Thou'rt kind as heaven's angels."

She made no reply to this but brought a spoonful of gruel to his lips.

"Thy name is Eric Stavelot?" she asked in her tremulous whisper, glancing quickly up at his eyes.

Eric swallowed the gruel. "Aye, that it is. And thine?"

Once more she said nothing. Three more spoonfuls came his way in silence. On the fourth she spoke again. "Thou—thou hast a family—a mother—who cares for thee? Who would be worried to know thou wast being kept here?"

A vision of his mother flashed through Eric's mind, and he thought of how she would cry if she knew where he was, and in what condition. His mother had always been one who lived in fear for her family's safety. When any of them had been sick or hurt she had gone into a panic, hovering over them constantly and fearing the worst. He remembered the many nights she had sat up with him when he had fallen ill, making certain that he had every comfort and caring for him as tenderly and lovingly as only a mother could. She would always weep when he had finally gotten well, simply out of relief that one of her children hadn't been taken away from her. When his father and Jaufre and he had returned home from the war she had sat on his father's lap in the great hall and cried and laughed for a full hour, sometimes reaching out a hand to touch either Jaufre or himself, who had sat nearby patting her and winking at one another in amused understanding.

"Aye," he replied quietly, "I've a very beautiful mother, and she would be most unhappy to know I was being kept prisoner here. 'Twould break her heart, most like."

The woman swallowed heavily and looked as if she was going to cry again. She brought another shaking spoonful to his mouth.

"She has been good to thee, thy mother? She has always loved thee?"

He chuckled and wondered why this stranger should be so interested to know whether he had been loved. Perhaps her fear had given way to pity and she found it hard to believe that anyone could love such a one as he. The idea was not so unusual. He had had the same thought many times himself.

"She has been the finest mother God e'er sent to earth," he declared. "And, aye, she has always loved me, much more than I have ever deserved and much more than I can sometimes believe."

"Oh! Thank God!" the woman said so suddenly and passionately that it surprised him. "May God bless her all her days!"

Bemused, Eric agreed, "Amen!" Then he laughed a little and wondered at what an odd person this serving maid was.

The chamber door opened, squeaking on its hinges again, and the woman turned quickly to replace everything on her tray, suddenly nervous again.

Margot walked into the chamber first, bound only

by her hands now; behind her came Black Donal, prodding her roughly along; behind him came two more guards.

"Margot!" Eric cried, his heart leaping painfully at the sight of her.

"Eric!"

She would have flown down the few stairs and run to him, but Black Donal reached out, grabbed a fistful of her unbound hair, and forcefully yanked her back. The fingers of one gloved hand sank into the soft flesh of her arm until she winced from the pain.

"If thou dost not behave thyself, my lady, thou wilt find thyself more than sorry for't. I shall give thee over to my men to use for their pleasure once my master has had done with thee, and thou wouldst scarcely find their company amusing, methinks."

He gave her a rough shaking before letting her go so suddenly that she stumbled the rest of the way down the stairs.

"Bastard!" Eric rattled the steel rings he was tied to. He'd never felt so impotent in his whole life, or so furious. If he could somehow have gotten free he would surely have killed the devil with his bare hands.

Black Donal ignored him, however, because he had suddenly caught sight of the darkly clad woman standing so nervously with her tray. He carelessly picked Margot up by one arm and shoved her into a nearby chair, all the time never taking his eyes off the woman.

"Adela, why art thou here? How hast thou come to be here?" It was the first gentle tone Eric had ever heard the man use.

The woman began to cry. "Why didst thou not tell me, Donal?" She sobbed pitifully. "'Twas my right to know! Why didst thou keep it from me?"

Black Donal reached the woman in two angry strides, grabbing her by both arms and sending the tray clattering onto the floor. "'Twas for this that I kept it from thee! I knew thou wouldst only be overset, and so thou art! Why should I see thee made so miserable after he has gone? Thou knowest full well Ravinet will not let him live!"

Crying even harder, the woman beat at Black Donal's chest with two thin fists. She shook her head violently back and forth. "Nay! I'll not let him! I'll not! He is my son! Mine! I'll not let Terent take him away from me again!"

Eric felt as though his heart had stopped beating.

"Silence, Adela!" Black Donal shouted, shaking the woman viciously. "Silence or I'll make thee silent, I swear't! Terent has arrived. E'en now he comes to see his captives, and I'll not have thee anger him any more than he is already like to be by thy presence here!"

Eric forced himself to take deep, steadying breaths. Could it be true? Could it be possible? Were these two people his parents then? Black Donal his father and the darkly clad woman his mother? The thought of being sired by such as Black Donal was so terrible he could not even consider it, but the woman had been kind to him, had given him water and bathed his face when she had not had a need to do either. Oh, God, he thought suddenly, she wasn't frightened of me. She wasn't frightened of me.

The door squeaked on its hinges once more and every eye turned to it. Two solemn guards came through first, and then, slowly and deliberately, Terent of Ravinet walked into the room.

Margot gasped audibly.

Eric stared at Ravinet and shook his head in shock and disbelief.

"Nay," he whispered. "Nay!"

All his life he had waited for this moment, had prayed for it even, yet now when it arrived he could not bear the truth of it. Pain, worse than any he had ever known before, swept his body in a great wave. He began to cry, unable to stop himself and barely aware that he was doing so.

"Oh, God! Nay! Please, nay!" The words came screaming out of him, as from a man in torment, and he fought helplessly at the bonds that held him. It could not be true. It *could* not be. "Nay, God, nay!"

And he was lost, lost completely in a darkness so great he could not see out of it. He wanted to die and hoped he would. No thought he had ever had in his entire life had even approached the horror he felt at knowing the truth, and he cursed all his foolishness as well as his existence and wished Black Donal would kill him soon.

"Eric!" Margot's sobbing voice broke through to him, like a light in darkness. She was crying his name

over and over, her own voice as tormented as his. He
opened his eyes and looked at her, saw that she was
standing now, her bound hands stretched out toward
him pleadingly. But she seemed very far away, so far
that he wondered how he was able to hear her.

"Eric, th-thou m-m-must remember thy p-p-p, thy
p-p-p—" And she burst into horrible tears, unable to
finish the word because of her agitation and fear.

"My pledge," Eric whispered, completing her sen-
tence out of sheer habit. She nodded into her hands.
He blinked his own tears away and began to pull the
scattered fragments of his mind together. The pledge
he had made to her in the cool, wooded place by the
river seemed to have been an eternity ago, but it came
back to him slowly, and with it came memories of
Margot's sweet kisses and of her never-ending professions of love for him. He swallowed with difficulty
and shook his whirling head. He had pledged to love
faithfully and protect Margot for as long as his life
lasted. He had made his pledge before God. He must
keep it. He must, no matter what horrors befell him.

"Margot," he murmured, "I forget not my pledge
to thee."

"How very affecting," Terent of Ravinet said pleasantly, casually traversing the few steps into the dungeon proper. "I see thou wast not telling me false-
hoods, Donal." He strolled closer to Eric and eyed
him critically. "Not only do I have a son, but a gallant
son, it seems."

Eric turned to meet his father's gaze, though it was
so much like looking into a mirror that he shuddered.

Terent of Ravinet was shorter than he, as well as less muscular, but in every other way he was a replica of Eric himself.

"Greetings, my son," Ravinet murmured with some amusement, a smile curling his lips. "Thou'rt not pleased to meet thy esteemed parent, I gather. Or perhaps I should have said parents, for thou hast already met the mother who bore thee." He glanced briefly over his shoulder at Black Donal and his sister. "Good eve, Adela. Canst believe this giant we created betwixt the two of us? God's wounds! I should think the brute would have rent thee asunder when thou didst birth him!" He took up his perusal of Eric again, looking him over appreciatively from top to toe. "Had I known he would turn out so sturdily, I do believe I might have decided to keep him. Just think what a help he might have been had he been properly raised!" He chuckled. "Why, I imagine whole armies have trembled at the very sight of him! Owain would have his precious Wales by now if the son of Ravinet had been on the other side, methinks."

"I am no son of Ravinet," Eric said.

"The giant speaks!" Terent of Ravinet raised his eyebrows slightly and grinned. "And what? No son of Ravinet? But thou art, indeed, Sir Eric Stavelot of Belhaven. No man in his right mind could look at either of us and not find the match. In sooth, I did not raise thee, but I am the one who gavest thee life. Thou didst spring from the seed of my loins, just as thy many brothers and sisters did, and thou hast

Ravinet blood running through thy veins. There is no way thou canst escape that blood unless thou dost spill it out at thy life's end, as thy brothers and sisters did." He reached out a hand and touched Eric's chest briefly, pulling it back when Eric recoiled. "Thou'rt the only one who hath escaped the death I gifted my children with at birth, and only because I placed trust in a man whom I thought to be a faithful servant." He pinned Black Donal with a momentary glare. "A servant who apparently put his sister's whinings above his master's commands. But that is no matter to us now, is it, my son?"

"I am not thy son," Eric stated, the effects of his initial shock wearing away in the face of his hatred for this man. "Sir Garin Stavelot is my father. I shall never call another man such."

Terent of Ravinet gave a shout of laughter. "Garin! Hah! Yes, I can see thou hast been well muddled by his upbringing, God save us!" He turned from Eric and strolled to where Margot sat. She shrank from him as he approached, but he grabbed her by both arms and drew her to himself. "So," he said, looking her over, "this is my lovely, rich new bride, is it? She looks no happier to see her bridegroom than her lover is to see his father. Such ungrateful children! But she is much more beautiful than I thought she would be or, at least, shall be more beautiful once her tears have ceased and her face has regained its color." He placed one hand under her chin and smiled when she twisted in revulsion to be free of him. "What dost thou think, Donal? Shall I make a fortune from her as

I did from Adela? She would bring a pretty price, I vow, better than thy sister ever did, from many and many a man who would be willing to pay for her favors. Old Stareton shall have to be first, methinks. He'll set a goodly price for the others to follow, though perhaps the others will be willing to pay a little more in order to watch whilst they await their turns."

"Aye, that they would, my lord," Black Donal replied obediently.

Margot could not bear to look at the man who held her, who was smiling at her and stroking her cheek with his hated hand. She could not bear to see her Eric's every beloved feature repeated on the face of such a devil.

"Look, she closes her eyes against me!" Terent said, amused. "Methinks she likes not the face of her husband-to-be, though 'tis the same as that of her lover." He leaned closer to whisper near her ear. "In sooth, thou shouldst be pleased, my dear. When I've mounted thee this eve thou will be able to imagine 'tis thy Eric riding thee. Will not that be something to be grateful for, sweet?" He laughed again when she squirmed, and he cast a glance to where Eric stood furiously rattling his bonds. "I darest not hope that my son hath been so gallant as to have not gone before me." He shoved Margot aside and walked toward Eric again.

"Now there is an interesting idea," he said thoughtfully, his eyes roaming Eric's face. "What wouldst thou say, son, were I to offer thee a chance to save thy life and to wed the woman thou dost evidently desire?"

Eric felt amazingly calm now, as though the intense torment he experienced earlier had never happened. This man was not his father, and it was easy for him to say the words in his mind. Aye, he'd sprung from the devil's seed, true enough, but that only made the man his sire, not his father.

"I'd say, Terent of Ravinet, that my life is not in thy hands, neither to give nor to take away."

The lord of Ravinet was momentarily surprised by this curt response, but after a moment the surprise passed and he chuckled again. "Thou'rt bold, lad, e'en before thou hast had a chance to hear what I propose. But I like boldness in a man, and thou'rt a man, true enough, as well as my son. There is greatness in thee, Eric of Ravinet, no more of Belhaven, and such greatness could verily be a boon to a man like myself, nay, indeed, to any man. Too long hast thou been kept under the thumb of Garin Stavelot, who hath kept thee all these years as a great jest on me, no doubt. But I can set thee free, son, if thou wilt only let me!" His tone grew persuasive, caressing. "Come, join forces with thine own father and live with me as my rightful son. I've both power and riches which shall one day be thine, and thou canst marry thy lady love and take all that comes with her marriage as well. Betwixt the two of us we could verily rule the whole island! Only think how grateful Glendower and his cohorts will be when we've handed them the key to Wales! Thou shalt live as a prince, my son, as a prince! No longer shalt thou be called bastard, nor wilt thou live as one beholden to another for his keep and feed. What sayest thou? Shall it be death at the hand of my servant, or life and all that thou hast e'er dreamt of?"

Eric shook his head. "The life thou hast described has ne'er been my dream. Mine has always been to be the true son of my father, Sir Garin Stavelot. Verily would I choose death before I would shame him by taking another man's name."

"Garin of Stavelot is not thy father!" Ravinet snapped angrily. "Canst thou not see how that demon hast made use of thee for his own amusement all these years? The man hates me and has always done so. E'en when we were fostered together he wast jealous of me, he and that simpering fool Walter le Brun, whose death I shall celebrate whence the deed is done!"

Margot cried out but Ravinet ignored her.

"Always did they wish to humiliate me in any manner they could do so, and what better way than to flaunt publicly my bastard son?"

"My father never flaunted me!" Eric shouted furiously, his clenched fists straining at their ropes.

"Idiot!" Ravient spat. "Thinkest thou he knew not whose son thou wast? Any man having seen the both of us would know it! The king, Prince Henry, any nobleman of rank who has known of me and who has seen thee at court or on the battlefield, all would know the truth at once."

Eric blinked, stunned by the truth of the man's

words. He swallowed heavily and shook his head. "My father," he insisted, "my father did not know. He would have told me the truth had he known it. He knew how much it would have meant to me to know the truth."

Terent laughed in disbelief. "My God! Thou'rt a blind fool! The man who has called himself thy father all these years has done naught but lie to thee! He knew who thy real father was and ne'er told thee, and that is the truth of it! Why should he tell thee the truth? 'Twould only have caused him to lose thee, for surely thou wouldst have sought thine own father out. 'Twas better for him to keep thee for his own folly, to make the son of Ravinet his slave and jester. Canst not imagine the many times he laughed o'er thy ignorant devotion?"

"My father never, *never*—"

"Oh, aye, he did laugh, foolish boy! Long and hard, I'll wager. But I'll not waste my breath speaking of the likes of Garin Stavelot. I want an answer from thee, lad, and want it now, else thy life is over and I'm off to marry thy lady love. Come! The priest waits abovestairs e'en now to make one of us her mate. Shall it be me or thee, my son? Answer me now!"

Eric hardly needed to think the matter over. The lifelong love he'd borne his family was too much a part of him, was too heavily ingrained in him, for there to be any choice. Perhaps his father had known all these years. Indeed, he must have, for it seemed unlikely that anyone would not have known, just as Terent of Ravinet said. It disturbed Eric to think that

Father had never told him the truth, and it hurt a little, too, for surely his father knew how much it would have meant to him to have known something about his family, regardless of how terrible the truth might have been. But that little pain paled in the light of the hundreds and thousands of memories Eric had of his father's love for him, indeed, of his whole family's.

There was the time he'd been knighted, when Father had given him his sword, when he had nearly given way to tears for the first time in Eric's memory. There were the times he and his father had gone hunting together, either alone or with James and Jaufre and Aleric along, when Father could never quite keep from showing the pride he felt for all of them, equally, whenever one of them felled their game. There was the first time he had been wounded in battle and had wakened to find James sitting beside him, holding his hand and praying while Father and Jaufre paced agitatedly in the background. He remembered what he had said when he'd focused his eyes—"Thou shouldst have gone into the Church, James"—and how relieved his father and brothers had been to hear him speak. It had taken all three of them to carry him off the field, and it took all three of them to hold him down on the cot to keep him from going back out to fight again. And there were all the many family celebrations, when Eric had known the love of his family, when he had never felt the difference that the truth of his birth should have made. He remembered the time Liliore had sewn him a beautiful tunic for his birthday, and how she had cried because it hadn't fit perfectly. For once something had actually been too large for him. He had kissed her and wiped her tears away and promised that he would grow into it very shortly, and indeed he had kept his promise. He'd worn the tunic on his next birthday, and it had looked very fine on him, or so he'd thought. Liliore had been pleased, he remembered, and that was all that had mattered.

He met Terent of Ravinet's eyes steadily. "I am not thy son," he repeated. "Sir Garin Stavelot of Belhaven is my father, and shall be until I last draw breath. As to the lady Margot," he said, his gaze falling on her, "she knows how I love her and that my whole heart is hers so long as it beats with life. I should never bring her pain by marrying her falsely and by having a part in her father's death. 'Twould be better to die than to live and see such pain light her eyes."

Margot's lips trembled and she nodded silently at Eric.

Terent of Ravinet scowled. "So be it. Thou hast sealed thine own fate, then. Thou hast no other to blame but thyself. Donal, thou must do as thou shouldst have done three and twenty years past, but this time thou must not fail me. Do it after I have gone. I've no wish to watch this particular child die."

The words were barely out of his mouth when both Adela and Margot cried, "Nay!"

Both women flung themselves at Eric, Adela hugging him with both arms and Margot pressing herself firmly into his chest.

Ravinet easily threw Margot aside, but Adela proved more difficult. She clung to Eric tenaciously, her nails digging into the skin of his back to make herself more immovable.

"Damn thee, Adela!" Black Donal shouted, coming forward to take hold of her, but Terent of Ravinet grabbed his minion by the front of his tunic first, stopping him only inches from his sister.

"I've had enough of thy sister's whinings, and I've no patience left! 'Tis time and since one of us took a firmer hand with her, Donal, and thou hast proven useless in doing so."

"My Lord Ravinet, I swear by God that I shall—"

"Cease!" Ravinet bellowed, shaking the muscular man as though he were a child. "I shall have the saying of her, or 'tis I shall have the death of her! 'Tis only a miracle thou hast kept my hand from her these many years, but, by God, thou shalt do so no longer! She wants her precious child? Very well! Let her have him! Let her watch him die at the hand of her own brother and then we shall see whether she is so quick to interfere again!"

Black Donal blanched visibly. "Please, my lord, I shall do thy bidding and kill him, but do not ask the other of me. I cannot do it if Adela watches. Please, my lord—"

"What in God's name is all that infernal racket!" Ravinet interrupted, nearly screeching in his rage.

There *was* an infernal racket sounding from abovestairs, and had been for several minutes, though now the sounds grew closer and closer. To

Eric's trained ears the noises sounded very similar to those of battle, and fierce battle at that.

The door to the dungeon flew open and one of Black Donal's men stood in the opening, his face pale and his breathing ragged. "My lords! The keep hath been breeched! They're swarming down on us like very demons, my lords! We've lost twenty men already, and there seems no way of stopping them!"

Both Terent of Ravinet and Black Donal moved toward the stairs, and Eric himself was so intent upon this new revelation that he barely noticed Adela's stealthy movements or that she was suddenly sawing with a small dagger at one of the ropes that held his hands.

"'Tis impossible!" Black Donal stated flatly. "This keep is too well guarded to be breeched in only a matter of minutes!"

Eric glanced at his mother's determined face as she kept up her efforts to free him. It was a difficult task; she was a tall woman, but even so she had to strain on her toes to reach the rope.

The man at the top of the stairs shook his head helplessly. "I know it well, my lord, but I swear 'tis the truth! Canst not hear them approach with thine own ears? They were on us before we knew what happened!"

"How?! How?!" Terent of Ravinet demanded.

"I do not know, my lord!" the man wailed, shaking his hands. "The gates were somehow all opened to them, as though by magic. They came in on all sides and all at once! Thou must hurry, my lord Ravinet, and escape ere they find thee!"

The man turned and raced back up the hall in the direction he had come. Black Donal cursed aloud and followed, running up the stairs with every guard in the room behind him.

One good tug severed the frayed rope, and Eric's hand fell free. Adela turned her attention to the second hand. She had only begun to saw on it when she gasped suddenly, and stilled.

Terent of Ravinet's eyes met Eric's, so close that Eric wondered how he had gotten there. The man was smiling at him, and he seemed to be hugging Adela, who had gone strangely limp all of a sudden. Ravinet stepped back, easily lifting Adela away, and he pulled the knife out of her back, chuckling at the look of horror on Eric's face as he did so. Adela's own knife clattered to the floor next to where Ravinet laid her.

"Oh, Adela." Ravinet sighed, kneeling over her and stroking her cheek once. "Thou never didst know how to please me, e'en when thou wast a child." He grinned at Margot, who had covered her mouth with her bound hands in an attempt to keep from being ill. "I do hope my wife shall be able to do better." He rose to his feet and sheathed his bloody knife, then turned to Eric.

"I wish I could kill thee, as well, son, but I lied not when I said I have no particular wish to see thee die. 'Twould not be easy to do as the others were. Killing a babe is not much different from drowning a kitten, really, but I fear 'twould not be so in killing thee." He shrugged and looked down at Adela, who stared up at him with wide eyes. Ravinet nudged her with one foot and watched her contort in pain. A pool of blood formed slowly beneath her thin body. "She'll be dead soon enough," Ravinet commented blandly, turning to Eric once again. "Thou shalt watch her die, my son. That will be my gift to thee, rather than the gift of death. I rather think I shall regret not having killed thee, but this at least I can give thee. A memory to haunt thee all thy days. The memory of thy mother's death."

"Oh, d-d-dear L-Lord!" Margot cried, taking a step toward the dying woman.

Terent of Ravinet stopped her. "But thou art coming with me, my dear. We've a wedding to attend." He stooped and slung her over one shoulder.

"I'll n-n-not w-w-w-ed thee!" Margot cried angrily, hitting his back and shoulders with her bound hands.

Terent of Ravinet only laughed. "Good-bye, my son. I've no doubt thou shall be free within a few minutes, and that thy friends shall soon be here to aid thee, but e'en so thou must say good-bye to thy lady. Thou shalt ne'er see her after this, I promise thee."

Eric lifted his eyes from the woman lying on the floor to gaze at the man. "The lady Margot is one thing thou shalt never have, Terent of Ravinet. She is mine. Always." His words were very deliberate, cool.

Ravinet chuckled and headed for the stairs, toting a struggling, cursing Margot with him. "It seems I already have her, son, and shall continue to have her 'til I weary of her. But thou hast thy recompense and must not complain." He laughed a little harder. "After all, lad, have I not left thy dear mother to thee?"

His laughter echoed into the room even after he had left it, closing and bolting the door behind him. The only other sounds discernable above the noise of fighting were Margot's angry screams, but even for that Eric could spare no thoughts. The moment the door shut he began to tear at his bonds with his free hand.

"Don't die!" Eric pleaded furiously, cursing the impossible ropes that bound him. "Please, don't die!"

At last both his hands were free, then one foot, then both. He was kneeling beside his mother seconds after he was unbound, gently touching her face with his large, callused hands. She kept trying to speak to him, but her voice was so faint he couldn't hear her. Slowly, carefully he slid one hand behind her head, then another beneath her shoulders to lift her into his lap.

"Robin," she whispered. "My own Robin. How I prayed to have thee back again. Every night I prayed for thee."

Her life's blood was everywhere, all over the floor, all over her, all over him. Eric had seen too many men die in battle not to know that her wound was fatal. He began to weep.

"And I prayed to find thee, Mother. I prayed that I would know thee."

She trembled as though cold, and Eric gathered her close.

"I always loved thee," she told him. "Never would I have let thee go. Never."

"I know," he murmured, kissing her wet cheeks. "I know."

"God bless the woman who kept thee for me, who loved thee as I would have done. God bless her."

"He hath done so, Mother."

She closed her eyes. "Mother," she repeated softly. "Mother. 'Tis sweet to hear thee say it, my beautiful son. My beautiful Robin. I am sorry I was not a better one, but I always loved thee."

She was silent after that, her breathing slow and shallow, and Eric gently stroked her hair until her breathing slowed, then finally ceased altogether.

He did not know how long he stayed thus, holding the body of the woman who'd given him life, rocking her back and forth and stroking her hair. He did not know how long he wept. He only came to his senses when he heard his brother's voice speaking somewhere above him.

"Eric! Thank God thou'rt all right!" The relief in Jaufre's tone was distinct. In a moment his brother stood beside him, his hand firm on his shoulder. "God's mercy! Eric, what has happened here? Who is this poor woman?"

Eric turned his tear-stained face to Jaufre's. "She was my mother," he whispered.

"Oh, God, Eric. Oh, dear God." Jaufre knelt beside him. "Tell me what happened, lad."

The story was told numbly, haltingly. At the finish of it he gently laid his mother's still body down again.

He carefully arranged her to his satisfaction, pushing the hair out of her face and setting her hands just so. When he had finished Jaufre placed one of his hands over Adela's folded ones.

"I'm so sorry, Eric," he said. "I know thou hast wanted to know thy true parents all thy life."

Eric nodded, but pushed the sad thoughts away. "We must find Margot," he said, standing. Jaufre stood beside him. "Ravinet hath taken her. We must catch them ere he does her any harm."

"The lady Margot is safe, Eric. Sir Allyn has her well guarded. Ravinet did try to take her with him, but one of his own men, named Jason of Welshore, managed to wrest the lady Margot from him and carry her to safety. Black Donal put an arrow in the man's back and I do not think he will live long, but he was able to save the lady Margot from Ravinet's clutches."

Eric felt as though he could breathe again. "Thank God thou breeched the keep when thou didst, Jaufre."

"'Tis thy Thomas thou must thank, and none other. The lad was able to make his way into the keep without remark and unlatched each entry unseen. Without him we'd ne'er have found so easy a way. He's the bravest lad I've ever known."

"Good, brave Tom," Eric murmured, his gaze on the body lying at his feet. "I owe him my life." He held out a hand. "Give me thy sword then, brother, and let me join this fight. I'll see Black Donal dead this day, I vow, and shall gladly take every man who stands in the way between him and me."

"There is no need, lad. The fighting is nearly over now. There is no way for Black Donal to escape. Ravinet managed it, but just barely. Black Donal shall be thine if thou dost wish it."

"I do wish it."

"Then thy wish is granted," came a voice behind them.

Jaufre alone turned to see Black Donal standing at the top of the stairs. He came into the chamber, his eyes fixed on the body of his sister. Slowly, slowly he moved around Eric until he was on the other side of him, and slowly he knelt beside Adela.

"Adela," he whispered, pulling his gloves off. He reached a bare hand out to touch her face.

"Do not," Eric warned, stopping the man. "Do not touch her."

Black Donal's pale blue eyes turned up to him.

"She was my sister."

"She was *my* mother."

Black Donal shook his head. "Thou didst have her but an hour," he said. "She was all I had my entire life. Thou wilt kill me as thou may, but thou shalt not keep me from Adela."

He waited for no permission but turned back to his sister's pale face and touched her cheek.

"Adela. Adela," he crooned as though he were trying to rouse her from slumber. The hand stroking her cheek trembled. "Thou wast cruel to leave me thus, sweet girl. Did I not always love thee? Did I not need thee more than he? Oh, Adela, thou foolish, foolish girl."

Black Donal bent to kiss her, but Eric noticed that he did not cry for his sister. It angered him, but perhaps the man was too far removed from tears.

"She was only ten and three years of age when she gave birth to thee," he said quietly, "and only ten and one when our Lord Ravinet began taking her to his bed. Our parents had died and we were his wards." He shrugged. "There was naught we could do to stop him. We thought—we both thought he would marry her when she came of age, and she thought she loved him a little." He moved his hand down to take hold of one of hers. "Ravinet said naught when he learned she carried his child, and Adela only thought perhaps he would marry her sooner than he'd planned, in order to give the child a proper name." He shook his head. "What fools we were! What fools!"

There was a short silence before Black Donal continued, more calmly than before. "I was ten and eight and had pledged my fealty to Ravinet, when thou wast born. He'd introduced me to many pleasures by that time, and thus had bought me, body, soul, and spirit." He faltered a moment, then went on. "He told me to kill the child when Adela birthed it, and I swore I would do so." He lifted his eyes to gaze at Eric. "I loved my sister more than my own life, but I was determined to do as my lord bade me. But she cried so pitifully when she realized my intent." He brought his sister's hand up to kiss and hold against his cheek. "It nearly broke my heart.

"We were not here when she gave birth to thee, but were traveling home from Ravinet. Our lord could no longer abide to see Adela in her condition there, and he did not wish to be present when the child was born. He bade us return to Beronhurst, and she felt her first labor pains when we were halfway home."

"Near Belhaven," Eric said.

Black Donal nodded. "Aye, near Belhaven, though I did not know it at the time. She nearly died giving birth to thee, and e'en for that I would gladly have killed thee, but she begged me and begged me to leave thee with some peasant folk. She swore she would not tell Ravinet of my deception and that she would ne'er speak of the matter again, if only I would let thee live. I'd planned to take thee from her and kill thee then, but she made me vow I'd not kill thee with mine own hands, so I could not do so."

"But thou didst abandon me at the very first opportunity," Eric stated angrily.

"That is so," Black Donal admitted. "But I did not kill thee by mine own hand, thereby keeping my promise to Adela." He sighed. "She grieved for thee every day of her life since that time. Every single day. Robin, she called thee, after our father. I wanted to spare her pain, but there was naught I could do, and now her grief has brought her to this. Oh, Adela," he said miserably. "My foolish Adela."

Eric was unmoved by Black Donal's obvious affection for his sister, by the man's cold grief. He stood over them, watching, his hands folded together. "I shall take my mother to Belhaven for burial," he told his uncle. "And I shall fight thee fairly ere I kill thee."

Black Donal didn't look up. He only shook his head. "Adela must be buried here. Beronhurst was our home. Our parents, our ancestors, all are buried here. She would wish to be near them and not laid down amongst strangers. As to the other, thou may kill me if thou dost wish it, but I shall not fight thee. The morn shall not dawn on me again, regardless. I shall go with Adela, as I have always done, and we shall be together, as we have always been. There is no need to trouble thyself, nephew, unless thou dost wish to spill my blood. I give thee my vow thou shall see no more of me once thou hast quit this place."

"Eric," Jaufre said quietly, "the man speaks the truth."

For some odd reason that Eric could never after explain, he began to weep again, as silently and calmly as before. He nodded and wiped at his tears, embarrassed that Jaufre should see him so unmanned. "I know," he said with difficulty. "It shall be as thou hast said."

Black Donal bent and kissed Adela once more, very gently. "Beronhurst shall be thine tomorrow day. There are no others to claim it. Thou'rt the last of our line."

"I want it not," Eric said.

"Then let it fall to ruin, as perhaps it should. 'Twas once the proud barony of a proud baron, but now 'tis a place of shame. Adela would not want thee to cling to it. She always hoped thou hadst found a place in the world with a better family than ours, and so, it seems, thou hast. Thou must leave this place and ne'er look back, Eric of Belhaven. Thou must return to thine own and take thy place with them. There is naught for thee here, not even a name to take with thee."

"B-bury her well," Eric choked out.

"I shall. There is a priest abovestairs, remember, though he hath planned to perform a happier ceremony than this."

"Eric," Jaufre said, "let us leave now. There is naught thou canst do here, and we needs must get the lady Margot to Belhaven. Come along, lad."

It was good to give in to the pressure of Jaufre's hands, which turned him toward the stairs. He followed his brother numbly, and Jaufre guided him as gently as though he were leading a little child.

They stopped at the top and Eric turned to look once more at his mother and uncle. Black Donal was holding Adela's hand to his cheek again, but he turned to look at Eric. His white-blue eyes held a world of meaning in them.

"Thou must kill Ravinet when thou dost see him again. Tell him, then, that his faithful servant awaits him in hell. Tell him that for me."

23

"*Thank God! There it is!* Was ever a sight more welcome, lads?"

Aleric reined in beside his brother and shook his head. "Never, Jaufre, and glad I am to see it! I'll ne'er leave home again, i'faith!"

Jaufre laughed. "Methinks I remember a lad who was more than happy to leave it some weeks past, all ready to go out and have adventures."

"I've had enough adventure to last me a lifetime," Aleric replied with feeling, "and shall henceforth be content to live a peaceful, scholarly life." Minna, riding with him, smiled upon hearing these words.

"Then Father shall be well pleased with thee, lad," said Eric, reining in on Aleric's other side. "God's mercy!" he exclaimed, gazing at the valley lying below him. The afternoon sun was already stretching shadows across the fields and into the walled town beyond, and all looked very peaceful—the ripe, as yet unharvested fields, the lazy river, the tall spires of Castle Belhaven—all seemed beautiful to him. "Belhaven! What a blessed sight!"

Margot, sitting in front of him in the shelter of his arms, was likewise stricken with awe. "Oh, Eric! 'Tis m-more beautiful than I thought it w-would b-be! What a l-lovely place!"

"The loveliest in all the world to these weary eyes," he agreed, though in truth he felt the oddest combination of joy and sadness. He had never been so glad to see home in all his days, nor so miserable. The men behind him were murmuring, unable to contain their longing to be home, and their horses stamped impatiently as though they were going to charge.

Sir Allyn rode up and demanded, "By the Fiend's foot! What are we waiting for? Someone to trumpet us down?"

Eric glanced over Aleric's head and grinned at Jaufre, who was grinning back, then he lifted himself slightly from his saddle and looked around at his restless men. "We're home, men, may God be praised! Let's get us to Belhaven!"

A great cheer went up and the whole assembly started forward, practically flying down the mountainside. The three brothers in front raced, laughing, and Margot and Minna held on for dear life. But when they were halfway there Eric was seized by a sudden panic, and he pulled back on Bram's reins.

"What's amiss?" Margot shouted above the noise of the men passing them by. "Why hast thou s-stopped?"

He squeezed her more tightly and waited until the very last man had gone by. When the sounds of the horses' hooves had died enough he stopped Bram entirely and gathered Margot more fully into his arms.

Crushed in his embrace, Margot's laughter was smothered in Eric's chest. She pushed at him to force a space, then smiled into his unhappy face. "Thou'rt m-most romantic to s-stop for an embrace, Sir Knight, but d-dost thou n-not wish to be home?"

If he lived to be a hundred, Eric thought, he would never understand women. How could she be so happy at a time like this?

He lowered his mouth and kissed her gently, then drew back so he could look into those amazing blue eyes which were twinkling happily back at him. "My love," he said, "this shall be the last time I feel thee in mine arms. Ever. Once we pass through those gates I lose thee. I should be the greatest liar in all the world were I to say I want that. Much as I'm glad to be home I'm tempted to turn around and take thee away from here and keep thee with me forever."

Margot graced him with an ecstatic smile. "And I'd g-go w-with thee, my Eric. Anywhere in the w-world, if thou didst wish it."

Eric swallowed hard, shaking his head slightly. "I love thee, Margot. Kiss me now, one last time, and I shall live on't the rest of my days. Kiss me and I shall not care whether the entirety of Belhaven watches from the town walls."

He lowered his mouth to hers again and kissed her

as though he meant to devour her, his lips, tongue, hands all grinding her into himself until Margot thought he was going to meld their two bodies together. She returned the kiss wholeheartedly, though she knew full well it was not their last.

He looked very much like he was reconsidering turning around when the kiss ended, and Margot had to bite her lip to keep from giggling. She kissed his chin and smiled up at him again. "Take me home, my l-love. Thy p-parents will be w-wondering about us."

Eric's face was a picture of misery as he took up Bram's reins. Their ride to the gates of Belhaven was a slow one, and just outside the town walls Eric hesitated again, stopping and considering the gates to his home as though they were the gates to his doom. But just inside them he could see that all the townspeople had lined up and were cheering, and he supposed it would be more than rude not to ride in to greet them.

The sight of so many familiar faces warmed Eric's heart and made him smile in spite of himself.

His family was in the courtyard, already greeting the others who had arrived before them, and Liliore fairly screamed when she caught sight of him, causing everyone else to turn and look.

Always before when Eric had come home, either from some journey or war, the reunions with his family had been occasions of great joy, yet, at the same time, there had always been some semblance of order to them. But this time, at the mere sight of those whom he loved so well, his father, his mother, his sister, his brother James, some deep, wild emotion sprang loose within him, and he was off Bram and running to them without even knowing how he'd gotten down to the ground and without realizing that he was dragging Margot along with him, one of his strong arms circled firmly around her waist.

"Mother! Oh, God! Mother! Liliore!" He took both of them into his embrace, crushing Margot into it as well.

"I thought I would never see thee again!" his mother sobbed, kissing him over and over. "I was afeared thou wouldst never come home to me!"

"I was afeared, too," he said. "And I'm so glad to be home!"

Margot casually tried to pry herself out of this intimate family reunion, but Eric would have none of it. He didn't include her in the embrace, exactly, for he didn't seem to have any intent of introducing her to the people she was being smashed up against, and yet he wouldn't let go of her, either. His arm about her waist was like a steel manacle, and there seemed no way to get him to loose it.

He dragged her over to his father, next, where she found herself crushed between the two tall, rock-hard bodies.

"My son!" his father said, his strong arms encompassing both Margot and his son. "I nearly gave way to thy mother's prayers and came to find thee, thou wast gone so long, and yet I knew thou wouldst not fail me. I am very proud of thee, Eric."

"'Tis glad I am to see thee again, Father," Eric told him fervently. "Thou canst never know how glad."

His brother James stood beside their father, and Margot was next pulled into his embrace as well.

"James!" Eric exclaimed, hugging his shorter brother so hard he actually lifted him off his feet. "James, how good it is to see thee! It has been so long! Thank God thou hast returned from London!"

"I would not miss thy triumphant returning, lad," his brother said, clasping Eric by the back of the neck. "I only wish I had been home to go with thee on thy journey." He turned his blue eyes and handsome face on Margot, and smiled at her. "Who is this lovely lady who has been crushed by us all, Eric? Can it be the lady Margot, of whom I have heard much of late?"

Eric suddenly realized he was still holding on to Margot, and he instinctively pulled her behind his back as though to protect her from his brother. Only a second passed before he recalled himself and slowly drew her forward again. James was smiling very openly at Margot, and Eric felt like clobbering him. He saw it as a possessive smile, as James looking over his new bride, whom he had obviously been told of, and it infuriated Eric so that he wanted to wipe that smile off his brother's face, regardless of how glad he was to see him again.

But he didn't have a chance to make any introductions, for Margot was suddenly squealing with joy.

"Father! Father!"

And she twisted out of his arms and shot off toward Sir Walter le Brun, who held his arms open to receive his only child.

And this reunion, too, filled Eric's heart with a strange and unbidden jealousy, surprising him with the intensity of it. Sir Walter le Brun was Margot's father, a man who had every right to his daughter's love, a man who Eric himself had fought beside during many battles, and a man who was about to become a member of his family by marriage. Why, then, did Eric feel like marching over there, taking hold of Margot, and dragging her away to some safe place where only he could have her love and attention?

James's hand on his arm turned him from the affecting scene. "I've a surprise for thee and Jaufre and Aleric in the great hall," he said with a wide grin. "In sooth, we were in the midst of a little celebration when the page came to tell us of thy arrival. Now thou'rt home we've even more to celebrate. Come inside."

Eric cast a glance at Margot, only to find that her father was already leading her indoors.

Jaufre came up beside him, laughing. "Come on, lad! Let's see what delight James has waiting for us. Thou hast plenty of time later to pine o'er the lady Margot."

Since it would have been impossible for every person in the courtyard not to have heard Jaufre's booming voice and the words he said, and since everyone who heard those words immediately laughed afterward, Eric found himself not only turning bright red but also having to restrain himself from pummeling his obnoxious younger brother.

His father came up behind him and placed one large warm hand on his neck. "Come along, son," he said, chuckling and pushing him toward the open doors. "Let's all get us inside."

The great hall of Castle Belhaven had never seemed so warm and welcoming to Eric as it did at that moment. What James had said was true; there was a celebration of sorts going on. The fires had all been set to blazing, the tables had all been laid full with every manner of food and drink, and there were a great many people present. Some Eric knew—the servants, who stopped what they were doing long enough to greet the new arrivals, several of his father's managers and vassals, his mother's attendant ladies—and some he didn't know, though he recognized their wealth and nobility from the fine manner of their dress. He glanced at his own unkempt state with regret.

Sir Walter had already led Margot to the high table where he was introducing her to an elegant gentleman and two finely dressed ladies. Eric kept his eyes on Margot, who curtsied with perfect grace and who looked so beautiful that it seemed every man in the room was staring at her. For the very first time Eric felt angry that she hadn't covered her hair. It suddenly seemed perfectly obscene to him that any man other than he should be able to gaze upon it unbound.

James walked ahead of them, and Eric assumed it was because he wanted to claim Margot's attentions as soon as he possibly could. But when he reached the table, it wasn't toward Margot that James walked but around her, toward one of the ladies to whom Margot had just been introduced.

"Well, well." Jaufre made a clucking sound.

They neared the table and Margot turned, caught sight of Eric, and smiled so beautifully that he couldn't seem to keep himself from moving to stand beside her. The whole family crowded around, his mother and sister, Jaufre, and Aleric, who had dragged Minna along and who stood with her now, holding her hand with open affection for all the world and his parents to see. Eric wished he could hold Margot's hand or, better yet, put his arm around her waist. But he couldn't. He would never be able to touch her again, never be able to kiss her sweet lips again, or even be alone with her, if he knew what was good for him. He suddenly felt very weary and wondered how long he would need to stay in the great hall being polite before he could excuse himself and go upstairs to his much-longed-for bed.

Father was on the other side of the table now, beside the elegant gentleman who stood there smiling benignly at what Eric guessed must look like a very ragged group indeed.

"Lord Parvel, these are my remaining sons, of whom I told thee and who have just now returned successfully from their journey. This is my next eldest after James, Eric, and after him, Jaufre, and my youngest, Aleric. Eric, Jaufre, Aleric, may I present Lord and Lady Parvel and their daughter, Margaret?"

The three brothers nodded and murmured polite

rejoinders. Eric glanced curiously at James, who was standing with the daughter, his face beaming and one of his arms around her tiny waist. She was a pretty little thing, very petite and delicate. Her heart-shaped face, framed by dark brown hair crowned with a gold circlet, held a sweet, somewhat shy countenance, made even sweeter by the fact that she was blushing so deeply. She hesitantly lifted her blue eyes to gaze at the group before her, then smiled and blushed even more.

James bent and whispered something in the girl's ear that made her giggle, then he slowly led her forward.

"Thou didst tell me thy next eldest was something of a giant, Garin, but never did I expect such a man as this!" Lord Parvel was saying, though Eric only seemed capable of watching James and the girl's approach. "Thou must be very proud of him!"

"Aye, indeed I am, my lord. I truly am. And of all my sons, i'faith!"

It was a terrible moment for Eric. His head was actually buzzing from the awfulness of it. James stopped right in front of them and smiled broadly. The girl kept blushing.

And when James opened his mouth to speak Eric knew, he *knew* what his brother was about to say. "Eric, Jaufre, Aleric, I'd like thee to meet Margaret, my new wife."

He was so proud he looked as if he might burst from it.

"Thy wife!" Aleric gasped.

Jaufre hooted and laughed. "Thou sly dog! What's the meaning of getting wed whilst we're out risking our necks! Come here, sister Margaret, and give thy new brother a kiss!"

"Thy wife?" Eric repeated slowly, disbelieving. Jaufre finished kissing the giggling creature and set her down again. "Thy wife!" Eric said again.

Aleric dragged Minna forward to kiss Margaret and to congratulate James and introduce Minna.

"Thy wife!!" Eric shouted, causing everyone to grow quickly silent and to look at him.

"N-now, Eric," Margot said calmly, putting one hand on his arm.

James looked at him curiously, and the lady Margaret looked positively terrified.

"Eric, what's amiss? Art not happy for us?"

"Happy? *Happy?!*" Eric thundered, feeling every muscle in his body grow tight. "How couldst thou do such a thing? How, James? How?!"

"Eric! Hast lost thy senses?" his father snapped angrily, stepping forward as James and Margaret stepped back. "Hold thy tongue!"

"Thou wast to have married the lady Margot!" Eric went on heedlessly, his hands now clenched into two great fists. "How couldst thou have shamed her so? And in front of witnesses, by God!"

He lunged toward James, nearly overturning the table in the doing. His father, Jaufre, Aleric, and Sir Walter all pounced on him at once, trying to hold him back, but Eric's fury was too far gone to be contained.

"Damn thee!" he snarled at an amazed James, who had pushed the lady Margaret back toward the safety of her parents. "Damn thee for setting her aside so coarsely, as though she was naught! She's the most beautiful woman in England! The finest woman on God's own earth!"

Sir Allyn and several of the men-at-arms had joined in trying to hold him down, but Eric still made exceptional progress toward the object of his wrath.

"Someone hit him on the head, for God's sake!" Sir Allyn shouted, his arms wrapped around Eric's neck.

"The candlestick!" Garin shouted as he tried to shove his huge son back. "Someone hand me that damned candlestick!"

"'Twill be too light!" Jaufre grunted beneath one of Eric's massive arms. "Better get a hunk of wood!"

"Someone get this rotten brat off me!" Aleric yelled, trying to shake Thomas off. Thomas, bound and determined to help his beleaguered master in any way he could, bit Aleric's shoulder and pulled at his hair.

"P-pardon me, I have s-something to s-say!" Margot shouted above it all. "If everyone will p-please b-be quiet! I have something important to s-say!"

No one paid her any attention, least of all Eric, who just about had James cornered against one wall.

"I said," she repeated more loudly, "that I have s-something important to s-say!"

No response.

She sighed, climbed up on the high table, picked

up a huge glass bowl and flung it with all her might against the nearest wall. She followed this with a brass pitcher, a large copper tray, and several plates. When she heard, to her satisfaction, that the only person making any noise in the room was herself, she stopped.

"That's b-better," she said, wiping her hands. Eric and his assailants had all stopped what they were doing to gape at her. In fact, every person in the room was gaping at her, and she smiled graciously.

"I have s-something very important to s-say," she repeated in a normal voice, "and I w-would be m-most grateful if thou wouldst all l-listen to it." She looked at everyone present to make certain that she had their full attention, then she continued. "L-Lords and l-ladies and all those who c-can hear me, I am a woman scorned. 'Tis t-truth, I assure thee!" she said quickly when a few gasps went up, including her father's. "I have g-given my heart, my l-love and my whole b-being to one m-man, and that m-man, though telling me he l-loved me as well, has refused to w-wed me. In sooth, he hath m-made it his wish that I should wed his own b-brother. One n-night," she said, gazing at the table in what she hoped looked like embarrassment, "believing that he truly loved me, I shared a b-bed with this m-man, willing to hold n-none of myself from him." More gasps went up. Her father shouted, "What!" and Eric begged "Margot!" but she went on determinedly. "The next night, after he hath p-pledged his undying l-love to m-me, we slept t-together again."

"Margot, cease!" Eric pleaded.

"And yet he s-still refuses to w-wed m-me," she said sadly.

"By the Rood, he shall wed thee!" her father thundered. "What is his name, daughter?"

Margot didn't reply, she merely turned great, innocent blue eyes on the biggest man in the room, whose loud groan answered the question better than she ever could.

"Eric!" his mother cried, disbelief in her voice. The next second she began to cry.

"Mother, nothing happened!" Eric vowed fervently. "I never—"

"I can scarce believe it of thee, son," his father said with more censure. "Thou hast shamed thy mother and me!"

"But naught happened!" he insisted helplessly, "'Twas all innocent, I swear it!"

"Thou'rt saying thou didst none of these things with my daughter?" Sir Walter demanded, his face a picture of fury. "Thou wilt solemnly vow thou hast ne'er laid hand to her?"

Eric felt like a drowning man. Every face turned toward him, save Margot's, Jaufre's, and Thomas's, was damning.

"Well, I cannot say *that* exactly, but I can promise that we ne'er shared a bed as a man and woman might."

The assembled looked back at Margot, who still stood on the table. She smiled happily and with one hand pulled a folded piece of parchment from out of the bodice of her surcoat.

"I have here," she said, holding the parchment aloft for all to see, "a s-signed s-statement given by M-Michael and Leatie of D-Dunleavy which attests to the f-fact that S-Sir Eric S-Stavelot and myself s-spent the n-night in their home and that we sh-shared the s-same room alone together. It also s-states that Sir Eric introduced us as m-man and w-wife. Wouldst care to read it, F-Father?"

Eric groaned aloud again and covered his eyes with one hand.

"Garin," said Sir Walter, "fetch the priest."

24

"*I say we take hold of him* and drag him up there. It's six against one and he's on his third tankard of ale. We ought to be able to manage it."

Garin shook his head. "I'm not so certain, Jaufre. I disremembered how strong he is when he's angered, and if I've e'er seen Eric angry, 'tis now."

"He's a sick boy, that lad of yours," Sir Allyn commented somewhat dryly. "'Tis certain I'd ne'er spend *my* wedding night thusly, not when I'd the loveliest bride in all Britain waiting abovestairs for me."

"It doth seem rather odd," Sir Walter agreed. "I know he'd no desire to wed my Margot, but up 'til she made her announcement I'd the notion he favored her. Thus it seemed, at least. Why else would he try to kill his own brother?"

"'Tis true, I've ne'er seen Eric so furious before," said James, scratching his chin thoughtfully. "He seemed fit to kill me for what he saw as a slight to the lady Margot, and he hath ne'er done so much as to disagree with me before."

"I'd feel that way if someone slighted Minna," Aleric put in rather quietly.

His father laughed and put an arm around his youngest son's shoulders. "Thanks for the warning, lad. We'll all of us know not to say a word about the fair Minna, then."

They all laughed, including Aleric, who had turned an interesting shade of pink under his father's teasing scrutiny.

Eric scowled in the direction of the group of men standing on the other side of the room. They were laughing, all of them, his father and brothers, his friend Sir Allyn, his new father-in-law, Sir Walter. It seemed impossible that anyone in this entire household should have anything to laugh about. *He* certainly couldn't think of anything humorous at the moment. In fact, he could hardly think about anything at all. He was still in a state of shock.

He was a married man. A *married* man. It was incredible to consider, yet it was true. It had all happened so quickly he could barely remember how it had taken place, or how he had allowed it to happen. One moment he'd been trying to explain himself to his furious father and his weeping mother, and the next he'd been standing in front of the priest, surrounded by people, agreeing to accept Margot le Brun as his lawful wife.

How in the world had he been made to say *that?* he wondered. It must have been the sight of all those happy faces. Everyone, from Jace to Liliore and especially Jaufre, had been smiling so happily, so expectantly at that point that he felt compelled to do it. His mother had ceased her weeping and his father's face had softened—what else could he have done? And Margot, she'd been the worst of all. She'd stood right beside him, gazing up at him adoringly, looking like a very angel, so that he hadn't even been able to say the words with the fury he'd been feeling.

At least his Thomas hadn't deserted him, Eric thought gratefully, glancing at his faithful squire, who even now was attending him and keeping his tankard full. The lad had stood close by, scowling through the whole ceremony—the only one who'd supported him at all.

The whole episode had been disgraceful. Totally, completely disgraceful. At least he hadn't given her the kiss of peace and had left the priest shaking in his shoes when that man had tried to force him to it. And at least he'd given Margot a piece of his mind after the whole farce was over. He'd dragged her off in order to give her a sound, much-deserved talking-to, and once they were alone in his father's private solar he'd slammed the doors and started in on her without delay.

She'd stamped her foot. "'Tis thine own s-s-self thou hast to b-blame!" she'd argued. "I t-t-told thee we w-would be wed! If thou hadst n-not b-been so stubborn I w-would never have b-been forced to s-such extremes!"

"And I told thee we would not be wed!" he'd shouted. "Dost have any idea what my parents think? What thine own father thinks? Thou lied to them!"

"I lied n-not!" she shouted in return, surprising him with her anger. "I t-told only the t-truth! If they choose t-to th-think otherwise th-then th-that is their prerogative. And I w-w-warned thee I w-would make an honest m-m-man of thee!"

"My God, woman!" he'd thundered furiously. "I am not a child to be tricked into doing what he will not! I'm a man, and I'll wed when *I* say I shall wed and not before! And that, as I have told thee many and many a time, shall be never!"

He'd been towering over her when he'd made that statement, but Margot refused to be cowed. She'd placed her fists on her hips and faced him down.

"Thou shalt h-have to m-m-make the b-best of it, then, f-for thou art w-wed n-now! I am thy legal w-wife!"

"Not for long! Tomorrow I'll find a way to have the thing annulled. Not e'en the king himself would find that ridiculous ceremony legal."

That had taken a little of the wind out of her. Her eyes had widened and she'd shaken her beautiful head. "B-But . . . thou canst n-not have it annulled. We have b-been l-legally wed in f-front of a p-priest . . . and witnesses!"

"'Tis not legal 'til it hath been consummated, and that it shall never be."

"But why?" she'd wailed miserably, so that his heart had softened almost at once. "Thou hast said thou d-dost l-love m-me!"

It had been a struggle not to take her into his arms once she'd started crying. He'd had to back away toward the doors just to keep from doing so.

"Thou knowest why. Thou hast only refused to listen to me," he'd said more quietly. "If I loved thee less I would have thee abovestairs even now, making thee my wife in truth, but I love thee too much to consign thee to a life of sharing my shame. I shall have the thing annulled tomorrow, and afterward thou shalt marry Jaufre, or some other, since my brother James hath made such a mess of things."

"Nay!" she'd cried, stamping her foot angrily again. "I'll w-wed n-none other than thee!"

"Then we shall both live a life of loneliness, my lady. At least some other poor man shall be spared thy willfulness. Good eve."

He'd gone back to the great hall after that, with the intention of getting drunk, and she had gone running up the stairs, crying. He'd seen her go. Everyone had seen her go, since everyone had been watching the solar doors to see in what mood they would emerge. His mother, sister, Minna, and Jace had all gone upstairs after her, and Eric had promptly given all of the curious onlookers a good scowl. It must have been sufficient in indicating that he wished to be left alone, for he had been until his father and brothers had shown up with Sir Walter and Sir Allyn. They were still standing together across the room, talking and laughing and looking at him. They would come over to him in a few minutes, he was sure, or at least his father would, probably to try to talk him into going upstairs to Margot, who Thomas had told him earlier had been ensconced in his bedchamber. Let them come; he wasn't moving from this bench tonight, and he certainly wasn't going to go up to his bedchamber, no matter how exhausted he was.

Thomas refilled Eric's tankard, keeping a wary eye on the group of men across the room. "I think they mean to take thee, my lord."

"They may mean to, Tom, lad, but I doubt they'll try it. Not when I have thee here to help me."

Thomas turned to look at him, and he frowned. He set the pitcher he was holding down very carefully, and met Eric's eyes. "Why dost thou not wish to stay wed to the lady Margot? Thou hast told me thou dost love her."

Eric sighed and rubbed his tired eyes.

"Sit beside me, here, Tom." He patted the bench. "And I'll try to explain."

Thomas sat, continuing to stare at him.

"Thou must understand something of my birth, since thou hast been on this journey with me. Thou dost understand that Sir Garin and Lady Elaine are not the parents of my birth?"

The boy nodded solemnly. "That evil man was thy first father," he said.

"That's right. That evil man gave life to me, and I did spring from his seed and have his blood in me. I know not why I have been so fortunate as to escape being like him, but that doth not mean that his blood, his evilness, might not be born in a child of mine, were I to sire a child. And it would be very wrong of me to do such a thing, knowing what a curse I might visit upon the earth. Dost understand, Thomas?"

Thomas frowned again. "Canst thou not be wed to the lady Margot and not have children?"

Eric hadn't counted on this. He wasn't about to explain the facts of life to the boy. "Well," he began uncomfortably, clearing his throat, "when a man and woman are wed they generally . . . have children. Sometimes they don't have any choice in the matter."

Thomas tilted his head confusedly.

Eric cleared his throat again and took a long drink of ale.

"So thou dost not wish to wed the lady Margot because thou dost not wish to give her a child," Thomas stated carefully, thinking it over.

"That, and other reasons," Eric replied, feeling more miserable than angry now. "I am not much of a prize for any woman, especially not one as fine as the lady Margot."

That Thomas firmly refused to believe. "It's because thou dost not want to have a child," he insisted. "Like me."

Eric misunderstood the boy, thinking he meant to make a sacrifice of himself and follow in his master's chaste footsteps.

"Like thee, lad?" He chuckled. "Thou'rt rather young to make such a decision."

"Nay, I mean thou dost not wish to have a child like me. A bad one."

Eric nearly choked on his ale. "Thomas!" he sputtered, shocked. "Thou'rt not bad! Whatever gave thee such a ridiculous idea?"

"Well, my father's a bad one," the boy replied openly, "and his father was even worse than he, so I must be too. I have their blood in me, don't I? Thou didst say 'twas in the blood."

Eric shook his head. "I did not mean thee, lad. There is naught but good in thee, and bravery and selflessness. If any man should dare to say thou wast anything else I'd most like knock his head in. Ne'er again let me hear such nonsense on thy lips."

"But, thou didst just say—"

"Never mind what I said!" Eric nearly shouted. "Thou'rt not bad and that's that! If thou ever sayest so again I'll turn thee o'er my knee!"

Thomas didn't display even the slightest bit of fear over his master's threat. Instead he shook his head and stood up to resume his duties. "Thou dost not make any sense, my lord. I'll have to think on't for a while. Grown people don't always make sense." He picked up the empty pitcher. "But I still wish thou wouldst stay married to the lady Margot."

"Dost thou, lad?" Eric asked rather wearily, wishing he could lie down somewhere and go to sleep.

Thomas nodded. "She's nice and pretty. And she smells good."

Eric was about to reply that he was quite right, on all counts, when his father's cheery voice interrupted him. "Eric, lad, 'tis time and more since thou wast off to bed. Thy bride will be thinking thee ill mannered if thou dost not make an appearance. Come now, and don't be stubborn about it."

Whatever softening Eric had begun to feel fled, and his stubborn pride made a strong return. Always before he had obeyed his father to the letter, and always before he had wanted to, but in this instance, at least, he would be his own man. He'd already been thrust into wedded bliss; he'd be damned if he'd be forced to consummate the marriage, too! A man had to have some control over his own life, for God's own sake!

He lifted his eyes to meet his father's gaze. All six men were there, smiling down at him with infuriating amusement.

"I stay here. Let my *bride* think what she will."

His father chuckled. "Now, son, thou'rt being unreasonable. Take my word for't, thou wilt not stay here."

"I stay," Eric replied stubbornly, growing tense all over.

His father shook his head. "Thou wilt not. Thou dost not think I'd let a son of mine so disgrace the name of Stavelot, dost thou? Thou hast thy duty to perform, and thy mother and I are hoping for grandchildren ere long. Thou must get to't, son!"

All those assembled, save Thomas and himself, laughed heartily. Eric himself felt as though he were actually blushing. His father made him feel like a horse put out to stud. He hadn't been this embar-

rassed since his father had accidentally walked in on
him bedding a particularly curvaceous tavern wench
at one of the many inns they'd stopped at on their
way to Shrewsbury. She wasn't the same girl his
father had seen him taking up to his room earlier, but
was another, who'd come up after Eric had finished
with the first one. The sight had amused his father no
end, though he had tactfully withdrawn from the
room and taken his laughter away with him. For the
rest of the journey, however, Eric had had to endure
merciless teasing from his father and brothers
regarding his sexual prowess, and had had to relive
that embarrassing moment over and over and over.

"If 'tis grandchildren thou dost desire, Father,
then send James about his business. Thou shalt have
none from me."

"Is that so?" his father replied with pleasant disbelief, still laughing a little. "We shall see about that.
Now, wilt come willingly or unwillingly?"

Thomas set the pitcher down and pushed the
sleeves up on his thin arms. Eric clenched his fists.

"I do not come at all, Father," he gritted through
his teeth. "I stay here!"

His father laughed again and rolled up the sleeves
of his own tunic. "Gentlemen," he said, smiling,
"methinks we've our work cut out for us."

Margot had just fallen asleep when she heard the
loud commotion outside the bedchamber door. There
was a great deal of laughing and cursing and grunting

and groaning going on, and the door itself was pushed at and battered against so often that she thought it might give way at any moment. She sat up, tucking the covers carefully under her arms, and waited to see what would happen.

A sheer second later the door swung open, so hard that it bounced off the wall to which it was attached, and Eric was shoved inside. He made a valiant, furious effort to force his way into the hallway again but was pushed back into the chamber by a whole crowd of laughing men.

"Damn!" he swore out loud, plunging toward the door once more just as it was slammed in his face.

He pounded on it then, and put all his weight behind shoving at it so roughly that Margot was truly amazed the wooden thing didn't splinter into a thousand pieces. And he continued to swear, words that Margot had never even heard before, and words that she had certainly never expected to hear on her Eric's lips. The men outside held the door fast and laughed and hooted and shouted all kinds of extremely ribald suggestions to him. Eric replied with a few suggestions of his own, so incredible that Margot actually felt her ears burning.

Finally Eric gave in. He rested his fists and his forehead against the door and grew quiet and still, save for his laborious breathing. After a few minutes he lifted one hand and bolted the door, very resignedly, and after a few more minutes the laughter and hooting in the hallway died away.

It was very dim in the room, so that when Eric

finally turned she wasn't able to see his face, though she could tell he was looking directly at her. He stared at her without moving.

"I'm sorry," he said after an awkward silence. "It did not occur to me that thou wast listening to us. I'm sorry."

Fresh tears stung Margot's eyes, though she had thought only minutes before that she must surely have cried away every tear in her body. It was her wedding night, a night she had dreamed of for so long, and her husband didn't want to have anything to do with her. He probably hated her. He certainly didn't desire her. He'd had to be delivered to his own bedchamber against his wishes by a group of men who'd obviously had to fight him every step of the way just to get him there. And tomorrow he was going to have their marriage annulled.

Margot didn't say anything to him. She wasn't able to. She lay back down in the huge bed, turned on her side away from him, and closed her aching eyes. Let him do as he pleased. He could go away again in a few minutes and probably would; there wasn't anyone left in the hallway to keep him from doing so.

She was naked beneath the covers, Eric thought with a silent groan. It was the first thing he'd thought of when he'd turned to find her sitting in his bed, the covers tucked primly beneath her arms. Her smooth white shoulders had fairly shone out at him in the dim light of the room, and it had only taken his reeling brain a moment to realize that she wasn't wearing anything at all. It was a great shock to a disgruntled man to be tossed into his room where a naked woman lay waiting in his bed. Greater yet for Eric, where a naked Margot lay. His Margot. The woman he loved more than anyone or anything in the world. And the one whom he'd hurt so badly.

He pushed away from the door and took a few steps into the room, drinking in the welcome familiarity of it. Everything seemed so much more beautiful to him in the glow of the candle- and firelight than it had when he last left it: the beautiful, hand-carved Italian furniture, the colorful tapestries his mother and sister had sewn for him, his huge, comfortable bed, in which Margot lay so quiet and still. His over-large tub was sitting in front of the fire, on the other side of the bed. It was still filled with water which would have been kept warm from the fire. Eric sat in the nearest chair and began to take his boots off.

The sound of a boot dropping on the floor got Margot's attention. He was undressing! Her eyes flew open and her body stiffened. What in the world did that mean? Was he going to come to bed? Was he going to consummate their marriage after all? God's mercy! Why in the world had she allowed Minna to talk her into going to bed without a stitch of clothing on?!

Eric contemplated Margot's bare back and shoulders as he pulled his tunic off. Her golden hair covered part of it, but otherwise he could see most of the white skin down to her waist. Did it feel as soft as it looked? It must, he thought, and he wondered what she would do if he tried to touch it.

Eric walked into her view before Margot even realized he'd finished undressing. She'd been listening
for him, straining to hear what he was doing, but she
hadn't heard him walking behind her until he actually came into view. He was naked, stark naked, and
she automatically closed her eyes against the sight.
Water splashed. He was going to take a bath. She
opened her eyes again and drew her breath in
sharply. He hadn't lowered himself into the tub yet,
but was standing in it, turned toward her, gazing at
her. The fire behind him caused his body to glow
with a golden light, and Margot let her eyes run
slowly over him. He was magnificent, more beautiful
than she had ever thought any man could be. His
whole body seemed made of muscle covered by
smooth, golden skin and thick mats of hair on his
chest and arms and legs. She had touched his chest
once before, she remembered, and had felt the softness of the curling hair there. How she longed to
touch him now!

When her eyes lit on his manhood she swallowed
hard. He was fully aroused, and as large there as he
was everywhere else. She thought perhaps that it was
just as well he had decided not to consummate their
marriage. If he had, he probably would have killed
her. She lifted her eyes upward to look at his face,
and they gazed at each other in silence for a full
minute before he lowered himself into the water.
Margot closed her eyes again and buried her face in
her pillow.

The warm water felt good and Eric bathed very

slowly, enjoying the luxurious feeling of being able to stretch out in his big tub. He watched Margot, though, as he quietly soaped and rinsed himself, and he wondered what she was thinking. Her eyes hadn't been shy when they'd taken him in so thoroughly a few moments before, and he'd felt an exultation in her perusal that he doubted he would have felt even if her hands had wandered everywhere her eyes had. She hadn't seemed afraid of him, of his size, and he'd been on the verge of stepping out of the tub and going to her. But she had closed her eyes again and had turned her head into the pillow, and his heart sank. Perhaps it was too late to make things right. Perhaps he had hurt her too much. And he had hurt her, with his foolish male pride and his ridiculous notions he had hurt her badly.

He supposed any man who was a man would have had his pride wounded to have been married off in just such a way, especially when he'd already made a fool of himself by declaring over and over that such a thing would never happen. Indeed, his pride still felt bruised and tender. He'd been proved a liar the whole day long. First he'd been married when he had said he never would be, and then he'd been bested by a mere five men and one boy, all weaponless, who had somehow managed to carry him, against his will, to his own room, where he'd been thrown in as if he were a bad boy. It was humiliating beyond belief, and yet, yet, what was so terrible about it? He was married to the woman he loved, whom he had never dared dream he could wed or would even be allowed to wed. How could masculine pride possibly stand up against such a miracle?

As to his notions about bad blood, well, Thomas had fairly well done those in. Eric had meant what he said about bashing in the head of any man who would dare to suggest that Thomas was other than the fine boy he was simply because of who his parents were. The mere idea of anyone saying such a thing infuriated him. Perhaps badness was something carried in the blood . . . perhaps not. Perhaps he and Thomas had merely been the odd ones in their family lines, good come out of evil. And perhaps he would watch his and Margot's children grow with wariness, always keeping an eye open for any sign of an evil mind, always fearing lest he should see something of his birth father in them. But he would love them, regardless, and he would do his best to raise them with the kind of love and care his own parents had given him. And he would pray for them every day of his life, on his knees, that God would keep them from being cursed as Ravinet was.

And then there was the very last difficulty: the fact that he wasn't good enough for Margot. He was still amazed that her father had allowed her to wed him on the basis of such weak evidence as having merely shared a bed together. It would have been an easy thing to have fetched the leech to verify the fact of her maidenhead. Why in the world hadn't Sir Walter done that before dragging them both off to the altar, especially knowing, as he most surely did, who Eric's sire was? The man had almost eagerly stood by and watched as his only child had been put into the care of the son of Ravinet, the son of the man who had tried to kidnap that same child and who had planned on killing Sir Walter himself. It seemed witless to Eric. He certainly wouldn't have been so eager if the daughter had been his. And yet Sir Walter had done it and had blessed the union aloud. Amazing.

Now Margot was bound to him, unless he was able to find a way to annul their marriage, and that didn't seem likely. At least not now. The only thing that did seem likely was that he was going to consummate their marriage in a few minutes, and that nothing short of a raging fire in the castle would stop him. It didn't seem fair that Margot should have to live with him for the rest of her life. She was so incredibly beautiful, and he was so incredibly plain. She was so nobly born, while he had been born out of wedlock, the product of an ill-used child and an evil man. She had a title, wealth, land, and he was naught but a lowly knight with no rightful claim to any of those things, save through the merciful kindness of the man who had raised him and to whom he owed a lifetime of fealty and service. He had almost nothing to offer her, and less than nothing, not even a name that was truly his own. But he loved her, he loved her as purely and as passionately as a man could love, and he would be able to keep her safe, at least, from the hurts that a man who loved her less might give her. And he would devote himself to making her happy, to seeing that she never had a reason to be unhappy again.

Margot didn't open her eyes again when she heard him getting out of the tub. She closed them more tightly, in fact, and kept them closed while she listened to the quiet sounds of him drying himself. And she held her breath, a moment later, when she felt him pulling the covers back on the other side of the bed, and when she both heard and felt him climbing in beside her.

His weight didn't dip this bed as it had the last one they'd shared, and Margot relaxed the hand she'd dug into the mattress in order to keep herself from rolling over into him. She thought he would merely stay on his side of the bed and sleep, but he didn't. He got into the bed and kept coming toward her, moving slowly until she felt the heat of his naked body pressed against her back. Her eyes flew open, and she gasped out loud with surprise. His hand, warm and gentle and slightly moist, slid over her shoulder.

"Margot," he whispered near her ear, his warm breath fanning her face, sending shivers over her skin.

"I'm s-s-s-sleeping," she stammered nervously, shutting her eyes tightly again. There seemed to be nothing she could do about the trembling of her body.

"Nay, thou art not." He pressed his lips softly beneath her ear, and Margot's breath came a little faster. "Turn and look at me, love."

His hand gently persuaded her shoulder down until she turned and was lying flat on her back, nearly beneath him. She kept her eyes squeezed shut, afraid to look at him.

He didn't seem to mind. She felt him bend to her again, felt his moist mouth brush against her closed eyelids, then her nose, and lastly on her lips in a soft, tender kiss. She sighed when he lifted his head, and she opened her eyes at last. His dark eyes gazed deeply into hers as his hand moved to her other shoulder. He stroked her there with his fingertips, very lightly, then ran them lingeringly down the soft skin of her arm until she trembled. When he reached her wrist he drew his hand across her body, until his palm lay warm against her bare stomach. Margot shuddered uncontrollably, but Eric only continued to gaze at her. His hand stilled where it was, though his thumb brushed gently against her skin.

"I'm sorry that I ruined our wedding day," he whispered. "I shall try to do better on our wedding night."

"On our—" Margot repeated with surprise. "Th- thou hast changed thy m-m-mind, Eric?"

His eyes were so dark they seemed fathomless. "I'll not tell thee," he murmured, lowering his head again. "I'll show thee."

His mouth covered hers softly at first, moving lightly, tasting her and letting her taste him, nibbling and caressing until Margot thought she might melt from the tenderness of him. His tongue gently pressed at the seam of her lips, licking very slowly over them until they parted. He slid it all the way into the heat of her mouth to explore the moist flesh there and to tease her tongue gently into mating with his.

The heat of his body was an incredible thing, and he brought it closer to her still. One of his long, muscular legs moved until he had lodged it between both of hers, and he shifted his whole self carefully until the length of him was pressed against her. She could feel his arousal hard against her hip, and felt afraid again.

"Eric," she gasped, pulling her mouth from his.

"Mmmmm?" he replied, touching her naked breasts for the first time and thinking that he had never felt anything so soft in all his life.

"I don't—I d-don't think this is g-going to w-work," she said miserably, sounding like she was going to cry.

Eric lifted his head and looked at her. "Why, my heart? What's amiss?"

"I think—" She gulped. "I d-do n-not think w-we w-will f-f-fit. I think I'm t-too s-small for th-thee."

For the first time in hours, Eric smiled. If he had a gold coin for every time a woman had said those very words to him, he'd have been a rich man long since. He briefly considered telling her that his size had never killed a woman yet but prudently decided to put it another way.

"We'll fit, my love," he assured her tenderly. "Don't worry o'er it. 'Twill hurt a little this time because thou'rt a maiden, but after 'twill only be pleasure. I shalt make it so." He kissed her again, then lowered his head to her breasts. "I give thee my solemn vow," he whispered before his warm mouth covered one aroused peak.

"Oh," Margot replied stupidly, her hands twining in Eric's soft hair. She had thought to say more, but very soon forgot what. Eric's gentle hands and seeking mouth seemed to make her forget everything, and her last coherent thought before she finally gave herself up to pleasure was that none of her dreams had ever been like this.

25

It faintly amused Eric to think that a person could spend so much time in bed and yet feel more exhausted at the end of that time than he had when he'd first climbed in between the sheets.

A pale light was just beginning to show itself through his thickly glazed bedchamber windows, and Eric smiled at the sight. He supposed he had snatched a few hours of sleep between all the lovings he and Margot had shared, yet he felt as weary as though he'd not slept even a moment. But, tired as he was, Eric believed he had never felt so happy or content. His arms were filled with the woman he loved, who was sleeping very deeply at the moment and who was all twined and curled around him, and it seemed nothing could touch him that could make life seem less than perfect.

It still seemed odd to him that he was married,

especially to a beauty like Margot, but it was true nonetheless. Last night they had confirmed the fact several times over, so he supposed there was no going back on the thing now. Not that he wanted to go back. Far from it. Having made Margot his wife in truth had created a possessive feeling in him that was so intense it was rather frightening. Any man who tried to take her away from him now would be in grave danger of losing several limbs, both eyes, one nose, and probably his life.

She was his wife. *His.* And she was a part of him, now and forever. He had felt it to the very core of his being each time they'd come together, so deeply that he'd felt both stunned and awed. It was a feeling he would never grow used to, he supposed, and one which he wanted to know forever.

Margot shifted in her sleep and sighed, her breath warm on his shoulder where her head lay. Sated and content, Eric placed a gentle kiss on her forehead. He wished he could join his beautiful wife in slumber, but something remained for him to do, and no matter how weary he was he knew he could not sleep until he saw to it.

If it seemed amusing that he could feel so tired after having been in bed so long, it seemed witless to leave that same bed when a soft pillow and a softer woman were waiting there for him, but regardless, Eric carefully moved until Margot no longer lay twined with him, and he slipped out of the bed to get dressed.

*   *   *

As was his early morning custom, Garin Stavelot was working in his private solar when his son walked in. He glanced up when he heard the door opening and was surprised. Eric stood in the doorway, looking both disheveled and slightly chagrined, his dark hair an unruly mess and his huge feet bare. Garin wanted to laugh at the sight his second son presented, but he did not. It was obvious that Eric had done his husbandly duty the night before, for the only sounds to be heard at his bedchamber door several hours after he'd been forced inside were sounds of pleasure, and the very state of him only confirmed what had transpired, for it was quite evident that the boy hadn't had much rest.

"I, uh, thought thou wouldst be here, sir," Eric said rather foolishly.

Garin could see that his son was nervous, but he refused to smile and offer him relief. The boy had behaved badly the day before. Let him sweat awhile and think his father was still angered with him.

"As thou seest," he answered curtly. "What dost thou want of me, Eric?"

Eric swallowed uneasily. "I've a need to speak with thee, if thou canst spare me the time."

Garin leaned back in his chair and motioned for Eric to take the one across from his working table.

"Of course I can spare the time. Come and sit." When Eric had quietly closed the door and begun to walk across the room he added, "Dost not think it odd that a man should be away from his new wife so

early on their first morn together? I hope thou hast
not been unkind to the lady Margot."

Eric blushed so deeply as he took his chair that
Garin had to bite his lip to keep from grinning. His
son couldn't even meet his eyes but focused on his
bare feet. "I believe I owe thee an apology, sir, for my
behavior of yesterday. I can assure thee that my—
wife—and I have come to an—understanding. As to
this morn," he said, glancing at his father briefly, "I
believe she's too weary to notice my absence."

It would have been impossible for any father to
have kept from chuckling at that point, Garin supposed, and he gave way to his mirth. Eric looked back
at his feet and reddened, but Garin felt so pleased it
was difficult to take pity on the lad.

"Thou'rt a true credit to the Stavelot name, son,
and I'll accept thy apology as given. Thou hast many
more to make this day, but I've no fear thou wilt do
as thou must, for thou wert ever a good lad. Only give
Sir Walter and thy mother and I as many grandchildren as we can manage and the whole matter shall be
forgotten." He added this last very lightly, thoroughly
enjoying Eric's discomfiture.

Eric mumbled something about doing his best and
Garin finally took pity on him.

"Very well, lad. Now, what is so urgent that thou
hast felt compelled to leave thy warm bed and lovely
bride so early in the morn? I'll wager thou'rt eager to
be back to them, so speak what thou must. I'm a
ready audience."

A chill of dread crept into Eric's heart, and he

found it difficult to even meet his father's teasing gaze.

"Eric?" There was a note of concern in his father's voice now.

Keeping his gaze on his toes, he took a deep breath. "Did Jaufre have a chance to tell thee much regarding our journey yet, Father?"

"Nay, not Jaufre. He was too weary last eve to relate any more than the least of it. 'Twas Sir Allyn who gave us the tale."

"He told thee that the lady Margot and I were taken captive, then?"

"Aye, he did do so. Eric, what is the matter, son?" His father's voice grew achingly tender and gentle, so that Eric felt his eyes begin to sting. "Dost think I'm angered that such a thing happened? Far from it, lad. Far, far from it. I'm proud of thee, for thou didst not give way beneath thy enemy's hand. Allyn and Jaufre both assured me that thou hadst no chance against Ravinet's men, yet even so thou didst fell more than half a dozen before thou wast taken. There was naught else thou couldst have done, and neither I nor any other man could have done more nor better than what thou didst do, and most would have done much worse, i'faith."

The dread in Eric's chest had become painful, and he wondered if his heart was going to burst from beating so hard and fast. His mouth was dry, he still couldn't meet his father's gaze, and he couldn't think of what words to use. If he had ever seemed less worthy of his father's good opinion, it was now. How weak and useless he felt, and how miserable. His voice, when it came out, was a rasping whisper.

"Did—did Sir Allyn tell thee that I met Terent of Ravinet?"

"Aye," his father replied without delay.

Finally Eric lifted his eyes, more out of surprise than anything else. Didn't Father understand him? Was it possible that he didn't know, that he had never made the connection between himself and Ravinet? A small hope surged within him.

"He told thee of the woman Ravinet killed? The sister of Black Donal?"

His father frowned. "A woman? Killed by Ravinet? Nay, he told me of no such thing. Who was this woman?"

The hope in Eric died, and the vision of his dying mother made the tears that were already so close upon him spring into life. He blinked them away furiously and struggled to keep control of his voice.

"She was my mother," he whispered, losing his struggle. The warmth of silent tears touched his cheeks.

His father stared at him, stunned, and the silence stretched between them.

"Eric—" Garin began quietly.

"Why didst thou never tell me?" The words were out of Eric's mouth before he even knew it, as though they'd been said by someone else. He and his father shared the surprise of them. When his father only shook his head, Eric pushed on. "Why didst thou never tell me that Terent of Ravinet was my father?"

His father shook visibly, as though Eric had physically struck him. "He is not thy father!" he said through his teeth. "I am thy only father, Eric!"

"Thou'rt my father in truth," Eric replied readily, wiping at his tears with the palm of one hand, "for which I thank God every day of my life, but he was the one gave life to me."

The words were barely out of his mouth before Garin was on his feet and slamming one mighty fist on his working table, causing it to shudder beneath the blow.

"*I* am the one gave thee life!" he thundered furiously. "Ravinet gave thee only death! He left thee in the forest to die when thou wast barely born, to be eaten by wolves or to die from want! I am the one gave thee life that day, and thy mother is the one suckled thee at her breast to keep thee alive! Ravinet has naught to do with thee. Naught!"

"Is that why thou didst ne'er speak of him to me, then?" Eric asked, pleading for an answer. "E'en when thou didst know how much I longed to know something of the people I came from?"

"What should I have told thee?" Garin demanded. "That the bastard who sired thee was the wickedest man in England? Aye, I knew Ravinet was thy sire, but he ceased to have aught to do with thee once he left thee to die. I have never thought of him as thy father, nor e'en as thy natural parent. I ne'er deceived thee by my silence, Eric. God gave thee to thy mother and me just as surely as He gave us Jaufre and James and Aleric and Liliore. Ravinet hath never had a right

to thee, in any way. Thou'rt thy mother's and mine
and ours alone by the laws of both Heaven and earth!
I tell thee, son, nay, I swear to thee, had I set eyes on
the man just once these many years past I would have
killed him! Not for what he is, but for what he did to
thee, to *my* son, and no man on earth would have set
blame against me for doing't!"

His father's passionate words soothed the ache in
Eric's heart, yet still he felt deeply confused. "But—I
look like him. 'Twas like looking into a mirror to see
his face."

Garin could see the pain in his son's troubled eyes,
and his anger melted away. He coursed the table and
leaned against it, directly in front of Eric. When he
spoke, meeting his son's eyes, his words came out
both gently and firmly.

"Eric, Ravinet was to thee as a rutting stag is to
his offspring. He took his pleasure of some poor
maid and that was all the thought he ever gave thee.
Those few moments were all thou didst mean to him.
'Twas unfortunate that thou didst inherit the look of
him, just as a deer might inherit the markings of its
sire, but that is all the man e'er gave thee, and that
he gave unknowingly, not even wishing to give thee
life. And that link is so fragile, Eric, that it can hardly
be counted a link at all. 'Tis true thou dost bear his
physical resemblance, but in thee 'tis noble while in
him 'tis evil. Thy inner self doth change it, son, so
that no man hath e'er mistaken thee for his son
rather than for mine, or for thy mother's. Thou must
have heard her say so many times, just as I have, that

thou'rt special to her out of all her children because
thou dost take after her dark coloring. After all these
years she hath come to believe it, as though she had
truly given thee birth, and if thou didst suggest otherwise to her she would be full broken-hearted. There
is something more precious even in that small thing,
my son, than in anything thou hast had from
Ravinet."

"No man hath e'er named me Ravinet's son?" Eric
asked hopefully.

Garin shook his head. "No man hath e'er asked
nor commented such a thing. I cannot say no one
hath e'er thought it, but none hath e'er said any such
to thy mother or me. And hast thou not always been
accepted as our son, Eric? Hath there ever been anyone, man or woman, who hath treated thee differ-
ently than James or Jaufre or Liliore or Aleric?"

"Nay," Eric admitted.

"Yet thou'rt still uneasy," Garin said. "What did
Ravinet say to thee which hath overset thee so badly?"

"He said that thou didst only keep me as a joke on
him, and that thou hadst only amused thyself these
many years by making the son of Ravinet thine own.
He said thou didst surely know that he was my true
father but kept the truth from me so thou couldst
humiliate him by flaunting me as thy slave and jester,
and that thou didst laugh o'er my ignorant devotion."
He looked back up at his father. "I did not believe
him, not for any of it," he vowed solemnly. "I have
known too much of thy love to have believed him.
Thou hast done naught but treat me as if I was thine

own, as if I had been wrought from thee. None of his words e'en made sense to me, so mad they were. But I did wonder, Father, why thou never told me of him. I did wonder that."

His father's eyes narrowed. "Did he say thou wast his son, Eric? Did he name thee such and say thou wast his?"

Eric had never seen such an expression on his father's face before. "Aye."

Garin released a taut breath. It seemed as if he had been waiting for this moment ever since the day he had found Eric lying abandoned in the forest, and now that the moment had arrived he almost felt relieved. He knew what he must do. He would do it immediately, today, in fact, or rather tonight. But before he did he would make certain that his son's mind had been put at ease.

Eric was looking at him rather worriedly, probably thinking he'd made him angry by saying the wrong thing. Unlike Jaufre, who said whatever he damn well pleased whenever it damn well pleased him, Eric was sensitive about the feelings of others, especially when those feelings belonged to members of his family. It had always amazed Garin that a man as large and lethal as his son was should occasionally have the sensibilities and tenderness of a lamb, but so it was. Although it was the last thing in the world that Garin felt like doing, he forced a smile.

"'Tis all right, son. What Ravinet said hath no importance. The man is a liar through and through, and I'm grateful to know thou dost trust and love me enough to know that the things he told thee were lies. I only regret he made thee listen to such dross. Wilt put the man from thy mind now? Canst accept my reasons for not telling thee of him?"

"I can accept, Father. As to Ravinet, I know not if I will ever be able to put him from my mind, but I shall try. I give thee my promise I shall do my best." He hesitated before adding, "I should like to accompany whatever men are sent to apprehend him, sir, and would like to join his guard on their way back to London."

"What! And leave thy bride of only one day? Absolutely not! Sir Walter would be furious!"

"Margot will understand, my lord," Eric replied firmly, " and I will make all well with my father-in-law before I leave. 'Tis important to me to be able to do this, if thou canst arrange it with King Henry. I shall make it up to my wife when I've returned."

Garin shook his head. "I'm sorry, lad, but 'twould be impossible. I sent my fastest messengers on their way to London the moment thou didst arrive home safely, and I've no doubt the king hath already sent his own men to the task. If thou didst join them now thou wouldst only get in the way of their duty. Nay, son, thou wilt remain at Belhaven and enjoy thy lovely wife. Let Ravinet be dealt with by others."

"But, sir, I must—"

Garin held up one hand to silence him. "I've said nay, Eric, and nay is what I mean. If I must call upon thy vow of fealty to ensure thy obedience, I will. Wilt force me to do so, or wilt promise to obey me without it?"

Frustrated, Eric replied, grudgingly, "I shall obey thee. With or without my vow."

"Without it, then," Garin said with relief. He put a hand to his eyes and rubbed them, feeling suddenly weary. "Eric, I would be certain thou hast unburdened all that is on thine heart. We have spoken only of Ravinet thus far, and I hope we shall ne'er have need to speak of him again, but thou hast said thou didst also meet the woman who gave birth to thee." He gazed at his son, whose eyes held pain in them again. "And thou didst say Ravinet killed her. I'm truly sorry for't, my son. But if thou hast aught to tell of her, thy mother and I should like to hear it. We have always wondered about her, just as thou hast, and if thou wouldst share with us, we would be grateful to hear."

A lump so large formed in Eric's throat that he had difficulty speaking around it, and he felt embarrassed that his father should see him thus. He hadn't cried very much during his life, especially during his adult years, but over the past few days he seemed to have become as weepy and mawkish as an oversensitive female.

Because he was reasonably certain he was going to make a fool of himself through the entire telling of his tale, he thought it might be best to get that fact right out in the open, to give Father a chance to get used to the idea.

"I'll probably cry," he stated.

His father answered with a gentle smile. "Why, son, I might, too."

Eric was shocked. "Thou?"

"Aye, e'en me," Garin replied, putting an arm around Eric's shoulders as the two men walked toward the chamber door together. "Thou wilt find that there are some things a man cries o'er no matter how fierce he may be. One of those things is his wife, the other is his children, yet another is his parents, and also his friends. Thou wilt cry o'er the loss of the woman who gave thee life, and I shall cry because my son is in pain, but hopefully thy mother will cry more than both of us put together." He grinned at Eric and opened the door. "So we'll not be too embarrassed, shall we?"

26

"I have never," stated Jaufre, "seen so many lovebirds in one afternoon. If matters continue on as they are, I'll soon be the only single member of my family." And the very idea surprised him, so that he added, sincerely, "What a dreadful thought!"

Jace, sitting on one side of him on a bench in the castle gardens, seemed unperturbed by the several couples strolling through those gardens, all in their own separate worlds.

"My love songs will be well requested this eve, methinks. I'd best make certain there's a tuned instrument ready."

Thomas, sitting on Jaufre's other side, only seemed confused. "Are they all sick?" he asked.

Jaufre and Jace both laughed.

"Aye, sick as men and women can be, i'faith!" Jaufre told the boy. "But 'tis a sickness thou wilt catch one day as well, lad, so thou must not feel too harshly o'er these poor souls. They cannot help themselves."

Thomas shook his head vigorously. "If I e'er catch it, I'll kill myself! I'd rather be dead than make a cursed fool of myself!"

Jaufre and Jace laughed again and were largely ignored by the others who occupied the gardens. Margot was farthest away, all alone but obviously very happy. She was cutting roses from several of the bushes there and placing them into a basket she held on one arm. It was a long time since Jaufre had seen her so finely dressed, as befit her station, and he thought she looked radiantly beautiful in her surcoat of embroidered gold-and-white silk. Her hair was covered with a white silk mantle topped by a circlet of gold and sapphires. There was a glow about Margot that told better than any words could of how well her marriage night had gone, and Jaufre could scarcely wait until his lazy brother finally got himself out of bed so that he could tease him mercilessly.

There were three couples walking in the gardens as well, each representing what Jaufre concluded were the three different stages of a romantic relationship.

Sir Allyn and Liliore walked together, not touching but very intent upon one another. Sir Allyn did much of the talking, probably telling some of his more repeatable adventures, Jaufre guessed, and Liliore responded with laughter and blushes every few words. It seemed obvious to Jaufre that the two were at the very beginning of something deeper, and he was only amazed that his father should allow Liliore to be out walking with Sir Allyn at all. In sooth, if his father and Sir Walter hadn't mysteriously left Belhaven some few hours earlier, she probably wouldn't be allowed to do so, though Jaufre couldn't be sure of that. Sir Allyn was a crafty, determined fellow. His ability to get whatever he wanted was renowned, and if anything could be told by the present expression on his face, Liliore was going to be the next thing he wanted. Father might just be able to respect that in a suitor. After all, hadn't he himself kidnapped Mother many years before, when her father, Jaufre's grandfather, had refused to give her to a Stavelot in marriage?

Aleric and Minna were the second couple strolling, though their relationship was rather more advanced than Sir Allyn's and Liliore's. The two young people were walking hand in hand, so deeply involved in their conversation that they threatened to walk into a shrubbery every few minutes. Aleric was so lost in his first infatuation that he seemed to be unable to keep from gazing at Minna each moment of the day, a circumstance Jaufre found most amusing. He remembered his own first love and hoped and prayed that he hadn't walked around with such a slavish expression upon his face both day and night.

James and his new wife, Margaret, hardly walked at all. They would stroll a few steps down one of the garden paths, though as they now appeared to be physically attached to one another in the manner of twining roses it couldn't accurately be called stroll, and then James would stop, take his wife up into his arms, and proceed to kiss her so hotly that Jaufre had twice made Thomas turn his head. The couple had been in the gardens only three quarters of an hour, yet they had barely gotten halfway down the first path. Jaufre and Jace made a wager that by the time they finally reached the end of the path they'd probably decide they'd had enough fresh air and return to their bedchamber.

"Here comes Sir Eric," Thomas spoke up hopefully, his despondent mood suddenly replaced by expectancy.

"So he does," Jaufre said, smiling at the sight of his older brother walking toward the gardens. He'd never seen Eric look so rumpled, though he had obviously shaved and cleaned up a bit. He'd probably only been out of bed a few minutes before starting in search of his wife, and he must have been certain she was in the gardens, for he was striding toward them with real purpose.

"Look, he's seen James and Margaret. I do believe he's about to make an apology," Jaufre mused.

"Dost think the lady Margaret will forgive him?" Jace asked. "Or thy brother? Sir Eric did try to kill him."

"Oh, well, that's not much betwixt brothers," Jaufre assured him readily. "And James loves Eric well. They've ne'er fought before this, and methinks James will understand what a man in love will do when his lady hath been insulted, albeit innocently.

And," he added, "there's neither man nor woman on earth who can withstand Eric when he makes an effort to charm. Thou'lt see. He'll have the lady Margaret half in love with him shortly."

And it was true. Over the next few minutes, as the three males on the bench watched, Eric proceeded to make all well with his brother and to charm his new sister-in-law utterly, who giggled and blushed and allowed Eric to lift her from the ground and kiss her.

"I'm glad we didn't have a wager on that," Jace remarked. "It looks as if he's going to go collect my Margot lady now."

"Collect appears to be a most appropriate word," Jaufre agreed.

Once Eric had made all well with his brother and new sister, he immediately turned and sought out his wife, who, catching sight of him in the gardens, gifted him with a brilliant smile. Eric smiled in answer and crossed the distance between them rapidly. He kissed her the moment he reached her, then whispered something into her ear. Margot laughed and Eric stooped and lifted her into his arms, kissing her again and causing her to drop her basket of roses onto the lawn. A moment later he was carrying her back inside the castle, both of them laughing and neither concerned that they had a full audience watching.

"Well, we'll not see them for the remainder of the day," Jaufre commented.

"Or night, probably," Jace added.

Thomas sighed sadly and rested his chin in his cupped hands.

Jaufre placed a hand on the boy's neck. "What's amiss, lad? Art missing thy master so soon? Thou shalt have to make do with me for a while, I fear, or at least 'til Eric hath more time to settle thee in."

"'Tis not that," Thomas said, his gaze on the ground. "I have to go see my father."

"Ah," said Jaufre, "the brute. That's right. I'd forgotten about him, but I suppose thou must let him know thou'rt alive and well and living gainfully at Castle Belhaven. Shall I go with thee, then, since thy master is busy? I'll not let thee come to any harm."

Thomas turned serious eyes up to consider Jaufre. He looked at him as if seeing him for the first time, and as though he were taking his measure, which he evidently found wanting.

"He's mean, my father, when he's been drinking. And he's big."

Jaufre tried hard not to laugh. "Thou'rt kind to worry o'er me, Thomas, but I assure thee I've not the slightest fear of thy father. I know I'm but a puny runt compared to my older brother, but I think I might manage to hold my own against the man."

Thomas thought it over for a long moment, then gave Jaufre a decisive nod. "Very well. I can always hit him on the head with the cooking pot if he gets out of hand."

Jaufre's laughter, loud and unrestrained, could be heard in the gardens even after he had followed Thomas out toward the village. Jace listened until the sound died away, then he yawned, rested his head in one hand, and went back to watching the happily strolling couples.

Setting his goblet aside, Terent of Ravinet sighed and let his gaze drift toward one of the fires in the great hall.

This was his last night in England. The knowledge burned in him as hotly as those flames. Tomorrow he would be leaving his birthplace indefinitely, possibly even permanently, and the idea filled him with a great sadness. There was no choice, of course, for he had realized as soon as he escaped that chaotic mess at Beronhurst that everything was over. All his dreams, his plans, everything. All over. He had let his son live and had lost his grip on the girl and thus had lost her, and now King Henry would have every bit of evidence he needed in order to drag him to court to stand trial for treason. There wasn't any doubt in his mind that the king's troops were already on their way to Castle Ravinet in order to seize him. They would arrive tomorrow day, or on the next day at the very latest, and so he had no choice but to flee. He would be gone when they arrived, to France, or to Italy. He would be gone, and unless Henry was dethroned soon he would most likely have to stay away from his beloved England for the rest of his life.

Thinking on it, Terent of Ravinet vaguely wished that he had killed Sir Eric Stavelot of Belhaven, son or not.

"Ravinet."

It was a voice Ravinet hadn't heard in many and many a year, and one that was warped with unmitigated disgust, yet he knew at once who it was. He lifted his head slowly.

"Good eve, Stavelot. What an unexpected surprise." His eyes met and held those of his intruder. "I never thought of this. How very lax of me."

Since Ravinet had known him, from the days of his youth, Garin Stavelot had been an imposing figure, but he had grown even more so during the years since their fostering days. He'd gained in both height and width, and the muscular quality of his arms and chest testified to the strength of the man. He had entered the castle from one of the long windows, evidently having found a way to scale the wall in order to reach it, and he stood there now, just inside the room, dripping wet from the downpour of rain, his long blond hair plastered against his head, a long sword clutched in one hand. The expression on his face told Ravinet exactly why he'd come, and what was about to happen.

"Aye, lax indeed," Garin replied, his fingers straining against the handle of his sword.

"How didst thou manage to get past my guard?" Ravinet asked with perfect ease.

"'Twas not difficult. Most of thy men gave way at once when they saw the size of my column. Some in the castle still hold fast, thus the necessity for my climb, but Sir Walter hath them nearly vanquished, or shall very soon."

"Thou hast come on behalf of my son, I take it?" Ravinet asked.

The red fury that Garin had held so tightly in rein began to seep through him, renewing his strength, firing him.

"Eric is *my* son, Ravinet. *Mine.* I'll not give thee, or any other man, leave to call him thus."

Ravinet chuckled pleasantly. "But thou must, Garin, for 'twas I gave him life. Thou wouldst not have him at all were it not for me."

Garin frowned grimly. "I barely had him as it was. Thou didst leave him to die, bastard. 'Twas God's own miracle led me to him that day, and God Himself gave him to me, in place of thee. Thou didst throw away the finest treasure a man can call his own, Ravinet, a noble son of whom thou couldst have been proud. Thou didst throw him away, man. And thou hast no right to call him thine now."

"I have every right, Stavelot. He is the flesh of my flesh, born of my seed. And he looks like me, does he not?" Ravinet smiled at Garin's flushed face. "How thou must have hated me when thou didst finally realize who had sired him."

"Aye, I did hate thee," Garin admitted, "but not because thou sired him. Any man can tumble a maid and create a life, there is naught to hate in that save perhaps to despise him if he chooses to do naught for the child. Nay, I hated thee not for the life thou gave him, but for the death thou gave him."

"But I have made recourse for that," Ravinet pointed out, hoping to say anything that might save his life. "I gave him his life but a few days since, when I could have killed him. I did so because he is my son. Doth that count for naught?"

"For less than naught," Garin replied heatedly. "Thou didst not kill him because it would have been unpleasant for *thee*, not because of any love thou didst bear him. Thou wouldst have let another take his life's blood."

Garin took a step closer and Ravinet stood, trembling. "Thou canst not kill me, Stavelot! The king would hang thee for't!"

Garin shook his head and continued his slow advance. Ravinet stepped behind his chair for protection.

"He'll not hang me, for he'll ne'er know 'twas I did it. But e'en if he should find out, I'll have no regrets. I made a vow to my son when he was but ten years of age, and I always keep my vows. Especially when I've made them to my children."

"Thou wilt kill me for the sake of a vow?" Ravinet screamed, panicked as Garin drew closer.

"Aye," Garin replied, following as Ravinet backed away from him, "for the vow that I'd kill any man who laid a claim to him, as thou hast done. I've heard thee claim him with thine own lips, Ravinet, and so I shall kill thee."

"I'll—I'll ne'er do so again, Garin, I swear it! Tomorrow I shall be gone from England forever. Thou shalt ne'er see me again, nor even hear of me."

Again Garin shook his head, almost sadly this time. "Nay, I shall ne'er see nor hear from thee again,

Ravinet, and I wish to God I'd not had to see nor hear thee this night. Thou'rt foul as a week-old carcass left out in the sun to rot. The very stench of thee sickens me."

And he took another step.

27

Margot and Eric came out of their bed-chamber only briefly over the next three days. James and his new wife did likewise, and the rest of the family soon grew used to catching only glimpses of the newlyweds.

On the morning of the third day Margot woke to the pleasant sensation of her husband's gentle hands lazily stroking her back. She was sprawled comfortably atop his massive chest, still in the same position in which she'd fallen asleep some hours earlier, and his hands and fingers moved over her slowly, softly.

She lifted her head to look at him and was surprised to find that he was frowning—frowning and staring stonily at the ceiling.

"Eric?"

His eyes snapped downward, as though she'd taken him unawares. Then a slow smile spread on his face, and he lifted his head so that he could kiss her. "Good morn, my beauty," he murmured. "I thought thou wouldst sleep much longer, thou didst seem so weary last eve."

"I was," she admitted, a little embarrassed. "I am."

He kissed her again, cradling her head with one hand. "Return to sleep then, love. I'll wake thee later."

Margot shook her head and scooted up so that their faces were level. With her free hand she touched his face, running her fingers over his stubbly chin.

"Why wast thou f-frowning, Eric? Wast thinking of s-something s-sad?"

"Was I frowning? I was not aware of't." His hands began moving over her again, more meaningfully this time. "I was wondering how I'm going to keep thee, and trying to think of where and how we shall live."

Margot smiled. "Thou w-wilt be the l-lord of Reed one day, and we w-would be welcome there. My f-father will be eager to t-teach thee regarding the management of his m-many estates."

Eric grimaced. "Aye, it doth seem that I shall one day be the lord of Reed, a fact of which I can only hope thy good father will neither regret nor sorrow o'er. I can hardly believe it myself, still. But there is another matter to consider, Margot. I have given my father my vow of eternal fealty, and such as that cannot be broken. I cannot leave Belhaven without his consent."

"We could s-stay here, then," Margot conceded. "Methinks I c-could m-make myself useful to thy m-mother and sister."

"We could stay here," Eric agreed hesitantly, "but 'twould not be fair to thy father or to thee. Thy father would be alone at Reed, then, for he hath only thee to call his own, and thou wouldst be living far beneath thy station. Thou'rt used to being the lady of thine own home, Margot, and that is what thou'rt born to. 'Twould not seem meet were thou to take place behind Mother and Liliore."

"Mayhap 'twould not s-seem m-m-meet," Margot said, bending to kiss his unhappy frown, "but 'twould n-not trouble me to d-do s-so, either. I w-want only to be where thou art, my Eric. If I am w-with thee, I shall be happy, whether we dwell in the f-finest castle or the l-lowest hovel. As to my f-father," she said, her voice a little less sure, "he hath m-much to k-keep him busy and f-from feeling too alone. Mayhap we could v-visit him sometimes." This last came out very hopefully.

"Oh, Margot." He groaned, responding to the wistfulness in her tone. "Thou shouldst never have wed with me. There are so many others—better men—who could have given thee all thou dost deserve. If only thou hadst not been so stubborn!"

"But n-none other could have g-given m-me love as thou canst do," she argued, tickling his face with rapid kisses, "and I could l-love n-none other as I do thee, so 'twould have been a m-miserable, lifelong m-mistake."

Eric rolled suddenly so that Margot lay beneath him, cradled within the grip of his arms. "Love I can give thee," he whispered before finding her mouth with his for a thorough kiss, "and all the affection thou canst abide, but what if thou dost grow weary of such? Will there not come a day when thou wilt long for the life of a lady as thou didst once have? When thou wilt wish for the wealth and standing thou didst enjoy at Reed?"

Margot shook her head. "I want n-not those things. I w-want only thee."

"But I would give them to thee if I could," Eric vowed fervently. "Thou dost deserve them."

She smiled and stretched lazily beneath him. "I w-will be content with thy love, and with all the affection I c-can abide. I d-do believe I can abide a little now, i'faith."

"Thou dost mean to distract me, woman, when I am all in earnest," Eric said, chastising her with mock irritation.

"Aye," she admitted, "that I do."

He kissed her. "Being married to thee will be a sore trial, I fear. Thou wilt be a demanding wife, methinks."

"Mmmm," she mumbled as he kissed her again.

"'Tis well I am a stout, long-suffering man, is it not?" His lips pressed warm kisses along the prominent bones of one cheek, then skimmed the slender column of her neck and on to her shoulder.

"Aye. M-most well."

"And dutiful," he added, sucking lightly on the tender skin at the base of her neck, "a most dutiful husband."

"Aye."

"Sweet Margot," he murmured, finding her mouth with his again, "I do love thee. Never shall I grow weary of joining my body with thine. Never shall I grow weary of loving thee."

And as if to prove it to her, Eric proceeded to love Margot with a passion and ferocity that afterward left them both stunned.

"M-my," she whispered, her eyes closed. one hand lightly stroking the back of his neck.

"Great Lord," he said from somewhere in her shoulder, against where his face was pressed. He lay heavily atop her, so drained and sated he could not move.

Margot moved her hand up into the softness of his hair and began to tease the damp curls there. "Thou'rt m-most skilled in the art of l-love, my lord. I kn-knew it would be thus."

Eric slowly lifted his head, which felt heavy as a boulder, and grinned at her, amused and pleased. "Didst thou, love? I am glad thou hast not been disappointed." He chuckled and added, "I shall endeavor to make certain it is always so. I did say I was dutiful, did I not?"

"Aye," she said, smiling. "My f-father will be w-well p-pleased with such respect for duty. He hath commanded that w-we produce a grandchild before the f-first year of our marriage is out."

"God's mercy! Mine hath commanded the same of me! I imagine they would lock us in here night and day, only allowing food and water to be brought us, if we showed no inclination to do so on our own. But," he bent and kissed her lightly on the nose, "as we are such dutiful children, I suppose we shall have to do our best to obey them."

"Mmmm." She nodded. "Methinks 'twill be demanding w-work, my lord."

"Most demanding," he agreed with a sigh, "and likely most tiring. We shall need our strength if we're to do as we've been told. Art thou as hungry as I, love? Shall we go down to table and share the midday meal with our families? Or shall we eat in our chamber again?"

"Downstairs, p-please. I should l-like to see my f-father."

"Downstairs, then," he said, finally disengaging himself from her warm body and groaning aloud as he did. "My love." He moved to one side of the bed and collapsed. "Thou wilt be the death of me. I feel half-dead already."

James and Margaret decided to come out of their bedchamber for the midday meal as well, and the entire Stavelot family was wholly reunited for the first time in several days. The wedding guests had also remained, including Margaret's parents, and with Sir Allyn and Sir Walter all of these combined to make for a very full, very merry table.

"Thou must leave tomorrow day?" Eric asked his brother James with true dismay. "But we've barely had a chance to see each other! God only knows when we shall be together again!"

"Aye, truly," James agreed, "but there's no help for't. King Henry gave Margaret and me only so long for our wedding trip, and he desired his good cousin back at his side quickly," he said, indicating Lord Parvel, his new father-in-law, with a smile, "so we needs must get us back to London."

"We'll miss thee and thy lovely Margaret, I vow," Eric said. "I wish thou couldst stay longer."

"'Twould do thee no good were thy brother to stay, lad," Garin said, reaching for another ripe plum. "Margot and thou shall be leaving Belhaven by weeks' end, to return to Reed with Sir Walter."

Both Eric and Margot nearly choked on the food in their mouths. Eric reached a hand around to pat Margot's back, while he himself eyed his father with shocked disbelief. "I beg thy good pardon, sir. Methinks I misheard thee."

Garin exchanged looks with Sir Walter, who shook his head. "I've not had a chance to talk with them yet, Garin." He sent a wry smile toward his daughter and son-in-law. "They've been too busy. I was thinking to do so after today's meal."

"It matters not," Garin said with a slight shrug, turning his eyes back to Eric's. "Sir Walter would like Margot and thee to return to Reed with him so thou canst give him aid in the management of his estates. Thy mother and I have agreed that it shall be so, though I told him I'll have the Fiend's own trouble running my own estates with my two eldest sons gone from me." He grinned at his third, who was trying to avoid meeting his gaze. "I suppose I'll needs must dust Jaufre off and set him to work, and Aleric as well."

Jaufre grimaced visibly. "Work!" he muttered. "I knew I should have gotten wed when I'd the chance!"

Aleric looked pleased and smiled at Minna, who smiled back. Margot, watching this exchange, realized that if she did go back to Reed it would be without her good friend.

"But, Father, art certain of this?" Eric asked uneasily. "What of my vow of fealty? I had meant to serve thee at Belhaven."

Garin smiled at him. "Thou canst serve thy mother and me best at Reed, son, and by doing thy utmost to keep thy lands peaceful and prosperous and by making sure that those who live beneath thy hands are happy and well. Do these things and we shall be well pleased."

"Well," said Eric, still rather stunned. "Well, I suppose that is what we shall do then." Though it was certainly something he had never thought he would do. He'd always thought Belhaven would be his home. He looked at Margot. "Wilt make thee happy, will it not, love? To return to thy home at Reed?"

"Thou kn-knowest full well what shall m-make m-me happy, Eric."

He grinned and covered her hand with one of his. "To be with me?"

She nodded.

"Then we shall be together at Reed." He glanced at his father-in-law. "I thank thee, sir. I vow to do my best for thee."

Sir Walter looked as pleased as though he'd suddenly inherited a vastly valuable treasure.

"However," Garin said, frowning at his friend Walter a little, "thou must promise to come home at least once a year to visit, just as James and Margaret have promised to come. I'll let my sons go for a good cause, but I'll not let them go forever, by God!"

"We'll come," Margot promised. "Once a year at l-least."

"Now that that's settled," said Sir Allyn, mischievously, "which of thee will present thy parents with the first grandchild, lads?"

"By the Rood!" Eric laughed aloud, along with James, with whom he exchanged incredulous looks. "Is that the only thought in all thine minds? We've only just wed, for mercy's sake!"

"I've put my money on Margaret and James," Aleric confided to Sir Allyn. "They've a three-day lead on Margot and Eric."

"God's teeth!" Jaufre laughed. "There's a challenge thou canst not let pass by, Eric! Take it up and I'll place my money on thee!"

Eric laughed again, as did everyone at the table, including Margot, and he said very graciously, "I—we," he corrected, setting an arm about Margot, "accept."

"The race is on!" Sir Allyn shouted, lifting his tankard aloft.

More laughter followed until Eric added, "Before we're exiled to our respective bedchambers by this crowd of gamblers, however, we'll eat. We need to keep up our strength, do we not, James?"

The laughing and teasing continued throughout the remainder of the meal, until the end of it, when Garin had only just stood in order to make a toast to the two newlywed couples.

He lifted his goblet and prepared to speak, but was stopped by the arrival of several of the king's soldiers. They clattered into the great hall uninvited, ignoring the protests of the servants and guards, and their leaders, two harried-looking knights, immediately headed for the long table.

Garin set his goblet down; James stood up. Everyone else fell silent and watched the soldiers approach.

"Salton, Fincet, what is this?" James demanded with a frown.

The men immediately recognized the face and form of the king's newest regent and steered toward him, one with arm outstretched.

"Sir James! Thank a merciful God thou'rt here!"

James clasped the man's arm. "What's amiss? What hath brought thy men and thee to Belhaven?"

The man surveyed the gathering at the table with unease. "May we speak privately with thee, sir? And with Sir Garin and Sir Walter, if't please thee?"

James shot a glance at his father, who nodded solemnly. Sir Walter stood and the three men followed the knights some distance across the great hall, where the sound of their voices was dim and unintelligible.

Beneath the table Eric took hold of Margot's hand, squeezed it, and smiled encouragingly at her. Margot gazed back at him with a worried expression, for she feared her father was about to be sent into some kind of danger again.

After a few minutes' discussion, the knights went back to where their men stood and directed them to sit and eat at one of the lower tables, where servants were already setting out food and drink for them, and Garin, Sir Walter, and James returned to the long table, closely watched by one and all. Sir Walter and James took their places again.

Garin continued standing at the head of the table, where he addressed his curious onlookers. "There is no great tragedy to tell thee, friends," he said. "These men were sent by King Henry to apprehend a traitor to the crown, one known to us as Terent of Ravinet, the baron of Ravinet. He was to have been taken back to London to stand trial for his crimes, where he surely would have been found guilty and suitably sentenced, for there was more than ample proof of his treason." His gaze fell briefly on Eric, then moved away. "However, when these men arrived to arrest him, it was to find the man dead." A gasp went up. "He was killed by an unknown assailant who has yet to be apprehended." Garin stopped speaking, leaving only a gaping silence at the table, and he sat down, his face and manner indicating that his announcement had been nothing out of the ordinary.

Eric felt as though he had turned to stone. He could barely feel Margot's tight grip on his fingers, could barely hear her say his name. His father's eyes rested meaningfully on him once more, then broke away. Eric, however, couldn't keep from staring at him still. It wasn't the surprise of Ravinet's death that shocked him, Eric had long since reconciled himself to the fact that the man's life would find its end soon, it was the instant realization, as his father had spoken, of who had done the deed.

"My God," he whispered, shaken by what it all meant.

Only Margot heard him say it, for the conversation at table had slowly started up again. Jaufre, sitting across from Eric, watching him carefully, saw Eric's mouth make the words.

"Eric," Margot said again, sliding one hand up his arm. He turned to gaze at her beautiful face, so full of concern, and he smiled, then bent to kiss her. "'Tis all right, love. I'm all right."

He felt Jaufre's eyes on him, too, and smiled across at his brother. "I'm all right, Jaufre. Never fear. It distresses me not."

Both Margot and Jaufre looked at him skeptically, so far from believing him that Eric actually laughed.

"I feel free," he insisted, and he meant it. His heart felt lighter than it ever had before. He had seen his father kill many a man in his day, and he'd seen him save many a man's life; those who had died had been more than deserving of it, and those who'd been saved had been worthy of that as well. It had never pleasured his father to kill, but at times it had been necessary. Eric understood this very well. He'd had to kill men himself and had never enjoyed doing so, yet he harbored no guilt over those who had died at his hand, for they'd been wicked men, or the enemies of his country and people. He would have killed Black Donal with ease had that man not promised to put an end to his own miserable life, and there was certainly no doubt that Ravinet's black heart would have found its end with a stroke of the axman's instrument of death.

But his father had killed Ravinet. His father had done it and had done it so that Eric himself could be set free. He remembered the promise his father had made him so many years before, when he had been only ten years old, and now his father had made good on that promise. He had done it out of love as well as duty, and he had done it knowing what dangers there were for him in the doing. He had done it so that no other man would be able to lay a claim to his son.

For the first time since he'd learned the truth of his birth, Eric was able to identify himself. He was Eric Stavelot, the son of Garin and Elaine Stavelot, the brother of James and Jaufre and Liliore and Aleric Stavelot, and a higher price had been paid for him by his parents than the mere price of birth.

It was difficult to hold back his tears as he stood, and even more difficult as he made his way to the head of the table, where his father stood and made ready to receive him.

Eric hugged his father in a painful embrace, and when he let him go they were both smiling. No words passed between them, for words meant nothing at the moment.

Garin squeezed his son's shoulders too tightly, he knew, but he couldn't seem to stop himself from doing so. A whole tableful of people watched them, unable to know what only he and Eric would ever be able to share, and Garin didn't mind at all. He kept squeezing Eric's shoulders as though to take a part of him away on his fingers, somehow, and be able to keep some of him at Belhaven.

"I'll miss thee when thou'rt gone," he said finally.

Eric nodded. "I'll miss thee, sir," he whispered.

"But I know thou wilt make me proud, as thou hast always done."

"I'll make thee proud, Father," Eric vowed.

It was difficult, but Garin let him go. Eric smiled at him once more, brilliantly so, then turned to scoop his mother up out of her chair. He hugged her so hard that Elaine squealed and laughed. Liliore, who sat next to her, received the same treatment.

Sir Allyn, sitting beside Liliore, admonished jokingly, "Best not harbor any ideas about doing that to me, lad."

"Never fear." Eric laughed, setting his sights on Margot, who was standing beside her chair, waiting for him. "I've a greater beauty than thee to tempt me."

He went to his wife and kissed her there in front of all the assembled, ignoring their laughs and hoots.

"I love thee, Margot," he whispered when he had lifted his head to gaze wonderingly at her.

She lifted one hand and touched his cheek, as unembarrassed by their audience as he. "And I l-love thee, my Eric. What a l-long t-time I have had to w-wait for thee."

"How glad I am thou didst wait, love," he said, grinning. "Mayhap I should show thee how glad."

She lifted an eyebrow. "Thou'rt f-feeling m-more alive than d-dead now, my lord?"

He laughed delightfully, then bent and took her up into his arms. "Fully alive, sweet, and I'll prove't to thee." He turned his grin on those assembled.

"I hope thou will pardon us, good lords and ladies, but as I'm certain thou will recall, my wife and I have a wager to win."

A roar of laughter rose from the table, though Eric and Margot didn't stay to listen to it. Eric carried Margot toward the stairs, whispering promises of love to her every step of the way. The laughter, full of as much cheer as humor, drifted upward after them, all the way up the stairs, until they closed their bedchamber door.

AVAILABLE NOW

CHEYENNE AMBER by Catherine Anderson

From the bestselling author of the Comanche Trilogy and *Coming Up Roses* comes a dramatic western set in the Colorado Territory. Under normal circumstances, Laura Cheney would never have fallen in love with a rough-edged tracker. But when her infant son was kidnapped by Comancheros, she had no choice but to hire Deke Sheridan. *"Cheyenne Amber* is vivid, unforgettable, and thoroughly marvelous."—Elizabeth Lowell

MOMENTS by Georgia Bockoven

A heartwarming new novel from the author of *A Marriage of Convenience* and *The Way It Should Have Been*. Elizabeth and Amado Montoyas' happy marriage is short-lived when he inexplicably begins to pull away from her. Hurt and bewildered, she turns to Michael Logan, a man Amado thinks of as a son. Now Elizabeth is torn between two men she loves—and hiding a secret that could destroy her world forever.

TRAITOROUS HEARTS by Susan Kay Law

As the American Revolution erupted around them, Elizabeth "Bennie" Jones, the patriotic daughter of a colonial tavern owner, and Jon Leighton, a British soldier, fell desperately in love, in spite of their differences. But when Jon began to question the loyalties of her family, Bennie was torn between duty and family, honor and passion.

THE VOW by Mary Spencer

A medieval love story of a damsel in distress and her questionable knight in shining armor. Beautiful Lady Margot le Brun, the daughter of a well-landed lord, had loved Sir Eric Stavelot, a famed knight of the realm, ever since she was a child and was determined to marry him. But Eric would have none of her, fearing that secrets regarding his birth would ultimately destroy them.

MANTRAP by Louise Titchener

When Sally Dunphy's ex-boyfriend kills himself, she is convinced that there was foul play involved. She teams up with a gorgeous police detective, Duke Spikowski, and discovers suspicious goings-on surprisingly close to home. An exciting, new romantic suspense from the bestselling author of *Homebody*.

GHOSTLY ENCHANTMENT by Angie Ray

With a touch of magic, a dash of humor, and a lot of romance, an enchanting ghost story about a proper miss, her nerdy fiancé, and a debonair ghost. When Margaret Westbourne met Phillip Eglinton, she never realized a man could be so exciting, so dashing, and so . . . dead. For the first time, Margaret began to question whether she should listen to her heart and look for love instead of marrying dull, insect-loving Bernard.